Mrs Huds

MRS HUDSON AND THE SAMARKAND CONSPIRACY

MARTIN DAVIES

CANELO

First published in the United Kingdom in 2020 by

Canelo Digital Publishing Limited
Third Floor, 20 Mortimer Street
London W1T 3JW
United Kingdom

Copyright © Martin Davies, 2020

A CIP catalogue record for this book is available from the British Library.

Print ISBN 978 1 78863 825 8
Ebook ISBN 978 1 78863 708 4

Look for more great books at www.canelo.co

Printed and bound in Great Britain by Clays Ltd, Elcograf S.p.A.

So much has changed since those days that sometimes I find it hard to believe I was ever such a young girl, dashing around Baker Street in so much haste, at the height of a sweltering summer. Hard too, in these different times, to imagine a desert city seething with spies, or the envoys of a great empire fleeing in disguise across steppes and seas and mountains, hunted by a ruthless enemy. All that belongs to another world, a lost world, the stuff of storybooks.

But sometimes, when the temperature in my rooms becomes unbearable, I slip on my sensible shoes and take a walk along the Serpentine, to a particular bench, where I sit and look out over the water and see, not ducks or toy boats, but the minarets of Samarkand and the domes of Tashkent, and the dust of horses galloping towards the shores of the Caspian Sea. And perhaps, sometimes, if I close my eyes, instead of the laughter of children, I hear a band playing, and then a whistle, and the roar of a shuddering locomotive as it plunges at speed into the gaping mouth of a coal-black tunnel…

And then I blink and stretch, and calm myself by watching the ducks' careless manoeuvres.

However warm it is, however sticky the season, it is never as warm as that one I remember.

Part I

Nothing Happens in Baker Street

Chapter One

It was so hot that summer you could have fried on egg on the pavement outside our front door. Or so Dr Watson declared, although I don't think anyone would ever have attempted it; the pavements were too thick with dust, whirled up from the cobbles by the passing hansoms and coating everything and everybody, from the wilting flower girls to the dispirited sparrows; it crept under the starchiest collar and eddied under ladies' skirts, so that by the end of the day, when you came to wash, you found yourself dirtier beneath your clothes than above them. It would have been a terrible waste of an egg.

Mrs Hudson, who believed in clean aprons even in the hottest weather, had me running errands to the laundry twice a day, and three times on Tuesdays when the coal-wagon made its calls. But despite the dirt and the dust and the terrible smells that sometimes rose from the gutters, our shady kitchen – so much lower than the street – remained cool and soothing, a little sanctuary from the fevered world around us. And we avoided the worst of the coal dust, for that summer, from the beginning of July to the middle of September, Mrs Hudson refused to light a fire.

'No need for one, Flotsam,' she assured me. 'With all our neighbours out of London and their houses all but empty, it would be foolish to heat up *this* house instead of theirs, wouldn't it, my girl? We made similar arrangements in St Peter's Square back in '68, and it worked very well. So Mrs Johnson, the housekeeper at 197, is going to provide boiling water for all of us at pre-arranged times. Mrs Turner and Mrs McFarland will provide baths for those of us left below stairs, and the gentlemen can bathe next door, in the Jenkinsons' rather grand porcelain tub. In return, we shall be generous with the iced white port, which all three of those ladies enjoy greatly, and come the autumn you and I will help with their airing and the parquet floors. And, as for cooking, well, Flotsam, fruit and salads are what's needed this summer. Bread and cheese, cold meats, good chutney, plenty of Derbyshire water. A chilled soup from Lamington's, perhaps, if the gentlemen wish it, and a good supply of light Moselle to wash it down. But I promise you one thing, Flotsam, whether Mr Holmes likes it or not, nothing hotter than a bunch of grapes is coming out of this kitchen until the weather breaks. And hopefully, before then, something will happen to distract our two gentlemen from this terrible heat.'

But in Baker Street that summer, apart from the dust-spirals and the grumbling victorias, and the reluctant pedestrians hugging the shade, nothing did happen. It was far too hot for crime. Mr Holmes complained that London's most significant villains had all left town, and that those who remained were too befuddled to be interesting. And Dr Watson, driven by days of sullen inactivity to brave the glare, reported that over in Scotland Yard, where the dust was even thicker, Inspector Lestrade and his colleagues had nothing to do but pore morosely over the documents of unsolved cases. Meanwhile, on the streets, our local bobbies spent their days perspiring into their uniforms and their nights breaking up the tavern brawls that sparked into life as soon as darkness fell.

Had it not been for a deranged sultan, a foreign spy and a peculiar piece of railway timetabling in a remote corner of Europe, we might all of us have gone mad before the end of August.

The morning Mrs Hudson sent me to St Pancras to ask about ice was as hot and breathless as any other. It was that part of the summer when the pace of the city slowed and the streets were less frantic, and I made my way to the station past grand houses closed up for the summer, and past shops that were barely less quiet, the shop-keepers leaning in their doorways with folded arms, or sheltering in deep shade beneath their awnings. By the time I reached St Pancras my crisp, new petticoat was limp and clinging, my summer skirt already streaked with grime.

There, beneath the station's thrusting tower, I found my old friend Scraggs, the grocer's boy, selling overpriced paper fans to desperate passengers. Business was brisk, but his face was flushed and his forehead dripping, although it was barely nine in the morning.

'Hottest day yet, Flot,' he told me cheerfully, 'or so I'm told by the lad who shines the station master's boots. And what brings you to this particular part of the furnace?'

'I've come to see the iceman,' I told him. 'And then I'm to go to Fotheringill's for raspberry syrup.'

'Ah! One of Mrs Hudson's summer punches!' He grinned happily. 'Then I'll make a point of dropping in later on.' He paused to dab his brow with a shirt sleeve.

'What I don't understand, Flottie, is why you're all still here. Old Sherlock could afford to get out of town, couldn't he?'

It was a very fair question. Ours was, by now, the only front door on our side of Baker Street that had not been bolted for the season. But the great detective remained stubbornly at his post. Since his sensational triumph in the affair of the opera-singer's lizard, he had barely ventured beyond his own study, waiting in vain for the challenge that would rouse him from his torpor. Listless and out of sorts, he passed the hours staring at his fingertips or playing 'The Arab's Farewell' on the violin with such intensity of feeling that Dr Watson had to beg him to stop.

'I'm not sure Mr Holmes feels the heat,' I explained to Scraggs, 'and, besides, he says he needs to stay where he can be found.'

Scraggs didn't even attempt to reply to this. He merely shook his head in bewilderment and pointed out that, so great was the heat in Trafalgar Square, even the pigeons had left for the country.

And I couldn't blame them. By then, the long days of breathless, unstirred heat had turned London's streets into open ovens, the brick and stone still hot to the touch long after the sun had set. And the nights were worse than the days. People kept their windows closed to exclude the dust and the stench, and because the air outside was hotter than the air within. But the stillness of those sweltered rooms pressed down so heavily upon the occupants that, all across the city, sleep came and went in restless, ragged fragments. Nearly all the travellers who approached Scraggs for fans had about them an air of long-suffering weariness.

6

'So, Flot, if you're going to be here all through the summer, you could go to the Survivors' Ball. It's at the Mecklenberg Hotel this year.'

The Survivors' Ball! He said it very casually, rearranging the fans on his tray as he spoke, and he didn't look up when I laughed. Because the Survivors' Ball was, in those years, a hugely famous institution, and the grandest, poshest, most spectacular event that anyone in service could ever imagine attending. It was organised by old Lady Townsend, who never left London during the summer months, and took place every year on the last Saturday of August. It had begun as a simple thank-you dinner for her own servants, a reward for surviving summer in the city. Gradually it had grown to include the households of other aristocratic families, until it had become the stuff of legends, and the object of a thousand below-stairs fantasies. Its fireworks were spectacular, its orchestra the very finest, and the food was as sumptuous as the most lavish London banquet. All the grandest families subscribed.

'But, Scraggs,' I pointed out with a smile, 'I would never receive a ticket, and neither would you. We'd have to find employment in much grander homes first. I believe Lord Brabham's household all used to go, back when he used to stay in London all summer with the stud books. But now he closes down the house in Bloomsbury every August. And I don't know anyone else who ever goes.'

'Well, you never know, Flot...' Scraggs looked up from his fans, and instead began to examine a locomotive that was building up steam on a nearby platform. 'If I thought you'd like to go... I'm very friendly with the boot boy at Lady Townsend's, you know. And ever since I helped him out with that bunion cream, old Perkins the butler thinks of me as a favourite son.'

'Really, Scraggs!' I laughed again. 'Last time I saw you and Mr Perkins together, he was throwing a rotten cabbage at you!'

He had no option but to smile at that.

'But fondly, Flottie. Very fondly.'

He turned back to me, and we grinned at each other.

'And he missed, remember, which shows his heart wasn't really in it. Anyway, think about it, Flot. Meanwhile,' he added, 'if it's true about Mrs H's punch, I'll be around about four. Unless the points melt before then, and all the trains get cancelled. But I don't think that will happen. Reliable things, railways.'

He paused and both of us considered the hissing locomotive in front of us – fifty tons of hefty, ponderous iron.

'Solid,' Scraggs pointed out. 'Predictable. A locomotive may run late every now and then, Flot, but you always know where you are with trains.'

And I smiled. I thought so too.

–

I returned to Baker Street that morning considerably hotter and considerably dirtier than when I left it. But if I had hoped to rest – and a lie-down in my under-garments in the cool of my little box bed would have been very welcome – Mrs Hudson had other ideas. I found her in the shadiest corner of the kitchen, chopping cucumbers. It was something she could do with breathtaking speed, and apparently without effort, her roundly muscled forearms barely moving, only the slightest twitch of her wrist setting the blade a-blur. Even one of the giant cucumbers sent to us from Petworth was reduced in seconds to a series of perfect, paper-thin discs.

'More sandwiches,' she explained. 'Mr Holmes has a fancy for them, and if they serve to keep him off the violin until lunchtime, they will be performing a service to us all. You can take them up in a minute or two, Flotsam, but, first…' She gestured with one elbow towards a pitcher and bowl on the kitchen table. 'There's fresh water there, and I've put out a clean flannel for you.'

The water was miraculously cool. I cupped my hands and buried my face in it, then held the damp flannel to the back of my neck until I could feel little droplets creeping down my spine. By the time I was finished, the sandwiches were ready, arrayed in a delicate spiral around a Wedgwood platter, each one of them so thin they were practically translucent.

The sandwiches reached Mr Holmes just in the nick of time, for I found him pacing his study listlessly, violin in hand, a look of indecision on his face.

'Come now, Watson, you decide. Is it to be "Merry Maids of Maidstone" or "The Fairy of the Glen"? I am proficient in both.'

Dr Watson managed only a grunt in reply. For weeks the study's shutters had not been opened beyond a quarter, and the room was swathed in a soft, seductive gloom, but it was still unbearably hot. Dr Watson's armchair had been turned towards the window in the hope of attracting a cooling draught – a vain hope, I was certain, for any breeze from the street that reached him there must certainly have been hotter than the stale air within. He brightened considerably at my entrance.

'Ah, Flotsam! We were just speaking of you. And refreshment too! Excellent.'

'Indeed,' Mr Holmes concurred, 'you are most welcome. It is the time of day when we require your assistance. Dr Watson will do the post if you take on the press. But he may bring greater attention to the task if you were to recharge his glass.'

This brisk utterance made more sense to me than you might suppose, for latterly a routine had been established. More often than not, after Mr Holmes had smoked his third pipe of the morning, I would be summoned to his study, where Dr Watson and I would read aloud any items of interest we were able to discover in that day's post-bag, or in the late editions of the morning's newspapers. It felt a great honour to be trusted with such a task, and I longed to discover some fascinating curiosity that might capture my employer's interest and restore him to his usual vigour. But never had I met with any success.

That morning, too, there proved to be slim pickings. The front pages of the newspapers were largely given over to diplomatic rumblings in Persia, and to rumours that poor growing conditions in the hop fields of Kent might lead to future beer shortages.

'Well, Holmes,' Dr Watson began, his countenance glum, 'I can't say today's post is looking very promising either. There's a bill from my tailor, but that won't interest you. And one from that chap who sends you organs in jars. But from potential clients...'

He tailed off with another grunt, and fanned himself for a moment with a sheet of writing paper, one of several, of various sizes and hues, that were stacked beside his chair.

'For instance, here's another one about a missing cat,' he continued, gathering himself and peering at the paper in his hand. 'And this one here, the one on pink notepaper, is from a woman who claims she can identify the whereabouts of any felon we happen to be seeking using only playing cards and a divining rod.'

'Do you know, Watson...' Mr Holmes was eyeing the platter of sandwiches. 'The nutritional value of a cucumber sandwich is almost negligible, thus making these, in all practical terms, next to useless.'

He selected a sandwich from the platter and examined it carefully, then took a little bite.

'And yet there is, nevertheless, something strangely restorative about their consumption. They elevate the spirits in mysterious ways, in ways that would appear to defy all rational explanation. Is there anything else, my friend?'

'Two more from householders convinced their servants are pilfering from them, and two from servants who feel their employers are unfairly withholding their wages. Oh, and one here from a woman in Yorkshire who wishes to know what brand of tobacco you smoke.'

'Astonishing.' The detective shook his head and sighed deeply. 'Now what about you, Flotsam? Have the gentlemen of the press managed to unearth any items that might interest us?'

I had taken the armchair commonly occupied by Mr Holmes himself, and had spread the newspapers across my lap.

'Very little, I'm afraid, sir. Three more stabbings, all in public houses.' I said it timidly, knowing my employer's scorn for such things. 'And a gentleman in Clapham has slain his brother-in-law with a reproduction Viking battleaxe.'

Mr Holmes rolled his eyes as though such acts of barbarity, even when committed with historical weaponry, were intended purely to vex him.

'Watson, please tell me you have come across something better.'

'Well, Holmes, there's an undertaker in Somerset who has been sold a potato that resembles the Kaiser. He believes it to be evidence of a German plot against the nation. Oh, and this very last one is from a lady in Hampshire whose husband keeps losing his spectacles. Not sure what she expects *you* to do about it though, Holmes. Find 'em, I suppose.'

Mr Holmes stopped pacing and closed his eyes.

'Sometimes, Watson, I feel we would be better to seal up our letterbox and have the Post Office redirect all our mail directly to the bottom of the Thames.'

'Please, sir,' I interrupted, trying to conceal my sudden excitement. 'Please, sir, here's something that's a bit different. I know it isn't really any concern of ours, but even so…'

Despite my efforts to the contrary, my excitement must have been evident in my voice, because Mr Holmes opened his eyes and cast an appraising glance in my direction.

'Read on, then. Flotsam. Read on.'

It was only short, a Stop Press item on the front page of *The Clarion*.

> *Predeál, Rumania. Railway officials report express train missing in Carpathian Mountains. Rumanian officials state special charter from Bucharest*

> *to Cluj entered tunnel in Tömös Pass, Monday*
> *morning. Witnesses confirm train never emerged.*
> *Local service which followed passed through tunnel*
> *without impediment. Officials report tunnel single*
> *track throughout, no branches or sidings.*

I looked up from the newspaper. For a brief moment Mr Holmes appeared to be studying the pattern in the carpet, then he approached my chair and gently removed the paper from my lap so that he might read the mysterious paragraph for himself. There was a gleam in his eye as he did so, a gleam I had not seen there since before the hot weather began. But it was Dr Watson, sitting forward in his seat, who spoke first.

'My word, Holmes!' he declared. 'That sounds like a rum sort of business. What do you make of it?'

'What do I make of it, Watson?' The eminent detective placed the newspaper back into my hands and reached for another sandwich. 'I make very little of it. It is a tantalising fragment, nothing more. To speculate without further data would be an unforgivable waste of our energies.'

'But Holmes! A disappearing train!'

In reply, his companion reached to the mantelpiece for a short pamphlet about strangulation, and began to fan himself.

'Of course, Watson, there *are* certain conclusions we can draw, are there not? For instance, the tunnel in question is of unusual construction and considerable length. The missing train carried no more than half a dozen passengers, consisted of a single carriage and was driven by an unmarried Rumanian national with no close family. That much is obvious. Would you not agree?'

I had known Mr Holmes for too long to gasp out loud at such bold statements, but I do believe my jaw dropped a little. Dr Watson, however, looked less surprised.

'I would agree without hesitation, Holmes, for you clearly know much more about this business than you led us to believe.'

'Oh, come now, Watson!' Mr Holmes waved his pamphlet with a flourish. 'I know no more than any other reader of *The Clarion*. Yet I am confident that, within a fortnight, I shall have been proved correct on all counts.'

'Sooner than that, Holmes!' Dr Watson countered. 'For I think we can expect much fuller reports of the business in tomorrow's papers.'

'Perhaps, Watson, perhaps.' The eminent detective appeared to be gazing intently at a small indentation in the opposite wall, the result last autumn of a misguided experiment with catapults. 'But it is just possible,' he added firmly, 'that the British press will say no more about this incident in the coming days. And if that is the case, my friend, then we should rejoice.'

'And why is that, Holmes?'

'Because it will prove beyond the tiniest fragment of doubt that, in some matter of quite extraordinary importance to this country and her citizens, something has gone very badly wrong. And that the nation is threatened, not by some belligerent monarch or blustering demagogue, but by an opponent of unparalleled ingenuity and imagination. After all, Watson, one does not make an entire train disappear without considerable amounts of cunning, a quite extraordinary determination, and an uncommon helping of panache.'

'Well, really, Holmes,' Dr Watson objected, 'I can't see why we should be rejoicing at any of that!'

'Not at that, my friend. But we may very reasonably rejoice at the upshot. Because, if I'm right, Watson, and I have every confidence that I am, then we shall very shortly be receiving a visitor, recently arrived from the Carpathians, with a truly remarkable story to tell.'

Chapter Two

The following day there was no mention of the missing express train in *The Clarion*, nor in any other of the newspapers. I know this because, the next morning, as I made my way from Baker Street to Bloomsbury, I bought a copy of every London daily I could find. But not one of them contained any interesting item of news, only the usual monotony of diplomatic communiqués on the front pages and news of tavern brawls inside. None of them saw fit to mention the mystery in the Carpathians, not even *The Planet*, which so enjoyed reporting cases of the bizarre and mysterious that it sometimes made them up. It was as if the disappearing train had disappeared all over again.

My outing to Bloomsbury was not an errand in the usual sense. Bloomsbury Square was home to the Honourable Rupert Spencer, a dashing young gentleman and an amateur scientist, and the nephew of the famously short-tempered Earl of Brabham. As a rather mischievous child, Mr Spencer had some dealings with a certain stern housekeeper, and his respect for Mrs Hudson lasted well into adulthood. So when Mrs Hudson had decreed that I should have an education, and that my education should include a knowledge of the sciences, Mr Spencer had agreed with good grace to act as my tutor.

So every week after that, and sometimes more than once a week, I could be seen making my way to Bloomsbury dressed in my smartest clothes, trying my hardest to look like a lady, and calling, not at the familiar rear entrance that led to the cosy servants' hall, but at the grand front door, as bold as any duchess. But it was hard to appear ladylike when the heat was melting the cheese in the grocer's window and I was staggering under a thick pile of heavy papers; by the time I reached Bloomsbury Square, the hot newsprint had smudged from the pages all over my hands and sleeves. Reynolds, the butler, and an old friend of mine, appeared as impassive as ever when he opened the door, but took the unusual step, before announcing me, of packing me off downstairs to clean myself up in his pantry.

'I shall deliver the newspapers to the library,' he told me solemnly, 'where Miss Peters is waiting to pour tea. Miss Peters,' he added, even more solemnly, 'has a new bonnet. I believe fulsome praise, and a great deal of it, would be the tactful course.'

Hetty Peters, the ward of the Earl of Brabham, and a young lady of great vivacity, was required for the sake of propriety to attend all my lessons with Mr Spencer, while never ceasing to insist that absolutely none of them made any sense to her. Her admiration for Rupert Spencer, however, comfortably outweighed her horror for the sciences, and as a result I believe she looked forward to my visits even more keenly than I did myself. When I entered the library she was standing before one of the glass-fronted bookshelves, admiring in reflection an extraordinary item of headwear.

'Flottie, darling!' she cried when I entered, 'what do you think? Isn't this just the most marvellous creation? The silk is French, the lace is Nottingham, the pink bit is some sort of old rope, by the look of it, and this bit in the middle isn't a real bird's nest, it just looks like one.' She poked it merrily with her forefinger. 'The fruits are wax, I think, because the lady in the shop warned against wearing it outside until the weather is a bit cooler. But milliners are always far too cautious, aren't they, Flottie? And what's the *point* of making bonnets that can't go out in the rain, or in the sun, or in the wind, or on a Tuesday, or whatever? If we aren't going to wear them whenever they make us happy, why bother with them at all? We might as well just wear bowler hats or mortar boards or pith helmets.'

'But, Hetty!' I replied, blinking, caught off-guard by the eccentricity of the garment. 'Where *could* you wear a bonnet like that? It's so... so striking,' I finished lamely, suddenly recalling Reynolds' excellent advice.

Miss Peters mistook my hesitation for awe.

'It *is* striking, isn't it, Flottie? And no one else has one like it, absolutely no one. Not even the Moresby sisters, who own ostrich farms. I shall wear it to the Wymondham's this year. It will be the talk of the county.'

I feared this was true, but before I could think of anything else to say, the door of the library had been flung open and the Earl of Brabham himself was striding into the room.

I had met the Irascible Earl on many previous occasions, and for all his bristling manner he had always been – in his own brusque way – reasonably polite towards me. Even so, I confess I always quailed slightly in his company, and it was clear from the manner of his entry that his mood was not a good one.

'Hetty? You still here? Drinking tea again? Tea! Ghastly stuff. In my day a girl of spirit quaffed champagne in the afternoon and brandy in the evening, then *chartreuse* between the sheets. And she'd have told you very prettily exactly where to put your tea! Who's this?'

He turned to examine me, his dark brow furrowing to a point above the bridge of his nose in a manner which made him look, I always thought, a little like an angry seagull.

'This is Miss Flotsam, Uncle,' Miss Peters explained with a sigh. 'You've met her before.'

'Flotsam? Flotsam? Oh, yes, I remember. The sensible one. How d'you do? God in heaven! What *is* that nightmare on your head?'

To my relief, the question was not addressed to me but to Miss Peters, who drew herself up to her full height and eyed him coldly. Although I could not always bring myself to admire Miss Peters' taste in hats, I invariably admired her courage.

'This, Uncle,' she told him loftily, 'is the Very Latest Thing. It looks strange to you because you stopped noticing the latest fashions at about the time of the first Ashanti War. But I shall wear this at Lord Wymondham's house party, and when I do, I shall be the envy of every lady there.'

'Great heavens!' The elderly peer looked in genuine pain. 'And to think I was planning to attend! Must write to Wymondham at once to tell him I'm going to be overseas. Might actually have to *be* overseas if there are going to be bonnets like that one around this season.

19

Looks like a half-eaten flamingo! And a messily eaten one, at that. Now, where the devil's Rupert? Want to ask him something. Never here when you need him, confound the fellow!'

'*Sometimes* here, Uncle.' A pleasant voice from the doorway signalled that the gathering of the household was now complete. 'How can I help?'

Mr Rupert Spencer was a brown-haired and undoubtedly handsome young man, with eyes that crinkled at the edges when he smiled, and an air of calm about him that was often, I felt, sorely needed in the house in Bloomsbury Square. He advanced into the room as he spoke, and greeted me with a friendly nod while the Irascible Earl gathered himself for his next assault.

'Need to tell you something! About a friend of yours. That damned nuisance Broadmarsh. The cheek of the man! If I were a younger chap, I'd horsewhip the fellow for his impudence, although horsewhips nowadays probably aren't up to the job. What the devil does the fellow mean, sending me ridiculous telegrams?'

'Do you mean *Professor* Broadmarsh, Uncle?' Mr Spencer was clearly surprised. 'I haven't heard a word from him for months.'

'Yes, Broadmarsh! Didn't I just say as much? You remember the fellow! You invited him round here once. Brought a dead cat with him! And had the effrontery to put it on the table in the card room. I made Reynolds throw him out, remember? And the cat too! Told Reynolds I'd tip him a guinea if he could hit the blighter with the cat, but the fellow ducked in the nick of time.'

'Ah, yes, Uncle, I certainly remember the incident. I had invited the professor here to demonstrate a certain technique of dissection.' Mr Spencer grimaced slightly at the recollection. 'Fortunately, he bore no grudge. He is a gentleman with a very well-developed sense of humour.'

'Sense of humour! Sense of humour!' I thought it quite possible that the Earl of Brabham might explode, right there in the middle of the library. 'Sense of humour, be damned! The fellow wrote to me the following day, apologising for the cat, saying he had no idea I objected to felines, and promising to bring a sack of dead rats next time he called.'

I confess I struggled to suppress a smile at this, and Miss Peters actually spluttered into her tea.

'You see!' Lord Brabham continued, apparently inter-preting her reaction as one of shared outrage. 'Clearly the man's an idiot as well as a lunatic! Dead cats on the card table, indeed! Rats in sacks! I remember I wrote back telling him that if he ever contacted me again I'd take his communication directly to the Home Secretary and ask for him to be committed to an asylum. Broadmarsh to be committed, I mean, not the Home Secretary. Though, come to think of it, both would benefit equally.'

'And Professor Broadmarsh has been in touch again, Uncle? Completely out of the blue, you say?' Mr Spencer clearly considered this a surprising twist. 'It is unlike Broadmarsh to over-play a joke,' he explained to me and to Miss Peters.

'Call it a joke, call it what the devil you like!' the earl retorted. 'I call it insanity. The fellow's unsafe! And now he's sent me another damned impertinent message. By telegram! Arrived a week ago, but I mistook it for a reminder from my bookmaker, so I only just got round to looking at it properly. Wish I'd just thrown it on the fire, but the weather's too hot for fires. Makes no sense at all, and no reason given! The fellow's clearly a lunatic. Knew it all along!'

'Do you have the telegram here, Uncle?' Mr Spencer asked patiently.

'Well, of course I have it here! Where else would it be? Want your help with it, said so when I came in, remember?' Lord Brabham pulled a crumpled piece of paper from his waistcoat pocket. 'Thought you might know the quickest way of getting the man locked away, that's all. I've already fired off a note to the Home Secretary, but I just wondered if the Archbishop of Canterbury needs to be involved.'

Mr Spencer took the paper and glanced at it, and immediately I saw his smile turn to a look of genuine surprise.

'Well, Uncle, for once I would have to agree with you. This is a genuinely strange communication. And sent from abroad, from Constanta, on the Black Sea coast. I wonder what old Broadmarsh is doing there?'

'Oh, really, Rupert! Don't be so utterly annoying!' Miss Peters burst out, snatching the telegram from his fingers as she did so. 'I'm sure Flottie and I can make some sense of it.'

But neither of us could. The message was easy to read but very, very difficult to understand. Apart from the sender's surname, it consisted of a single word:

SULPHUR

On my return to Baker Street, I found Dr Watson settled at our kitchen table, feet up, head back, and balancing a piece of ice on his forehead. Around him were spread the gutted remains of a pile of newspapers as big, if not bigger, than my own, and behind him Mrs Hudson stood polishing punch glasses with a cotton leather, unflustered and impossible to fluster, and apparently unperturbed by the gentleman's singular antics. The kitchen was notably cool, more comfortable even that Lord Brabham's airy library, and I was not greatly surprised to find that Dr Watson had sought sanctuary in its shadows. The unmistakeable sounds of 'Once I Kissed a Jolly Jack Tar', rendered expertly on the violin, were filtering down to us from upstairs.

'Ah, Flotsam!' he remarked when I entered, scrambling to his feet and nodding to me, while all the time holding the piece of ice to his brow. Then, observing that I too had been collecting the day's news sheets, he sighed and sat down again.

'Not a word about it, I'm afraid,' he grunted. 'A great deal about Russian posturing over Afghanistan, and something about unrest in the Trans-Caspian, but nothing at all about vanishing trains. Holmes pretty much predicted as much.'

'Then do you think, sir,' I asked hopefully, 'that somebody really *will* want to consult you and Mr Holmes about it? It sounds terribly exciting!'

The doctor removed the ice cube from his forehead, slipped it down the back of his neck, then sat up a little straighter.

'I suppose they might. And I suppose we'll discover Holmes was right about all that other stuff too, but I'm dashed if I know how he could be so certain of it all.'

I cast a proud little glance over at Mrs Hudson; I had spent a great deal of the previous evening giving her my views on the subject, and now I interpreted her slight nod of the head as permission to repeat them.

'Well, sir,' I began a little nervously, 'Mrs Hudson and I were talking about those things last night, and I think I understand the bits about the tunnel. Mr Holmes said it must be an unusual one, and quite a long one – and of course most tunnels are straight, aren't they? The engineers want to keep them as short as possible and as straight as possible, because straight tunnels are easier and cheaper. But this one can't be straight, sir, it must have a curve in it. It must be impossible for someone looking into the tunnel from one end to see straight out of the other. Because trains don't just disappear, do they, sir? If they go into tunnels and don't come out again, then they must still be in there somewhere.' I turned to Mrs Hudson for support. 'And someone must have thought to peer down the tunnel when the train went missing, mustn't they, ma'am?'

'You would certainly hope so, Flotsam,' she concurred. 'Now, perhaps while we're chatting you'd be good enough to give that table a quick wipe?'

'And do you see, sir,' I went on, looking around vaguely for a cloth, 'that must be one reason why Mr Holmes thinks the train was made up of a single carriage. Because a short train would be easier to hide in a curved tunnel than a very long one.'

'Well, yes, my girl.' Dr Watson was looking a little more cheerful. 'That all sounds sensible enough. No special Holmes magic required there!'

'And if the train was a special charter, sir, it might very well be a small train, wouldn't it? If it was being chartered by a single person, they'd only need one carriage or perhaps two at the most, isn't that true?'

Again I turned to Mrs Hudson for confirmation, and again she replied with a nod.

'The table, if you please, my girl. PC Mawkins had his boots on it earlier.'

'But one moment, Flotsam...' Dr Watson was pursing his lips. 'Holmes can't be sure about that, can he? It's only a guess. The train might just as easily have been chartered by a huge group. It might have been for a factory outing or a sight-seeing trip organised by some large society, or it might have been a regiment of soldiers on the move.'

'But, sir, I think Mr Holmes was very likely right. Because if a great many individuals had vanished into thin air, the item in *The Clarion* would surely have mentioned them, wouldn't it? It would have been a story about *people*, not about locomotives. Or at least that's how Mrs Hudson put it last night, isn't it, ma'am?'

'Very possibly. I should try the stiff brush first, Flotsam, if I were you, taking great care not to scratch.'

Dr Watson, realising that this item was within his reach, passed it to me, but his thoughts were clearly elsewhere.

'I think you're right, Flotsam. Because the London papers could hardly keep quiet about a whole train full of people vanishing into thin air, could they? That would be an international sensation. It would be the talk of every city in Europe.'

'But if there were only one or two people on the train, sir, and if there was some special reason why someone wanted them to disappear...'

'...And if,' Dr Watson continued, following my line of thought, 'if, for the same reason, someone else wanted the papers to keep quiet about it... If it were a British official on board, for instance!' Dr Watson beamed. 'But what about the driver? All that stuff about no family, and about him being a Rumanian?'

'I suppose, sir, that if the driver had a family, they would make a great deal of fuss about him disappearing. But if he were an unmarried man with no dependents...'

'Of course! You can't make a train disappear without a bit of planning, and if you want to avoid an army of grieving relatives creating an uproar, then it would make sense to choose a driver who can disappear without causing an outcry.'

'And if the plot was hatched in Rumania, then perhaps the plotters might feel that a Rumanian citizen would be more trustworthy?'

'My word, Flotsam! I think we've cracked it! What do you think of that, eh, Mrs H?'

The housekeeper raised one eyebrow a fraction of an inch.

'I'm not convinced, sir, that any mystery is worth the pointless ruin of a good table top. A gentle scrub only, Flotsam, if you please. But if Mr Holmes' predictions are as accurate as you both believe, then no doubt we shall be hearing more about the incident at some point in the next few days. Until then, Flotsam has a scullery to sweep, and judging from the appalling noise upstairs, sir, you might set about persuading Mr Holmes that a brisk walk, despite the heat, would do him the world of good.'

And yet, for all Mrs Hudson's sound common sense, I'm not sure that either Dr Watson or I was able to put the business out of our minds in the days that followed. The rooms in Baker Street, though as hot as ever, and certainly no less airless than before, had a different feel to them. The lassitude and irritability of the previous weeks had been replaced by an air of expectation; and every time a carriage paused outside our door, our heads would turn, eager to discover if anyone would alight.

A long week followed, but at the end of that week, the message came. A short note on thick, creamy notepaper with an elaborate heading, from a gentleman well connected in the highest circles of government. *Sir*, it read.

> *I would be greatly obliged for your assistance in a peculiar matter that has been brought to my attention. A young man recently returned to London from the Carpathian Mountains brings with him a tale that I believe you will find of interest.*
>
> *I have asked him to call upon you at the earliest opportunity. His name is Charlesworth. I believe him to be reliable and trustworthy. You would be well advised, however, if you value your sanity, to avoid engaging him in any discussions of Eastern European linguistic forms.*
>
> *Faithfully,*
> *Franklin*

Chapter Three

The following day, for the first time in weeks, Mr Holmes and Dr Watson went out. Mr Holmes, it seemed, buoyed by the knowledge that a matter of substance was finally to be brought to them, was suddenly revitalised. The violin was put away, the cucumber sandwiches declined, and, having resisted Dr Watson's urgings for more than a month, the suggestion of an outing was seized upon with enthusiasm. So that morning the gentlemen set out with the intention of returning a quantity of borrowed scientific paraphernalia to its various owners. None of it would be greatly missed; it was far too hot for practical experiments and, besides, in the last four months there had been no new bloodstains on which to practise.

Their departure, however, meant a great deal of work for those of us who remained, representing as it did a rare opportunity to give the gentlemen's study a thorough and sorely needed clean. Mrs Hudson and I set about the task with great vigour, aware that the occasion might be a fleeting one. So despite the breathless heat we worked like Trojans, tidying, dusting, polishing, and scrubbing from the floorboards various sticky residues that defied all attempts at classification.

We had no fear of interruption, for there had been no callers at the front door for nearly three weeks, and such was the energy with which we went about our tasks that at first I mistook the little knocking noise from down below as the tap of a gentleman's cane as it passed along the street. Only when it came again a second time did I realise the sound was coming from our front door.

'You had better go, Flotsam,' Mrs Hudson advised, proving that she had heard it too. 'Your apron is marginally less filthy than mine. And when you return, perhaps you could bring with you some extra dusters and a little more of the sugar soap.'

There was no further knocking as I made my way downstairs, and by the time I reached the hallway I was quite certain that the person who had tapped so timidly must already have changed their mind and gone away. But when I released the bolts and opened the front door, she was still there, still on our doorstep, but turning away, as if preparing for flight. At first I couldn't see her very clearly – the street was so bright after the sepulchral shade of our hall that I was dazzled for an instant by the sunlight, while at the same time the raw heat of the day wrapped itself around me with such suddenness that I stepped back, my hand shading my eyes, struggling to focus.

'Forgive me,' our visitor began, apparently realising that I had caught her in the act of departure. 'I hadn't really expected anyone to answer.'

Her voice was hesitant, but soft and pleasant, and as my eyes narrowed I could see that she was a lady of perhaps twenty-five years of age, beautifully dressed in the lightest and airiest summer fabrics, her face shaded by a hat which, in terms of elegance and simplicity, put to shame any number of Hetty Peters' remarkable bonnets. One gloved hand held a furled parasol, the other a calling card which she seemed oddly reluctant to surrender.

'I had come to see Mr Sherlock Holmes,' she went on, 'but of course, now I think of it, he is surely out of town at this time of year...'

'Mr Holmes is not at home, madam,' I told her formally, then, taking pity on her: 'I mean he *is* in London, ma'am, but he really is out. We're not sure what time he'll be back. And this evening he's busy. Perhaps if you were to call again tomorrow?'

But the lady in front of me gave a little shake of her head.

'I am in town only for a few hours,' she told me. 'I came in the hope... I had hoped...' Then she smiled and shook her head a second time. 'Well, it is not to be. My apologies for disturbing you.'

And before I could prevent her, before I could assure her that her visit, regardless of its purpose, would surely be very welcome, she had turned and stepped away. I watched her make her escape down Baker Street, and as she went, I wondered why she had come.

When another knock interrupted our labours a few minutes later, before I'd even made a start with the sugar soap, my first thought was that our timid visitor must have returned. But this was a knock of a very different sort, firm and confident, and repeated three or four times. This caller, too, was a lady, only five or six years older than the first, and also well dressed, not in the same sumptuous fabrics, but neatly and sensibly and with evident good taste. Her face had none of the blushing prettiness of the first lady but was handsome and firm, and when she spoke her voice was kindly.

'My name is Mrs Esterhazy,' she told me, 'and I have called to see Mr Sherlock Holmes.'

She didn't seem at all put out when I explained that Mr Holmes was not at home, but nodded and gave me her card, on which was printed her name and an address in Hampshire.

'Please tell Mr Holmes that I shall call again. I have already written to him but have not yet had a response. It concerns my husband and his spectacles, which repeatedly go missing, and I am growing increasingly anxious about the matter.'

Then she too turned and made her departure. I watched her make her way up Baker Street with brisk, purposeful strides, but this time I had no thought of trying to detain her. To be honest, I think I was lost for words.

–

That evening passed slowly. The sun slipped below the line of the rooftops but there was no abatement in the heat. Even the shadows seemed to swelter, and upstairs, in the gentlemen's study, the airlessness was exacerbated by the gentlemen's barely concealed impatience. I was occupying myself washing and re-washing lettuces when we finally heard a carriage rumble to a stop outside our front door.

'Go on, then, Flotsam,' Mrs Hudson told me, before there had even been a knock. She was busy folding pillow cases, her sleeves rolled up, her great rounded forearms pale in the gloom of our shady quarters. 'You can do the honours, my girl. Better slip on a clean apron, mind. We don't want to welcome our visitor with salad smudges, do we?'

The gentleman I ushered into Mr Holmes' study that sultry evening did not look like a bringer of mysteries. He looked rather nervous and very hot, a slight, pale-skinned young man with thinning hair, a round face and round spectacles. He stood on the doorstep rotating his hat between his fingers like an anxious curate contemplating his first sermon.

'Mr Erasmus Charlesworth, for Mr Holmes,' he told me apologetically. 'I believe he is expecting me. But perhaps you would be good enough just to make sure? Perhaps the hour is too late? Perhaps Mr Holmes is occupied on other business?'

'Mr Holmes *is* expecting you, sir,' I reassured him firmly, shepherding him indoors. 'You are to go straight up.' I had no intention of letting him slip away.

If poor Mr Charlesworth had appeared nervous on the doorstep, he looked a great deal more so on arriving in the study. Mr Holmes, who was not always the warmest or most welcoming of hosts, advanced upon him out of the shuttered gloom with an enthusiasm and vivacity that even I found a little alarming.

'Welcome, sir, welcome! Dr Watson and I are delighted to make your acquaintance. Ever since we received the note from Sir Torpenhow Franklin, we have thought of little else. Please, come in, come in. Watson, mix Mr Charlesworth a drink. No? Very well. Tea? Water? Yes, of course, later perhaps. Come in, come in.'

And I swear the great detective actually put an arm around his shoulder and drew him into the room, as if fearful that the long-awaited caller, if not held firmly, might simply melt away into the heat of the night.

Only when Mr Charlesworth had been positioned squarely in front of the fireplace did Mr Holmes turn to me.

'That will be all for now, Flotsam,' he informed me crisply, 'but I believe the silverware needs some attention and this would be a very convenient time to see to it. It will save us all a lot of bother, one way or another.' His manner was brisk and business-like. 'And please leave the door open a little as you leave. Our guest will appreciate some circulation of the air.'

If Mr Charlesworth thought it strange that Baker Street's famous detective took such a personal interest in the minutiae of our domestic arrangements, he showed no sign of it. Visitors to Mr Holmes' establishment had come to expect eccentricity, I knew, and no doubt Mr Charlesworth thought this a perfect example.

I, on the other hand, understood exactly what Mr Holmes had in mind, and was delighted by his words. For it was a quirk of our living arrangements that the small box room where the silver was stored stood directly opposite Mr Holmes' study. When both doors were slightly open, a young girl hard at work with the silver polish couldn't help but hear what passed in the room opposite; and should she happen to look up from her work, she would find that relatively small gaps at both thresholds afforded her a surprisingly wide view into the heart of the study.

It had not, of course, taken Mr Holmes very long to understand these things, and although none of us ever alluded openly to the arrangement, he clearly derived satisfaction from the idea that Mrs Hudson and I had some knowledge of the cases in which he was engaged. Perhaps this was simply his eccentricity; or perhaps he believed that by understanding the outline of any new case, we would be better able to anticipate his requirements. Confidentiality, I knew, was something of an irritant to Mr Holmes if it became, in any way, an impediment to efficiency.

Over the years, therefore, I heard many remarkable things while hard at work on the silver, but few tales were as bewildering as the one told that night by Mr Erasmus Charlesworth in the gloom of the darkened study.

'First, gentlemen, please let me introduce myself.'

The young man's voice as he began to speak still wobbled slightly, as though from nerves.

'I am, by training, a scholar of European languages, with a particular interest in the rare and ancient dialects of the Carpathian Mountains and of Trans-Danubia. Unfortunately I was not born with the means to indulge this passion for its own sake, and so for most of my adult life I have been forced to take employment as a private tutor, teaching – for the most part – French.'

He spoke the word with a shudder, as though recalling the pain of countless brutal assaults upon that language by countless brutal pupils.

'My last employer, however, Lord Whortleberry of Whortleberry-cum-Magna, was most generous. Against all expectation, I succeeded over the course of twelve months in teaching his eldest son very passable Portuguese, which enabled his lordship to win a substantial wager involving very large quantities of unbottled port.

'His lordship's gratitude took monetary form, and as a result I was able to fulfil my lifelong dream of moving to Transylvania to make a study of the dialectic variations to be found in its mountainous regions. Why, within only the first few months I had identified a variation of the local linguistic forms which had never previously been recorded. It took the form of...'

Mr Holmes gave that curt little cough I knew so well.

'I strongly suspect, sir, that it was not your achievements as a student of rare languages that recommended you to Sir Torpenhow Franklin. Perhaps if you were to tell us precisely why he asked you to call...?'

'Yes, of course, of course. Sir Torpenhow. Yes.'

Even from my remote vantage point I could see our visitor blush, but he collected himself bravely and carried on.

'After various travels in the Carpathian region, gentlemen, I settled in the small town of Predeál, which nestles on one of the high passes between the Kingdom of Rumania and the Hapsburg Empire. I find it a delightful spot, short of luxuries, certainly, but a place of simple joys and honest pleasures. The people are good-humoured, friendly, and not uncultured by the standards of the region. I am happy there, and the joy of giving no lessons and of speaking no... French...' He shuddered again. 'That joy has been considerable. I live very simply, but from time to time I have supplemented my meagre funds by penning short articles about Carpathian life for some of the more erudite British journals.'

I saw Mr Holmes nodding sagely, although I knew that such publications did not feature very prominently in his own bookcase.

'As a result of this,' Mr Charlesworth went on, 'it seems that my name became known in certain writing circles, and I was surprised a few months ago to receive a letter from a Mr Murgatroyd of the Foreign News Desk at *The*

Clarion asking me for a paragraph about the forthcoming visit to the region by one of the Rumanian princes. The level of remuneration I received for this simple task came as an extremely pleasant surprise.'

Mr Charlesworth cleared his throat, clearly a little embarrassed to have raised, in polite company, the treacherous subject of money.

'I was therefore delighted,' he continued, 'to hear from Mr Murgatroyd again, a month ago, suggesting I send him a short report on Predeál's famous Tunnel Ceremony.'

Dr Watson, who had been fanning himself with a slim volume of essays about spiritualism, appeared to sit up a little in his chair.

'Eh? What's that? Tunnel Ceremony? Can't be that famous, can it, Holmes? Don't think we've ever heard of it!'

Mr Charlesworth flushed again, even more deeply than before.

'My apologies, Doctor. I used the phrase loosely. The ceremony has a certain local renown, and this year, because an official from our embassy in Vienna had been invited to attend, it had come to the notice of Mr Murgatroyd at *The Clarion*.'

'Your account is admirably clear, sir.' Mr Holmes' voice was soothing. 'But perhaps, given our ignorance, it would be helpful if you could tell us a little more about this Tunnel Ceremony of yours.'

Mr Charlesworth paused to mop his brow with a modest, cream-coloured handkerchief.

'Certainly, Mr Holmes. It must all seem very whimsical to you, but it is quite an occasion in Predeál and the surrounding area. Predeál, you see, stands just inside

Rumania, at one end of the Tömös Pass. A few years ago, to facilitate the construction of the railway between Bucharest and Cluj, a tunnel was cut through the pass, a tunnel which begins in Rumania and ends on the other side of the border, in Austria-Hungary, by the little village of Tömös. There were, in medieval times, periods of great hostility between the villages on one side of the pass and the villages on the other, and I think it is fair to say that the opening of the tunnel caused a certain amount of trepidation among the simple folk on both sides – fears that it would be used in some way by marauding raiders to pillage across the mountains.

'But the story goes that when the very first train passed from Rumania through the Tömös Pass, a local youth had a happy idea. Boarding the train in Predeál, he stood on the footplate playing his flute, entertaining the towns-folk with traditional songs of the mountains. On arrival in Tömös, he then repeated his performance to great applause before returning to Predeál. By making the point that the towns and villages on both sides of the border were united by a common musical tradition, he ensured that, from that day forward, the railway – and the tunnel it ran through – were celebrated rather than feared.'

Dr Watson, I noticed, was fidgeting slightly.

'A good story, Mr Charlesworth. Quaint and heart-warming, and all that. But I can't quite see why a man like Torpenhow Franklin would be interested in any of this. For all his high standing in matters of state, he is, I've always thought, rather a dry old stick. Surely not one for peasant folk music?'

'No, sir.' If our visitor disagreed with this assessment of Sir Torpenhow's character, he did not betray the fact. 'But

I am merely explaining how the modern ceremony came about. From then on, you see, on the anniversary of that opening, it has been the tradition that a band of Rumanian musicians travels to Predeál by train and performs for the townsfolk from an open railway carriage before passing through the tunnel to be greeted by villagers and dignitaries on the other side. There they perform for a second time, again from the open carriage, before the train returns to Predeál for a third and final performance, followed traditionally by much feasting and merriment.'

'A very pretty ritual,' Mr Holmes commented, 'and I begin to see its relevance to the events recently reported in *The Clarion*. Please continue, sir.'

'Well, Mr Holmes, this year, because of my commission from Mr Murgatroyd, I observed the ceremony with great care. In Predeál, on the Rumanian side of the border, the guest of honour was a local count whose family had given up some of its lands to allow the railway to be built. On the Austrian side of the border, in Tömös, a minor member of the Hapsburg royal family was attending, accompanied by Sir Humphrey Ward-Smythe from our embassy in Vienna. Sir Humphrey, you will recall, is a student of music and an eminent amateur composer. Please note that I observed events from the Predeál end of the tunnel, but had an opportunity two days later to compare notes with Sir Humphrey in person.'

Dr Watson, who had shuddered slightly at the words 'eminent amateur composer', gave a confident nod.

'I get the idea. A reliable witness at either end. So one of you was bound to witness any monkey business, eh?'

'I would certainly have thought so, Doctor. But as events transpired...' The speaker shook his head, apparently struggling for adequate words. I noticed he was no longer looking at either of his hosts, but gazing at the floor as though lost in a very different time and place.

'Gentlemen, I think it best if I spare you most of the detail of that day, all the colours and sounds, and the various sentiments expressed by the speakers. But there is one detail that is significant. The opening concert lasted noticeably longer than in previous years, because of a change to the local railway timetabling. You see, the officials in Predeál had been informed that the local train – the one pulling the orchestra's open carriage – could not depart until a special charter had passed through the station. While we waited, the orchestra continued to play. Only when the special charter train had passed through, into the tunnel, was the signal given for the local train to follow.'

Mr Holmes was leaning forward in his seat, his eyes bright with interest.

'So you actually saw the special charter train enter the tunnel? Excellent! Then please tell us everything you remember about it.'

Our visitor nodded.

'Of course, sir. I recall that it was an express locomotive, pulling a single carriage. It slowed slightly as it passed through the station but it didn't stop, which is, I believe, the usual practice of the fast trains that run through to Cluj. Other than that, I remember very little. It was travelling too quickly for me to notice any passengers other than one gentleman, a gentleman with red hair and a short beard, who had pulled down his window and was looking out. But he was gone in an instant, and that is all I remember seeing.'

The great detective looked satisfied with this, and leaned back in his chair.

'That is all very interesting, Mr Charlesworth. Now, please go on.'

'I fear, sir, that there is very little more to say. When the special charter had passed, the signal was given for the local train to move. The orchestra waved, the train pulled out, then they too disappeared into the tunnel. There followed a hiatus of an hour or two, while the townsfolk of Predeál awaited the return of the train. Some drifted away, some produced food and made a picnic of it right there at the station. The dignitaries were escorted to the house of the mayor for refreshment. I stayed, notebook in hand, feeling it was my duty to continue to observe.

'But there was nothing untoward to report. At the appointed time, the local train returned, and the musicians played again. Shortly before six o'clock in the evening we waved them off and their train continued in the other direction, back to Bucharest, where the orchestra was scheduled to disembark. No other trains passed through the station during that time, and in fact none were scheduled for the rest of that day, the usual timetable having been amended on account of the ceremony. In fact, Mr Holmes, everything was exactly the same as every year, except for one thing.'

Outside, the street was very quiet, and I could hear the footfalls of a single weary carthorse passing our front door. But in Mr Holmes' study the silence of that moment had a different quality – intense and exciting and pulsing with energy.

'I didn't become aware of it, gentlemen, until after the musicians had departed, when I noticed the local station master looking troubled. He was a man I was well acquainted with, and he seemed relieved to be able to confide in me. At about five o'clock that afternoon he had received a telegram from the railway officials at Tömös asking him about the special train. It was a rather bad-tempered telegram apparently, asking why they had not been informed of its rescheduling, and wanting to know what time they should be expecting it. Well, of course he had replied promptly, telling them that the special train had left Predeál on schedule and what did they mean by their absurd message? A rapid exchange of telegrams ensued, with each side accusing the other of mendacity or incompetence or both. It was not until the milk train from Cluj arrived the following morning, bringing with it the station master from Tömös, that the true nature of the conundrum became clear.'

If Mr Charlesworth had begun his tale nervously, no trace of those nerves now remained. He weighed his words carefully, looking from Mr Holmes to Dr Watson and back again.

'Gentleman, let me simply state the facts. The tunnel between Predeál and Tömös is single-track, it has no sidings, no spurs, no branch lines. There exists but one way in and one way out, and one line of track along its entire length. I watched the special train enter that tunnel, and I watched the local train follow it, with the orchestra waving from an open carriage. Those waiting in Tömös at the other end of the tunnel witnessed the local train emerge and heard the musicians play. They watched it re-enter the tunnel and return to Predeál. But not a single person in Tömös, from the Hapsburg prince to the humblest beggar, saw the special train emerge from the tunnel. That train went in, Mr Holmes. But it never came out. And for the other train to pass through the tunnel without hindrance, not once but twice… Well, to put it plainly, sir, that charter train had simply vanished, had simply dissolved into thin air.'

Chapter Four

When I recall the events of that evening, so many pictures remain vivid in my mind: Mr Charlesworth planted firmly by the fireplace, no longer nervous, waiting while his words sank in; Dr Watson putting down his fan and quietly reaching for his glass of brandy-and-shrub; Mr Holmes rising from his armchair and stalking to and fro in silence, his eyes narrowed in thought. I don't recall anything about the interior of the silver cupboard that evening, not even the heat, although it must have been unbearably hot in there. So great was my concentration on Mr Charlesworth's tale, so engaged was I in the mystery he'd brought us, that I didn't notice any discomfort at all. Any silver I attempted to polish that night must surely have required further attention at a later date.

Mr Holmes was the first to speak.

'Excellent! A fascinating tale, and every bit as intricate as I'd hoped.'

Having vacated his chair, he now gestured for Mr Charlesworth to replace him there; not, I think, out of any concern for our visitor's comfort, but simply to allow himself more room in which to prowl.

'The solution, of course, will not detain us long. But first I must ask the obvious questions. You will forgive me, sir, if I clarify one or two points?'

'Of course, Mr Holmes. I will help in any way I can. But the fact remains that the charter train really had vanished. If it had left the tunnel, at either end, there would have been witnesses galore. But if it had remained *in* the tunnel, the orchestra train could never have passed through.'

'Yes, yes.' Mr Holmes waved away these objections with a flourish of his pipe. 'Now, let us begin at the start of the day. The orchestra, you say, travelled to Predeál that day from Bucharest?'

Mr Charlesworth nodded. 'It was not, of course, a large orchestra – about fourteen musicians in all, carefully selected from the students at the King Michael Academy in the capital. They were very good.'

'Of course, yes.' It wasn't clear if my employer was commenting on the size of the orchestra, or the training of its members, or the quality of their performance. 'And the train they travelled in… You call it a local train, but clearly it began the day in the capital city and returned there that night.'

Mr Charlesworth blushed again.

'I stand corrected, Mr Holmes. There are various fast trains that pass through Predeál without stopping, and we always refer to them as express trains. The trains that stop at the smaller stations, and therefore all the trains that stop at Predeál, are routinely referred to as locals. The orchestra's train was referred to as a local train for that reason, but of course it was really a special train in its own right, laid on by the company especially for the orchestra and stopping only at Predeál and at Tömös.'

'So it carried no passengers?'

Mr Holmes' questioning was crisp and certain. I was given the impression that he already knew the answers.

'No, sir. The orchestra train consisted of a locomotive, a standard second-class carriage for the musicians and their instruments, and one of those old-fashioned open carriages from which they were to play. The Rumanian railways still own a few of those and they are not an uncommon sight, especially during the warmer months.'

'Kissed a girl in an open carriage once,' Dr Watson recalled fondly. 'It was Derby Day, back when I was a slip of a lad. Long time ago now,' he added quickly, blushing slightly.

'So, to be clear, Mr Charlesworth, a specially selected band of musicians set off from Bucharest that morning in a second-class carriage, taking their instruments with them. The first stop was Predeál, where they moved to the open carriage and performed to the gathered crowds. When the mysterious charter train had passed through the station, the musicians' train followed it and arrived safely in Tömös. The musicians were no doubt questioned?'

'Yes, sir. I was even invited by the authorities to travel to Bucharest to interview them myself. But they all said the same. The train had run through the tunnel in the normal way. There had been no stopping, no sudden breaking, no shunting, nothing out of the ordinary.'

'And what is your recollection of the orchestra on the day itself? Did they seem in any way affected by the experience of travelling through the tunnel?'

Mr Charlesworth took a moment to think back.

'I don't think so, Mr Holmes. They were a strikingly young and dashing group of fellows, and their playing was as accomplished for their last performance as it had been for their first. I remember wondering if the double bass might have been slightly out of tune, but apparently not, for Sir Humphrey Ward-Smythe, who knows much more about these things than I do, declared the performance of every instrument excellent.'

'And what about the driver of the orchestra train? Were you able to speak to him?'

'Indeed. He and the fireman are both Bucharest men with many years of service, and are very familiar with the line that runs through Predeál. And both told the same story. They had waited for the appropriate signal before entering the tunnel. They had proceeded slowly, at the speed laid down for that stretch of track. All the signals were in their favour, and they arrived at Tömös without incident. And the return journey, by both accounts, was similarly straightforward. They saw no sign of any train ahead, and both are adamant that it is the people at Tömös who are mistaken, that the charter train must have passed through the tunnel in the normal fashion.'

'But of course one of those people at Tömös was Sir Humphrey Ward-Smythe,' Mr Holmes pointed out, 'and although the British public might be persuaded to believe that any number of Austrian princelings had failed to notice a fifty-ton locomotive passing by them, they would be inclined to take the word of an English gentlemen, albeit a self-confessed amateur composer.'

'That's right, Holmes,' Dr Watson concurred. 'Can't imagine Sir Humphrey would be wrong about a thing like that. It seems to me pretty obvious that there must have been some funny business in the tunnel. I suppose the express must have derailed, eh? Then the other train could pass through perfectly normally. And I suppose it's just possible the driver and the rest of them might not have noticed. It must be pretty dark in there.'

'But, Doctor,' our visitor protested, 'there's not enough space in the tunnel for two trains to pass, even if one of them had come off the rails. In fact there's not even enough space to come off the rails, really. The tunnel is notably narrow, you see. If a train breaks down in there, there's only just room for the mechanics to squeeze through between the carriages and the tunnel walls. The passengers could wriggle out to safety if they needed to, but they'd probably have to leave their luggage behind. Even a small trunk would be too big to manoeuvre through the space available.'

I swear that Mr Holmes rubbed his hands at this.

'Mr Charlesworth, your little problem does not disappoint. The elegance! The simplicity! I am lost in admiration. Now, tell me, you mentioned that you noticed one passenger in the charter train as it passed, a red-haired gentleman, I think you said. What else have you found out about that train?'

'Very little, I'm afraid, Mr Holmes. The train driver...'

The great detective held up his hand.

'I have already explained to Dr Watson that he was unmarried and with no close family. Am I correct?'

Although I had seen the same expression many times, and on many different faces, I couldn't help but revel in Mr Charlesworth's look of undisguised astonishment.

'Perfectly correct, Mr Holmes, though I'm at a loss as to how you know.'

'And the fireman is the same, I take it? Yes, of course. And the passengers, Mr Charlesworth? What can you tell us about them?'

But here our visitor shrugged.

'As I said before, I fear I can tell you very little. I made enquiries, of course, but could discover only that the train had been chartered from Bucharest to Cluj, and from there on to Vienna. No passenger list has been published, and no further details released.'

This reply seemed to affect Mr Holmes greatly. He paused in his pacing and studied his visitor closely. I could tell by his expression that the answer surprised him in some way and I thought he was about to remonstrate, but after a long pause he looked away and resumed his restless progress from the window to the corner and back again.

'I almost forgot to ask the most obvious question, Mr Charlesworth. You have come here tonight on the recommendation of Sir Torpenhow Franklin, but you have not yet explained what interest Sir Torpenhow takes in the matter, nor why you have abandoned your beloved mountains to be here tonight. I hope that this little mystery has not soured your positive feelings for the area?'

'Not at all, Mr Holmes. I would not have left the region at all had it not been for Sir Torpenhow. Shortly after the incident he sent a telegram to Sir Humphrey in Vienna, urging most insistently that I should return to London at once to place the matter in your hands.'

'But he has made no effort to explain his interest to you? And you have not wondered why Sir Torpenhow Franklin is so concerned about the disappearance of a foreign train?'

The question caused our visitor some confusion.

'Well, sir, it was a very remarkable event. It certainly caused something of a sensation locally. Surely anyone would want to know...' He tailed off, apparently examining his own logic for the first time, and finding it wanting. 'You know, Mr Holmes, I *was* surprised that Sir Torpenhow wanted me back in London with quite such urgency. The embassy in Vienna arranged the whole thing for me. Fast trains, first-class tickets. But I suppose I just thought the Foreign Office liked to keep itself abreast of strange events.'

'Well, indeed it does. On occasions.' Mr Holmes favoured his visitor with a warm smile, the sort of smile which indicated that the interview was coming to an end. 'You may tell Sir Torpenhow Franklin that we have greatly enjoyed your visit, and that the conundrum you've brought us poses no great difficulties. If he wishes to learn how the charter train was made to disappear that day, he only has to call upon us here and ask. But he should not attempt to do so until he is prepared to surrender some information in return.'

'Information, Mr Holmes? What information do you seek?'

'Sir Torpenhow has lost a diplomat, Mr Charlesworth. That much is obvious to me. And if he wishes to engage our help in finding this missing person, he must be willing to tell us all about him, about his reasons for being on that train, and the plain truth about his mission. Until he is prepared to share with us the full story, sir, then we are most certainly not prepared to furnish him with any answers.'

It was nearly ten o'clock when Mr Charlesworth departed but, when he stepped outside, Baker Street seemed even hotter than when he'd arrived. That evening, as nearly every evening of the whole blighted summer, the setting sun had drawn a thin layer of cloud over the city – a layer that would have been hailed as a glorious blessing during the daylight hours, but which at night only served to press the heat more firmly upon the airless streets. Few people had ventured out that night. In December, at the same hour, to cross from one side of Baker Street to the other without being struck by a carriage would have required quick wits and not a little agility; that evening I could have performed hand-stands in the centre of the thoroughfare and still have come to no harm.

But Mr Charlesworth was not our last visitor that night. Mrs Hudson and I had completed our chores for the evening and were just settling ourselves down for a moment of quietness before bedtime when we were disturbed by a diffident tap at the area window, followed a moment later by the appearance of Mr Rumbelow, the solicitor, an old acquaintance of Mrs Hudson's, looking horribly hot in evening dress, with a crumpled top hat beneath his arm.

'Mrs Hudson, Flotsam, my apologies. So late to call. Happened to be passing. Dinner at the Empedocles Club, then lingered a long time over an iced crème de menthe because it was just too hot to walk home. Saw your light and thought I'd pop in. My visit is not inconvenient, I trust?'

Mrs Hudson, who had been busying herself hulling strawberries, signalled for me to provide the perspiring gentleman with a chair, and he sank down next to me, clearly much relieved to feel the weight off his feet.

'So *very* hot out there, Flotsam,' he explained a little breathlessly. 'And rather a lengthy walk in this heat. Eerily quiet, too. I would have taken a cab, but there were none to be found.'

Mr Rumbelow, a comfortable and portly figure not greatly given to exercise, was clearly in need of further refreshment, and before he had even rested his hat beneath his chair, Mrs Hudson had provided it.

'An iced Riesling, sir. Just the thing for these terrible nights. And Vichy water for you, Flotsam, straight from the cellar so beautifully cool. The strawberries will go well with both, though not too many just before bed, my girl. And, yes, on this occasion, you may indeed float one or two in your drink.'

'Ah, Mrs Hudson...' Our visitor surveyed the scene. 'I've often said there is no more welcoming place in London than your kitchen in hot weather. Perhaps you would permit me to loosen my collar a fraction? That's better! Of course, you must not think I have called tonight simply because I was hoping for a fine glass of wine. That would be quite wrong of me, quite wrong. Although it would be dishonest of me not to admit that the Alsatian wines you have served me here quite surpass those available at the Empedocles Club. A gift from Lord Ellesmere, perhaps? I know he has, in the past, sent you some excellent white port.'

Mrs Hudson nudged the bowl of strawberries a little closer to him.

'Certainly not, sir. Lord Ellesmere has an excellent port cellar, and is always very generous. He also has some surprisingly fine Iberian wines. But I would never recommend his hock. This particular wine is purchased from Arwell Brothers on Greek Street. The elder brother has not left Alsace in thirty years.'

'Quite so, quite so.' Mr Rumbelow examined his wine more closely, perhaps wondering if the waiting list at Arwell's was still as long as it had always been. 'But as I was saying, Mrs Hudson, it was not the prospect of a restorative glass – not *purely* the prospect of a restorative glass – that brought me here tonight.'

Mrs Hudson made no reply, but settled comfortably into the chair next to mine and quietly topped up our visitor's glass.

'You see, there's something I'd quite like to discuss with you. I had a strange consultation this afternoon, and I can't quite put it out of my mind. Have you ever heard of a fellow called Broadmarsh?'

'*Professor* Broadmarsh, sir?' I found myself sitting forward in my chair, suddenly much less tired than I had been. 'The scientist? I believe he's a friend of Mr Spencer.'

'That's the chap, Flotsam. He's a popular and well-connected fellow. But not *universally* popular. It so happens that from time to time his brother, Mr Ezra Broadmarsh, consults me in a professional capacity. And without betraying any professional confidences, I believe it is fair to say that the two brothers do not always see eye to eye.'

Mr Rumbelow sipped his wine and sighed.

'Mr Ezra Broadmarsh is undoubtedly a difficult fellow, rather thin-skinned and litigious by nature. On many occasions now it has been my duty to dissuade him from taking legal action over perceived slights. And that was also the case today. Mr Ezra fancies himself as something of an amateur lawyer, and he was seeking my assistance in having his brother charged under the Offences Against the Person Act of 1861. He felt certain that his sibling's actions constituted an assault upon him under Section 35 of the act. However, that section, when I looked it up, concerns causing bodily harm by wanton or furious driving, so was clearly not applicable. Then he thought it must be Section 36, but that one outlaws the obstruction of a clergyman in the performance of his duties. Eventually we agreed that the part of the act he had in mind was Section 16, Threats to Kill, but I advised him most firmly that, even under that section, no reliable case could be made.'

'But, Mr Rumbelow, sir,' I interrupted, unable to contain myself, 'what exactly had Professor Broadmarsh *done*?'

The solicitor sighed and mopped his forehead again.

'Well, it appears the two brothers have not spoken for some months, and their last meeting ended badly, with my client, by his own confession, losing his temper somewhat. Now, I am aware the professor has a somewhat mischievous sense of humour, and I suspect that he likes to tease his brother on occasions. But, even so, the telegram he sent this week seems a strange response. You see, there is no message, as such. The telegram consisted of a single word: *Arsenic.*'

I think I must have let a little gasp escape me, for both my companions turned to look at me. Before I could explain myself, however, Mr Rumbelow continued.

'Well, of course, I explained to Mr Ezra Broadmarsh that sending someone arsenic in a physical sense – in a bottle, for instance – might be considered tasteless, might even in some circumstances be considered to constitute a threat to the person. But simply sending someone the *word* arsenic, by telegraph, would not, in the eyes of a well-directed jury, be considered on offence under the act.

This was not what Mr Broadmarsh wished to hear, and he became rather heated, insisting that his brother was trying to play tricks with his mind. And it is not hard to understand that such a communication might unsettle someone. I don't know if the professor intended it as a joke or as some sort of insult, but I do believe it was slightly shabby behaviour.'

'Was the telegram sent from abroad, sir?' I asked eagerly.

Mr Rumbelow looked surprised.

'Why, yes, Flotsam. I believe it was.'

So I explained about the similar telegram received by the Earl of Brabham, and the general bemusement Mr Spencer felt about his friend's behaviour.

'It's very odd, isn't it, sir? For him to send two telegrams so similar, and for no apparent reason?'

'Indeed, it is! *Sulphur, arsenic*... I know the fellow is a scientist, but even so...'

Mrs Hudson had risen from the table and had moved to the dresser, where a pile of napkins waited to be folded.

'Do I recall that Professor Broadmarsh recently did some work for the government, sir? Last year, I think it was. Something to do with mineral rights in Persia?'

'I believe you're right, Mrs Hudson. I know they think very highly of him in diplomatic circles. Nowadays he is as much a special envoy as he is a scientist.'

'Why, I remember him now!' I cried. 'I knew I remembered the name. You pointed him out to me in the street once, ma'am, shortly after he returned from that expedition. Just outside Covent Garden it was.'

'That's the gentleman, Flotsam,' Mrs Hudson confirmed. 'And I'm sorry to say it, but I believe he is currently in some danger.' She paused, and I noticed the smallest trace of a frown form on her brow. 'I hope, for the professor's sake, that Sir Torpenhow Franklin calls upon Mr Holmes as quickly as possible. The sooner it is all sorted out the better.'

'You mean, ma'am...?'

But Mrs Hudson, perhaps fearing a long explanation so late at night when our visitor was so clearly weary, changed the subject swiftly, inquiring after the health of Spendlehume, the veteran steward at the Empedocles Club, who had been a fixture there since Mrs Hudson was a girl.

It was only later, lying practically naked in my little cupboard bed, too hot to sleep and with my mind still racing, that it all fell into place, and I wondered that I had not seen it all before. Just two simple things occurred to me as I lay there, two things I already knew but which made the other things fit together: firstly, that the town of Constanta stood on the Black Sea coast, in the Kingdom of Rumania; secondly, that the man I had seen near Covent Garden, the man who had been pointed out to me as the notable Professor Broadmarsh, scientist and special envoy to the crown, had been a striking looking gentleman – striking, for the most part, because of his head of blazing red hair and his impressive red beard.

Chapter Five

The next morning found me at the house in Bloomsbury Square, bright and early and full of news. I found the house serene, with no sign of either Miss Peters or Lord Brabham. Mr Spencer was taking coffee in the drawing room, and rose when I came in. An enormous leather-bound atlas lay open on the table in front of him.

'I attended a lecture last night at the Galen Society, all about the Comoros Islands,' he explained, 'and I emerged extremely well informed about the habits and culture of the people there, but still a little hazy about exactly where the islands are to be found. Now what brings you here so early this morning, Flotsam?'

'I'm really on my way to Lamington's to talk about cold meats,' I told him, 'but Mrs Hudson said I may call in on my way. You see, I think I have some news about your friend Professor Broadmarsh.'

'Then you must sit down and allow me pour you some coffee. Reynolds has already laid an extra cup.'

While Mr Spencer attended to the coffee pot, I allowed myself to recover my breath for a moment, for I had rushed to Bloomsbury Square at a considerable pace, and even at that early hour, the streets were still too hot for rushing. But the drawing room at Mr Spencer's house was an airy room, with high ceilings and north-facing windows, and certainly considerably cooler than the world outside.

'It is funny you should bring up Broadmarsh again,' Mr Spencer commented as he helped me to cream. 'After reading that strange telegram of his, I asked around about him and found that none of his regular acquaintances had any idea where he was. Most assumed that he was simply out of town somewhere, but it seems no one has seen him for the last two or three months. Then, last night, at this lecture, I learned certain things that captured my attention.'

He placed the coffee cup and saucer in front of me and leaned back in his chair.

'First of all, someone told me that Broadmarsh had recently been in touch with his banker, old Plumstead of Gerrard's. The chap who told me about it didn't know much, simply that he'd overheard someone say that Plumstead had some sort of problem and had been trying to find Professor Broadmarsh in order to sort it out. I wonder if that means the professor is in some sort of financial difficulty?'

'I'm afraid the professor's difficulties might be of another sort altogether,' I told him. 'But, please, go on. What was the next thing?'

'Well, this one's similarly vague, I'm afraid. For a bunch of people who profess themselves interested in the sciences, the members of the Galen Society always seem rather better at gossip than at facts.'

Mr Spencer smiled at me. He had a very nice smile.

'Anyway, one fellow heard me asking about Professor Broadmarsh and told me that *he'd* been talking to someone who was just back from Persia, who claimed he'd bumped into Broadmarsh in Tehran. Broadmarsh had behaved rather oddly, apparently, and had practically snubbed the fellow, but he did learn from an ostler who had been travelling with the professor that the two of them had just arrived from Ashkhabad. Do you know something, Flotsam?' He smiled again. 'I have no idea where Ashkhabad is.'

'It's a city in Turkestan, sir,' I told him promptly, for I loved maps and had long ago memorised every page of Mr Holmes' copy of *Butler's Atlas*. 'It's a very long way away. I wonder what the professor could have been doing there?'

Mr Spencer had turned to the relevant page of the tome in front of him.

'Here we are...' He placed his forefinger on the city of Ashkhabad. 'And here's Tehran... and here's Constanta, on the Black Sea coast, where he sent my uncle that telegram. Why, he *has* been getting about, hasn't he? That's quite a journey. From Central Asia, heading west, south round the Caspian, then up to the Black Sea and into Europe. I wonder where he is now?'

'But that's just it, sir. That's why I came. You see, Professor Broadmarsh got as far as here...' I pointed, as nearly as I could, to the spot in the Carpathians where the railway line ran through the mountains. 'And then he disappeared.'

And slightly breathlessly, but as clearly as I could, I told Mr Spencer the story of the disappearing train, concluding with Mr Charlesworth's sighting of a red-headed man leaning from the window.

'Of course, I can't be *certain* that was the professor,' I confessed. 'But the professor was definitely in Constanta, and if he was trying to get home from there he might very well choose to take the train through Rumania and on to Vienna. And we know that something strange was going on, else why would he have been sending such peculiar telegrams? And, from what I understand of the region, a gentleman with blazing red hair would be something of a rarity there.'

Mr Spencer closed the atlas with a soft, rather satisfying thump.

'You are almost certainly correct, Flotsam. And you say that Sherlock Holmes is likely to be engaged in the case?'

'Mr Holmes thinks so. And Mrs Hudson hopes he will be.'

Mr Spencer rose.

'Then the fate of the professor is in reliable hands. But there is something that you and I could do to help, Flotsam. That business about his banker... Plumstead will still be at home at this hour, and if you are heading to Lamington's, his residence is not greatly out of the way. So, come, let us go and pay a call. Just this once, the cold meats can wait.'

I went with him happily, delighted to be following a trail which, however convoluted, might eventually lead us to the truth behind such strange events. As we made our way up Bedford Place, Mr Spencer had me take his arm. I suppose I should have been feeling fearful for the unfortunate gentleman missing in the Carpathians, or at the very least anxious that Lamington's would be selling out of Parma ham. But I wasn't. It makes me sound silly and shallow to confess it, but as I walked along at Mr Spencer's side that morning, I felt full of a warm, frothy happiness.

And fortunately the interview with Mr Plumstead did not last very long, so in the end there was plenty of time for me to place my orders at Lamington's. The banker turned out to be an elderly gentleman, bald but for grey side-whiskers that clung to the side of his face like exotic and determined caterpillars. Mr Spencer introduced me as Miss Flotsam and we were both received very cordially in a study that was, apart from Mr Plumstead himself, dark brown throughout – from the floorboards, to the leather, to the spines of the books that lined the walls. We declined sherry, it being not yet nine o'clock in the morning.

'Yes,' he told us cheerfully, in answer to our question, 'I have the professor's telegram here. Somewhere in this drawer, I believe. It was a most puzzling communication.'

He began to rifle through a great many pieces of paper, some of which spilled onto the floor as he talked.

'I am, of course, very familiar with clients sending me instructions from abroad. Very frequently they find, when travelling in foreign parts, that they have urgent need of funds to be made available, often in remote locations, with a minimum of delay. But the instructions I received from Professor Broadmarsh were, I am forced to admit, more cryptic than most. I fear he is in need of funds, but how much, and in what precise location, I am unable to determine. In fact I felt unable to take any action at all, so unclear were his instructions. Ah! Here it is. I can only assume that the professor, if still in need, will contact me again shortly, and hopefully in rather more lucid prose.'

The telegram he held out to us was similar to the one received by Lord Brabham in almost every way. It too had been sent from Constanta, and on the same day, only a few minutes before the other. And like the other, the message contained a single word:

SILVER

As an instruction to a banker, it was certainly lacking. But no one could have complained it lacked for drama.

–

By the time I returned to Baker Street, it was already late morning. Mr Holmes and Dr Watson had departed early that day, their precise destination unclear, although Mr Holmes had talked about sending telegrams and Dr Watson had muttered cryptically about maps; so I had expected to find Mrs Hudson alone. But when I tiptoed down the area steps, I heard voices coming from our kitchen, and when I peered around the door, I saw a well-dressed lady sitting at our kitchen table, a brandy glass in front of her and a large carafe of iced water to her side. To my astonishment she was a lady I recognised.

'Ah, Flotsam,' Mrs Hudson welcomed me cheerfully. 'You have already met Mrs Esterhazy, I believe. She has come up from Hampshire in the hope of seeing Mr Holmes.'

The lady smiled at me, and I recognised her handsome features and determined expression from her previous call.

'I am afraid I was taken faint outside your front door,' she told me lightly, 'but fortunately Mrs Hudson came to my aid.' She spoke frankly, without embarrassment. 'It was the heat, I think. It is so *very* hot today, and this morning I had determined to remain in Baker Street, walking up and down, until Mr Holmes returned. I had resolved to talk to him today, you see, but I fear I had underestimated quite how hot it would be. We think the temperature is astonishingly high down in Hampshire, but in London it is clearly a great deal higher. I have never known the like.'

Mrs Hudson bustled over to the carafe and poured me a tall glass of water.

'Now, Flotsam, you take a seat here and recover yourself a little after your walk. I have persuaded Mrs Esterhazy to share her reasons for visiting Mr Holmes, and she was just about to begin. Something about your husband's spectacles, I believe?'

'That's right, Mrs Hudson. He keeps losing them. Oh, I know that sounds petty and ridiculous, but it really is a mystery, and I fear it may have a very sinister side to it. Of course, the police laughed at me when I tried to explain it to them, which is why I decided to seek out Mr Sherlock Holmes.'

Mrs Hudson did not join us at the table, but remained standing near the fireplace, rubbing the kitchen knives with vinegar paste.

'It all began about two months ago,' Mrs Esterhazy went on. 'My husband is a clergyman, the Vicar of Pinfold, and he spends most Friday evenings working on his sermon for the coming Sunday. This particular evening, however, he was unable to find his spectacles, and although we had the house searched, we never did succeed in finding them. I should state at the outset that our servants – a cook and a parlour maid – have both been with us since our marriage and are extremely reliable. And my husband is man of forty, in the prime of life, with an excellent memory and an organised mind. It is unheard of for him to mislay something out of carelessness.'

Mrs Hudson nodded, but the faintest wobble of her eyebrow betrayed her interest.

'In my experience,' she stated firmly, 'even in the best-run household, it is not impossible for something to be mislaid, and no one in particular to blame for it. Something is inadvertently knocked, for instance, it topples into a wastepaper bin that is promptly emptied, and its subsequent disappearance feels, to all concerned, like the greatest of mysteries.'

'And that is precisely the conclusion we reached,' Mrs Esterhazy assured her. 'My husband owns no spare pair of glasses, so we wrote to London for a new set to be made up to his requirements, and, apart from regretting the additional expense, we thought no more of it.'

She paused to take a sip of brandy and a sip of water, then continued.

'I should say that my husband, outside his ecclesiastical activities, is also something of an expert in the archaeology of the Celtic fringes. He has made a lifelong study of Neolithic artefacts, and is often invited to lecture by historical societies or other learned groups. A week after his new spectacles arrived, he gave a talk in Andover organised by a group of local enthusiasts. It was a popular talk, well attended by members of the public, many of whom stayed to chat to him afterwards.

'My husband, who, as I say, has a clinical mind, remembers most clearly placing his eyeglasses, in their case, on the edge of the podium when he finished his talk. He needs them most particularly for reading and for close work, you understand, and although he generally wears them throughout the day, he will often remove them on social occasions – out of simple vanity, I'm afraid, because he says they make him look like a clergyman.'

She turned to me and smiled.

'Yes, Flotsam, I know you're thinking that he *is* a clergyman, but, in his mind at any rate, there is a very great difference between *being* a clergyman and *looking* like one.'

She smiled again, rather a happy smile, I thought, and one that made me think Mr Esterhazy must be rather a good-looking gentleman.

'Anyway,' our visitor continued, 'my husband placed his spectacles on the podium before mixing with the audience, but when he came to leave at the end of the evening the glasses were gone. More bafflingly still, the empty case remained exactly where he had left it. It was not until some hours later, when he next opened it, that he became aware of the theft of its contents.

'For theft it must be, I fear. It is a strong word to use, but we can think of no other. If my husband is correct that the glasses were there – and I believe with all my heart he must be – then the only possible explanation is that some member of the audience must have removed them during the evening. Yet why should anyone do such a thing? They are made to my husband's own individual specifications – his left eye is very much worse than his right – so would be of no practical use to anyone else. You may call it a prank if you like, but, if so, it is a peculiar one, and most unamusing.'

There was something about Mrs Esterhazy that made me warm to her. I think perhaps it was her clarity and her determination. But sitting across the table from her that day, my head full of exotic locations, strange events in remote mountains, and a missing professor, possibly on a secret mission, almost certainly in danger, it was hard to share her sense of outrage.

But when I looked across at Mrs Hudson and saw one of her eyebrows raised by the tiniest amount, I realised that she was giving the problem her full attention.

'And yet, ma'am,' she suggested, 'had it not been for the first event, which we all agree could have been a simple accident, would the second appear quite so strange? Thefts do take place in public places, sadly, just as items can be mislaid around the home.'

'Again, I agree with you, Mrs Hudson, and my husband has convinced himself that the mistake was probably his. So unlikely was it that anyone would have removed the spectacles from their case deliberately, he believes it was his own memory at fault. I, however, cannot share this view, and later events, I believe, prove I am correct not to do so.'

She reached for her brandy glass, decided against it, and returned to her tale.

'Two days after the Andover lecture, you see, my husband gave a lecture in London to the Society of Antiquarians. This was a much bigger event and had received a gratifying amount of publicity in advance, so Emeric – my husband – insisted that it must go ahead. It was too late for a second pair of replacement spectacles to be made up before the talk, so as a desperate measure my husband borrowed some spectacles from his curate. They were considerably less efficacious than his own, but they did at least enable him to make out his own lecture notes.

'My husband travelled up to London by train that day. There had been some correspondence with Lord Digby, the Egyptologist, about meeting on board and travelling up together, but for some reason that plan fell through. Instead Emeric found himself sharing his compartment with a Dutch lady, a rather refined young woman travelling without a maid. The two fell into conversation, and enjoyed a pleasant and companionable journey. My husband had been wearing his spectacles when he set out, but when the two fell into conversation – and I fear once again that vanity was his motive – he removed the spectacles and placed them most carefully in one of the outer pockets of his leather document case.

'The Dutch lady left the train three or four stops before it arrived in Victoria, and she and Emeric parted with the usual courtesies. It was not until my husband prepared to leave the carriage that he realised the curate's spectacles had disappeared. The pocket of his document case – in which he had most certainly placed them – was empty, and, although he searched the carriage with great rigour, they were nowhere to be found. Since no one else had entered the carriage, he was forced to the conclusion that his fellow traveller must have stolen them from him at some point during the journey. But why would anybody do such a thing? And why would my husband's spectacles be stolen twice in three days, and each time by a complete stranger?'

Mrs Esterhazy opened a sturdy and serviceable Baude fan which had, until then, been resting on her lap. After a few vigorous wafts, she laid it on the table in front of her and continued.

'Frankly, Mrs Hudson, until I know the answer to these questions, I do not believe I will be able to rest easily. You see, that first pair of missing spectacles, which we had been happy to believe were simply lost, have now taken on a most sinister significance. My husband had placed them on the desk in his study. What if that pair had also been stolen? What if, unbeknown to my household, an intruder had stolen in through the open French doors and carried them away? Such an idea would have appeared absurd at the time, but now it begins to seem considerably less improbable. And although the problem of a rural clergyman being repeatedly deprived of his spectacles may seem a humorous situation to some, I absolutely refuse to spend the rest of my life worrying that someone whose name I don't know, and whose motives I don't understand, is tracking my husband's every move with some peculiar – and surely sinister – intent.'

I had smiled when Dr Watson told us about Mrs Esterhazy's original letter. And when she first called at Baker Street, I had been astonished that she was taking so seriously the loss of some reading glasses. But I wasn't smiling now. There was something about our visitor's unclouded reasoning that was hard to resist; and however trifling the subject of her concerns had seemed at first, now I fully understood – and sympathised with – her determination to arrive at a solution. No one likes to think they are being constantly observed. No one enjoys the attention of the unseen watcher.

Although what it all meant, I couldn't begin to guess.

Mrs Hudson, having listened to the tale, for the most part, with impassive features, now allowed her other eyebrow to twitch.

'So, tell me, ma'am, this lecture of your husband's… Was there anyone who might benefit if it did not go ahead? Any rival academic, for instance, who might otherwise have been asked to take your husband's place?'

'It is hard to think of one, Mrs Hudson,' our visitor replied firmly. 'And besides, the loss of his glasses did not prevent my husband from giving the talk. He likes to consult his notes as he lectures because he feels more comfortable when he can do so, but he has lectured many times previously without notes, and did so again on this occasion. If somebody wished to prevent him speaking to the Society of Antiquarians, then removing his reading glasses was neither an effective nor straightforward way for them to achieve their ends.'

'Very good.' I could tell that Mrs Hudson also appreciated Mrs Esterhazy's clarity of thought. 'And there has never been anything unusual about any spectacles your husband has owned, something that might give them special value?'

'Such as diamond encrusted frames, or a mysterious previous owner, or secret messages etched upon the glass?' Mrs Esterhazy gave us a warm, open smile. 'It sounds absurd, but really we have considered all those possibilities. Sadly, however, my husband, who has needed reading glasses since the days of his youth, has always patronised Coe & Snodgrass, just off Regent Street. They are a respectable but unremarkable firm, just as my husband's have always been respectable but unremarkable spectacles.'

Mrs Hudson pondered.

'And this Dutch lady, what does your husband remember about her?'

'He describes her a neatly dressed young woman, perhaps twenty-eight years old, with very dark hair that was styled simply beneath a simple navy hat, secured with a blue quartz pin. She introduced herself as a Madame De

Witt. She was below average height, and slight, with a fair complexion, a small nose, brown eyes and a small chin. She wore a pale blue day-dress, of good quality, cut in an English style. Her wedding ring was a plain gold band and she wore no other rings. She told Mr Esterhazy that her husband was a Dutch academic, in Britain to study forestry techniques, and the journal she was reading was entitled *Monthly Reports of the Ancient Society of Shropshire Dendrologists.* He noticed it was open on a passage about larch husbandry.'

It was unusual for Mrs Hudson to raise both eyebrows at the same time, but I believe she did so then.

'A remarkably detailed set of observations, ma'am. Was Mr Esterhazy wary of this foreign lady, to have taken such a close scrutiny?'

'Far from it, Mrs Hudson. My husband has an open and unsuspicious nature. But as I have already suggested to you, he also has an unusual clarity of thought. This is, I believe, a result of his upbringing. His mother died young, and his father was a rogue and a reprobate, given to drink and debauchery. He grew up surrounded by chaos, without rules or restraints.'

She shook her head sadly, as though pained by thoughts of her husband's past.

'In my experience, a child brought up in such an environment will take one of two paths. Emeric's twin brother took the easier of the two, revelling in the lawlessness that surrounded him, learning at a young age to fight, to cheat and to refuse all wise council. Benedict was, by all accounts, a brilliant marksman and an expert fencer. My husband, on the other hand, although also blessed with an athletic frame, had poor eyesight and very different tastes, and he chose the much harder path. He understood that only through diligence, sobriety and study, through a clear mind and ruthless self-discipline, could he hope to escape the world he inhabited. He determined to study for the Church, and did so, ignoring all impediments, with iron resolution. His twin disappeared abroad at the age of eighteen and died some five or six years later when a passenger ship sank in a storm off Havana. My husband's father died three months after that.'

Mrs Esterhazy did not even try to look sad.

'Happily, there remained a small portion of his father's fortune that had not yet been squandered, and the income from this inheritance allows us to live a comfortable life. But to this day my husband retains acute powers of observation and an excellent memory. He is also, against all odds, rather a nice man, and much better company than I make him sound. He does not deserve to be antagonised in this way.'

And this was a sentiment that Mrs Hudson clearly shared, for she put down the knife she was cleaning and came to join us at the table.

'It is a strange tale, madam, and it seems to me that you are right to seek an explanation. We cannot promise that Mr Holmes will be able to give it his immediate attention, of course, but I will inform him of your visit. Now, as I have explained, Mr Holmes may not return until a very late hour, and it is far too hot to linger in London a moment longer than necessary. Flotsam here will be delighted to flag down a hansom for you, to take you to the station. But I do promise you this, madam –

that your perplexing account will not be ignored here in Baker Street.'

She allowed herself the tiniest fraction of a smile.

'Flotsam and I shall make sure of it.'

Chapter Six

That particular afternoon was a quiet one, free from callers, and an opportunity for Mrs Hudson and I to address various small tasks that had been neglected. The pantry shelves had not been wiped down since the previous morning, and in that dustiest of summers the floors needed sweeping on an almost hourly basis. As we settled to our various tasks, the conversation inevitably turned to Mrs Esterhazy's visit, and Mrs Hudson was adamant that she had no theory that might explain that curious sequence of events.

'I really don't, Flotsam,' she insisted. 'It all seems rather baffling, and I feel for Mrs Esterhazy. But I can't imagine why anyone would be going to such trouble to separate Mr Esterhazy from his spectacles. Not unless... But, no, that is too far-fetched, the sort of device that occurs only in the most dreadful penny novels...'

I had read very widely in Mr Holmes' library, as well as in Mudie's circulating library, but my acquaintance with the sort of penny novels Mrs Hudson described was a great deal more limited than I would have wished. Therefore my mind raced as I imagined all sorts of bizarre and bewildering possibilities – none of which, however, came close to explaining the facts that had been laid before us. So instead I changed the subject.

'Professor Broadmarsh, ma'am... Do you think he really is in danger?'

Mrs Hudson continued to sweep, a pile of light brown dust accumulating near the area door.

'Well, Flotsam, that depends. Someone has gone to a great deal of trouble to make him disappear. But if their aim was simply to eliminate him, that could have been done quietly and anonymously in a back street, somewhere in Bucharest or Constanta or some such city, and no one would have been any the wiser. This whole nonsense with trains suggests that the professor is more important to them alive than dead.'

My spirits lifted slightly.

'That doesn't sound so terrible, after all.'

'Let us hope not, Flotsam.'

But the way she said it was not entirely cheering. I put down my cloth, miserable again, then suddenly brightened.

'But, Mrs Hudson, ma'am, what about these telegrams? It seems to me that the professor is sending us clues. Something that might help us to help him, perhaps?'

The housekeeper made no reply as she opened the kitchen door and, with three strong, deft strokes of the broom sent the entire pile of dust spinning out into the area. Then she closed the door swiftly and turned to me.

'Those telegrams are certainly intriguing, are they not, Flottie? Let's see, what do we have so far? *Silver, Sulphur, Arsenic.* And what do we make of those?'

'Well, ma'am,' I told her, 'all three are chemical elements, and they can be combined with other things to make compounds.' I said it proudly. Chemistry was a favourite subject. 'But I can't think of any compound which combines all three.'

'And who is to say there are not further telegrams that we don't yet know about, young lady? Mr Holmes would no doubt tell us that it is pointless to speculate without complete data.'

I nodded, disappointed, for I had often heard him say exactly that.

'Very like a cucumber sandwich, Flottie. A bit point-less, as we all know – and yet strangely pleasing nonetheless. Now, young lady...' She indicated the pantry shelves. 'No matter how many mysteries arrive at our door, those shelves will still need wiping. And our two gentlemen will no doubt be back shortly, and in need of cold drinks and refreshment. So we'd better jump to it.'

–

Mr Holmes and Dr Watson stayed out until the sun began to drop below the rooftops, and returned every bit as drained, and every bit as thirsty, as Mrs Hudson had predicted. They brightened considerably, however, when they saw the tray which followed them up the stairs.

'My word, Flotsam,' Dr Watson exclaimed, 'what have we here? Melon and Parma ham, vichyssoise, muscat grapes, and is that a guinea fowl? What do you say to that, Holmes?'

'I say it is no more than you deserve, my friend, for you have laboured indefatigably today in taxing conditions.'

Dr Watson appeared delighted by this praise.

'Well, I confess it *was* hot work. What do you think, Flotsam? Holmes here has had me running backwards and forwards between the Geographical Society and the telegraph office for most of the day. Which reminds me, have we had any replies? Any telegrams waiting for us?'

'One, sir. In the usual place on the mantelpiece. Should I fetch up the chilled Moselle now, sir?'

'One moment, Flotsam.' Mr Holmes had retrieved the telegram from in front of the carriage clock and was examining it thoughtfully. 'No other correspondence of any sort? Nothing from Sir Torpenhow Franklin?'

I shook my head sadly. It felt as though the true business of the summer could not properly begin until we had heard from Sir Torpenhow.

I hesitated while Mr Holmes began to study the telegram, not sure whether or not I should remain. Before I could decide, the great detective looked up, his expression triumphant.

'From Sir Humphrey Ward–Smythe, Watson. It is exactly as I expected. Here, Flotsam…' To my great surprise, Mr Holmes handed me the telegram. 'For you, to read at your leisure. You may fetch up those drinks now. And please tell Mrs Hudson that I shall require your services tomorrow, for the whole morning, at least. Dr Watson plans to abandon me for the day, so you must take his place.'

I returned to the kitchen slightly dazed by the improbability of this instruction, but bursting to relate it to Mrs Hudson.

'He said the whole morning, ma'am! Will that be convenient? What could Mr Holmes want me for? Will it be here, do you think, or will we be going out? Where do you think we shall go? And what should I wear? Oh, and there's another thing, a telegram from Sir Humphrey Ward–Smythe in Vienna. Mr Holmes gave it to me but I haven't even looked at it yet. Is that all right, ma'am? May I really go?'

'If Mr Holmes requests it, Flottie, then of course you must go. I have no idea where you will end up, but it will certainly be best summer clothes, and I will help you with your hair. Now, that telegram, Flotsam...'

I read it out to her twice, because on first reading it made no real sense to me. Sadly, it made no more sense on the second reading.

> CAN CONFIRM ATTENDED
> TUNNEL CEREMONY STOP
> SURPRISINGLY ENGAGING AFFAIR
> STOP CAN CONFIRM MUSIC
> EXCELLENT BUT ORCHESTRA
> CONTAINED NO DOUBLE BASS
> STOP CHARLESWORTH IDIOT STOP
> WARD-SMYTHE

However, if I had expected Mrs Hudson to share my mystification, I was disappointed. She simply nodded as though the telegram and its contents were no more and no less than she was expecting.

'I think Sir Humphrey is being a little unkind to Mr Charlesworth,' was the only comment she made.

'But, ma'am,' I floundered, 'what does it mean?'

She paused in her tidying and looked at me in surprise.

'Why, Flotsam, the double bass. As soon as Mr Charlesworth mentioned it, it was surely clear that the instrument hadn't been played to Sir Humphrey?'

I have learned since then that it is rarely sensible to pretend to a greater understanding than you possess. But, I confess, that evening, my pride got the better of me. I simply nodded wisely, and took the problem with me to bed.

–

I awoke the next morning tremendously excited, but also terribly nervous. The prospect of a morning in the company of Mr Holmes, taking the place of his most trusted companion, assisting with an investigation upon which someone's life might depend, and all this without the reassuring presence of Dr Watson or Mrs Hudson – well, I knew that many of the great detective's admirers would have given up their fortunes to exchange places with me, yet even so it was hard not to be a little afraid. I had spent a great deal of time in Mr Holmes' company, but very little of it alone. We had certainly never before left the house *a deux*.

Mrs Hudson did everything in her power to calm me, insisting that I should carry out all my usual breakfast chores exactly as normal, and telling me a long story about the chimney sweep's fear of swans which, with its surprising denouement, certainly succeeded in distracting me from other matters until it was time to change into my best clothes.

'And the big, velvet reticule,' Mrs Hudson advised. 'Anything smaller is pointless, anything larger too clumsy. Until women are allowed pockets, and sensible shoulder bags, it's the best we can do.'

Then she seated me by the kitchen table and arranged my hair, twisting it and turning it, and pinning it ruthlessly into the latest fashion, until I looked every bit the young lady.

'Now, just be yourself, Flotsam,' she advised me. 'Don't attempt Dr Watson's trick of trying to appear less alert than you really are. That's a tricky game, and I don't deny that Mr Holmes enjoys it, but you're a young woman, Flotsam, and there are already enough people trying to make out young women can't think for themselves. You are not to join them.'

I found Mr Holmes in his study, standing by the almost closed shutters, peering listlessly down into the street. However, my entry seemed to rouse him, for he blinked and nodded at me, and was suddenly filled with a blaze of energy, stalking from one point of the room to another, gathering up certain items that he stuffed into his pockets, others that he thrust at me.

'Magnifying glass… Safety matches… You have a bag? Excellent! And one that is not totally impractical, I observe. You have room for this? Splendid. I don't suppose we shall need a Rumanian phrasebook, but Dr Watson has been enjoying reading bits out over meals. Now, let us go! Our first stop is Savile Row.'

A hansom was quickly found, and in those sweltering streets the breeze generated by its forward motion came as a welcome relief. I had been worrying what Mr Holmes and I would talk about when alone in the cab, but found I was only required to listen. Mr Holmes had much to say about Dr Watson's absence, for it emerged that his companion's activities that day had no bearing on Mr Charlesworth's case.

'Gone off for a walk on the Downs,' Mr Holmes complained. 'In this weather too! With someone he became acquainted with during that business of the Malabar Rose. And wearing a patently ridiculous cravat.

Precisely why he feels this to be a sensible use of his time is unclear.'

I had a suspicion that I could probably answer that question, but, on this occasion at least, it seemed prudent to remain silent. I knew very little about affairs of the heart, but Mr Holmes, I think, knew even less.

I must have walked past the premises of the Royal Geographical Society a hundred times or more before that day, but I had never imagined going inside. And even as our hansom pulled up in Savile Row, I was far from sure I would be allowed in. Mr Holmes, when I expressed my nervousness, sought to reassure me.

'Don't worry about membership, Flotsam. They know me here, and you are my guest.'

'But is it the sort of society that permits women on its premises, sir?' I asked.

'Women?' The question surprised him. 'I've no idea. Why do you ask?'

Before I could think of a tactful way of answering his question, the door was opened for us by an ageing doorman with a pleasant smile, who seemed to entertain no misgivings about my gender.

'Good morning, sir. Good morning, miss,' he greeted us cheerfully. 'That volume you requested has been found, sir. I believe it has been laid out for you in the Tagus Room.'

We were escorted up an elegant staircase and along corridors panelled with rich, dark timber until we reached a small room containing a large walnut table, two old-fashioned dining chairs and bookshelves along three of its walls. The fourth wall was taken up by a tall window, its sash slightly raised, although no discernible breeze was venturing through the gap. By the standards of any normal summer, the room was uncomfortably hot and airless; but it felt so much cooler than the streets outside, it was almost a pleasure to sit there.

Someone had placed an enormous leather-bound folder on the table, and it was this that was to occupy us for most of the morning. It proved to be an unbound collection of maps, all of them of the Carpathian region, or of the wider Kingdom of Rumania.

'Our first task,' Mr Holmes complained, 'is to discard those that are not relevant to us. We are interested only in Wallachia, and in the areas of Transylvania that are currently within the borders of the Rumanian nation. Moldavia and the Black Sea regions need not concern us. Any that show in detail the area near the Tömös Pass should be put to one side for our particular attention.'

It did not appear to occur to Mr Holmes that the great majority of scullery maids, indeed the great majority of young girls my age, might not be instantly familiar with the geography of the Balkans; this was perhaps the first time in my life that my passion for maps had actually proved advantageous. But even so, the task was not an easy one, for the maps we discovered were not the clear and well-ordered items that I was familiar with from Butler's Atlas. Many were hand-drawn, to a variety of different scales, or to no scale at all, and some were clearly of great age. Some were labelled in a complicated script that I discovered was Cyrillic, others gave the names of towns in the Latin form, or in the German form, or in local forms that seemed to vary down the years – so that one village might appear under three or four different names depending upon which map you were looking at. So large was the pile of maps that the task of sorting them took the best part of an hour.

'Excellent,' Mr Holmes declared when the task was complete, 'now we can get down to the real work, Watson.'

'Flotsam, sir,' I corrected him, timidly.

'Exactly. Now let us begin with any one of these that shows us the line of the railway between Predeál and Bucharest. We are not concerned at the moment with the line beyond Predeál, through the pass and into Austria-Hungary.'

'And why is that, sir?' I ventured to ask, aware that the tunnel where the train vanished had entrances in both countries.

'Because this is clearly a Rumanian plot, Flotsam,' Mr Holmes explained patiently. 'There can be no doubt. All those implicated in the plot – the drivers and the orchestra – are Rumanians who hail from the capital city, and all three of the trains involved in that day's charade set out that morning from Bucharest.'

'*Three* trains, sir?'

'Yes, yes, Flotsam.' He was already studying one of the maps with a magnifying glass, and seemed only partly aware of my question. 'The special charter train, and both the trains used by the orchestra.'

'But, sir,' I persisted, 'the orchestra arrived on a single train.'

However, I spoke without conviction. Already my brain was frantically rearranging the many things I'd been told.

Mr Holmes looked up from his map, and studied me over his magnifying glass.

'Clearly they all *arrived* on the same train, Flotsam. But the second train used by the musicians that day must also have come from Bucharest, must it not? Presumably the night before, and with a high level of secrecy. Otherwise they would not have been able to conceal it in the tunnel without anyone noticing. Of course, the existence of the third train was obvious from the moment Mr Charlesworth began to explain the details of the affair, but it was not until he mentioned...'

'The double bass!' I exclaimed triumphantly, and the whole fantastic plot was suddenly clear to me. 'The third train explains everything *in theory*, doesn't it, sir? But the only *proof* is the double bass.'

Mr Holmes looked up from the papers.

'Precisely.' It was, I think, an approving look. 'I'm pleased you have grasped the salient points, Flotsam. The solution is, after all, blindingly obvious. So blindingly obvious that Mr Charlesworth and the others were, in fact, blind to it. It beggars belief that some people find the exercise of simple logic so arduous, so taxing on their brains, that they would prefer to believe in vanishing trains.'

'So, if you please, sir, just to make sure that I understand everything correctly, someone in Rumania arranged for two identical trains to be prepared for the orchestra at the Tunnel Ceremony. The first was sent ahead and hidden in the Tömös tunnel under cover of darkness. There were no scheduled trains that day, of course, because of the ceremony, so it could simply wait out of sight, until it was needed.'

'Exactly right, Flotsam. You will have noticed, of course, that they took care to select musicians from the state academy? Young men who were probably patriots in any case, but who would be sure to keep the secret if only to safeguard their future careers. And the drivers and firemen were all long-standing employees of the railway company who could also be trusted to stay silent.'

'Yes, sir. So, on the day itself, the driver of the special charter train drove into the tunnel, already knowing that the line ahead was blocked by another train. His orders must have been to pull up behind the first train and wait. And then, very shortly afterwards, the orchestra train arrived – the third train in the tunnel – and the musicians simply picked up their instruments and squeezed past the charter train, taking up their places in the *first* train in the queue, which looked identical to theirs. And that train carried on, out of the tunnel, to Tömös, where they played to Sir Humphrey and all the others. Except...'

'Except for the double bass player, Flotsam. Because no one had realised that the tunnel was far too narrow for an instrument as large as his to fit between the train and the tunnel wall. Which is why we could be certain, long before we received Sir Humphrey's confirmation, that the double bass had never made it to Tömös.'

'And after Tömös, sir, they all simply headed back into the tunnel, squeezed back into the original train, and continued back to Predeál, where they played for a second time to Mr Charlesworth...'

'...who noticed that the double bass was still out of tune. Had Mr Charlesworth not had a sensitive ear, Flotsam, he may never have mentioned the instrument in the first place.'

I thought of the three trains in the tunnel, the special charter trapped there while the musicians played.

'But, sir,' I asked, 'what about the passenger on the charter train? What was he doing while all this was going on? And what happened to him afterwards?'

'I would imagine, Flotsam, that he was sedated in some way. The most sensible course of action would have been to offer him drugged refreshments somewhere between Bucharest and Predeál. That would have allowed time for the drugs to take effect at around the time the train reached the tunnel. As for what happened next...' Mr Holmes indicated the maps in front of us. '...That is precisely what we are about to determine.'

And with that we set to work on the maps. Mr Holmes asked me to compile a list of all the possible stops the trains must have passed through that day – not only the actual stations, but any sidings or water-stops, or just any place close to a remote road or a good track which might have allowed passengers to disembark. Then we began to work through the list, item by item.

'Let us suppose, Flotsam, that the charter train was held in the tunnel until midnight. By then the crowds in Predeál who had gathered for the Tunnel Ceremony would surely have dispersed, and the station master would have been safely in his bed. The charter train – along with the orchestra train that still remained hidden – needed to make its way back to Bucharest that night before the normal timetables began to operate, so time would have been tight. But the crew had to make one stop along the way, so that their passenger – now their captive – might be removed from the train.'

'Could they not have taken him all the way to Bucharest, sir, and unloaded him there?'

Mr Holmes nodded, his attention apparently focused on my list of train stops.

'That was my thought too, Flotsam. But yesterday I sent a number of telegrams, and this morning's flurry of replies – which I fear must have disturbed your breakfast – brought me some helpful answers. As a result, I think it is highly unlikely the captive was taken as far as the capital. It appears there is a member of staff at the English library in Bucharest who is something of a train enthusiast. He is in the habit of spending much of his free time – both mornings and evenings – at the main station in the city, and he noted in his book the arrival of two empty specials that morning. *Empty*, you note. In addition, the danger of being observed in Bucharest, a city not without its share of foreign spies, must surely have deterred the plotters. Much safer for them to find a remote and rural location.'

He indicated the list in front of him, and began to cross out various entries with crisp, firm strokes of his pen.

'I am inclined to rule these out, Flotsam, because of the geography of the surrounding area. Look, this map of the physical geography of the region clearly shows where the line runs through flat or open country, where any nefarious activity might easily be observed. And these…' He crossed another dozen places from his list. 'These can be ruled out because of their proximity to towns or villages, or even to the rural hamlets shown on some of these maps. So we are left with these…'

We worked through them together, finding each one on a dozen different maps, working out how hidden they were from public view, how easily they could be accessed by road or track, and where those tracks might lead to. And one by one, the various options fell away.

'This one appears ideal, Flotsam, surrounded by the high mountains, and with a good track running beside the line. But where would they take their prisoner from there? Eastwards, the track runs into a sizeable village, and westwards it meanders for nearly twenty miles before it reaches that remote farmhouse. If it were me, if I valued secrecy, I would prefer a shorter journey.'

And finally, at about half past two, when the air of the book-lined room was heavy with the afternoon and both of us were sticky from the heat, only one place remained on my list.

'This one, Flotsam. It appears to be a seasonal stop of some sort – for hunters, or for moving livestock, perhaps – and it is hidden deep in the woods with high hills on all sides. But the track leading away from it is a good one, winding through the forest and along the valley floor to here.'

His fingertip came to rest on a tiny square – a building all on its own – with a label in German next to it.

'It would appear to be some sort of hunting lodge. No doubt we can easily discover its local name, and I confidently predict we will find it belongs to a substantial landowner, probably a member of the Rumanian aristocracy, someone sympathetic to the plots emanating from Bucharest. It would be the perfect place to hold a prisoner, Flotsam! They could have carried their victim here completely unobserved, knowing that the nonsense at the Tunnel Ceremony would kick up enough dust to hide their tracks for a week or two at least. We cannot be entirely certain, of course, but I think we can make a shrewd guess at the location of this missing diplomat. All that remains is for Sir Torpenhow Franklin to reveal that person's identity.'

'But, sir,' I exclaimed, trying not to sound too overexcited, 'I don't think we need Sir Torpenhow to tell us. I think we already know.'

And with a rush – surrounded by fusty maps and with an ink smudge on my finger – I told Mr Holmes all about Professor Broadmarsh's mysterious travels, his telegrams from Constanta, and, perhaps most importantly of all, about his bright red hair and lengthy beard. It was not quite a quarter to three, but I felt it had already been a good day's work.

–

I've often heard it said that time speeds up as you get older, but looking back from a great distance upon that burning, airless summer, I'm struck by the breathless pace at which events began to unfold. That afternoon, before we had even finished tidying away the maps, there was a knock at the door of our room, and the elderly doorman who had first welcomed us entered with an envelope in his hand.

'For me?' Mr Holmes asked, looking up eagerly, perhaps hoping for more information about his Rumanian researches.

But to the surprise of us both, the attendant shook his head.

'For you, miss.'

The appearance of the envelope he gave me was instantly familiar. I recognised it at once as one of those from Mrs Hudson's kitchen drawer, but it was addressed to 'Miss Flotsam', and the handwriting was Hetty Peters' exuberant scrawl.

Dearest Flotsam, it began.

> *Isn't it just too hot for words? I came all the way to Baker Street to find you, and the earl's carriage was so stifling I thought I might pass out, which would have been terrible, because the dress I'm wearing is simply too lovely to describe, and far too delicate for fainting in. Mrs Hudson is making me suck an ice cube to cool me down as she says it's too hot to boil the kettle and too early to pull a cork. Anyway, she tells me that the terrifying Mr Holmes has kidnapped you and has taken you to some dreadful learned society, so I'm sending this message there. Rupert took me to a talk at the Philosophical Society once, you know, and it was, by some distance, the most tedious afternoon of my entire existence, worse even that that time Lady Milton invited me to tea with the Bishop of Bermuda.*
>
> *You see, the thing is, Flottie, I've made a discovery and I need to tell you all about it. So as soon as you get this, tell Mr Holmes you have to dash off – tell him it's a sick aunt or something, that always works – and come and find me. I'll be at Frobisher's, looking at gloves. It's always cool at Frobisher's, except in the winter, when it's always deliciously warm, which is exactly as it should be, isn't it?*
>
> *No room for more,*
> *Hetty*

And it was true; there *was* no room for more. The last words, and Hetty's signature, had been forced by lack of space to turn the corner and to creep up the right-hand side of the writing paper.

'From Miss Peters, I take it?' Mr Holmes remarked when I looked up from the note. 'A guess, of course. I recognise Mrs Hudson's envelopes, but Mrs Hudson would only have interrupted us in an emergency, and in an emergency she would have felt it proper to address messages to us both. And however urgent her reason for writing, she would not have required more than one side of paper to explain it. Miss Peters, however, is a young lady who likes to express herself, and is also one of the few people I can think of who considers it acceptable to use violet ink.'

'She wants me to meet her at once, sir, at Frobisher's.' I explained. 'That's a glove-maker's.'

'We are finished here, Flotsam, so you may do as you please.' He smiled, almost to himself. 'Professor Broadmarsh, eh? Sulphur, silver, arsenic...'

He was still muttering the names of those chemicals to himself when the door closed behind me.

I found Miss Peters in the cool basement rooms of Frobisher's, surrounded by a great many flushed assistants and a great many more discarded pairs of gloves.

'Flottie!' she exclaimed, delightedly. 'You came! I'm so pleased that you did, because I can't decide which of these Rupert is going to buy me as an apology for his terrible behaviour at the Renfrews' party. He spent the entire evening talking to old Mr Renfrew about the evolution of shire horses, which apparently Mr Renfrew knows a lot about, and I can believe he does because he *looks* a bit like a shire horse, doesn't he? And Rupert had promised me he'd dance the mazurka, because he does dance divinely.

But when the mazurka came around, old Mr Renfrew was still in full flow and Rupert just kept nodding and saying, "Very interesting, sir," even though it clearly wasn't in the least bit interesting, even to him, and I had to dance the mazurka with Robbie Flinders, who might look like a Greek god but dances like an elderly farmer in the wrong sized boots.'

She waved at a pile of exquisite lace gloves.

'I think he will have to buy me the French pair with the little birds on them. He'll like the birds, I think, because he'll be able to persuade himself they're ornithology, not clothes.'

She peeled off the very beautiful garment she was wearing on her left hand and passed it to one of the assistants.

'Come on, Flotsam, it's getting a bit hot down here with so many people. Let's go and sit in the little salon upstairs for a few minutes. Rupert always says that it can help you to make a decision if you think about something entirely different for a time. But of course Rupert has never had to decide between two pairs of Frobisher gloves.'

The little salon was dark and shadowy, and very quiet after all the bustle downstairs. As soon as we were seated there, on a rather lovely chaise longue in red velvet, Miss Peters turned to me and grabbed my arm.

'Flottie, dear, I'm not really here to buy gloves at all, you know. Not this time, at any rate. Or perhaps only one or two pairs. I'm really just here to calm down, because Frobisher's is *so* calming, and I've been too terribly excited all morning because of my detecting.'

'Detecting, Hetty?' I'm ashamed to say that I felt a little nervous at the thought. 'What have you been up to?'

'Well, Flottie, I was lying in bed this morning thinking about how stinky Rupert had been at the Renfrews, and then thinking about how interested he'd been in Professor Broadmarsh and his silly telegrams, and of course I know that something bad might happen to the professor unless somebody does something to help him. And I do feel rather fond of Professor Broadmarsh, even though I've never met him, because of that note he sent my uncle about rats, because anyone who thinks it's funny to tease the earl must be a good sort, mustn't he?'

I agreed that was one way of looking at things, and allowed her to rattle on.

'Well, it occurred to me as I was lying there – in a rather lovely peignoir covered in very delicate silk peonies – it occurred to me that I know something about Professor Broadmarsh that Rupert doesn't. Although he *would* know, of course, if he went out a bit more often, or if he actually listened to introductions, and perhaps if he didn't think that gossip was some sort of frightful disease. You see, Professor Broadmarsh has a cousin, a Miss Blondell, who is a lot of fun and goes to all the good parties. Her father was incredibly rich, and when he died she inherited all his money, but the professor was given control of it all for about the next ninety years, or until she gets married. Apparently, that's one of the reasons the professor's brother is so disgruntled, because the professor is in charge of all that money, and receives some sort of stipend for looking after it, and gets to stay at Revennings as often as he likes. Revennings is Miss Blondell's family home down in Sussex, and is rather lovely apparently. And

Miss Blondell gets on very well with the professor, and doesn't seem to want to get married, so everything's fine really.'

Miss Peters paused for breath. Downstairs I could hear the sound of gloves being stored away in boxes.

'Anyway, Flottie, I'd heard that Miss Blondell has been up in town for a few days, something to do with comforting a friend who is being made to marry the son of a biscuit baron, so I thought I would seek her out and ask her about her cousin and his peculiar telegrams. And it didn't take me very long to find her, because she's a friend of Tilly Evergreen, and Tilly always knows where everyone is, so I persuaded Carrington – the earl's coachman, you know – to take me round to Tilly's father's place in Cavendish Square, because Tilly's father has to stay in London for the whole summer because the Bank of England depends upon him, and Tilly has to stay in London for the whole summer because Tilly's father depends upon her, because she's the only person who doesn't actually drive him mad. So I was pretty sure she'd be there, and she *was* there, and so was Miss Blondell, which was handy, wasn't it?'

I agreed that it was, and begged her to tell me what Miss Blondell had to say about the missing professor.

'Well, the thing is, Flottie, she didn't know he *was* missing. He'd told her that he was going abroad on business of some sort and would be away for three months or more, and would be far too busy to write. She didn't find this even slightly surprising, because he was always off in foreign parts looking at rocks and things, and he's not quite been away for four months yet, so it hadn't occurred to her to start worrying about him just yet. And anyway, Flotsam, and this is the exciting part, he'd sent her a telegram only a few days ago.'

Miss Peters took another breath and smiled beatifically.

'You see! I told you it was exciting. Can you guess what it said? No, of course you can't, because who could? It seems that Miss Blondell and the professor had a mild disagreement before he left, something about the best colour for new drapes at Revennings. Miss Blondell wanted them to be mauve, and the professor said he thought that was wrong, so she asked him what colour he thought they should be, and he said he didn't know but he'd have a think about it and let her know, and that once he'd offered her an opinion she was perfectly free to ignore it and chose any colour she liked. And then he went abroad, and she didn't give it another thought because she wasn't really very bothered about the drapes, and then suddenly out of the blue she received a telegram from him, and it just said one thing: *Neon*.'

Miss Peters looked at me rather proudly.

'Well, I was able to tell her that neon was a recently discovered gas, and quite inert, and that when you did the right things to it, it turned orange. And she looked a bit astonished that I knew so much, and told me that she'd had to ask the local vicar about it, and he'd mumbled something about orange too, and she thought orange was a perfectly acceptable colour for the drapes, so that's what she ordered.'

'But, Hetty,' I asked, quite diverted from the real point of her tale, 'how did you come to know so much about neon?'

At this, she blushed deeply. I have seen Hetty commit social *faux pas* that would have made the sturdiest of yeoman howl with embarrassment, and to carry them off without a care in the world. But now she flushed right up to the roots of her hair.

'Well, you know, Flottie, during all those lessons of yours with Rupert I'm nearly always thinking about much more interesting and important things, but very occasionally – very, very occasionally – my concentration just lapses and I find myself listening to bits of it. You *will* promise not to tell him, won't you?'

I promised, but I was already grappling with a different question. When, after a couple of deep breaths, Miss Peters carried on, it was as if she'd read my thoughts.

'Do you know something, Flottie? I don't think the professor's telegram was about the drapes at all. In fact, I'm sure it wasn't, because Rupert says the professor is a very well-turned out gentleman with excellent taste in clothes, and I've seen a painting of the Great Hall at Revennings, and nobody with any taste at all could possibly think that orange drapes would be the best colour for it. And anyway, if he wanted orange drapes, why not simply say "orange"? I know scientists can be a bit showy-offy, but if he was really bothered about the drapes you think he'd be a bit more specific about it.'

And I thought the same. I didn't know the professor at all, but I felt sure that there was some greater meaning behind his telegrams, and that the messages he was sending were intended for an audience much wider than those few recipients. But *sulphur, silver, arsenic, neon…* I still had absolutely no idea what the professor's message might be.

Chapter Seven

The letter from Sir Torpenhow Franklin – the one Mr Holmes had been awaiting so anxiously – never came. Instead, Sir Torpenhow came in person, that very evening, while I was still reeling slightly from all the discoveries I'd made that day.

However, there was no sign of him when I returned to Baker Street from Frobisher's, slightly after five o'clock in the afternoon. It was still very close to being the hottest part of the day, and our rooms were very quiet. Dr Watson had not yet returned from the Downs, and Mr Holmes was in his study with a bottle of brown ale and a bowl of cherries. From time to time, a hushed fragment of violin music reached as far as the kitchen, but it was too hot for a whole tune, and, from the silence that finally settled upon the study, it was my guess that the great detective had fallen asleep.

I would have done the same, for I found the kitchen immaculate, the hall and stairs freshly brushed, and the brass on the front door polished to a shine. Mrs Hudson had been busy, but now she was seated quietly at the kitchen table, writing letters, and it was she who suggested that I might benefit from a short lie-down. But before I could act upon her advice, there was a light tap at the area door and in walked Scraggs, flushed and dirty, but with a triumphant smile upon his face and a crisp, white envelope in his hand.

'Told you so!' he exclaimed cheerfully, brandishing the envelope in my direction. 'Didn't I say Lady Townsend's butler would deliver the goods? You'd better start thinking about dresses for dancing in, Flot!'

Mrs Hudson laid down her pen.

'Young man, if you feel that is a proper way to enter a room, then you need to learn some manners. And quickly too, if you are planning to attend the Survivors' Ball.'

Scraggs grinned, unabashed.

'Afternoon, Mrs H. Spotted the crest on this, did you? Well, you're quite right. *Oppida cessant, nos superesse.* That's the Townsend motto, all right. No idea what it means. Here, take a look, Flot.'

The envelope was thick and textured like linen, with the Townsend crest embossed in navy in one corner. It was not sealed, and it contained not one but two gilt-edged invitation cards. The first was made out to *Miss Flotsam, Baker Street,* the second to *Mr Ezekiel Scraggs, trade.*

'Ezekiel?' I exclaimed in astonishment. I don't think it had ever occurred to me before that Scraggs might have a first name.

'Ssssh, not so loud, Flotsam. It's my dark secret.' He looked genuinely embarrassed.

'Well, at least you *have* two names,' I pointed out. When I had first come to Mrs Hudson's attention — caught stealing by Scraggs and dragged through the fog to her kitchen— I had but the one name, one I had never once heard spoken except with scorn or unkindness. Later, with my education progressing, and faced with the form for Mudie's library, Mrs Hudson had firmly written

Flotsam in the column for surnames and *Flotsam* again in the one for Christian names, with the comment that it would do very nicely as both. And, to be fair, it always has.

'But Scraggs,' I protested, looking at the invitation again, 'the Survivors' Ball... It's a very grand affair. Can we really go?'

Experience had taught me that the servants of the great and good were frequently a great deal more aloof than their employers. And Lady Townsend's servants, who would be the hosts of the ball, were very grand indeed. But Mrs Hudson replied with something of a growl.

'You are invited, Flotsam. So you have quite as much right to attend as any other guest, and quite as much right to enjoy yourself too.'

She took up her pen again, and prepared to return to her correspondence.

'There's still some lemonade in the jug, and Scraggs here looks thirsty. And always remember, my girl,' she added, firmly, without looking up, 'you are going to face quite enough obstacles in your life as it is, without having to stop and construct your own whenever you think one's missing.'

'No lemonade for me,' Scraggs put in, retrieving his own invitation and leaving mine in the envelope on the table. 'I have to see a man about a crate of Gentleman's Relish.' He paused at the door and looked back. 'You do know, don't you, Mrs H, that Mr Perkins would be delighted to send you an invitation too? But he says you always decline.'

'Indeed I do, Scraggs.' She didn't look up from her writing. 'Invitations are limited, and somewhere there is

97

someone who will appreciate a place at the Survivors' Ball a great deal more than I would. But it was kind of you to think of me. Happily, the days when I took pleasure in dancing all night in hot clothes on the hottest night of the year have long since past.'

Scraggs bowed gravely in reply, then turned to me with a grin.

'The last Saturday in August, Flot. It's coming right up! Better start thinking about what to wear.'

–

There were, no doubt, many girls my age in London that summer who, on receiving an invitation to an event as splendid and spectacular as the Survivors' Ball, would have gone to bed that night thinking of absolutely nothing else. And no doubt, under normal circumstances, I would have been one of them. But that evening, a little after nine o'clock, Sir Torpenhow Franklin paid his call.

He did not arrive alone, and the two gentlemen I showed into Mr Holmes' study that sultry evening seemed unlikely companions. Sir Torpenhow was tall and gaunt, and at least seventy years of age, dressed, despite the heat, in immaculate evening dress. The other gentleman, a much younger man, was round and fleshy, and wore a linen suit of the type generally sported by English travellers in the world's warmer regions. Judging by his appearance, he might have come to us directly from the boat train.

Yet it was this gentleman who seemed most oppressed by the temperature that evening, slumping in his chair, dabbing at his forehead with a crimson handkerchief and occasionally tugging at his collar with his forefinger, while his companion remained standing, apparently impervious to discomfort.

'Sir Torpenhow Franklin and Mr Albert Asquith,' I announced as they entered.

Dr Watson, rising from his chair at these words, advanced to meet them, fanning himself vigorously, still in excellent spirits after his day on the Downs. But Mr Holmes, I noticed, remained by the fireplace, filling his pipe, although I knew he wouldn't smoke it. The room was stuffy enough without adding tobacco smoke, and Mr Holmes' pipe had rested untouched on the mantelpiece since the warm weather began. By way of welcome, he gave his guests a curt nod.

'Good evening, Sir Torpenhow. We have been expecting you, haven't we, Watson?'

'We certainly have. Thought you'd want to get this train business cleared up, sir, and we're delighted to see you. It must be a couple of years since your last visit? That business of the Baltic financier, if I recall rightly. I hope your dog has recovered fully?'

As Sir Torpenhow replied, Mr Holmes beckoned me over.

'Flotsam, to the silver cupboard, if you please.' He spoke in a low voice – not quite a whisper, but crisp and firm. 'Apron off, you understand, and ready to come when I call.'

Then he turned around and addressed Sir Torpenhow in quite a different tone.

'Now, sir, to business. Of course, you wish to consult Dr Watson and myself about the disappearance of Professor Broadmarsh in Rumania. If I may say so, you have done an excellent job of keeping his name out of the papers. A missing train cannot be an easy story to suppress.'

I did not see Sir Torpenhow's expression when he heard these words because I had left the study and was taking up position in the little box room opposite. But I can imagine it. I have seen it before, on the faces of other visitors to Baker Street.

'You astonish me, Mr Holmes,' our visitor began. 'There are only six people in London apart from myself who know the identity of our missing envoy. Or so I had thought. And I would have vouched for the cast-iron integrity of every one of those six. Yet clearly someone has spoken out of turn.'

'Calm yourself, sir. I assure you that no one has betrayed your trust. Now, as I understand it, when the professor went missing in unusual circumstances, you immediately summoned Mr Charlesworth to London in the hope that he could enlighten you about the professor's fate. And when he could not, you sent him here, in the hope that we might extract some sense from his account of events.'

The two men had been facing each other, both standing at different ends of the mantelpiece, but now Mr Holmes returned to his armchair, his unlit pipe in his hand.

'Of course, you consider Mr Charlesworth your only witness of value, though I can assure you, sir, that Sir Humphrey Ward-Smythe's importance as a witness is equally significant.'

'But, Mr Holmes,' Sir Torpenhow pointed out, 'Sir Humphrey simply listened to the music and left. He witnessed nothing of significance.'

'My point precisely. Now, sir, we have heard Mr Charlesworth's account and we are aware that Professor Broadmarsh was the passenger on that train. All that remains is for you to tell us why the professor was there, and why his disappearance is causing you such consternation. Until we know the full story, we cannot offer you a full explanation.'

'Very well, Mr Holmes. As I explained to the Foreign Secretary only this morning, the sooner we furnish you with all the facts, the better for the country. But before I begin, let me introduce you to Mr Asquith. Mr Asquith is one of those invaluable Britons who lives in remote and uncomfortable areas, and who not only knows them intimately, but is also prepared to share that knowledge with those of us back home. In short, Mr Asquith is our eyes and ears east of the Urals.'

Mr Asquith stopped mopping his brow for a moment, muttered something about hoping to be of service, then continued to mop.

'I know this a bizarre business, Mr Holmes,' Sir Torpenhow went on, 'but it is also an extremely grave one. As you have somehow discovered, an envoy is missing, and with him a vital message. That message could lead to untold benefits for this country, adding hugely to our wealth and security. Unfortunately, were it to fall into the hands of our enemies, Mr Holmes, we might find ourselves plunged into the bloodiest and most desperate of conflicts. A conflict on such a scale that there could be no winners, and one, I fear, in which our own defeat would be inevitable.'

'Hmph. An exaggeration, surely!' Dr Watson was looking sceptical, but Sir Torpenhow continued regardless.

'The root of our problem, gentlemen, is, of course, Afghanistan. Russian influence grows there by the day, and with it the threat to our Indian possessions. Ignoring danger in that region is a luxury we can't afford, and I don't need to tell any of you how dearly we have paid for it in the past. So the desire to find a way to put an end to Russian meddling – once and for all – is very great.'

He paused to clear his throat for a moment; a dramatic pause, I thought, intended to allow the seriousness of his message to sink in.

'You will have heard, gentlemen, of Alim Khan, the Emir of Bokara? His name has been in the newspapers once or twice in recent months.'

'I remember the fellow.' Dr Watson rallied bravely. 'Didn't the Queen send him one of her horses recently?'

Sir Torpenhow nodded.

'A polo pony, Doctor. Although I don't believe the Emir is a player. Bokara, though, enjoys a uniquely significant position along the north-western border of Afghanistan. The Russians think of it as their own playground, and for a long time the Emir of Bokara has been merely a puppet, ruling only with St Petersburg's permission. But of course, gentlemen, if he were ever to swap sides...'

He said it slowly, as though he relished the idea so greatly that the words themselves felt good on his tongue.

'...If the Emir were ever to swap sides, it would change the situation in Central Asia beyond recognition. Were he to accept British protection – and a substantial British military presence in Bokara – it would, at a stroke, cut off Russia's access to the Afghan tribes, and would secure the north-western frontier for generations to come.'

Dr Watson straightened in his chair.

'The British in Bokara!' he exclaimed. 'But that's impossible, surely? The Russians would never allow it. Nor would the French. Or the Germans. You say you don't want a war, but that strikes me as a very certain way of starting one!'

I could hear the alarm in his voice. He, better than anyone, understood the dangers and hardships of military adventure in those parts. But when Sir Torpenhow replied, his tones were calm.

'Of course, Doctor. The balance of power in Europe is precarious. If it were proved we were negotiating in secret to turn Bokara into a British protectorate – behind the back of our allies and in defiance of reassurances previously given to them – not only would it encourage the Russians to take up arms, but we would not have a single ally prepared to stand with us. Worse than that, with "perfidious Albion" as their cry, our neighbours might well see the advantages of uniting against us. It is not impossible that we would end up facing the Russians in Asia, the French in Indo-China, the Germans at sea, and all of them in Africa. It would be a world-wide war of a sort never known before, and the casualties – even for the winners – would be unprecedented.'

He paused again, this time apparently to pick his words with care.

'And yet, if we were able to secure the Emir's signature in total secrecy, if he were to frame the treaty as a request for assistance from Britain and other western powers against the tyranny of the Russian Bear, and if our presence in Bokara were presented to the world as a *fait accompli*, it is not impossible that we might bring our allies round to the idea. In fact, provided we are not seen as the instigators of the plot, provided we can deny all charges of negotiating with the Emir, I am extremely confident a peaceful accommodation could be found. There would be suspicion, certainly, and a great deal of name-calling, and some liberal horse-trading of favours in other parts of the world, but most importantly, no war.'

Mr Holmes had listened to this with his pipe to his lips, but now he lowered it.

'You astound me, sir. To gamble the safety of the empire – and the lives of so many of its citizens – on such a high-risk venture smacks of almost cavalier irresponsibility. The dangers are enormous.'

Our visitor nodded politely in reply.

'But the rewards even more so. And there really is very little risk, provided the plan remains secret. That is why it was agreed in the very highest circles of government that we should open negotiations with the Emir.'

Dr Watson drew in his breath sharply.

'My word, sir. If a whisper of that got out...'

Sir Torpenhow waved this away with a sweep of his hand.

'We don't worry about whispers, sir. There will always be whispers. For our enemies to act against us they will need proof. And we were confident no such proof would be available to them until the deal was done and it was too late for them to unify against us. That polo pony, for instance...'

He allowed himself a small, dry smile.

'You may recall that twenty-seven other minor rulers also received polo ponies that month, all sent in an effort to disguise our true intentions. Many of these unfortunate animals were delivered by British dignitaries of significant standing. Poor old Lord Malmesbury, for instance, has still not made it back from Kazakhstan. But the trio who accompanied the Emir's pony to Bokara were not individuals of any great international reputation: Harry Barrington, the nephew of Sir George Barrington, and a safe pair of hands; old Stoughton-French, the explorer fellow, who was in Bokara back in the '60s, during the Persian Cat Crisis; and, as you have somehow discovered, Professor Broadmarsh, the scientist and geologist, whose purpose was ostensibly to visit the limestone caves of Bokara-Qut.'

The great detective pondered these names for a moment or two.

'An interesting choice of delegates, sir. I'm not familiar with the man Barrington, but Professor Broadmarsh has a reputation for shrewdness and quick wits. And Major Stoughton-French, although by no means a young man, must know as much about the region as anyone in England. So tell us, sir, were their negotiations successful?'

'They were, Mr Holmes.' Sir Torpenhow said it with such pride that I realised he himself must have been one of the principle architects of the plan. 'They found the Emir deeply resentful of his Russian protectors. A number of small slights in recent months had left him angry and unusually defiant, and more than ready to listen to our proposition. Harry Barrington is a fine diplomatist, and Professor Broadmarsh is a very affable fellow, and a bird-fancier to boot, so was apparently very good with the Emir's falcons.'

Dr Watson nodded shrewdly.

'Very keen on their hawks in those parts, Sir Torpenhow. Once met a fellow near the Ghibli Pass who'd trained a goshawk to fetch his slippers. Nice chap, but I sometimes wonder if that bird might have stolen a pair of my socks. Anyway, a deal was done, was it?'

'An agreement *was* reached, and a document signed by the Emir, but there could be no question of any British envoy returning with it about his person because if they were found with it in their possession, the consequences would have been catastrophic.'

Sir Torpenhow reached for his handkerchief a second time. In the dim light of that shaded room, his sharp features seemed more pronounced with every moment that passed. If Mr Asquith had the appearance of a man melting in a furnace, Sir Torpenhow Franklin seemed to be doing the opposite, as if the heat was slowly drying him out like a prune.

'So it was agreed the Emir's own agents would bring the treaty with his signature on it to Britain in the strictest secrecy. That way we could deny all knowledge of it until it was safely under lock and key in Whitehall. The Emir, in turn, insisted that the document, when it arrived on these shores, should be delivered to Harry Barrington in person, and to no one else. Nor would he have the thing delivered to any official address, in case it were being watched, and not to Barrington's home, either, for the same reason.

'Now, it happens that his vizier, or chief advisor, is an elderly fellow and very sympathetic to Great Britain – an avid reader of *The Lady* magazine, apparently – and he came up with a time and place where the signed treaty could be handed over to Barrington in total safety.'

'Clever fellow,' Dr Watson commented, still fanning himself with some vigour, 'though I'm not sure reading *The Lady* is time well spent. What place did he suggest?'

But Mr Holmes shook his head.

'Really, my friend, do you think our visitor would be here now, on an evening as hot as this one, if things were as straightforward as that? I think we can safely assume that details of the time and place for the handover of the treaty were entrusted to Professor Broadmarsh.' He turned back to Sir Torpenhow. 'Which would make his recent dramatic disappearance particularly awkward.'

Our visitor nodded.

'Awkward and extremely worrying, Mr Holmes. The Emir, being a man of convoluted cunning, and having no wish to end up with his head upon a spike, split the information about the rendezvous into three parts, entrusting each of our three envoys with one of them, and insisting they should return home by different routes. If all three returned safely and the messages were put together, the meeting place would be apparent and the Emir would feel confident in our ability to keep our promises. And, of course, if any one message was intercepted by an enemy, that single message in itself would not be enough to betray the rendezvous.

'The downside of this arrangement from our point of view is obvious, gentlemen. Because if any of those three sections fail to make it back to London, we will never know the full details of the handover. And if Barrington fails to appear at the appointed time and place, this will be seen by the Emir as evidence of ineptitude on our part, and the signed treaty will be destroyed by the Emir's agent. Worse still, if any hostile party were able to discover the rendezvous and intercept the document, then our dealings with the Emir would be revealed for all to see, with disastrous and bloody consequences.'

Dr Watson scratched his head.

'Sounds dashed complicated. Couldn't his agent over here just pop the thing in the post?'

Sir Torpenhow, who did not seem to smile very often, allowed himself a slight crinkling of the lips.

'I'm afraid, Doctor, the Emir doesn't share your confidence in the British postal system.'

'I always find it pretty reliable myself. Still, even though Bokara's a long way away, you'd expect all three of Her Majesty's representatives to make it back safely enough. Must have been a terrible shock to you when the professor went missing.'

'Far from it.' The elderly statesman gestured towards his companion. 'And I have brought Mr Asquith with me this evening to explain why. Mr Asquith…'

I saw the second of our visitors edge forward in his seat, until he was poised on the edge of his armchair. He still looked hot, but he did not appear embarrassed by the attention now being paid to him.

'Gentlemen,' he began, 'I first became aware of an unusual gathering of spies and plotters in the city of Tashkent at about the time Sir Torpenhow's envoys were arriving in Bokara. Rumours abounded almost at once, and I was made aware of the names of various individuals – veteran intriguers and spy-masters – who simply by their presence in the region were enough to ignite my suspicions. So I made it my business to discover theirs.'

'You must remember, gentlemen,' Sir Torpenhow interjected, 'just how many nations would be suspicious of a British triumph in Bokara. The Turks, for instance, fear that a bloody nose for the Russians in Central Asia might turn the Tsar's attentions back towards the Ottoman Empire. The Hapsburgs fear it might redirect Russian ambitions to the Balkans. The French and Germans fear it would strengthen our influence in Persia and greatly disrupt the balance of power. Greece, Bulgaria and those other new Balkan nations believe any action of the Great Powers in the East constitutes encirclement. And in Central Asia itself, well, the Tajiks loathe the Emir, the Afghans loathe us and the Turkmen loathe almost everyone.'

His companion nodded.

'So it is perhaps unsurprising,' Mr Asquith added, taking up the tale, 'that so many unscrupulous and dangerous parties were prepared to come together in secret, in such a remote location, united in a determination to obtain evidence of our dealings with the Emir and to expose our plans to the Russians and to the world. This gathering is being referred to in Foreign Office circles as the Samarkand Conspiracy.'

Dr Watson, still alert despite the heat, frowned at this.

'But surely Samarkand is nowhere near Tashkent?' he pointed out.

'Indeed, Doctor. It is an unfortunate misnomer, but sadly not everyone in the Foreign Office has your grasp of the region's geography. Now, gentlemen,' Mr Asquith continued, 'I have some useful contacts in Tashkent, and in Bokara too, and pretty soon the word was out that three English envoys were at large in the region, travelling incognito, and that the agents of the Samarkand Conspiracy had sworn to hunt them down.'

Compared to the dry, diplomatic phrasing of Sir Torpenhow's narrative, Mr Asquith's words sent something of a shiver through me. Until now, I had been guilty of seeing the professor and his telegrams as some sort of clever puzzle, to be enjoyed until a solution was found. Now, for the first time, I imagined him pursued, living on his wits, making his way across dangerous, exotic landscapes of deserts and oases, while faceless conspirators contrived to bar his way.

'We don't, unfortunately, know as much as we would like about that gathering of conspirators,' Mr Asquith continued, 'but I do know it was convened and inspired by a shadowy figure who goes by the name of Andreas Weiss. We have come across him often, both in Central Asia and in Europe, but know little about him. He appears to have impressive connections in the courts of Europe, and is able to call upon an informal network of spies and informers throughout the Balkans and Central Asia. As well as working on behalf of the French, we believe he is also close to senior figures in Bulgaria, Serbia and Germany, and many say he is the dark hand behind a secret treaty between the Austrians and the Kingdom of Rumania.'

Mr Asquith spoke soberly, but I'm sure I detected a trace of admiration in his voice as he listed these devious accomplishments.

'No one seems to know precisely where his loyalties lie,' he went on, 'but more than once we have detected his hand in events that have been of great detriment to our interests abroad. One might almost think his sole purpose was to undermine Great Britain and her interests.'

'Hmph. I know the type.' Dr Watson observed. 'Sour grapes, usually. I've met a few of his sort.'

'Indeed, Doctor. And thanks to him, as a result of the gathering in Tashkent, every foreign agent between China and the Channel was suddenly on the lookout for our unfortunate envoys.'

'So now we come to it...' The satisfaction in Mr Holmes' voice was undisguised. 'A train disappears in a remote corner of Europe, the newspapers say nothing about it, and Sir Torpenhow Franklin's carriage stops at Baker Street one breathless summer evening. The pieces fall most prettily. Now, sir, we already know that Professor Broadmarsh hasn't made it home, but what of the other two? And why did these foreign agents – the Samarkand Conspirators, if you like – go to such lengths to spirit away the professor? Why not simply overpower him on the road and steal the message?'

Even from where I stood, in the stuffiest room in London, surrounded by unpolished silver, I could see that our visitors did not greatly relish Mr Holmes' enthusiasm. It was Sir Torpenhow who replied.

'The message was not stolen, Mr Holmes, for one simple reason – no part of it was written down. The Emir insisted that each man should commit his section to memory and should share it with no one until he reached these shores in safety.'

'I see.' Mr Holmes seemed in no way dampened by this correction. 'So, unable to steal the message, your enemies have been forced to steal your messenger. Tell us, Mr Asquith, how did the other two envoys fare?'

'I will start with Harry Barrington,' our visitor explained, 'as we have his story from his own mouth. Barrington's idea, and it was a startlingly good one, was to travel home by way of the lion's den itself. Word of the Samarkand Conspiracy had reached him and his companions in Bokara, so he decided to travel north, incognito, into Russia itself – possibly the last place they would expect him to go. And his ploy worked admirably, gentlemen. Barrington made his way by horseback all the way to the Aral Sea, then onwards to Ekaterinburg, then by train via Moscow and Paris to London. He arrived nearly six weeks ago.'

'And Stoughton-French?' Dr Watson, clearly gripped, had stopped fanning himself. 'How did he get on?'

Mr Asquith sighed.

'I'm afraid that Major Stoughton-French's journey did not end happily. The major, remember, was over seventy at the start of the expedition, and by the time he reached Bokara his health was already failing. Barrington reports that the old man was debilitated by an intermittent fever, and that even on arriving in Bokara he looked a sick man.'

'But he's still going, surely?' Dr Watson protested. 'I run an eye over the obituary columns every day – cheers me up, I find – and if I'd certainly remember if I'd read anything about old Stoughton-French.'

'The obituary will appear next month, Doctor,' Sir Torpenhow explained. 'We felt it better, for now, that his fate should not be advertised.'

'And what precisely was his fate?' Mr Holmes asked quietly.

'The major got as far as the western shore of the Caspian,' Mr Asquith told him. 'I know that much for certain. The actual story of his last few days remains unclear, but it appears he succumbed to the fever about a month later, in a bordello in Baku.'

'And his message, sir?' Dr Watson's anxiety was clear from his voice. 'Surely it cannot have been lost?'

'No, Doctor,' Mr Asquith assured him. 'Somehow it survived and reached London. I've pieced things together as well as I can. Before the major died, it seems he whispered his part of the message to a young Azeri courtesan, begging her to pass it on to any traveller bound for London. London-bound travellers, however, are not common in Baku, so she did her best, passing it to a Lebanese horse dealer bound for Kars. He in turn passed it to an Armenian grain merchant, who possibly relayed it to a Moroccan bookbinder, although the exact route remains unclear. But remarkably, a rather austere Spanish lady turned up at the Foreign Office here in London last month saying that the mistress of an Algerian fencing master had asked her to deliver a message. So we have, we believe, the second part of the Emir's instructions safely in our hands. But, of course...'

Mr Asquith looked across at Sir Torpenhow.

'But, of course, Mr Holmes,' the older gentleman explained, 'we cannot be certain how many others have also shared it. In fact, it seems impossible that the content of the message, after passing through so many hands, has not also fallen into the hands of our enemies. So we are forced to conclude that, while we have exclusive possession of Barrington's section, we share Stoughton-French's section with the agents of various foreign powers. Which makes it all the more important that we obtain the final section as promptly as possible.'

'And that brings us to Professor Broadmarsh.' Mr Holmes turned to Mr Asquith. 'Dr Watson and I already know that the professor has disappeared in the Carpathian Mountains. Do you have any information that may be relevant to us about his journey up to that point?'

Mr Asquith tugged at his collar again, so firmly this time that I believe a stud might have popped. His collar certainly remained crooked for the rest of his visit.

'I know he reached Constanta by fishing boat from Odessa, Mr Holmes, and that he travelled by train from there to Bucharest, where he remained for some days. There is an English bookseller in Bucharest, a reliable fellow called Robinson, and Professor Broadmarsh sought him out, looking for advice about a place to stay where an English traveller would not attract attention, somewhere he could lie low while he waited for a companion to join him.'

'A companion?' Dr Watson looked astonished. 'We didn't know anything about that, did we, Holmes? Who was this companion, sir?'

'Well, Doctor,' Mr Asquith explained, 'we can't be sure, because the story he told the bookseller seems impossibly far-fetched. He told Robinson that he'd tele-graphed ahead sometime before, from Tehran, I believe, to the staff at his cousin's country home, a place called Revennings. He had been giving instructions – and Robinson was absolutely clear about this, you understand – giving instructions for the head gardener there to meet him in Bucharest.'

At that point in Mr Asquith's narrative, and to my eternal shame, I dropped an enormous silver candelabra. It hit the floor with such a crash it must surely have been heard on the other side of the street. Yet so dramatic and unexpected was Mr Asquith's revelation, that I don't believe the gentlemen gathered in Mr Holmes' study that night were even aware of it. Perhaps only Sir Torpenhow, who, after all, had heard the story before.

'The *gardener*?' Dr Watson's astonishment clearly matched my own.

'Yes, Doctor. Of course, this man Robinson assumed the professor was joking. But it seems...'

Again Mr Asquith looked across at Sir Torpenhow, and it was that gentleman who continued the tale.

'I had one of my officials visit Revennings, gentlemen. The house actually belongs to a Miss Blondell, the professor's cousin, but she was up in town, so my man spoke to the servants. Or attempted to. It seems they were rather tight-lipped. And when he asked to meet the gardener, whose name is Thompson, every single servant maintained that Thompson was visiting a sick aunt in a remote part of Scotland and had the professor's permission to remain away indefinitely. No address, of course, nor any name of the aunt. Not even any clear idea about which part of Scotland.'

'But surely, sir,' Dr Watson persisted, 'this fellow must be more than just a simple gardener? You made enquires, of course?'

'Naturally, Doctor. But, although it pains me to say so, everything we were able to discover suggests that Thompson really *is* just a gardener. He has worked at Revennings since he was a boy, and has rarely left the place. His father was the head gardener there before him. He is about sixty-five years of age, and, from what we've been told, he's never before travelled further than

Cornwall, and that was to make arrangements on the professor's behalf for the purchase of a specimen palm tree. The aunt in Scotland, if she exists, has never been visited before.'

'Clearly he and the professor have a shared interest in horticulture,' Mr Holmes observed. 'But I think we can assume that it was not the purchase of palm trees that required the fellow's presence in Bucharest.'

Mr Asquith cleared his throat.

'One thing we do know, Mr Holmes, is that the rendezvous in Bucharest was successful. The day before he left that city, the professor informed Robinson that his gardener had arrived safely, and that a special train had been chartered – under an assumed name – to rush the two of them to Vienna, with a view to getting home as quickly as possible. He seemed in extraordinarily high spirits. It struck Robinson that a huge weight had been lifted from his shoulders.'

'Pleased to see the fellow, eh? And is that the last we heard of him?' Dr Watson asked.

'Not quite, Doctor. I've made enquiries about the professor's last day in Bucharest. It appears that, before boarding the train, the professor went to the telegraph office and sent five telegrams. Of course, the content of any telegram he sent would almost certainly have become known to his pursuers, and the professor was aware of that, so I cannot believe he would have risked sending his precious message down the wire. And yet perhaps he did, for he visited Robinson for one last time that day, and said something that must surely be significant. "I've stayed on the tight-rope this long," he told him, or words to that effect. "I've stayed on the tight-rope this long, but it's all a bit touch and go, so I've built a safety net in case I fall.'"

A short silence followed, then Sir Torpenhow cleared his throat.

'I would give a great deal, Mr Holmes, to know what vital information Professor Broadmarsh attempted to communicate in those last hours before his inexplicable disappearance.'

I watched Mr Holmes smile – a little inward smile – then get to his feet.

'Inexplicable, sir? Hardly. I can see it is high time we gave you some answers.'

Then, to my surprise, he strode to the study door.

'Flotsam,' he called, 'Could you step into the study, please? Sir Torpenhow Franklin requires your assistance.'

Chapter Eight

Mrs Hudson once told me never to be nervous in the presence of important people because I was every bit as important as they were. And I know, had she been with me in the silver room at that moment, she would simply have nudged me forward and told me to be myself. Which would, of course, have been exactly the right advice.

But even good advice isn't always easy to follow, and it is hard to put into words the nervousness – almost the dread – I felt as I entered Mr Holmes' study that evening. I had shown a great number of Mr Holmes' clients into that room in the past, but never before had I been asked to join them. And Sir Torpenhow Franklin was no ordinary visitor; he was one of the most powerful men in the country. Feeling important in his presence – even just a little bit important – wasn't at all an easy thing to do.

'Gentlemen,' my employer began briskly, as though my presence there was the most natural thing in the world, 'let me introduce you to Miss Flotsam. She has been assisting Dr Watson and myself with this case.'

'But, Mr Holmes…' For a moment I thought the great Sir Torpenhow was lost for words. 'Isn't that the girl who showed us in?'

'Indeed.' Mr Holmes seemed utterly unperturbed. 'Flotsam's abilities know no bounds. Now, please sit, gentlemen. Make yourselves comfortable.'

He signalled for Sir Torpenhow to take one of the vacant chairs, then ushered me into the spot by the fireplace where he himself so often stood.

'Flotsam,' he began, 'our visitors have been asking about the contents of Professor Broadmarsh's last telegrams. Perhaps you would be so kind as to tell them what you know of the matter.'

And so I did. A little hesitantly at first, but growing in confidence, I listed the four recipients we knew of, and the messages they had received.

'But that is absurd, child!' Sir Torpenhow exclaimed. 'Even if those messages made any sense, how could you possibly know all this?'

'Please, Sir Torpenhow…' Mr Holmes' tone was stern, and a little icy. 'There will be time for explanations later. Now, Flotsam, that disappearing train… Sir Torpenhow remains baffled.'

'Well, sir…' I must have sounded a little timid, because it isn't an easy thing to explain to one of the most eminent men in the country that he hasn't been thinking very clearly. 'The train didn't really disappear. Of course it didn't. It just stayed in the tunnel until no one was looking.'

And between us, Mr Holmes and I explained how the vanishing trick had been achieved, from the careful selection of the orchestra to the problems with the double bass.

'But why go to so much trouble?' Mr Asquith asked. 'If the Rumanian authorities were determined to seize the professor, they could have done it with perfect ease on the streets of their capital.'

'But not without a scandal,' Sir Torpenhow interjected. 'The British government would have a thing or two to say about something like that, and a country like Rumania can't afford to fall out with us so openly. But this way, because the train – and the professor – disappeared in the tunnel between two countries, each country is able to blame the other. The Rumanian ambassador is telling us the whole thing is an Austrian plot, while the Austrians deny all knowledge of everything. And until we know more, there's not a lot we can do about it.'

'It seems to me that your problem, sir, is one of time.' Mr Holmes stretched himself again, his long legs reaching almost to the hearth rug. 'To succeed in their first aim, your enemies do not need to obtain the professor's portion of the Emir's message for themselves. It is sufficient for them to prevent you from receiving it. That way, Barrington is unable to make his rendezvous, and all your plans fail. So, if I were to furnish you with the professor's precise location – and I shall do so presently – it will not be enough to rescue your treaty. To extract the professor from captivity, whether by direct or diplomatic means, will be a lengthy process, and time is not on your side.'

'Exactly right,' Sir Torpenhow agreed. 'The Emir hinted to Barrington that the coded messages refer to a rendezvous in late August, so it could be any day now. Indeed we might already be too late.'

'Then we must decipher Professor Broadmarsh's telegrams as swiftly as we possibly can. Tell me, Flotsam, what is your view on those peculiar communications?'

I paused before speaking, to gather my thoughts.

'Well, sir, I think it's clear that the words in the telegrams are not the actual message he was bringing back from the Emir. That would have been too risky. I think they are his way of pointing us in the right direction. I suppose we'd have to say they are some sort of code.'

'My thoughts precisely,' Mr Holmes concurred. 'Now, sir,' he continued, turning to Sir Torpenhow, 'it is time for you to share with us the two portions of the Emir's message that you do have – the Barrington and the Stoughton-French portions. I assume you have them on your person? Let's get them out and see what we can make of them.'

I saw Sir Torpenhow's hand begin to move towards his chest pocket, but then the gentleman paused and looked across at me.

'Mr Holmes, this is some of the most sensitive information imaginable. I have explained to you the lengths some people would go to – have gone to – to obtain it. I hardly think…'

My employer rose briskly to his feet.

'You do not wish to share it with us?'

Sir Torpenhow seemed to pick his words carefully.

'With *you*, Mr Holmes. And with Dr Watson, of course…'

The great detective sighed ominously, and began to move towards the door.

'Let me bid you good evening, sir,' he declared. 'If at any point you choose to reconsider your decision, then you know where to find us.'

For the first time that night, Sir Torpenhow Franklin appeared at a loss.

'But, Mr Holmes, I merely meant...' he began, and then, perhaps observing the expression on the detective's face, he seemed to change his mind. 'My apologies, Mr Holmes. I have no desire to question anyone's integrity.'

Without a further word, he drew a paper from his pocketbook and handed it to his host, who opened it, then propped it up against the mantelpiece clock so that Dr Watson and myself could both examine it.

If I had hoped for answers, I was severely disappointed.

Message One (Barrington)
M N H I A M T C T O E E Y V A U

Message Two (Stoughton-French)
D G L R Y N A U H S W T E N G T

–

Later that night, long after Sir Torpenhow and his companion had rattled off into the darkness, that same piece of paper was laid out on Mrs Hudson's kitchen table while Mr Holmes, lounging outrageously, his bottom on one kitchen chair and his feet on another, concluded an admirable summary of our visitors' story. Opposite him, Dr Watson listened intently, watching the ice melt in a glass of brandy-and-shrub, and I sat between the two, pleased to have it all repeated, desperately trying to make sure I'd grasped every detail. Mrs Hudson remained standing, cloth in hand, drying repeatedly, and with great care each time, a delicate porcelain soup tureen.

'And that, I think, is about the sum of it,' Mr Holmes concluded. 'Would you agree, Watson?'

'Certainly, Holmes. Puts it very nicely.'

Both men had changed into smoking jackets, and both had dispensed with their collars, although neither smoked.

'Beats me how you keep it so cool down here, Mrs H,' the doctor went on. 'I'd sit here all night if you allowed me. So what do you make of it all? It strikes me as a bit of a tangle.'

Mrs Hudson ran the cloth slowly around the rim of the tureen.

'It strikes me, sir, that Sir Torpenhow Franklin has been extremely reckless, and thoroughly deserves the position he finds himself in.'

Mr Holmes smiled.

'You are not impressed by his diplomatic manoeuvres, Mrs Hudson?'

'He would appear to have embarked on a very dangerous game, sir, and might have anticipated a mess of this sort. Also, although it's hardly my place to say, I'm not at all sure that the Emir of Bokara is the sort of gentleman Her Majesty's government should be doing business with. Were he a tradesman in London, I'm far from convinced I would open an account.'

'Hmm, you do have a point there,' Dr Watson agreed. 'Thought the same thing myself. Wasn't he the chap who had those French missionaries whipped in public? Bit of a tyrant, by all accounts. Not sure that it sounds entirely right, sending the fellow polo ponies.'

Mr Holmes shifted his feet so that he was sitting slightly more upright.

'But surely, my friend, regardless of moral scruples, you would not have that treaty fall into the hands of our enemies? As Sir Torpenhow points out, the consequences might be unthinkable, and we may pay the price in human lives.'

'Well, of course, Holmes, we can't have that.' Dr Watson looked down at the ice in his drink, found it melted, and looked up again. 'But there's not much danger of them getting hold of the treaty, is there? They may have Stoughton-French's section of the instructions, but they don't have Barrington's, and I can't believe Professor Broadmarsh will give up his section of the message, however long they hold him for.'

'Not willingly, Watson.' Mr Holmes pursed his lips. 'But I believe they must have drugged the professor when they took him from the train, and there exist fiendish concoctions that can loosen a man's tongue as efficaciously as strong liquor. And if our enemies hold two of the three sections, they are definitely still in the game.'

Dr Watson was looking around for the ice bucket.

'So what do we do about it, Holmes?'

His companion turned to me.

'Flotsam?'

I'd been itching for him to ask, and I had my reply already rehearsed in my head.

'First we need to understand the professor's telegrams, sir, because they will surely lead us to the last portion of the Emir's message. So our first step is to find the telegram we don't already have. And it must have been sent to a friend of the professor, or someone he has business dealings with. It can't be impossible to find out who. Then, when we have the professor's portion of the message, the challenge is to understand the Emir's code. I suppose that is another of the Emir's tests, sir. But if we can manage that, then Mr Barrington can be in the right place at the right time to receive the signed copy of the treaty.'

'Admirable, Flotsam.'

'And I'll tell you what, Holmes,' Dr Watson added, 'the first thing for you and I to do is to head down to Revennings sharpish, to see if those telegrams mean anything to the people down there. And to find out a bit more about that gardener fellow at the same time.'

'Quite wrong, Watson.' Mr Holmes, who had been nursing a slim glass of chilled Moselle, placed the empty glass on the table. 'The professor's servants would tell Sir Torpenhow's men nothing. They will almost certainly tell us the same thing. Now, if someone else were to go...'

'We could go, sir!' I blurted out excitedly. 'Mrs Hudson and I! They might talk to *us*. Don't you think so, ma'am?'

'If Mr Holmes wishes it, Flotsam.' The housekeeper placed the well-polished tureen on the sideboard and began to fold the cloth. 'A day out of the city would do you the world of good.'

'Excellent!' Mr Holmes swung his feet down to the floor. 'You and I, Watson, will make some enquiries about the last of the professor's telegrams. And then, perhaps, we could call on Mr Barrington. After spending all that time with the professor in Bokara, he may well know more about the business than he realises.'

'He did awfully well, didn't he, sir?' I added. I'd formed rather a favourable opinion of Harry Barrington. 'Avoiding all those spies, I mean.'

'Humph!' Dr Watson took a sip of his drink, then placed his glass on the table. 'Can't say I'm altogether convinced by all this spy nonsense. The Samarkand Conspiracy, indeed! Makes 'em sound more important than they are. They're not really conspirators, just a group of underhand foreigners skulking about in the back of beyond, hoping to do whatever they can to land a blow on the British Empire. Sometimes I think those fellows at the Foreign Office like to imagine dastardly plots because it gives them something to do. What do you say, Mrs H?'

But Mrs Hudson was refilling Mr Holmes' wine glass, and when she'd finished, she examined the label on the bottle of Moselle.

'I don't think of it often, Doctor,' she replied, 'but as a very young girl I was, very briefly, lady's maid to an impressive young lady from Baden-Baden who had married an Irish peer. She spoke very good English, but I did pick up one or two German words.' She studied the label more closely. 'As I often say to Flotsam, it's a good thing to learn other languages, even if it's only a word or two. You simply never know when they will prove useful.'

And, with that solemn utterance, she placed the soup tureen on the table in front of us with such finality that it was clear to all of us the evening was at end.

–

To my surprise, Mrs Hudson and I did not set off for Revennings the following morning, or indeed the following day. After receiving such explicit instructions from Mr Holmes, I'd expected to be rushing to the station before breakfast and leaping aboard the first train. But Mrs Hudson, although she was up early, showed no signs of packing. She laid out the breakfast things with her usual unhurried patience, and directed me to clear the tray from the gentleman's study.

'They called for tea very early, Flotsam,' she explained, 'and were out with the first sparrows. It's good to see them active again, isn't it?'

'But, ma'am,' I asked, horrified by her lack of bustle, 'shouldn't we be active too? Don't we need to be getting to Revennings? Everything may depend on it!'

'First things first,' she replied with maddening calm. 'And the first thing you must do is eat a good breakfast. The baker's lad has already been, and there are peaches and figs from Glendenning's, and a slice of melon, too, if you have room.'

'But Revennings, ma'am! The professor's messages! His gardener!'

'We'll go tomorrow, Flottie. I think we can get everything done by then. Now, once we've got everything straight here, we need to be on our way to Shepherd's Bush before it gets too hot.'

'Shepherd's Bush, ma'am?'

It was hardly the stately country house I'd been anticipating.

'That's right, Flotsam. There is a hostel there for retired policemen, and I'd like to pay a visit. And after that, perhaps to Mr Rumbelow, who might agree to ask one or two questions on our behalf at the Empedocles Club. And then I would like to write to Mrs Esterhazy, to reassure her of our best intentions. And after that, we might take the opportunity to move the gentlemen's big leather sofa. I know for a fact we haven't had a brush under there for nearly two weeks.'

I think my disappointment must have showed, for on the way to Shepherd's Bush Mrs Hudson made a great effort to chat to me about the excitements in store for me at the Survivors' Ball; and I confess her description of the Mecklenberg Hotel *en fête*, decorated as smartly as it would be for the grandest ball of the season, did go some way to placating me.

'And the band plays till dawn, Flotsam, because it is a point of pride at the Survivors' Ball that everyone must still be dancing at daybreak.'

The contrast between these visions and our destination in Shepherd's Bush was stark. The building Mrs Hudson led me to was a drab red-brick affair, two storeys high, but extending a long way back, like a long, low warehouse. We entered through a blue door which needed repainting, and Mrs Hudson led me down a dark, rather dreary corridor, then up a flight of steps, before knocking at one of the many identical plain black doors. This was opened to us by an elderly man with cropped grey hair, out of breath and slightly stooped, but broad in frame – so broad he filled the doorway. When he saw my companion, his face lit up.

'Why, it's young Hudson! Good to see you, young lady. Though not so young nowadays, eh? None of us are, I'm afraid, none of us are. Come on in, come in. I've tidied up a bit since you were here the other week.'

'Good morning, Joe.' Mrs Hudson's voice was soft with affection. 'Flotsam, I'd like you to meet Sergeant Minders. The sergeant and I go back a long way. Joe, this is Flotsam, who works with me.'

The old policeman favoured me with a little bow, then coughed to clear his throat and led us very slowly into a tiny living room. There, he pointed us towards the room's only two chairs.

'Please, take a seat, young lady. I don't entertain often nowadays, but there's a boy who will bring tea if I call. Or I could offer you something stronger, Mrs Hudson, although it's hardly the weather.'

'Flotsam will be very comfortable on the stool, won't you, Flotsam? No tea, thank you, Joe. It's too hot to send the boy off for boiling water.' She placed a linen bag by his feet. 'Here. I've brought you some more plums and some Clawson stilton, and another bottle of the rosehip syrup you like.'

The old man's face lit up.

'From Dillford Abbey? Ah! There's nothing better for keeping the aches away. Remember the first time our paths crossed, Mrs H, chasing that young viscount fellow into the wild rose hedge? So prickled he was, that they had to cut him out with nail scissors before they could arrest him. I've had a liking for their rosehip syrup ever since.'

'It was a close thing, Joe. If he'd picked the other hedge, he'd have got clean away from us, you know.'

The two of them both grinned, two old friends rehearsing a familiar joke.

'He would, too, but then he'd have run slap into Lady Dashwood's mother, who'd have got him with the stuffed fish, and we'd have ended up with a murder on our hands.'

They both laughed out loud at that. I'd often seen Mrs Hudson solemn, sometimes seen her fierce, but I'd don't think I'd ever before seen her so skittish.

'I was a little younger then, Flotsam,' she explained, 'and Sergeant Minders here was the only one who'd listen to me about the viscount's collar studs.'

'It was PC Minders then,' he pointed out. 'I always say it was them studs that got me my promotion. Them and the rose bushes, of course.'

More recollections followed, all of them light-hearted, none of them explained in quite as much detail as I'd have liked, until Sergeant Minders was interrupted mid-sentence by a fit of coughing. When he'd recovered, he smiled apologetically at Mrs Hudson.

'Now, young lady, it may be a while since I was in the uniform, but I don't have to be one of those detective chaps to know that you've got something to ask me. So out with it, before my lungs give up altogether.'

Mrs Hudson nodded.

'I need to pick your memory, Joe. It's probably nothing, but someone told me something the other day and it's been preying on my mind. Do you remember that business with the Plinlimmon emerald?'

Sergeant Minders coughed again, but he was nodding as he coughed.

'I do indeed. A funny one that, wasn't it? Coming so soon after the Plinlimmon diamond affair, everyone thought it must have been the same villain coming back and pulling the same stunt. The diamond culprit was that fellow Fogarty, wasn't it? The one who went on to cause so much trouble later on.'

I felt a little shiver run through me at the mention of his name; I had run into Mr Fogarty myself once, and it had not been a happy experience. But Mrs Hudson seemed less perturbed.

'It wasn't Fogarty the second time, though, was it, Joe? Because by then Fogarty was posing as an Italian fencing master, and blackmailing the Duke of Ferrara. It was that very young fellow who Lord Plinlimmon had employed to catalogue his library.'

Joe coughed again. It was a deep, troubling cough that clearly caused him some pain.

'That's right, Mrs H. He'd worked out for himself how Fogarty pulled off the diamond affair, and then he scraped acquaintance with the Plinlimmons so he could try it for himself. And if you hadn't warned the ostler to watch out for scratches on the stable floor, he'd have got away with it. Clever young fellow, wasn't he?'

'And a dangerous one, I seem to recall. He bore a grudge, you see, Flotsam. And a villain driven by a grudge is a great deal more dangerous than one driven by simple greed.'

'That's right,' Sergeant Minders confirmed. 'As I remember, his father was killed when the Royal Navy bombarded Kagoshima, and his brother died in Fort Marabout, when it was fired on by the *Condor*.'

'So he was a foreign gentleman, was he?' I asked.

'Not that you'd have noticed, Flotsam,' Mrs Hudson explained. 'I believe his mother was English, and he might have been taken for a young English gentleman, but I'm told he could just as easily pass for French or Spanish or who knows what else. Rumour has it that later on he posed as a Spanish count and married a French countess, only to discover that the countess was as big a fraud as he was.'

Joe Minders laughed, then coughed, then laughed again.

'Of course, I never saw the fellow myself, Mrs Hudson. He was gone by the time the alarm was raised.'

'And I never saw him either, Joe. But I was wondering if perhaps you could remember the name he was using at the time? I have a name in mind, but would very much like to have it confirmed.'

'If I remember rightly, Mrs H, he was using a foreign name when he gave us the slip at Dover. I can't remember what. But I can remember the name he used at the Plinlimmon's right enough, because it was me who had to write all the reports. He was going under the name of White back then, wasn't he? Andrew White, he called himself. But he probably hasn't used that name since. Is it important?'

Mrs Hudson pursed her lips and her eyebrows straightened slightly.

'Perhaps not. As I said, something I heard the other day made me think of it, that's all.'

Sergeant Minders smiled.

'Another jewel robbery, Mrs Hudson? Or a peer being blackmailed?'

'No, Joe.' She shook her head, as though shaking off a troublesome thought. 'No, it was a couple of things, but nothing like that. One of them was a missing pair of spectacles, believe it or not. Now, tell me, is there anything else we can get you, or any errands we can run while we're here?'

We remained another twenty minutes, chatting and reminiscing, before gathering up our things. Before we left, while I was busy with my bonnet by the front door, I saw Mrs Hudson take the old man's hand.

'How are you, Joe?' she asked very quietly, and I realised it was the first time she'd asked the question. In reply, the old man shrugged and gave a slightly sad smile.

'There are more bad days than good ones,' he told her, 'but this is a good one.' He lowered his voice so that I could barely hear him. 'But my lungs are gone, young Hudson, and some nights the cough is very close to carrying me off. It will be quite soon now, I think.'

I saw her hand tighten around his, and they stayed like that for a few moments, very still, her standing, the sergeant still in his chair. Then Mrs Hudson spoke very softly.

'Thank you, Joe,' she said.

And he looked up at her then, turning his big frame in his chair so he could see her properly.

'It's been my pleasure,' he replied.

The two smiled, hands still joined, then the old policeman coughed and Mrs Hudson poured him a little measure of the rosehip syrup she'd brought, and then we left.

Walking back, through the baking, breathless streets of Shepherds Bush, my desperation to get to Revennings had begun to seem a little unworthy.

–

We found Mr Rumbelow in his office, looking very hot and rather bothered.

'I really think it is time for me to leave London,' he announced, waving us into the leather armchairs that flanked his desk. 'Until now I have been detained by this business of the banks selling people worthless canal stocks. A most lamentable affair. Honest people who failed to read their loan agreements properly and ended up inadvertently buying shares in the Bridgwater and Taunton Canal. Anyway, I'm happy to say I have brought the matter to a satisfactory conclusion, and now I think a visit to my cousin in Cornwall is in order. I'm really not sure that I can take another week of this terrible, spiteful heat.'

Mrs Hudson agreed that it *was* very hot and added that Cornwall was very lovely, but she didn't sound like someone desperate to escape London herself. I have a suspicion that Mrs Hudson, like Mr Holmes, enjoyed being at the heart of things.

'I have placed those advertisements you requested, Mrs Hudson,' Mr Rumbelow went on. 'In the academic and trade journals, and also in the *Timber Trade News*, just in case. Too soon for any replies, of course, but I'll let you know.'

I had no idea what request he was referring to, but, before I could ask, Mrs Hudson had made another.

'We were hoping, sir, that you could make some enquiries at the Empedocles Club on our behalf. In particular, I was hoping to identify any professional men Professor Broadmarsh might have had dealings with. He presumably has someone who looks after his legal affairs and such like, and perhaps a land agent he's close to. We are, of course, trying to identify anyone who might have received one of the professor's cryptic telegrams. We know he sent two to members of his family, one to his banker and one to the Earl of Brabham. The fifth remains unaccounted for.'

Mr Rumbelow nodded happily.

'Of course, Mrs Hudson, of course. And is there anything else I can help you with?'

'Only this, sir. Tell me, if someone repeatedly stole your spectacles, someone who didn't need them for themselves, what would you think they were up to?'

Our old friend sat back in his seat and pondered this with impressive gravity.

'Well, Mrs Hudson, pranks aside, I'm a bit short-sighted nowadays, so I'd probably conclude that there was something they didn't want me to see. Like the tiny print about canal shares at the bottom of those loan agreements, for instance. Either that...' His seriousness deserted him and he chuckled. 'Either that, or I'd be forced to conclude that someone thinks I just look a lot better without 'em!'

Mrs Hudson and I both smiled at that, even though I wasn't sure that it was particularly helpful. After all, Mr Esterhazy was not a man concerned with controversial legal documents; and it was hard to imagine that anyone would go to such great lengths simply to alter a vicar's appearance, no matter how unsightly his spectacles.

Which just shows that, on this occasion at least, my imagination was sorely lacking.

Part II

Summer in the Country

Chapter Nine

We sent off for Revennings the next morning, and the joy I felt on escaping the city is hard to describe. Waterloo station held the heat like a crucible, bubbling and hissing and screeching, while the locomotives belched smoke, and sweating passengers swirled around each other in complicated patterns, like currents in a boiling sea. By the time we were seated in a stifling third-class carriage that smelled of hot tar and hair oil, I was so limp I could barely hold up my own head.

But then the doors began to thump shut and a whistle blew and we began to move, and with motion came the breeze – a hot, dry breeze, admittedly, but still like heaven on my hotter skin. And as we edged out of London, nudging through the suburbs, through Vauxhall, past Clapham Junction and Wimbledon, past new houses being thrown up on old fields, I began to revive; until suddenly we were in the countryside, and the train was flickering past golden acres of corn and fields of rough plough, past cows sunk to their haunches in reed-fringed ponds. An old church dashed past, and a thatched village, and a stand of trees as old as England; and I, who for so much of my life had known no landscape but brick and stone, felt my heart fill as it always did when these simple and amazing things were rolled out in front of me.

Around me, passengers dozed – even Mrs Hudson's eyelids began to droop from time to time – but I felt more alive and less like sleeping with every mile that passed. When the train pulled into the little station at Milford and Mrs Hudson gave me the signal to alight, I practically danced down the step to the platform. Mrs Hudson followed me, tossing down our neat overnight bags before she clambered down, for it had been arranged that we should stay the night at Revennings and return the following day.

'We have Miss Peters to thank for that,' Mrs Hudson explained. 'She wrote to Miss Blondell at my request, though precisely what she said, I shudder to think.'

Our anxiety on this front only increased when we met the driver of the trap sent to collect us. He was a craggy, unkempt fellow in a slouch hat, but he leapt down at our approach and saluted us as though we were royalty.

'Trap for Revennings, ma'am,' he mumbled. 'I'm Ridley, work on Bottom Farm, sent to meet you, great honour. Mrs Watson, the housekeeper, she's looking forward to welcoming you, she is.' He handed us up into the trap before stowing our bags with such care they might have been made of china. 'Mrs Watson... No relation to the great man of your acquaintance, ma'am, though people often ask her. She likes to read his accounts though. Never misses one. We know all about your two gentlemen down here.'

'Really, Mr Ridley,' Mrs Hudson began politely, once he'd turned the pony and got us underway, 'it is very good of you to take the trouble to come for us. Was there no member of staff at Revennings who could come and meet us in the trap?'

'No, ma'am. It's not a big place, Revennings. Small but friendly, that's the truth. It's always Thompson the gardener who meets the trains, but he's away, so Mrs Watson asked me to help out.'

'Away?' Mrs Hudson sounded astonished. 'This is surely a busy time in the garden.'

'Arr.'

It was not clear if Mr Ridley saw this as confirmation or denial. But it was clear that he felt no further answer was required.

'Perhaps he is away on gardening business?' Mrs Hudson persisted.

'Arr,' Ridley said again. 'That's the house, there.'

And he pointed with his whip towards a cluster of mellow stone chimneys rising above the trees.

I will never forget my first view of Revennings. I think it was the most beautiful house I'd ever seen. Not grand, not even very big, but perfect in its proportions, and built from a warm, brown stone that seem to smile at us in the heat. Its fine front door stood open, and so did its long, elegant windows, but most breathtaking of all were the climbing roses that clung to it, neatly trained around the windows and the door. I don't know what magic had been brought to bear on them so late in the season, but even in the burning heart of that burning August, they were festooned with yellow flowers – scented clusters so perfect that they might have been painted there by an artist.

Behind the house, the rising woodlands were a dark green backdrop that made the stone and the flowers stand out, and in front, the lawns were a softer shade, leading your eye to the house itself. Nothing complicated or exotic caught the eye; the allure of Revennings was its simplicity.

'A tidy little place,' Mrs Hudson commented, and Ridley acknowledged the compliment with a nod, and I could tell from the softness of his expression that he shared her appreciation.

Mrs Watson, the housekeeper, greeted us at the back door with open arms and a beaming smile.

'Mrs Hudson! Flotsam! *So* pleased to welcome you to Revennings. When Miss Blondell told us that you were to break your journey here, we were all aflutter. But I thought, "well, this is just the place for them to pass a quiet, restful stay after all their adventures." You two poor souls must be utterly exhausted after chasing those jewel thieves through the night. And on a camel too! How lucky that you knew how to steer one! Miss Blondell says that Sherlock Holmes would never have caught them if it hadn't been for you.'

I confess I blushed and even opened my mouth to protest, but Mrs Hudson's solemn expression silenced me.

'I can tell, Mrs Watson, that Miss Peters has been extremely detailed in explaining the reason for our visit. She is a most exuberant young lady. And it is true that Flotsam and I are looking forward to a few quiet hours before we return to our duties in Baker Street.'

'Of course, of course.' Our hostess gestured towards a tiny housemaid who had been cowering, awestruck, behind the pantry door. 'Nessie here will show you to your room. Tubbs – Miss Blondell's butler – will be back from Godalming in an hour or two and is looking forward to meeting you both. And when you've had a chance to wash and rest, Miss Blondell would like to see you in the Great Hall.'

The room we were to share was at the top of the house, with a low ceiling but two reasonably sized beds and a generous window. The sash was open, and gave us an astonishing view of Revennings' lawns and the golden fields beyond.

'This will do us very nicely, Flotsam,' Mrs Hudson remarked. 'It's warm enough up here, but after London this room feels extremely pleasant.'

'What do you think Miss Peters has said about us, ma'am?' I asked, still slightly aghast. 'What *was* she thinking?'

Mrs Hudson's mouth twitched at the corners.

'I don't suppose Miss Peters was thinking at all. She is a young lady from whom words just flow out. I told her that you and I were anxious to have a look at Revennings, and suggested she might drop a line to Miss Blondell. I also pointed out that it wouldn't do for anyone to know we were looking for information about Professor Broadmarsh. The servants here had clammed up when asked by Sir Torpenhow's man, and I didn't want them to do the same with us.'

'But all that stuff about jewel thieves, ma'am?'

'Who knows, Flotsam? I suggested to Miss Peters that you and I might very reasonably be interested in seeing Revennings' famous Great Hall, and Miss Peters said, "yes, you *will* need a good reason to visit, won't you? Don't worry, Mrs H, I'll think of something." It was, perhaps, an error on my part to leave it at that.'

Her eyes moved to the window.

'Have you noticed how very perfect the gardens are looking, Flotsam? It's not what I was expecting. Now, let's get our faces washed, and then get up to the Great Hall to see Miss Blondell. But before we do, Flottie, we have one important thing to decide.'

'And what's that, ma'am?'

'Was it you, Flotsam, or was it me, who proved so adept at steering that camel?'

–

The Great Hall at Revennings was every bit as striking as I had been led to believe – lofty, arched and incredibly ancient – and made even more striking by the dramatic orange drapes that hung from every stone pillar.

'Rather loud, aren't they?' Miss Blondell remarked when Mrs Watson had made the introductions. 'But Prof – that's my cousin, Professor Broadmarsh – was so keen on them that he telegraphed me all the way from who-knows-where, and I don't mind really. He loves Revennings much more than I do – I'm more a Mayfair and Park Lane girl myself – and he looks after the place beautifully. All the servants here adore him – he used to come here all the time when he was a boy, so he's known Tubbs and Watson since he was a tot – and sometimes I feel rather guilty that it belongs to me and not to him.'

Miss Blondell was a cheerful young lady of around twenty years of age, plump and comely, with hair that was not quite fair and not quite red.

'And is the professor here at the moment?' Mrs Hudson asked innocently. 'I think Miss Peters mentioned that he'd been away.'

'Oh, and he still is. I can't remember where, exactly. I'm sure he'll be back before the end of the month, though, because he won't want to miss the Wymondham's Ball over at Montrachute House. *Everyone* goes, and Prof likes a good waltz as much as anyone.'

'It must be a comfort to him to leave the place in such good hands.' Mrs Hudson was all formal politeness. 'We were particularly struck by the neatness of the grounds. You must have an excellent gardener.'

'Oh, yes. Thompson. He's a treasure.' Miss Blondell looked a little vague. 'I do like the gardens to look nice, but they're Prof's department really. He's mad keen on plants and things.'

'Well, we'll look forward to meeting Mr Thompson during our visit,' Mrs Hudson commented gravely. 'I don't suppose he'll be hard to find.'

'Oh, no, I'm sure he'll be around somewhere.' If Miss Blondell was part of a conspiracy to conceal her gardener's whereabouts, she showed no sign of it. 'In the potting shed, no doubt. That's where I always run into him. Now, on a much more important subject, Mrs Hudson, I want to hear all about this business of the jewel thieves. It all sounds incredibly exciting…' She gave a little shudder. '…Although how you both survived in that room full of scorpions I simply can't imagine.'

Nearly half an hour later, we returned to the servants' hall in search of Mrs Watson. During that time we had convinced ourselves that Miss Blondell, although able to pinpoint very precisely the current location of a great many eligible young men, both in the Home Counties and beyond, had genuinely no idea that Thompson the gardener was not still in the garden, overseeing operations.

'Mrs Watson must know something, ma'am,' I urged. 'Why don't we just ask her where he is?'

'All in good time, young lady,' my companion replied. 'It may surprise you to know this, Flotsam, but there was a summer in my youth when I was taught fly-fishing by an Irish earl. He was a rather serious young man.'

'So… are we going fishing, ma'am?'

It seemed a strange way to go about things.

'Not this visit,' Mrs Hudson smiled. 'I only mention it because it taught me something that has often proved helpful: to achieve the best results, you don't always cast directly at your target. Unfortunately, the earl applied the same wisdom to his pursuit of a wife, and in such an exaggerated manner that it's unsurprising he remained a bachelor.'

At that point we were interrupted by Mrs Watson, bustling in from the boot room with a basket of dirty washing, and showering us with offers of food and refreshment.

'We were just heading into the gardens,' Mrs Hudson explained to her. 'Flottie here is something of a botanist, and we're looking forward to a chat with the gardener. Thompson is his name, I believe?'

Mrs Watson's warm and effusive countenance changed in a moment. She looked embarrassed, I thought, but more than that. I thought she looked afraid.

'I'm sorry to say Thompson's away at the moment,' she told us, looking at the washing, then at the basket, then at a small crack in one of the kitchen tiles. 'Visiting a sick relative, you know. But, of course, you're very welcome to explore the grounds. Miss Blondell says you are to have the freedom of the place.'

'Thompson is away?' Mrs Hudson was all astonishment. 'But the gardens look so immaculate. I imagine he must have planned his absence, and left very clear instructions for the under-gardeners.'

'Oh, no, far from it.' The housekeeper clearly felt on firmer ground. 'The summons was quite sudden. But the under-gardeners are very competent, and then there's Agnes.'

'Agnes?'

Mrs Watson sighed.

'Agnes is quite hard to explain. I suppose you'd call her Thompson's apprentice, though it's not a formal arrangement. She's a peculiar little thing. She turned up here about ten years ago, when she was no more than four or five. Starving, she was, just a tiny little waif. No family, no shoes, and barely any clothes. Thompson found her picking flowers in the water meadow.'

'Picking flowers?' I asked. It seemed an odd thing for a hungry child to be doing. I'd known for myself what hunger feels like.

'That's what surprised Thompson. He's an expert at chasing off urchins from the village, but instead of chasing off Agnes, he took her in and gave her something to eat, and she's been here ever since.'

'But where had she come from?' I wondered.

'Nobody knows.' Mrs Watson shook her head. She seemed much more comfortable now. 'She barely speaks to anyone but Thompson. No one's ever discovered how she got here or where she came from. But she knows everything about the garden, and she's good with his birds – Thompson keeps pigeons – and she sleeps on a pallet in his cottage, and never bothers anyone. I don't think Miss

Blondell even knows she's here, but Professor Broadmarsh is a great friend of Thompson, and he gets on very well with Agnes too, even though she hardly says a word. But if you're heading out into the gardens, you'll meet her for yourself.'

And we did. We had been strolling through the lavender walk that lay on the south side of the house when we spotted one of the under-gardeners, shears in hand and fork over his shoulder, talking to someone who I mistook for a child; a slim, slight figure in boy's clothes, with a boy's cap pulled low over the eyes. It was only when I watched for a moment that I realised the smaller figure was clearly giving directions to the larger, accompanying them with hand gestures to illustrate the point – a chop of the hand, or a sawing action with the arm – and the gardener was listening attentively, nodding all the time. Finally, he tugged respectfully at the brim of his hat, then marched purposefully upon his way.

'Agnes,' Mrs Hudson observed.

She turned when we approached her, and I saw a small, boyish face peeping out from below the cap. She had lively blue eyes and blonde hair, cropped very short, and she showed no wariness at our approach, but stood her ground, watching us. Hers was an unlikely figure to find in the timeless gardens of Revennings, but she appeared in no doubt that she belonged there.

As we came nearer, I saw her eyes switch from me to Mrs Hudson and then back again.

'Agnes?' I asked. 'My name is Flotsam. Mrs Watson told us to look for you. She says you know everything about this garden.'

She didn't reply, just tipped her head very slightly to one side and looked me up and down, and I had no idea what to say next. But sometimes, by pure luck, without plan or thought, we can find ourselves saying exactly the right thing at exactly the right time.

'I'm desperate to know something,' I told her. 'How can it be, in a summer like this, that your roses still look so perfect?'

She smiled at that. Not a grin, and not really directed at us, just a slow, happy smile that transformed her features.

'Follow me,' she said.

We spent nearly an hour with her that afternoon, moving from shade to sun, from the house to the rose garden, to the long pergola that swept down to the lake. It was a strangely silent tour; Agnes told us the names of every rose we passed, then showed with her fingers where they should be pruned, and very occasionally added some little comment: '*Eleanor's Glory*. Finished now. Smells like pear drops.' Then silence as she led us onwards.

From time to time Mrs Hudson surprised us both by putting the name to a flower before Agnes revealed it.

'*Comtesse de Chambord*,' she informed us on approaching a particularly ravishing pink-flowered shrub. 'They grow them at Cheveney. I was your age, Agnes, when I first saw them.'

And all the time I waited for Mrs Hudson to ask this strange creature a question – about the professor, or about Thompson, or about the strange telegrams. But it was not until we arrived at a round, stone building, hidden behind yew hedges, that the conversation moved away from roses.

'A very fine dovecote,' Mrs Hudson commented, 'and older than the house itself, by the look of it.' She looked at Agnes. 'Someone had already told us that Thompson kept pigeons. Do you like them too?'

The young girl seemed poised to reply, but instead simply nodded her head and led us towards the low door. The only light in that ancient stone room came from dozens of small openings near the point of the roof, but it was enough to show me that the walls were lined with nesting ledges set into the stonework. In the centre stood a post as tall as a maypole, with wooden arms branching off it, and a single ladder rested against one the arms. There was a very strong musty smell but the room itself felt cool, despite the temperature outside.

There were few birds to be seen, no more than a dozen, nestling on the top line of ledges, cooing softly together so that the room seemed filled with a very low purr. Agnes stood for a moment saying nothing, looking up at the birds, then she too made a cooing noise, and at the same time held up her hand. Almost instantly, and quietly as a leaf falls, a single pale bird glided down to rest upon it.

Still the girl said nothing, simply smiled at us, then back at the bird, and began to stroke the back of its neck with her finger.

'You must know them very well,' Mrs Hudson said softly.

'Thompson's birds.' Her eyes remained on the pigeon. 'Mine now, too. They love it here like I do. They always come back.'

'And where is Thompson now?' Mrs Hudson asked.

'Away.' She repeated the soft cooing noise she'd made before. 'I'm not to say where. A long way. I keep the garden right till he comes back.'

Mrs Hudson nodded as though none of that was in the least surprising.

'And what made him go? He must love it here in the summer.'

The girl nodded.

'A message came. Before the dahlias were out. The professor sent for him.'

'And do you know why, Agnes? Why Thompson had to go? Why did the professor want him?'

But Agnes barely seemed to hear, so engrossed was she in the small creature on her fingertips.

'Thompson and the professor... They both love the birds.' She lifted her hand a little higher, and the pigeon, as if following an unspoken command, returned with a flutter to its resting place. 'And I do too,' she added. 'The three of us. More even than the roses.'

'Yes.' Mrs Hudson remained very still, and I wondered what she was thinking. 'Yes, I can see that. And Professor Broadmarsh must be missing Revennings very much. Have you had any word from him since Thompson left? Any message at all?'

The question did not seem to surprise Agnes. She had moved to the door and was opening it for us.

'Nothing yet. But soon, I'm sure.' Her eyes moved away from the house, towards the path that ran down to the ornamental lake. 'He'll want to know about the mulberry tree. It's very old. He worries.'

We had to stoop to leave the dovecote, and as we stepped outside the warmth of the day embraced us again – no less hot than London, perhaps, but a gentler, less fierce sort of heat. Out there, among the fields and the trees, the weather might be debilitating, but you never felt it was actually trying to kill you.

'Well, thank you, Agnes.' Mrs Hudson straightened, still blinking slightly in the sunlight. 'Our tour of the gardens has been most enlightening. They are a great credit to you, and you should be enormously proud. I hope we shall meet again before we depart.'

But when we looked for her the following day, she was nowhere to be seen. It seemed to me that no one would ever find Agnes in the gardens at Revennings unless Agnes cared to be found.

Mrs Hudson waited until almost the last moment, when we were helping Mrs Watson clear away the breakfast things, before she returned to the subject of the absent gardener. When our hostess expressed the hope that our short stay had done us some good, Mrs Hudson nodded warmly.

'Indeed it has, Mrs Watson. Flotsam and I both feel greatly revived after our recent travails. The scent of camel is finally out of our nostrils, isn't it, Flottie?' She sniffed, as if in relief. 'We had heard so much about Revennings, and none of it was exaggerated. But we had hardly expected to discover a brand-new mystery within its walls.'

'A mystery, ma'am?'

I thought a shadow passed across Mrs Watson's face.

'Why, yes. About Mr Thompson and the professor. You see,' and here she lowered her voice dramatically, 'our two gentlemen – Mr Holmes and Dr Watson – are in the confidence of some very important people, and every now and then we can't help but overhear some trivial detail of their conversation. And a while ago we heard none other than Sir Torpenhow Franklin himself mention the professor's name, saying that he should be back in the country any day. But it seems the professor is still away, and no one seems to know where, not even Miss Blondell. And then – and it really is the strangest thing – a friend of Mr Holmes – because Mr Holmes has friends everywhere, you know – a friend wrote to Mr Holmes from Rumania of all places, saying he had met a fellow called Thompson who claimed to be Professor Broadmarsh's gardener! But everyone here tells us that Thompson is in Scotland. So how can that be?'

I watched Mrs Watson change colour. She really did. She actually went from rosy red in the cheeks, to a very pale blue-white, and then to a deep purple flush. Finally she looked around with that exaggerated caution that you see on stage, in amateur theatricals.

'Mrs Hudson…' She spoke in a strained whisper. 'There's no mystery here, but we *are* keeping a secret. About Thompson. And I will admit to you freely that we're at our wits' end. Tubbs and I, we don't know where to turn. Tubbs is so sick with worry he can hardly sleep. "Something's gone wrong, Mrs W," he keeps telling me, "something's gone terribly wrong."'

She began tugging at her knuckles until they started to click.

'You see, before the professor went away, he told us he might need Thompson to help him with something overseas. And if he did, he said, he would send for him by telegram, but no one else must ever know about it. He left Thompson the address of a man in London who would make all the travel arrangements, so all Thompson had to do was to pack his things and go, as quickly as possible. But the professor was most particular that we must say absolutely nothing to anyone about Thompson going, because it might bring trouble down on Revennings. It would only be for a week, or ten days at most, he told us. But it's been so much longer than that, and no word from Thompson. And now Tubbs says…'

She cast a glance towards the window, as if she half-expected to find someone listening there.

'Tubbs says something must have gone wrong, and something has happened that *will* bring trouble down on Revennings. Perhaps there are criminals following Thompson's trail back here. Perhaps Revennings is already in their sights. We're seeing strangers in every shadow, and every creaking gate sets us on edge. We can hardly sleep a wink for worrying about intruders. Yesterday a tinker appeared in the village selling clothes pegs who no one had ever seen before.'

'I can understand your concern, Mrs Watson. But Mr Holmes is looking into things.' She said it with such confidence that even I felt a little reassured. 'Now, tell me, was Thompson happy with these arrangements? I'm told he has rarely travelled very far from Revennings.'

'Oh, nothing upsets Thompson. He's… what's the word? *Phlegmatic.* He and the professor are thick as thieves, with their plants and their birds and their plans for the garden, so as long as the instructions were clear, Thompson would follow them. And he had Agnes to look after things here. I sometimes think, Mrs Hudson, that if all the staff left Revennings tomorrow, Agnes would manage things perfectly well without any of us.'

And to my great disappointment, Mrs Hudson left it at that. She offered more words of encouragement and reassurance, and more compliments about the house and its gardens, but asked nothing more. In return, Mrs Watson thrust various gifts of produce upon us, and, to take her mind off things, was persuaded to chatter about Miss Blondell's various suitors, none of whom ever seemed to find favour, and it was not until we were finally alone upstairs, packing our things, that I could ask the question that was burning my lips.

'But, Mrs Hudson, ma'am,' I spluttered, as soon as the door closed behind us. 'Aren't we going to ask Mrs Watson about *why* the professor wanted Thompson in Rumania? Surely that's the most mysterious thing of all?'

'Oh, I don't think we need to ask about that, do we, Flotsam?' Mrs Hudson was calming folding her night things. 'Mrs Watson has already told us more than she really wanted, and I fear it would make her very uncomfortable if we pressed our enquiries any further. No, I think we have already discovered everything we need to know here at Revennings, Flottie, and if we don't linger too long over our farewells, we should be nicely placed to catch the ten o'clock train back to town.'

But we did not, after all, return to Baker Street that day, because a telegram arrived at Revennings just as our bags were being loaded onto Ridley's trap. Miss Blondell came rushing into the kitchen with it, rather pink in the cheeks and glowing with excitement.

'Oh, Mrs Hudson, how lucky that I caught you! This arrived for me only a moment ago, but I rather thought you'd gone.' She thrust the slip of paper into my companion's hand. 'Really, the life you lead! It's all simply too exciting for words, isn't it?'

And the telegram did, perhaps, justify her enthusiasm, for it was an unusual communication.

PLEASE TELL HUDSON FLOTSAM
DIVERT FROG HALL ALTON STOP
BARRINGTONS IN URGENT NEED
GOOD COOK DINNER THIS
EVENING STOP BARRINGTONS
COOK VANISHED NO TRACE
HOLMES

Chapter Ten

Another house, another housekeeper. Miss Perch of Frog Hall was a gaunt, narrow-framed woman of sixty whose face fell naturally into an expression of anxiety; yet I believe she was every bit as pleased to see us as Mrs Watson of Revennings, and probably much more so. A party of twelve local dignitaries expected for dinner, all plans carefully laid, all preparations made, only to awake and discover the bed of your French cook unslept in, and the young woman herself quite disappeared – it is the sort of situation that might cause even the stoutest of housekeepers to quail.

We arrived at Alton station shortly after eleven o'clock, and were met in a four-wheeler by none other than Mr Barrington himself, with Dr Watson at his side.

'Welcome aboard!' Mr Barrington cried warmly. 'When I heard that you were coming to our rescue, I insisted on driving out myself. Dr Watson says that nothing can go wrong with you at the helm, Mrs Hudson!'

He was a pleasant-faced gentleman in his late thirties, with sandy hair and a sandy moustache, and a friendly smile. So affable was his manner that at first I took him for a much younger man, and it was only on closer inspection that I noticed some signs of age: the fine lines around his eyes, the tiniest sprinkle of grey at his temples, and, perhaps, I thought, an underlying seriousness that his cheerful ways could not quite hide.

'Mrs Hudson, Flotsam.' Dr Watson greeted us with a warm nod. 'Very good to see you. It's a funny business this. Holmes and I came down very first thing this morning and found the place in a bit of an uproar.'

'It certainly was!' Mr Barrington confirmed. 'We have been planning tonight's dinner for some time – ever since I returned from abroad – and to discover, this morning of all mornings, that our precious French cook has deserted us – well, you can imagine, Mrs Hudson, that emotions ran high.'

Our bags were swiftly stowed, and Mr Barrington himself handed us up.

'Keep an eye out for Mr Holmes,' he instructed us. 'He walked into the village earlier, intent on asking some questions about the wretched woman. He likes a mystery, doesn't he, Doctor?'

'On the contrary, sir, he *dislikes* a mystery. Yet sometimes mystery seems to follow him about.'

'So am I to understand that no note was left, or any other explanation given?' Mrs Hudson asked.

'None at all, Mrs Hudson,' Mr Barrington confirmed. 'Mademoiselle Le Blanc prepared an excellent dinner last night, and everything was very much as it always is. My wife spoke to her in the kitchen that evening, to inform her that Mr Holmes and the doctor here would be visiting this morning and might require luncheon. Everything seemed in order at that point. Yet by this morning, Mlle Le Blanc was gone. Frog Hall would seem to be cursed in the cook department just now.'

'You don't mean to say, sir, that something similar has happened before?'

'Well, not quite the same, Mrs Hudson. But a few months ago, Old Froggatt rushed home to Ireland and left us in the lurch somewhat. I was overseas at the time, and was rather sad when I got back and heard the news. I'm not sure she was ever the best cook in the world, but "Froggatt of Frog Hall" had a certain ring to it. Ah, here we are! And there's Perch waiting for you.'

Frog Hall was a striking residence, roughly similar in size to Revennings, but very different in appearance – a brick building of modern design and recent construction, with leaded windows and a gothic turret, and a great deal of dark, slated roof. Like Revennings, its grounds were neat and tidy, although to my eye its lawns and shrubs lacked something, like a very new suit of clothes which has not yet taken on the personality of its wearer. The gravel sweep where Miss Perch awaited us was very perfectly raked, and the servants' hall she led us to was large and well laid out, in the modern fashion. Even on first introductions, her relief was apparent.

'There's no denying I was at a loss,' she told us, shaking our hands warmly. 'At first, I had clung to the hope that she was coming back, that perhaps she had simply been taken ill somewhere. And then, well, I began to despair. I was relying upon her totally, and without her, well, we simply couldn't hope to deliver anything remotely good enough for tonight's occasion. And then when Mr Holmes mentioned your name, Mrs Hudson, I could barely believe our luck. You see, I remember hearing stories about a dinner you once prepared at Highbury Hall for the Spanish ambassador.'

'That was a very long time ago, Miss Perch,' Mrs Hudson pointed out, 'but certainly the circumstances are not dissimilar. And I'm sure between us we can serve tonight's guests something passable. You have the menu there, I see. Excellent. Then we have no time to lose...'

The rest of that day was one of hectic and unrelenting activity, for, as Mrs Hudson pointed out, much time had been lost and there were several dishes to prepare from scratch. Fortunately, Frog Hall's kitchen maids, Elsie and Leonora, proved as capable and confident as they were industrious, and Miss Perch pitched in gamely, overseeing the vegetables and the roast joints.

'It appears Mlle Le Blanc had already made a start on the *quenelles* for the consommé, Flottie, and the pigeon compôte is in excellent shape. But we have our work cut out with the sweetbreads, the mutton cutlets will take a little time, and it never does to rush a cucumber sauce.'

She studied the menu, frowning slightly as she did so.

'Now, what else...? Salmon-trout, whitebait, oxtail... They are all highly appropriate choices. And yet...' She turned to our hostess. 'I take it she was an accomplished cook, Miss Perch?'

'She was excellent, Mrs Hudson.' The housekeeper was already stuffing ducks with grim purpose. 'I had my doubts when the mistress first brought her down from London, her being quite youthful, and nothing like Old Froggatt, who was a terror. And she didn't really fit in with the rest of us below stairs, did she, girls? She was a bit too ladylike for my liking, and a bit too elegant in her manners, but perhaps that's the Frenchness coming out.'

Mrs Hudson was selecting artichokes from a large basket.

'I gather her predecessor left without proper notice, Miss Perch? In which case Mrs Barrington was fortunate to find someone so able.'

'It did seem like a blessed stroke of luck. Froggatt got a letter out of the blue telling her an uncle had left her a cottage in County Cork and three hundred pounds a year. She was always talking about an uncle who'd made good, wasn't she, girls?'

'Right boring about it she was,' Elsie confirmed. 'Told everyone for miles around. The old dragon,' she added under her breath.

'So when she got the letter, she was off in a flash,' Miss Perch continued. 'Burnt her bridges properly, she did. Told Elsie and Leonora they were both nitwits and would never find husbands.'

'Told Miss Perch she looked like a crow,' Elsie put in.

'And was bitter as a lemon,' Leonora added, with something of awe in her voice.

'Quite.' Miss Perch did not appear to share their pleasure in the reminiscence. 'So I think it's fair to say that Mlle Le Blanc was a very different kind of woman.'

'Ever so pretty she was.' Elsie's confidence was clearly growing.

'*Trés charmante,*' Leonora added, and both the girls giggled.

'And she got on ever so well with the mistress,' Elsie went on. 'They used to talk about fans and France and fabrics and things.'

'Could have been her companion, not her cook,' Leonora asserted, and might have gone on had Miss Perch not silenced her with a cough.

'That will do, girls,' she told them drily, then turned to Mrs Hudson. 'It was a difficult time for the mistress, with the master away for so long, and there being some talk of danger, and worry that something bad might happen to him in foreign parts. And Old Froggatt going without notice was a blow, because it never looks good for a young wife to start losing servants suddenly like that. But I remembered that we'd had a letter only a couple of days before from a French cook looking for work, with excellent references from grand houses in France, so Mrs Barrington wrote to her and interviewed her in town, and it was all sorted in a couple of days.'

Miss Perch sighed, and began work on the second duck.

'Now, I don't deny that the mistress became rather closer to Le Blanc than a lady should with her cook, but they were of similar ages, and both knew France, and the mistress speaks excellent French, and I think she was lonely, poor dear.'

'And now Le Blanc's gone.' Mrs Hudson rolled up her sleeves and got to work on the oxtail. 'Well, stranger things have happened,' she remarked.

And, as if to prove this sentiment correct, something fairly strange happened only a few minutes later. We heard light footsteps descending the back stairs, and Miss Perch, who had moved from the ducks to the beef, looked up.

'That will be the mistress now,' she told us, 'coming to see how we're doing.'

Then the door opened and a rather beautiful young woman entered the room holding a crystal vase full of ravishing orange-tipped heleniums.

'Miss Perch…' she began. Then, by chance, her eyes met mine, and she gave a little gasp, and the vase fell to the floor and smashed into hundreds of tiny crystal pieces.

–

'I must apologise for the mistress,' Miss Perch insisted, when she returned to the kitchen after helping Mrs Barrington to her room. In her absence, Mrs Hudson and I had exchanged a glance but had said nothing, letting Elsie and Leonora speculate to their hearts' content.

'Must have been feeling wobbly,' Elsie opined.

'Surprised to find strangers in her kitchen,' Leonora reckoned.

'Can't be that,' Elsie decided, 'because she knew Mrs Hudson was coming. Very pleased about it, she was.'

'But not Flotsam,' her friend pointed out. 'Mr Holmes never mentioned anyone else, only Mrs Hudson.'

Elsie looked at me appraisingly.

'Can't see why Flotsam would make anyone go wobbly. Perhaps it was them scrambled eggs you did for breakfast, Lee. I said at the time they looked funny.'

'Your kidneys, more likely.' Leonora turned to me and giggled. 'Mlle Le Blanc never let Elsie do the kidneys. She says she doesn't have *les doigts agiles*.'

Miss Perch's return put an end to the discussion. Her apologies were profuse.

'It is most unlike her, really it is. She is not the fainting sort of lady at all. I know she's seemed a little troubled recently, but she's never been nervy. She says it was a sudden dizziness, but she's having a lie-down now and I'm sure she'll be fine again in time for dinner. And me with the beef still to finish! My word, it's hot in here with

161

that oven roaring! I'm not surprised the mistress was taken funny.'

And it was hot. So hot that our clothes clung to our bodies as we worked and I could feel sweat prickling my scalp and trickling down the back of my neck. But I knew it was not the heat that had taken Mrs Barrington by surprise, and not the scrambled eggs either. Leonora had guessed right: it was the shock of seeing me that had made Mrs Barrington drop the vase. She had expected to find Mr Holmes' matronly housekeeper in charge of the kitchen; but she had not expected to come face to face for a second time with the little maid who'd opened the door to her that day she called – so very hesitantly – at Mr Holmes' house in Baker Street.

–

Dinner that night was served early, in the panelled dining room of Frog Hall, with the French doors open so that the soft breath of the evening could reach the diners. Mr Holmes and Dr Watson had been added to the party, but there was no shortage of food; the missing cook had made ample provision, and even though Mrs Hudson had struck the whitebait and the leg of mutton from the menu ('not enough time, and far too hot,' she had explained), there was still more than enough to eat. We watched it all being carried up from the kitchen with a strange elation, because during the course of the afternoon we had ceased to be an unlikely group thrown together by necessity and had become parts of a smooth, beautifully engineered mechanism, everything geared so perfectly that we stopped noticing the heat or the time, until suddenly, without us really knowing how, every dish was finished and we looked around at each other in a daze.

By the time it was our turn to eat, sprawled out around Miss Perch's table with the windows open and the night air flooding in, that elation was giving way to exhaustion, but I still felt a strange joy inside me. Miss Perch, who had struck me as dry and anxious on first acquaintance, now felt like an old friend, her work with the artichokes having bordered on the heroic; and towards Elsie and Leonora I felt a profound fondness, forged in the spitting heat of beef ribs and roasted ducks.

'*Très bon*,' Leonora concluded as we sat back at the end of our meal and feasted on a big bowl of Frog Hall's raspberries. The words seemed to sum things up very nicely.

'And *merci, mes anges*,' Elsie added. 'That's what Mlle Le Blanc always used to say to us,' she explained, 'though I'm not really sure what a *mezonge* is.'

'It is quite possible,' Miss Perch stated firmly, 'that Le Blanc left us so suddenly because she could no longer bear the terrible French she had inspired in you two. Now, Mrs Hudson, is there anything else we can get you this evening?'

'There was one thing...' Mrs Hudson considered the glass of chilled white port in front of her. 'It's a while since I've cooked for an occasion like this, and I was interested in the menu. Would you say tonight was typical of dinners here at Frog Hall, Miss Perch?'

'Of recent dinners, most certainly. A bit more lavish, of course, because we were entertaining. And very different from the days of Old Froggatt, eh, girls?'

'Old Froggatt would have thought a *quenelle* was some sort of illness,' Elsie giggled.

'And that a *fanchonette* was a bowl for washing your privates.' Leonora, who was sailing rather close to the wind, was silenced by a glare from Miss Perch.

'And presumably,' Mrs Hudson went on, 'Mrs Barrington would make most of the decisions about the food, in consultation with her cook?'

Miss Perch considered this.

'Well, not really, Mrs Hudson. When the Barringtons moved to Frog Hall, they inherited Froggatt from the previous owner, a northern gentleman who'd made a great deal of money from Kendall Mint Cake. They were newly married, and it can be hard to find a good cook, and Froggatt *was* good, in her own way. But she could be a bit fierce, and she had her own ideas about what constituted a good dinner, and I'm afraid the mistress used to defer to her rather. So when Le Blanc arrived, Mrs Barrington was in the habit of simply approving the menu rather than shaping it.'

'So tonight's menu was Mlle Le Blanc's work...'

Mrs Hudson's continued interest in the menu puzzled me, especially now we'd cooked it all and didn't have to worry about it anymore.

'I wonder,' she went on, 'what Mr Holmes discovered about the lady's sudden departure.'

We didn't have to wait very long to find out, because an hour later, just when we were about to retire for the night, Mr Barrington asked to see us in his library. We found him smoking a cigar by the French doors, while Mr Holmes and Dr Watson lolled in armchairs nearby. Dr Watson was also smoking, and Mr Holmes cradled a small glass of crème de menthe. When we entered, they rose to greet us, but it was Mr Barrington who spoke first.

'I wanted to thank you personally for your splendid efforts tonight. My wife is somewhat weary and has retired to bed, but has asked me to pass on her own thanks. Tonight's gathering was important to us, you see. I've been abroad for some months, and this was the first time we have entertained since I returned. My wife has been very proud of the new cook she found in my absence, and I'm afraid we had rather raised the expectations of our neighbours. So both of us, and my wife especially, would have felt it most keenly if we had disappointed them this evening.'

Mrs Hudson bowed her head solemnly.

'Thank you, sir. Flotsam and I were happy to help. But your thanks should really go to Miss Perch and the girls downstairs, who were quite magnificent. May I ask, sir, if anything further is known about Mlle Le Blanc's sudden disappearance?'

Our host turned to Mr Holmes, who shook his head.

'Very little, Mrs Hudson. I've been able to discover that she left Frog Hall at around four o'clock this morning. A local labourer saw her on the path to the village, although what *he* was doing out and about at that time I chose not to ask. It would appear she went straight to the station and waited there, because we know she caught the milk train to London. As to her motives in departing so suddenly, I don't suppose we'll ever know.'

'My money's on a love affair,' Dr Watson put in. 'French,' he added by way of explanation. 'That sort of thing always hits them harder.'

'Her motives are hardly any concern of ours,' Mr Barrington declared, his annoyance showing. 'She can take herself off to the devil himself, for all I care. She'll certainly be getting no reference from us.'

'Once or twice in my experience, sir,' Mrs Hudson appeared to be following her own line of thought, 'an employer has assumed that the sudden departure of a servant was prompted by baser motives. Can I assume, sir, that nothing has gone missing from Frog Hall in the last day or so?'

Mr Barrington shrugged.

'Not that we know of. I believe Miss Perch has checked the silver.'

'And your own personal effects, sir? Nothing missing there?'

He cast a glance towards his guests.

'Mr Holmes has already asked me the same thing. But my watch and cufflinks and the like are all in order.'

Mr Holmes cleared his throat and looked at Mrs Hudson very pointedly.

'Mr Barrington has assured me that there is nothing else of his at Frog Hall that anyone would particularly want to steal. No souvenirs of his recent travels, for instance. Nothing he has brought back from abroad.'

The message was clear enough, and Mrs Hudson nodded.

'Some travellers do prefer to commit things to memory,' she stated gravely, 'rather than to rely upon souvenirs. But, tell me, sir,' and she turned back to Mr Barrington, 'since your return from foreign parts, have you been aware of anything at all untoward at Frog Hall?'

I thought he paused for a fraction of a moment before replying.

'No, nothing at all. If that unreliable cook of ours is a thief, then she's found nothing here worth stealing.'

'If it's not a lover,' Dr Watson continued to speculate, 'then perhaps she simply lost her nerve? You know, first big dinner for a new employer, important guests, lots of courses, all that. Perhaps she wasn't confident of pulling it off.'

He looked across at Mrs Hudson, hoping for confirmation of his theory, and the housekeeper nodded her head.

'Yes, sir. I think you are probably right. It seems to me very likely that Mlle Le Blanc simply lost her nerve.'

But I was certain, even as Mrs Hudson spoke, that it had not been nervousness about the *quenelles*, or even the *fanchonettes*, that had caused the French cook of Frog Hall to flee so abruptly. Nor was it simple good fortune that the mistress of Frog Hall had been able to find so easily, and with so little fuss, such a capable young lady to take charge of her kitchen.

Chapter Eleven

The exact nature of Mrs Barrington's distress – and the reasons for it – became apparent the very next morning.

Mrs Hudson and I, assisted by Elsie and Leonora, had sent up a very fair breakfast, and the two girls had then been despatched to the village, ostensibly to buy bacon, but really, I knew, because an outing to the village was something of a treat for them, and Mrs Hudson was keen to reward them for their efforts of the night before.

So the two of us were alone in Frog Hall's big, modern kitchen when we heard footsteps on the back stairs and were joined by the lady of the house herself, as delicately beautiful as the day before, but considerably more composed.

'Mrs Hudson, Flotsam...' She nodded to us in turn. 'I have come to apologise for my strange behaviour yesterday afternoon. You will have gathered, Flotsam, that I was taken by surprise. It hadn't occurred to me that the maid I encountered that day in Baker Street might appear here in Frog Hall. And, you see, my visit to London that day was an indiscretion. I had some idea that the famous Sherlock Holmes might assist me in keeping a secret – one that I had not yet shared with my husband.'

It was, perhaps, not unheard of for the lady of an establishment to express her gratitude to members of the servants' hall who had done her a particular service. Nor was it unknown for such a lady to appear in person below stairs. But there was something in Mrs Barrington's manner, and something in the confidences she appeared to be sharing, that suggested she was eager to talk. Miss Perch had told us how close Mrs Barrington had become to Mademoiselle Le Blanc, and it struck me for the first time how lonely Mrs Barrington must be, with her husband away for long periods, and with few neighbours of her own age. The countryside can be very beautiful, but it isn't always the easiest place to find friends.

Mrs Hudson seemed to feel this too, for instead of responding to the young lady's words with the polite and formal acknowledgement I might have expected, she nodded gravely and indicated Miss Perch's high-backed chair.

'It is often easier to confide in a stranger than in a loved one, is it not, ma'am? And blackmail is such a dirty and distressing business that it can be hard to know which way to turn.'

At the word 'blackmail', Mrs Barrington gave a little gasp, but Mrs Hudson carried on without pause.

'Now, it's often been said that worries, like sugar lumps, will dissolve completely in a good cup of tea, and Flotsam here is just about to make a good strong pot.'

To my surprise, our hostess took the offered seat without demure.

'Blackmail...' She said the word thoughtfully, as though she were hearing it for the first time. 'How strange you should say it, Mrs Hudson, for you cannot possibly know...' Then she managed a proper smile, one full of warmth. 'Unless some of the magic of those rooms in Baker Street has rubbed off on you over the years.'

'I don't know about magic, ma'am,' Mrs Hudson told her gravely, 'but it is inevitable that Flotsam and I, in the course of our duties, are sometimes aware of certain things. And when a young diplomat is privy to information that a great many people wish to get hold of, and when that diplomat's wife appears in Baker Street in a state of distress – when something occurs in her life that is easier to confide to a famous detective than to the man she loves – well, ma'am, it doesn't require any great magic for the word "blackmail" to come to mind.'

'And you are right.' Mrs Barrington spoke firmly, confidently, as though she had just taken a decision. 'I have a secret, and that secret has become known to someone, and now both my husband and I are ruined. I don't know what will become of us. We must certainly separate. Possibly, if we do, Harry's reputation can be repaired, though his career is surely over. But only if I leave him forever and disappear from his life.'

It was a dramatic announcement, but she said it without any drama at all – just sadly and simply, as though she was stating an inescapable truth. And I confess my heart went out to her. Whatever she had done, however dreadful, I felt an urge to go over and comfort her, to put an arm around her shoulder and give her a hug. But it was hardly my place. Instead I busied myself making tea.

'Perhaps, ma'am...' Mrs Hudson lowered herself into the seat next to the young lady and dusted some imagined flour from her hands. 'Perhaps, if you were to tell us a little more, we might see if some of that Baker Street magic has rubbed off after all?'

'And why not?' Mrs Barrington smiled again, a small, lovely smile, and settled back into her chair. 'Even now my husband is sharing the whole sorry tale with Mr Holmes, and soon it will be the talk of every tavern and every drawing room in the land, so I can see no reason why I shouldn't tell you. Dr Watson has been saying how wise you are, Mrs Hudson, and I feel perhaps you will judge me less harshly than many others of our sex. It all began, you see, when I was very young...'

And so she told us her story. It was, in many ways, a sad tale, and my heart went out to her. She began with an account of her early years as the daughter of a dressmaker in a town on the south coast. Her mother was a widow, and times were hard, so the young Rosa Worthing, as she was then known, was no stranger to poverty, nor to the humiliations that so often accompany it. As a child she worked hard, learning her mother's trade, and gaining too the best education that lady was able to impart – reading and writing, enough arithmetic to be able to keep accounts, and a little French, because her mother considered it a ladylike accomplishment. More significantly, perhaps, her mother taught her that their impoverished circumstances were only temporary – that, someday, Rosa's charms and beauty would attract the attention of a proper gentleman, and from that day forward their problems would be behind them. Whether her mother was imagining that her daughter's salvation lay in wedlock, or in some other arrangement, was less clear.

'It was a difficult message to hear,' Mrs Barrington told us, 'for I was by nature a shy and quiet girl, and quite terrified by the idea that I would be expected to charm anyone, least of all a gentleman, for I met few men and was rather frightened of them. I allowed myself to hope my mother was wrong, and that it would be our skills in dressmaking that would one day make our fortunes.'

'And then, when I was fifteen, my mother sent me to buy ribbon at the Tuesday market, and while I was there I was spotted by a young gentleman on a jet-black horse who leapt down in front of me and demanded, with a laugh, that I should marry him on the spot. When I tried to step past him, he took my arm and insisted, at the very least, on a kiss. And when I blushed and refused him, he took it anyway, then tumbled into a string of the most gallant apologies, and declared that, to atone for his impudence, he should be allowed to buy me a twist of candied peel from the stall opposite.

'His name was Dick Eastwood, and he was about twenty-three years old then, but in terms of experience, of knowledge of the world, he might have been twenty or thirty years my senior. I don't deny that I was swept away by his attentions, perhaps from the moment of that very first kiss. Certainly, when he insisted on accompanying me home to my meet my mother, instead of resisting, as I should have done, I found myself floating on clouds of joy and excitement.

'And my mother was no less enthusiastic. Here, to her, was the gentleman of her dreams. He told her he was the only son of Sir Henry Eastwood, owner of ten thousand acres in Yorkshire. He told her that he was visiting the town for his health, and for adventure, and to seek out old friends, and hinted that a great many young ladies of fashion in London were awaiting his return. But he was wealthy enough in his own right, he told us, to marry any woman he chose, and stated plainly that beauty and simplicity were the only attributes that mattered to him, suggesting that he had found them both that very day in quantities that were greatly to his liking. When he invited us both to dine in a private room at his inn, my mother accepted with such alacrity that even I was a little ashamed.'

While she was speaking, Mrs Barrington had rested her hand on the table in front of her, and I think it was at this point that Mrs Hudson took it in her own.

'The deal was done that night,' Rosa Barrington continued. 'After a fine dinner and a great deal of wine, there was much talk about the darkness of the night, the strength of the wind and the hazards of the walk home. But it was agreed that my mother could not sleep soundly in an inn, for fear that her own little home might fall prey to thieves in her absence. Her daughter, of course, should not be exposed to the dangers of such a stormy night, and if it was true, as Mr Eastwood maintained, that a room at the inn was available for her, then the problem was solved. She left the inn that night knowing I was bound for the bedchamber of her new acquaintance, and confident that all her problems had been solved at a stroke.'

The day was already hot and the kitchen growing hotter, and I confess I blushed a little in appreciation of her predicament. But Mrs Barrington didn't blush as she told her tale. It was as though she had examined her own conscience and had found nothing there with the power to embarrass her.

'Of course, it was all lies. I soon discovered that Eastwood was but one of his names – Heywood and Vaizey were others he used – and that the wealthy Sir Henry was no more real that the private fortune or the acres in Yorkshire. But I didn't care. The discovery that my dashing lover was a gentleman of fortune, cheating and tricking his way through life, trading upon his charm and his good manners, adept at running and hiding and bluffing and bouncing back from any misfortune – it in no way diminished his allure in my eyes. Perhaps it even enhanced it.'

She shook her head, as if marvelling at her own stupidity.

'And the irony is that I insisted on him marrying me. That was no more a part of his plan than riding to the moon, but in those first heady weeks, when our shared bed was still a novelty to him, I found certain ways to persuade him. Had I not – had I been content to live as a fallen woman – how different things would be now! But at the time I felt blessed. I was as happy as Mrs Dick Vaizey as I was as Mrs Dick Eastwood, and at first I was blissfully happy as both. I left my mother without a care in the world, and followed my husband from inn to inn, from town to town, from scrape to scrape. He could charm any person he chose, and ride any horse he chose, and win any game he chose to play. He could fence, and dance, and with a pistol he could hit a sixpence from twenty paces. And for a time I think he was happy having me with him.'

She looked up at Mrs Hudson and I saw the older woman give her hand a squeeze. The tea was ready in its pot, but it didn't seem the right time to serve it.

'That didn't last, of course.' Mrs Barrington paused to fan herself, then continued with her account. 'Within a few short months, his interest in me was waning. And Dick had hit a run of bad luck – plans went awry, plots were discovered, card games were lost with catastrophic results. He came to believe I was the cause of his ill fortune – nothing of the sort had ever happened to him before, he told me cruelly. And now, so dire were our circumstances, so pernicious my influence, that we had no choice but to retreat abroad. He took me with him as far as Dover, where he left me at an inn while he looked for a ship to give us passage – and of course he never came back.'

Outside the kitchen window, a small brown bird was singing very loudly, so loudly that for a moment all three of us turned to watch it. When, after a few more seconds of song, it fluttered away, over the hedge of the kitchen garden, Mrs Barrington took a deep breath.

'It took me two days to believe he had really abandoned me, and another two to recover from the shock. But I had a bill to pay at the inn, and nothing but a gold chain and some cufflinks, won at cards on Dick's last night in England, with which to pay it. I had learned a great deal in the course of my marriage, however, including how to get the best price for gold. The second chapter of my life began there, in Dover, and until very recently it was a very happy time.'

And I had to agree that was true. The bird returned and sang again, a little further away this time, and while it sang Rosa Barrington told us how she had repaired her broken heart and her broken life; how, posing as a widow, she had found work with a seamstress in Dover; how she had saved enough for a passage to France, where, as a recently bereaved English dressmaker of uncommon talent and taste, her fortunes had prospered. It had been in Le Havre, some three years later, that she had met Harry Barrington, and the young diplomat had quickly found himself besotted with the shy but beautiful English widow who was so admired by the ladies of the town.

'At first,' she assured us, 'I could not reciprocate his feelings. I distrusted all men and had no wish to ever again allow one close to me. But he was most persistent, and to put an end to his suit I told him my whole life story, that I was married to a scoundrel, that I had lived the life of a scoundrel's wife, that my mother had traded her own daughter for some imaginary Yorkshire acres. My confession had exactly the effect I had hoped. Harry left Le Havre, and for three months did not return. But when he did, it was to tell me that he cared nothing for my past, that I was the only woman he could ever love, that he would have no one if he could not have me. And by then, everything had changed.'

Mrs Barrington was leaning forward now, closer to Mrs Hudson, and there was a gleam of joy in her eye as she recalled those times.

'You see, in his absence, word had reached me in Le Havre that my mother had died after a drunken fall from a cart. I therefore felt it incumbent upon me to return to my home town, to make arrangements for her burial and to sort out her affairs. I discovered a great many debts, which I was able to discharge by the sale of her house and stock. But I found something else, too. A letter. A letter addressed to me in Dick Eastwood's handwriting.

'It had been written about a year after his disappearance, and was sent from the island of Cuba. It was, I suppose, an apology of sorts. He told me that I should forget him, that he was about to take ship for South America where he would either make his fortune and live like a lord, or die a pauper in an unmarked grave – and that therefore I should consider myself a widow from that moment forth.

'Of course,' Mrs Barrington added hastily, 'it would never have occurred to me to take him at his word. I had passed myself off as a widow, true enough, but I knew myself to be married in the eyes of God, and in the eyes of the law, and no glib urgings from a rogue of a husband was going to alter that. But there was something tremendous in his letter, something that took my breath away. You see, Mrs Hudson, he mentioned the name of the ship on which he was about to embark – the *Conquistador*, bound for Pernambuco. And that name was familiar to me.

'The incident received much less attention over here, I believe, because there had been only one Englishman on board when the *Conquistador* went down with all hands. Even in England, however, because of the great many lives lost, reports of the disaster appeared on the front pages of the newspapers. But forty-three French citizens lost their lives on the *Conquistador*, so it was for many weeks a great talking point in France. That is why, even two years after the incident, I recognised the name of the ship immediately, and also remembered the fate of its passengers. One Englishman, Mrs Hudson! Only one Englishman on board, and I now knew, from his own letter, that man was my husband. Finally I was a widow in truth.'

Rosa Barrington looked across at me then, and there were tears in her eyes as she smiled.

'It must seem shameful to you, Flotsam, but the joy I felt on learning of my husband's demise knew no bounds. And as I read his letter, I learnt something else too. For on discovering myself free of him, it felt as though a dam had given way and bright water was flooding into me, and I was filled with the shocking realisation that I was in love with Harry Barrington.'

The tears were trickling down her cheeks now, but she looked more beautiful than ever.

'So when Harry returned to Le Havre to lay his heart at my feet for the umpteenth time, I was able to throw myself into his arms with a readiness that quite took him aback. I told him Dick was dead, drowned in the Caribbean, and that I was truly free to be his. His joy, I believe, was matched only by my own, and, for all our separations, for all the long days apart, ours has been a truly happy union. Or so I thought.'

All of a sudden, the young lady's face changed. Gone was the joy, gone was the defiance with which she'd told us of her past. She seemed to shrink a little into her chair, and her shoulders sagged; like a doll, I thought, with some of the rags removed from its stuffing.

'You see, Mrs Hudson, Harry and I have never truly been married. Oh, we thought we had. We thought we were the happiest married couple alive. No sin has been committed here, except through ignorance. And ignorance truly *was* bliss, until that day a few weeks ago when a letter arrived for me in a hand I did not recognise. Harry was not here. It was while he was away in Asia, on that latest mission of his. So I had no one to turn to, no one in whom I could confide. Only Mademoiselle Le Blanc, who sometimes seemed the one woman of my own age in this whole, pious parish!'

It seemed to me that Mrs Hudson's eyebrow twitched very slightly, but her expression didn't change.

'And this letter, ma'am?'

'It was the most mean and vile communication imaginable. It told me in the bluntest and most brutish prose that my first husband was alive, that he had not drowned, and that I stood before the law a bigamist. It told me that I should expect to spend the remainder of my youth in gaol, while my second so-called husband endured the disgrace and humiliation I had brought upon him. It stated that my crime should be revealed to the world if I did not follow the instructions of the writer, to be sent to me at a later date. And it told me, if I doubted the truth of these assertions, that I should be at platform three of Clapham Junction station at a certain time on a certain date, standing at a certain part of the platform. Arrangements would be made, the writer told me, for my first husband to appear before me in person.'

'But surely, ma'am,' I blurted out, unable to contain myself, 'surely your crime was unintentional, and committed through no fault of your own?'

She turned to me then with eyes full of feeling.

'All that is true, Flotsam,' she agreed, 'and a fair-minded court might believe it so. I might be spared a gaol sentence. But it would not be in their power to deny the bigamy. My marriage would be declared a sham, my reputation would be trampled into the mud, and Harry, even if he were to give me up, would find doors closed to him for the rest of his life. But I don't believe he *would* give me up, not willingly. He would want to go on living with me, outside wedlock, even though it would ruin us both. My only hope was that the letter was some sort of cruel hoax. And there was only one way to find out.'

Mrs Hudson stirred in her seat.

'That tea, Flotsam. I think this would be a good time.' But before I could bring the tray to the table, she turned back to our hostess. 'Do I take it then, ma'am, that you went to Clapham Junction?'

'I did.' Mrs Barrington fanned herself vigorously for a moment or two. 'I followed most exactly the instructions contained in the letter.'

'And this letter...' Mrs Hudson's eyebrow twitched again. 'May I ask if you still have it?'

'I'm afraid I destroyed it, just as soon as I had memorised its contents. I felt myself contaminated by it; tearing it to shreds was a relief of sorts. But none of that prevented me from taking the train to Clapham Junction, and I waited at the appointed place, just as I had been told. And it was all as horrible as I'd feared. I had waited no more than five minutes when a man in a cheap suit with a horrible little moustache and a bowler hat approached me. He spoke like an Irishman, and although he didn't introduce himself, he knew exactly who I was. He greeted me by name, then beckoned me to follow him, and led me to that part of the platform where the front carriage of any London-bound train would draw to a halt. He told me to wait, but it was not at platform three that the next train pulled in. It was at the next platform along, so I was separated from it by the width of a train track. But when the Irishman pointed, I could see quite clearly, through the window of the carriage, that it had one occupant only. And that occupant was undoubtedly the man I had married all those years before.'

I think she must have sensed that I was about to protest, for she silenced me with another of her smiles.

'I know, Flotsam, you will argue that I can't be sure – that there was a distance between us – that time must have changed him. But I assure you I was in no doubt. The man in the train was older, yes, but the folds of his face were set in exactly the pattern I remembered. The shape of his nose was precisely and unarguably the same. Even the little crow's feet at the corners of his eyes were as I remembered them – deeper perhaps, and perhaps a little more extensive, but forming the same distinctive fan shape as they had all those years before. It was my Dick, alive as the day I'd last seen him. The sight almost took my breath away, but never for a moment was I in any doubt.'

The temperature of the kitchen was still increasing, and perhaps that is why Mrs Barrington had begun to look so pale. But she continued her story, firmly and resolutely.

'He was too far away to hear me cry out, and he never looked my way. I confess I had wondered if Dick himself was the author of that letter, his intention being to torment me, and to help himself, through blackmail, to Harry's fortune. But seeing him in the train that day, I realised he was entirely unaware of the drama being played out on the adjacent platform. I have no idea how he survived the sinking of the *Conquistador*, nor what bitter chance had brought him to London, but I'm certain he was unaware of the villainy afoot that day.

'I suppose I only saw him for a few moments. By the time I had fully recovered my senses, his train had begun to pull away, in the direction of London. And when I turned around to question the man who had led me to the spot, I discovered he too had disappeared, slipping away in the moment of my greatest distress, leaving me alone and desperate on that crowded platform.'

She removed her hand from Mrs Hudson's and began to rub her temples in little gentle circles.

'I confess I spent the next few weeks in a turmoil of hope and despair. The letter was destroyed, and no further communication followed it. That day at Clapham Junction began to seem as unlikely and as insubstantial as a nightmare. I began to hope that perhaps my tormentor had forgotten about me, perhaps that he had found some other victim to torture. But then I would remember Dick's face in that carriage, and the blackness would engulf me all over again. Because even if my blackmailer remained silent for ever, the truth remained that I was a bigamist, that I had married one husband while the other still lived, that my marriage to Harry – the most precious thing in my life – was a sham.

'Even when Harry returned from Asia, I could not bring myself to tell him everything. I think I still hoped that perhaps Dick would disappear abroad again, and that without his presence as evidence against me, my crime would never come to light. It was in that troubled and uncertain state of mind that I travelled to London with the idea of throwing myself upon the mercy of the famous Sherlock Holmes. But I think, even before you had opened the door to me, Flotsam, that I had decided on the opposite course. I came home that day and immediately confided everything in my husband – for I still call Harry my husband, even though I know that, in law, he is not.'

'And the pair of you have confided all this to no one?' Mrs Hudson had risen from her chair and had moved to the counter by the kitchen sink, where she was idly examining the hem on a linen tea-cloth.

'Not until today, ma'am. But in the first post this morning, the second letter arrived. It was addressed to my husband this time. It appears Harry is privy to some piece of important, secret information. The writer of the letter has made it plain that this information is the price of his silence. There are elaborate instructions about how this secret is to be delivered, but the threat is clear. If Harry does not comply with these demands, his wife will be exposed as a bigamist and his career will be over.'

'And of course…' Mrs Hudson replied, still studying the tea-cloth, 'of course, your husband will not comply with those demands, because he is an honourable man who will not hesitate to put his duty to his country ahead of his own domestic happiness.'

Mrs Barrington sighed. 'Of course. It is one of the reasons I love him. And so, Mrs Hudson, my fate is sealed. In a matter of days, everything I hold dear will be destroyed forever.'

'Perhaps.' Mrs Hudson tossed the tea-cloth aside and looked at me. 'A fresh pot, I think, Flotsam. That one must be cold by now. And while it's brewing, Mrs Barrington, perhaps you would permit me to ask you a single question. On what date, as precisely as you can recall, did you confide the secret of your first marriage to your French cook?'

So unexpected and abrupt was the inquiry, that I almost fumbled the teapot. Mrs Barrington must have shared my surprise, for I saw a bright flush spread across her cheeks.

'Mademoiselle Le Blanc? You are quite right, Mrs Hudson. In a moment of weakness, I *did* take her into my confidence, although I don't remember the date. I was lonely, you see. My husband had been away so long, and

Le Blanc was so agreeable, so affectionate. One day she discovered an old book of verse among my possessions. It is one of the very few items I own that comes from that other chapter of my life. I had been given it by a customer of my mother's when I was a very young girl, and I have treasured it ever since. Mlle Le Blanc, however, had noticed my handwriting on the fly leaf. *Rosa Worthing*, I had written when I was a child, and later, in the first throes of wifely pride, I had crossed out the *Worthing* and replaced it with *Eastwood*.

'Well, it was obvious to Mlle Le Blanc that Eastwood was not the name of my current husband, and without ever really intending to, I found myself telling her the story of my first marriage. At that point, of course, I still believed Dick to be dead. It was around a month later that the dreaded letter reached me.'

Mrs Hudson listened to this in silence, then nodded her head gravely.

'Thank you, ma'am. Many things begin to make sense. Now, finally, that pot of tea, please, Flotsam, before we all die of thirst.'

'But, Mrs Hudson, ma'am!' I protested. 'Is there nothing we can do? Surely this horrible man must be stopped!'

'Please, Flotsam...' Rosa Barrington's voice was soft and strangely calm. 'Nothing can be done. But thank you for wanting to help.'

'Perhaps you are right, ma'am,' Mrs Hudson concurred. 'But we should never despair.' She brushed her hands together briskly. 'Now, Flotsam, as soon as we've drunk our tea, I would like you to go and find Mr Holmes. Please tell him that we shall be returning to

Baker Street by the next train. Then perhaps you would be good enough to find Miss Perch, and ask her for some writing paper and a copy of the *Peerage*.'

'Writing paper, ma'am? And the *Peerage*?' It was not, I fear, my proudest moment.

'Yes, Flotsam. You and I need to get a few things sorted before our gentlemen return. But first I would like to drop a line to Lord Digby, the Egyptologist. I don't know his lordship personally, but I've always heard he is a friendly enough gentleman. And then, I think, another letter to Mrs Esterhazy, warning her that we would like to visit. I have one or two urgent questions about her husband's spectacles.'

Chapter Twelve

I returned to the city that day with mixed feelings. We arrived at Waterloo a few minutes before noon, and after the green sweetness of Revennings and the airiness of Frog Hall, London came as a shock. As I stepped down from the carriage, the heat that rose up to meet me seemed thicker and somehow more malignant than the high temperatures of the countryside; and it felt much harder to breathe, too, as though the very air was being squeezed from the city's streets. But the smells of the station were rich and familiar – people and horses and hot tar, engine oil and coal dust, dusty leather and blocked urinals and the defiant drift of lavender from the flower girls at the platform's end – and the noise and bustle struck my ear like a welcome. For all its dangers and discomforts and iniquities, this was home.

It was well that Mrs Hudson and I had travelled ahead of the rest of our party, for the rooms at Baker Street felt stale and stagnant, as well as suffocatingly hot, when we arrived and threw open the shutters. And we had not been back many minutes – there had scarcely been time for me to unpack our bags and separate out the dirty laundry – when we were disturbed by a knock at the front door. Pausing only to pull on a clean apron, I opened it to a gentleman of perhaps forty or fifty years of age with a luxuriant and curly moustache, who, much to my surprise, was also sporting a delicate parasol in very fine French lace.

'My sister's,' he explained before I had time to say anything at all. 'I know it looks a little peculiar, but why not? Need all the shade I can get, and couldn't find an umbrella. And just you wait, if this weather keeps up, these things will be all the rage for the fashionable gentleman. Mr Holmes in?'

I explained that my employer was not expected home until the evening.

'Excellent. I'll pop back then.' He produced a striking card case of purple leather from inside his jacket, then, realising that he needed a second hand to open it, was forced to hand me his parasol before producing his card. 'The name's Alba, Egbert Alba. Please tell Mr Holmes that Sir Torpenhow Franklin has asked me to call, about developments in the Carpathians. Will that make sense to him, do you think?'

It was hardly my place to say, so I bobbed politely and took the card.

'No, seriously, child, I'd value your assistance. You see, I've no idea how much Sir Torpenhow has already told Mr Holmes, and if it isn't very much then I will have a lot of talking to do when I call. But I take it that the two have enjoyed quite lengthy discussions already. Is that right? I'm hoping your answer will be "yes", because I'm rather hoping to be away in good time tonight, to catch the fireworks down in Westminster.'

The gentleman twirled his moustache very playfully as he spoke, and he had a very winning smile, but I had been too well trained by Mrs Hudson to divulge information at the doorstep, even when I was holding a gentleman's parasol for him. So I muttered the conventional 'I'm sure I couldn't say, sir', and attempted to hand the thing back to him.

'You know what?' Mr Alba took a step back and, still smiling, looked me up and down. 'That thing suits you a great deal better than it has ever suited my sister. I think you should keep it. You have done me a great service, you see, because I suspect, from that little momentary frown of yours, that Mr Holmes *has* been briefed by Sir Torpenhow, for which information I am greatly obliged. I means I can look forward confidently to seeing some fireworks!'

It took me a moment to understand that he really meant what he'd said about the parasol, and, when the penny dropped, I attempted to follow him down the steps.

'No, please, sir, I couldn't possibly...'

But already he was turning away.

'You could. You can. You must!' He gave a little laugh. 'It's a good one, you know. It's by Duvelleroy. I will see you again, young lady. Perhaps not tonight, because, you know, with this busy life of mine, it's quite possible I might be detained elsewhere. But I now consider it a personal challenge to one day coax a smile to those firmly sealed lips of yours.'

And with that, he was gone, sauntering away south, towards Portman Square, as though, for him, flirting with parlour maids was the most unremarkable thing in the world.

It was not unheard of for one or two of Mr Holmes' callers to be a little on the flamboyant side, and in my experience debonair gentlemen from the Foreign Office were more likely than most to be a little unconventional, so perhaps I wasn't as perturbed by this encounter as I should have been. Admittedly, it was highly unusual to be presented with a parasol, but I didn't for a moment take seriously his suggestion that it was a gift. I placed it carefully in the umbrella stand behind our front door, and assumed that, in the next few days, a boy would be sent by its true owner with instructions to retrieve it. It was, I think, only when I described the interview to Mrs Hudson that my mind was changed.

'Again, Flotsam. Tell me again.' To my amazement, she was already stripping off her apron and moving towards the area door. 'Egbert Alba, did you say?'

'Yes, ma'am. A rather impudent gentleman.'

'And his card, Flotsam?'

'In the tray by the front door, ma'am.'

She nodded briskly.

'Never mind about that now. Come, Flotsam! He headed towards Portman Square, you say?'

And to my astonishment, we set off in pursuit.

It seemed an absurd undertaking, because a full three minutes must have elapsed since the gentleman had departed, and it was far too hot to hurry. But Mrs Hudson was up the area steps three at a time, still tying her bonnet strings as she went.

'But, ma'am,' I protested as I followed behind, 'he's too far ahead. And besides, he's coming back. He told me so.'

'I wouldn't be too sure of that, Flotsam,' Mrs Hudson replied, scanning the pavements in the direction Mr Alba had taken. 'Now, a light suit and a boater, you say. Sadly, that is the uniform of every second gentleman in London this summer, but it is something.'

And away we went, my companion bustling along with such haste that at times I had to trot to keep up with her. We had gone no further than the crossroads with George Street when Mrs Hudson waved down a hansom cab that was approaching us from the direction of Portman Square. The cab driver, a cheery faced old fellow wearing a fawn bowler hat, listened to Mrs Hudson's question with interest.

'Middle aged chap with a lengthy moustache, you say? Saw a gent like that catching a cab down in the Square a couple of minutes ago. Don't know if he's the same fellow, but he was wearing a boater right enough.'

We scrambled in, and, on Mrs Hudson's instructions, our driver turned his cab in the road and headed back towards Portman Square at a very fair lick. At the point where Baker Street joined the Square, he slowed and called out to the driver of another hansom.

'Hey, Arthur!' he called. 'Did you see which way Jeremiah went just now? He'd just picked up a fare in a boater.'

'Wigmore Street,' the other replied tersely, and pointed the way with his whip.

Our driver shook the reins and we were off again, east into Wigmore Street, jostling past hand barrows and heavy carts, swerving to avoid a stationery victoria that was badly parked near Duke Street. Near the top of Marylebone Lane we passed another hansom, and its driver hailed us politely.

'Afternoon, Gilbert. In a hurry?'

'Looking for Jeremiah Collins. Have you passed him?'

The other man gestured with his head as he went by.

'Saw him turning into the Lane just now.'

We clattered into Marylebone Lane at a fine speed, but instantly had to slow. The lane was much narrower than Wigmore Street, and much busier. Pedestrians crowed the pavements and we were forced to move at the pace of the slowest wagon ahead of us. At the end of Aldburgh Mews the traffic halted altogether, but our driver pointed over the tops of the various carts that blocked our way to another hansom, similarly marooned, some hundred yards further on.

'That looks like Jeremiah's cab, ma'am. We can keep on after him if you like, but to tell the honest truth you'd stand a better chance on foot.'

So we paid him and descended, taking our chance on the busy pavements. The hansom ahead of us was moving forward in fits and starts, but, even though our progress was not smooth, we were definitely gaining on it. Indeed, we had come within about thirty yards of it, and had it firmly in our sights, when its occupant, perhaps also despairing of his slow progress, jumped down.

I recognised him at once as the gentleman who had called at Baker Street, and from the languid grace with which he set off on foot, I could tell he had no idea he was being followed. That lazy saunter of his was deceptive though, for although Mrs Hudson and I were moving as quickly as we could through the crowds, we were struggling to draw much closer. He was still fifteen or twenty yards ahead of us when we saw him cross the lane and disappear into a public house called the Bag of Nails.

Mrs Hudson and I were quick to follow, but were delayed by a long coal wagon that drew to a stop in front of us just as we were about to cross the road.

'Don't worry, Flotsam. He must still be in there,' Mrs Hudson reassured me as we found our way around the obstruction. 'I know this pub of old, and there is no rear entrance. If we keep our eyes on that door, we can't miss him.'

'Couldn't we just follow him in, ma'am?' I asked, a little out of breath, and aware of the perspiration glistening on my forehead in a most unladylike fashion.

'I don't want to catch the fellow, Flotsam,' the house-keeper explained, 'but I would very much like to see where he goes.'

'But *why*, ma'am? He did flirt rather outrageously, I know, but apart from that, what's so special about Mr Alba?'

'Now, really, Flotsam,' Mrs Hudson tutted, her eyes never leaving the door of the public house, 'you have surely been taught enough Latin to know the answer to that.'

And it was true that I *had* been taught some Latin, by various butlers and clergymen at various times, once even – for three hours a week for a whole winter – by a defrocked priest working as an ostler for Lord Shrewsbury. But what the connection was between my very basic Latin lessons and the gentlemen in the Bag of Nails, I simply couldn't fathom – and before I could ask, the door of the tavern had opened.

We had taken up position beneath the awning of a draper's shop only a dozen paces away, and now we both leaned forward expectantly, but the person who emerged was an elderly lady of respectable but slightly dishevelled appearance, who was attempting to stow a bottle of gin into her slightly-too-small reticule. She was followed a few moments later by a clean-shaven gentleman in a dark suit and a homburg hat carrying a smart leather travelling case, and then by a man in workman's clothes and a flat cap accompanied by a greyhound on a lead. After that, for several minutes no one emerged, and I could feel myself growing nervous.

Finally Mrs Hudson tutted to herself.

'Come, Flotsam, it is too hot to stand here all day. We shall have to go in and look for our gentleman after all.'

But even before we stepped inside I had an increasingly unpleasant feeling that we would not be successful. And when we stood in the doorway, scanning the two dozen or so faces clustered in the public bar, I was not surprised that Mr Alba's was not one of them.

'Gent with a moustache?' An elderly man with a mottled complexion, seated very close to the door, pondered Mrs Hudson's question with a great deal of seriousness. 'Yes, I saw him. Came in, went straight to the yard at the back. You know, for a call of nature, like. Haven't seen him come back yet though. Perhaps he's trying to do the other sort.'

Mrs Hudson, I knew, was not one to be daunted by convention, so I caught her arm and held her back before she could stride out to the yard to investigate.

'Don't you worry, Flotsam,' she reassured me. 'I think I can survive the sight of men urinating in a gutter. I have, I regret to say, seen scarier things in my time.'

'No, ma'am, it's not that. It's just…' And here I paused, unsure how I was going to explain. 'It's just that, I didn't notice it at the time, but now I think back on it, I think perhaps the gentleman we were following has already gone. You see, that man in the homburg a few minutes

193

ago… I didn't look at him very closely when he walked past us, even though he tipped his hat to us, remember. He didn't have a moustache, you see, and he was wearing a dark, heavy suit, and his face seemed all serious and somehow much *older*. But now I think of it, I can't help wondering if that man wasn't Mr Alba.'

Mrs Hudson stood still for a moment.

'I see. Yes, Flotsam, that would make sense. He had a bag, did he not? For his change of clothes. And of course, when you are looking for someone with a very conspicuous moustache, all clean-shaven men rather fade from view. The gentleman has been very clever.'

'Perhaps not *that* clever, ma'am,' I exclaimed, my spirits rallying. 'His card, remember? He left Mr Holmes his card!'

But when we returned to Baker Street and examined the object in question, I suffered a further disappointment. Because the crisp calling card Egbert Alba had pressed into my hand did not contain his address, or even his name. It was, in fact, the business card of a cigar merchant on George Street, whose premises Mr Alba must have passed on his way to our door. When I recalled how easily this deception had been carried off, my cheeks flushed with embarrassment, but Mrs Hudson was quick to reassure me.

'You had no reason to look at the card, you know, Flotsam. In fact in my day it would have been considered very improper to have looked at it, if the gentleman had given his name.'

'But I don't understand all this, ma'am. If Mr Alba wasn't sent by Sir Torpenhow, who did send him? And what did he want from us?'

We were still standing in the hallway, but before she replied, Mrs Hudson beckoned to me to follow her downstairs.

'Nobody sent the gentleman, Flotsam. He came entirely of his own accord. As for why, well, I would say that he is the sort of man who likes to know his opponents' strength. Mademoiselle Le Blanc flees Frog Hall when she hears that Mr Sherlock Holmes is to pay a visit. And very shortly afterwards, a gentleman appears at our door asking questions. This wasn't just a piece of tomfoolery, Flotsam, this was reconnaissance.'

We had arrived in the blessed cool of the kitchen, and it was with enormous relief that I sank down onto one of the kitchen chairs.

'And we have to admire his cleverness, you know.' Mrs Hudson filled two long tumblers of water from a large earthenware jug and sat down beside me. 'Because he didn't really ask any direct questions, did he? He just asked you to confirm that Mr Holmes had been in discussion with Sir Torpenhow Franklin. And he mentioned the Carpathians. Even though you are far too sensible to betray any confidences on the doorstep, he was then able to form his own opinion based on your reactions. Because if you'd never heard of Sir Torpenhow, and never heard of the Carpathians, I think it's quite likely your ignorance would have been apparent.'

I considered this.

'So you think Mr Alba is in league with Mlle Le Blanc, ma'am?'

'I strongly suspect he is married to her.'

It wasn't like Mrs Hudson to speculate about such things, but I let it pass.

'And you think he is worried that Mr Holmes is on his tail?'

Mrs Hudson pursed her lips.

'Not worried, Flotsam. But wary, and perhaps it has given him cause for a little thought. But I suspect that the gentleman you met today worries about very little.'

I thought for a moment.

'He seemed like a very good-natured gentleman, ma'am. Though terribly flirtatious, of course.'

To my surprise, Mrs Hudson reached out and took my hand.

'Never be fooled by a charming veneer, Flotsam. You do not become an international spy master by tiptoeing around your own conscience, and no amount of charm can atone for the lives ruined by your schemes. So you can be quite sure, Flottie, that the architect of the Samarkand Conspiracy, a man who can make trains disappear, who is not afraid to kidnap British diplomats, a man who can be in Tashkent one day and London the next... You can be quite sure, my girl, that the man we are dealing with, for all his debonair manner, is a very dangerous man indeed.'

Chapter Thirteen

Mr Holmes and Dr Watson returned from Frog Hall that night tired, hot and in low spirits. The distress of the Barringtons had clearly taken its toll upon Dr Watson in particular, because when I took up a tray of iced lemonade to cool them after their journey, he was slumped in his chair, sighing softly to himself.

'I just can't see how we can help the young lady, Flotsam, short of locking up the blackmailer before he does his worst. But that only gives us till tomorrow night to find him, doesn't it, Holmes?'

Mr Holmes had taken up position by one of the windows, and was peering between the partly closed shutters into the street below.

'That's right, Watson. You see, Flotsam, midnight tomorrow is the hour appointed by the blackmailer. Barrington or his representative must be in position on a certain bench by the Serpentine at midnight, with his section of the Emir's code in a plain envelope, ready to hand over. If he is not there, or if the code is not handed over successfully, the blackmailer has sworn that the following day he will make public the Barringtons' unfortunate marital circumstances.'

'And I can't see how we can catch the fellow before then,' Dr Watson lamented, barely noticing the glass of lemonade I placed beside him. 'All we have to go on is the letter itself, and a lace handkerchief that Holmes here found in a hedgerow.'

'Come now, Watson.' The detective turned away from the window. 'Those things are not as negligible as you make them sound. Before we travelled to Frog Hall, we knew almost nothing of the forces ranged against us. Now at least we have a trail to follow.'

He reached for a tumbler of lemonade, tasted it, winced a little at its sourness, then drained the glass.

'I don't need to tell you, Flotsam, that the link between the French cook and the blackmail are obvious, and it tells us a great deal about the formidable planning and patience of our foes. Knowing that Harry Barrington had been entrusted with one part of the Emir's message, they were in action with impressive speed, even while Barrington was still pursuing his tortuous journey home through Russia. The conspirators were looking for a weak point, and they knew the best way of spying on Barrington would be by establishing a trusted agent in his household. Their methods were direct but highly effective.'

'You mean getting rid of that cook?' Dr Watson grunted.

'That's right, my friend. Everyone in the locality knew the Barringtons' rather garrulous cook hoped for an inheritance in Ireland. What easier than to fabricate letters and documents to convince her that her inheritance had finally arrived.'

Mr Holmes turned to me with a rueful smile.

'We've been sending and receiving various telegrams today, Flotsam, and just before we left Frog Hall we had a reply from a magistrate in County Cork who knew all about the woman known to the Barringtons as Old Froggatt. It is exactly as we all suspected: there was no inheritance. Far from it. In fact, Mrs Froggatt is currently working in the kitchen of a slightly disreputable hotel in Skibbereen. On arriving home, it appears she quickly discovered the inheritance was a hoax, but by then she had rather burnt her bridges at Frog Hall and was too proud to inform them of the deception.'

And Mr Holmes didn't need to explain any further. For our adversary, it had been a relatively simple thing to ensure that Froggatt's replacement was hand-picked by himself. A simple letter enquiring after employment, delivered at precisely the right moment, was all that was needed. And a cultured young woman of a similar age to Mrs Barrington was the perfect person to wheedle out any secrets that might lurk in Frog Hall.

'Stroke of luck for them, though, wasn't it, Holmes? Happening to have a French cook in their pay?'

'They made their own luck, Watson,' Mr Holmes replied with a smile.

'If you please, sir,' I explained to the doctor, 'Mrs Hudson says that Mademoiselle Le Blanc hasn't actually been a real cook for some time. She says she could tell that from the menu. Apparently it was all rather traditional, in a very slightly old-fashioned way. She's certain that Mlle Le Blanc must have trained as a young girl in an excellent kitchen, but she's sure that it's some years since she actually worked in one.'

'And we now know a little more than that about Mlle Le Blanc,' Mr Holmes told me, reaching into his pocket and producing a small lace handkerchief. 'Take a look at this, Flotsam. We found it in the foot of a hedgerow on the path Mlle Le Blanc must have taken to the railway station.'

It was an exquisite piece of work, a confection of the finest French lace, with the initials 'B. W.' embroidered in one corner in very narrow lilac thread.

'Revealing, is it not?' Mr Holmes asked me, and I knew him well enough to detect the very faint trace of a smile in his eyes.

'Don't let him tease you, Flotsam,' Dr Watson warned. 'It's just a handkerchief. We can't even be sure it's hers.'

'Oh, Watson!' Mr Holmes did not sound entirely displeased by his friend's scepticism. 'Flotsam will tell you that is an example of the very finest lace. French lace, and of a quality rarely encountered over here.'

'That's true, sir. Miss Peters was trying to get hold of something like this earlier in the year. From Rheims, I think it is – she showed me a sample. But they make so little, and all of it so painstakingly, that Miss Peters simply couldn't lay her hands on a set.'

'So you would agree, Flotsam, that this handkerchief was not dropped by any common passer-by?'

'No, sir. Not unless it had been given to them by some very grand lady.'

'And from what you know of Frog Hall and its environs, would you expect to find any such handkerchief in the immediate area?'

That was an easy question.

'I'd be surprised to find one anywhere in the country, sir.'

Mr Holmes turned to his friend. 'So I put it to you, Watson, that the only person in or near Frog Hall who might have owned such an item was the mysterious

French woman employed there. Would you agree, Flotsam?'

'Yes, sir. Especially now that I've had a sniff of it. Here, try for yourself, sir. That very slight smell of rosemary – the pillow cases at Frog Hall all smelled exactly the same.'

Mr Holmes looked delighted.

'So, Watson, if we assume this handkerchief belonged to the missing cook, what does it tell us about her?'

His companion grinned.

'Well, Holmes, it tells us her initials are B. W., and that she has expensive taste in lace!'

'Quite right, my friend. But there is more, is there not, Flotsam?'

I studied the handkerchief again, certain that it must have more to tell me.

'For instance, what if I said that the young lady is a married woman, that her maiden name began with the letter "F", that prior to her engagement at Frog Hall she had spent some time abroad, most probably in the Middle East or Central Asia, and that, while resident at Frog Hall, she was in correspondence with at least one person unknown?'

Dr Watson considered this.

'Well, Holmes, I surely know you too well by now to declare that everything you've just said is nonsense, but exactly how you have arrived at those conclusions is beyond me.'

'Flotsam?'

Much to my alarm, Mr Holmes was looking pointedly at me.

'Well, sir, I can see that there are marks in the fabric where the initials are embroidered – it looks as if something has been unpicked and stitched over. It's hard to make out what that might have been, but it does look as though the second letter was an "F". And if I owned a handkerchief like this one, and then got married, I would certainly be tempted to pick out my old initial and replace it with a new one.'

'And the rest, Flotsam?' Mr Holmes had returned to the window, and was once again looking out at the street below.

'Well, sir, this slight yellow stain in the corner… Mrs Hudson would know for sure, but I think it could be saffron. And if I'm right, I don't think that stain was made at Frog Hall, because I don't think there was a stick of saffron in the place. But it must have been made fairly recently, because however lovely the handkerchief, a lady wouldn't keep a handkerchief for very long if it was permanently stained. So it stands to reason that Mlle Le Blanc, or whatever her name really was, had been – fairly recently – somewhere where saffron was in common use. And it's the same for this stain here. It's only tiny, but it's clearly an ink stain, and it's an unusual shade of violet-blue ink, which is the sort they have in the ink wells at Frog Hall. But that's scriveners' ink, the sort that washes out easily, so the owner of this handkerchief has been putting pen to paper fairly recently, certainly since this handkerchief was last laundered.'

Mr Holmes turned away from the window with a warm smile.

'Excellent, Flotsam! Anything else, by any chance?'

'Not really, sir…' I tried to resist, but the temptation was too great. 'Only that the owner of this handkerchief is married to a man with brown eyes and a strong jaw, who is currently somewhere in London.'

Perhaps if I had been a little older, or a little more confident, I would have allowed this statement to resonate for longer, but the look of surprise on Mr Holmes' face was too much for me, and before either he or Dr Watson could expostulate, I found myself recounting the story of our earlier visitor, and of our fruitless pursuit.

'Mrs Hudson has had to go out this evening, sir. A friend of hers is very ill. But I know she's convinced that the gentleman was trying to find out about you, sir. She thinks Mlle Le Blanc panicked when she heard your name, which is why she ran away from Frog Hall. So Mr Alba came calling to find out if your visit there was a coincidence, or if you had been engaged by Sir Torpenhow to help with this Bokara business. And she says Mr Alba is not just anyone, sir. She thinks he is the man behind the whole Samarkand Conspiracy.'

'Does she, by Jove?' Mr Holmes' eyes had narrowed and I could tell I had captured his interest. 'I wonder why she thinks that? The fellow behind the conspiracy is a pretty big fish. What was his name? Weiss? Andreas Weiss? A man of mystery, by all accounts. So it's hard to imagine why Mrs Hudson would think she's able to identify him, right here on our doorstep. But then, of course...' And here he paused to run a finger along the line of his jaw. 'Of course, it's also true that Mrs Hudson's experience in the houses of the great and good means that she commands a remarkably wide range of esoteric information. Or, to put it more plainly, she probably knows something we don't.'

-

The messenger who'd called Mrs Hudson away that night had arrived at our kitchen door only half an hour before the gentlemen returned. He was a thick-set man of around sixty or seventy years of age with very little neck, and he was introduced to me as Sergeant McCafferty, although it was clear from both his age and his attire than he was now retired from the police force. He came with the news that Mrs Hudson's old friend, Sergeant Minders, had taken a turn for the worse in his room in Shepherd's Bush.

'Drifting in and out of sleep,' he explained, 'and breathing terribly badly. But he's asking for you, Mrs Hudson. If it's convenient, I think you should come at once.'

So Mrs Hudson had left me to look after our two gentlemen by myself, and I felt rather proud of my efforts. Not only had I made a very respectable examination of Mlle Le Blanc's handkerchief, I had also provided the two gentleman with chilled soup, a chicken pie from Towson's, a thinly sliced cantaloupe and bottle of hock from the coolest part of the cellar. Then I'd unpacked the gentlemen's bags, sorted their laundry, turned down the beds and tidied the kitchen, and by the time I was looking around for another task to occupy me, I was interrupted by another knock on the area door. To my surprise – for the hour was late – the caller was Mr Rumbelow, perspiring in evening dress, and rather out of breath.

'Ah, Flotsam! So sorry to intrude. Came straight here. Important. Mrs Hudson out, you say? Quite so, quite so. I can wait. Or I can entrust you with the message. Hock? Why, yes, most welcome. So hot out there! Yes, a seat. Thank you.'

For all his urgency, it must have taken a full two minutes for him to settle down at the kitchen table and recover his breath sufficiently to tell his tale.

'I've been at the Empedocles Club again tonight,' he explained. 'If you remember, Mrs Hudson had suggested that I ask a few questions about Professor Broadmarsh's associates, so I've been doing that. The professor's got lots of friends at the Empedocles Club, you see, so I explained that we were looking for anyone who might have received a strange telegram from him in the last few weeks. Said that his banker had received one, and wondered if there were any other professional men the professor had dealings with.'

Mr Rumbelow paused for breath, and for another enthusiastic sip of hock.

'Well, Flotsam, a couple of days ago a fellow called Peabody found me in the Reading Room and asked me if I knew about a chap called Reddleman. The professor is a scientist, you know, and does all sorts of experiments and what not, and this fellow Reddleman is some sort of chemical supplier. When Professor Broadmarsh needs supplies of anything a bit rare, anything that can't be supplied by a local chemist, Reddleman is the man he goes to. So yesterday I dropped the chap a note, and this evening, just when I was about to head home, he called in to see me at the club.'

I topped up the visitor's glass, being careful not to interrupt his flow.

'He's a funny little man, is Reddleman. Like something out of Dickens. About four feet tall, round as a ball, and cheeks like little fat robins. But he was most congenial, and didn't mess around, just cut straight to the point. Told me that it was totally usual for Professor Broadmarsh to send him lists of chemicals he wished to order, sometimes by letter, but once or twice by telegram. So when he received a message from the professor from foreign parts, it didn't strike him as at all peculiar.

'The telegram named a single chemical element, but specified no quantities, so Reddleman had simply checked his stocks, satisfied himself that he already held sufficient quantities of the substance in question in the most common chemical forms, and had thought no more of it until he received my letter. He'd simply expected the professor to write again, when he was back in the country, with more specific details of his requirements.'

I could contain myself no longer.

'But what was the chemical, sir?' I asked breathlessly. 'What did the professor's telegram actually *say*?'

'Well, Flotsam, it was just like all the others. Only with a different element, obviously. Don't know what to make of it, though. Seems to me just as meaningless as all the previous ones.'

The bottle of hock was still in my hand, and I began to wave it dangerously.

'The chemical, sir?'

He began to fumble in his waistcoat pocket and produced a crumpled slip of paper.

'Here we go. Made him write it down, just to be certain I couldn't forget. Begins with "K".' He peered at the paper more closely. 'No, it doesn't. That must have been a mistake. Begins with "P". Here it is: *potassium*.'

I honestly don't remember much about the rest of Mr Rumbelow's visit. I think he stayed and drank another glass of wine, then realised that sitting up with me so late, unchaperoned, might perhaps be considered a little improper. Once that thought had struck him, he flushed very deeply and mumbled such a confusion of apologies that I thought he would never leave. Which sounds terribly rude, because I was very fond of Mr Rumbelow and always welcomed his visits.

But that particular night, from the moment he passed me Mr Reddleman's scrap of paper, my mind was racing. I think it was the letter 'k', scribbled next to the word 'potassium', that jolted me into a state of understanding, and from then on only a tiny part of my brain was aware of Mr Rumbelow, while the rest of it played with letters, rearranging them in my head, until finally, a few minutes before Mr Rumbelow retreated up the area's steps, the light flooded in.

When Mrs Hudson finally made it home, a little after midnight, I listened as well as I could while she told me that she had left Sergeant Minders sleeping, that he was comfortable, but that his life was surely drawing to its close. They were sad words, and I felt genuinely sorry when I recalled the kind old man I'd met that day in Shepherd's Bush. But I was still a young girl then, and found it very difficult to suppress my excitement.

'Sergeant Minders sent for me this evening, Flotsam, because he'd remembered something he felt it important to tell me. It was good of him to think of us at such a time, was it not?'

'Yes, ma'am,' I nodded.

'It seems that, as he dozed, a name had come back to him. It was the name of a young foreign lady who, a few years ago now, was suspected of cheating an elderly peer out of a large sum of money. She had never been caught, and a year or so later someone had mentioned to Sergeant Minders that the lady in question was keeping company with another bad sort, the man who had almost got away with the Plinlimmon emerald. A man called Andrew White, if you remember?'

I nodded again, but the Plinlimmon emerald affair, though important to Mrs Hudson and to Sergeant Minders, seemed of very little importance to me.

'Anyway, Flotsam, he managed to whisper me the name. A French name: *Béatrice Flaubert*.' Mrs Hudson had finished hanging up her bonnet, and now she looked approvingly around the immaculate kitchen. 'And tomorrow, Flottie, I really must tell Mr Holmes everything I know about the whole business. And the sooner the better.'

'But, please, ma'am,' I burst out, unable to restrain myself a moment longer. 'Tomorrow we need to be out first thing. I've checked and there's an early train from Waterloo at three minutes past five. It should get us to Revennings before breakfast.'

'Revennings, Flotsam?' Mrs Hudson rarely looked surprised by anything, but one of her eyebrows most definitely lifted.

'Yes, ma'am. We need to do what Professor Broadmarsh has asked us to do. We need to ask Agnes.'

Chapter Fourteen

We crept out of the house the following morning long before the first fingers of light had begun to touch the London sky. It felt almost furtive, tiptoeing out so softly that the creak of the area door sounded as sharp and shocking as a knife. Arrangements had been made – hastily, and late in the night – for Mrs McFarland from next door to stand in for us at breakfast, and a note had been left for our gentlemen, explaining that a development had called us back to Revennings. But none of that made the early start any easier, and, as I climbed the area steps, I was yawning in a most unladylike fashion.

It was still dark when we left Waterloo, and we had a third-class carriage to ourselves. I'd expected to doze off as soon as we got underway, but in fact I sat beside Mrs Hudson and watched the sky turn to indigo, then navy, then to a pale, pink-streaked blue. Gradually our reflections in the train windows faded and the landscape became visible – first a church spire in silhouette against the sky, then clumps of trees, then paler fields and patches of bright water throwing the dawn back at us. For all my excitement, I felt strangely at peace. We were going to find our answer, we would crack the code, and everything would be all right.

As soon as it was light enough, Mrs Hudson drew a notebook and pencil from her bag and held it out to me.

'It was very late when you explained it to me last night, Flotsam. Just so I'm clear, we begin with *arsenic*, don't we?'

'That's right, ma'am. According to the times on the telegrams we've seen, that's the first one Professor Broadmarsh sent, although it took me a little while to work out that the professor, by sending the words in the correct order, had saved us the difficulty of sorting out the letters.'

'And the chemical abbreviation for arsenic is "As", you say?'

'Yes, ma'am.' I wrote the letters down in the notebook. 'I don't know why I didn't think of it before. It was only when I saw that Mr Reddleman had written the letter "K" next to the word potassium that I realised the chemical symbols were the key.'

'So potassium was next. Then silver, you say?'

I nodded happily.

'Silver and potassium are both tricky ones, because the symbols are nothing like the real words. So silver is actually "Ag".'

And I wrote down the letters for potassium and silver next to the symbol for arsenic: *As K Ag*

Mrs Hudson touched my hand fondly, then nodded at me to continue.

'Well, neon is fairly obvious, ma'am, and so is sulphur. Once I realised we just had to put them together in the order the professor sent them, it was all very simple.'

I looked at the message again. *As K Ag Ne S* – written down like that, it seemed remarkable that I'd ever found the telegrams cryptic or confusing.

'There is one thing I don't understand, though,' I confessed. 'The professor sent those messages as his safety net, to lead Mr Barrington and the others to his part of the code. Even if the foreign spies read the telegrams, even if they managed to decode them, they wouldn't know who Agnes was, or how to find her. But we *did* ask Agnes, didn't we? We asked her if she'd heard from the professor, and she said no.'

But Mrs Hudson was shaking her head.

'Agnes said "not yet", Flotsam. She was expecting a message, if you remember. And I think she was a little anxious that it hadn't come.'

'But how *could* it come, ma'am? The professor sent all those telegrams a little while ago, and almost straight after that, he disappeared. How could he possibly get a message to Agnes without it being seized by his enemies? And if he did manage to send some sort of message, why has it taken so long to arrive?'

At that moment, a train passed us in the opposite direction, so Mrs Hudson had to pause a moment before she replied. It gave me time to take in the look of surprise on her face.

'But surely, Flotsam, there's no mystery about that, is there? Why do you think Professor Broadmarsh summoned Thompson?'

I opened my mouth to reply, but could think of absolutely nothing to say.

'Why, Flottie, Agnes actually told us the answer, if you remember.'

But my expression must have remained one of total mystification, because Mrs Hudson simply shook her head. Behind her, the blue summer sky seemed to reach forever.

'The birds, Flotsam. I asked her why the professor wanted Thompson, and she told us it was because Thompson and the professor both loved the birds. And anyone who trains carrier pigeons would tell you that you don't entrust your best bird on a long journey to anyone but the most trusted of handlers.'

The early train ran smoothly and to time, and at Milford station the only other passenger to alight turned out to be a rather gallant medical man from one of the neighbouring villages who offered to take us as far as Revennings in his trap.

There, our arrival – unannounced and at such an early hour – caused a fair degree of consternation. Mrs Watson, the housekeeper, was convinced that we were coming to stay again, and that the letter informing her of the fact must have gone astray, leaving her utterly unprepared. Miss Blondell, on the other hand, was certain that we must be engaged in some frightful and complicated adventure, and had come to Revennings to seek refuge. Her disappointment on learning that no assassins were dogging our footsteps was at least as great as Mrs Watson's relief on discovering that ours was not to be an extended visit. Both looked bewildered on learning who we had really come to see.

'Well, of course, Mrs Hudson, anything you wish,' Miss Blondell told us graciously. 'I'm sure Agnes must be in the gardens somewhere. And then, afterwards, if you would like to join me in the Great Hall, I'm agog to find out what all this is about. I just know it must be thrilling.'

The gardens of Revennings at that early hour, with the morning dew not yet entirely burnt off, seemed full of enchantment. Wisps of mist still hung on the edges of the lake, and as we made our way down the meadow walk, a series of plump pheasants, startled by our presence, burst from cover in front of us. Even so, I was anxious that finding Agnes might not prove straightforward. The gardens were extensive, and Thompson's apprentice knew them better than anyone; I wasn't at all sure that she would welcome another visit.

But I had misjudged her. We found her in the doorway of the ancient dovecote, leaning against the stonework and eating an apple as though she had been expecting us. When I waved to her, she seemed to think for a moment, then replied with a nod of her head.

'I knew you'd come,' she told us as soon as we reached her, apparently feeling that any other greeting was unnecessary. 'I knew someone would come. The professor said so. And you two were the only ones who'd come before.'

Then she turned without waiting for a response, and led us into the dark interior of the dovecote.

Neither Mrs Hudson nor I said a word, because no word seemed necessary. We simply watched while Agnes raised her arm and repeated that little throaty, cooing sound we'd heard before. And again a bird responded; this time the creature that floated down to her wrist looked to me like a strange cross between pigeon and dove, its pure white patches mottled with brown and tortoiseshell.

'She came just after you were here before,' the girl told us. 'So tired she was. Almost too tired to drink. Such a long way. I don't think she found it easy. It's taken her so long. But she's better now.'

She raised her hand, and the bird lifted itself up to the dark heights of the dovecote where it settled in the gloom.

'See how she flies? With joy again. It will be the same with Thompson and the professor when they come home. They will be tired. But they will get well again.'

And such was the conviction behind those simple words, I believed her. They *would* get well again, I thought – if only because Agnes would make it her business to bring it about.

'And the message, Agnes?' Mrs Hudson asked. They were the first words either of us had spoken to her.

Without replying, Agnes reached into the pocket of the boy's jacket she was wearing and produced a very small slip of paper. The words on it seemed to have been written in a hurry, for the handwriting was something of a scrawl.

Dear Agnes, it said, *some friends will come asking for this note. Please give it to them with my compliments.*

Then, written underneath, was a string of letters, similar to the ones we'd seen before.

I I T B R O R H E U T N S E U S

And below that, a final line, one that made me smile.

> PS: *If the mulberry tree suffers from the heat, I recommend half a gallon of cold tea twice a week, applied to the roots.*

And that was nearly all that passed between us, that morning at Revennings. We thanked her profusely, and reassured her that her two allies, Thompson and the professor, would surely be home soon. Then we said our farewells and thanked her again, and then we left her where we'd found her, leaning in the doorway of the dovecote, a second apple in her hand, watching us depart.

It occurred to me as I turned away that, of all the people I knew, perhaps none was more quietly content than Agnes.

Strange to say, that interview in the dovecote was by far the easiest part of our visit to Revennings. Getting there had been very straightforward, but leaving was more difficult. Miss Blondell was eager to chat to us, and very determined to tease from us the reasons for our visit; and Mrs Watson, apparently anxious that we might have mistaken her consternation at our arrival for unfriendliness, was extremely insistent that we should sit down with her in the pantry over a piece of seed-cake and a cup of tea. Then there was further delay while we waited for Ridley from Bottom Farm to arrive with his trap, to take us back to the station – and all that time Professor Broadmarsh's note was preying on my mind, and I was all but consumed with impatience to return with it to Baker Street. The sooner we could place it alongside the other two messages, the sooner we could unravel the Emir's coded instructions, and make arrangements for the safe collection of the all-important treaty.

And I could tell that Mrs Hudson was also impatient to be gone. More than once I noticed her eyes move to the pantry clock, and while Ridley took his time adjusting his horse's bridle, she took it upon herself to hand me into the trap, then vaulted up beside me with undisguised briskness.

'Do we know when the next London train leaves?' I asked quietly, when the trap finally moved away.

'I'm afraid I don't, Flotsam,' Mrs Hudson replied, 'and I don't think we'll be taking it.'

She must have sensed my astonishment, for she was quick to explain.

'You see, Flottie, we're currently on the Hampshire border, and since we are so close to Mrs Esterhazy's establishment, I've a good mind to head in that direction. There are just one or two small things I'd like to clear up about that spectacle business, and this is an excellent opportunity.'

'But the code, ma'am! And Professor Broadmarsh's message! Surely we need to get these back to Mr Holmes as soon as we can? Sir Torpenhow says the safety of the nation is at stake!'

'And so it might be, young lady, but we won't save the nation by rushing our fences. And I think we'll save a lot of time later on by tying up some loose ends now.'

Which is why, when we left Milford station that day – carrying with us a clue so vital to so many people that its bearer had been pursued from the borders of Afghanistan to the shores of the Black Sea – we were not bound north, for London, where the authorities would have welcomed us with open arms, but south, for Portsmouth, where a change of trains would point us towards the rather sleepy village where the vicar's wife was worrying about his spectacles.

Chapter Fifteen

Mrs Hudson and I arrived in the village of Pinfold a little before noon, with the sun near its zenith and the sky a blanket of the most perfect blue. The nearest station was some three miles from the village, so our first sight of its square church tower and its cluster of stone houses was from the ancient dog-cart which had been waiting for passengers in the station lane. From there, Pinfold looked the very picture of the perfect English village, and the fields which surrounded it seemed to stretch themselves out and slumber in the sun.

It was hot though. So hot on the dog-cart that, even through my clothes, the wooden seat seemed to burn my legs; and often, when we looked ahead, the road before us was lost in a blur of rising heat. It came as something of a relief when our driver finally pulled to a halt outside the vicarage gate.

'Some would say,' Mrs Hudson remarked as she studied the building from the lane, 'that we are lucky to be here, Flotsam. That we are benefiting from the most enormous fluke. And yet...' She seemed to be speaking more to herself than to me. 'And yet, perhaps, in this hot summer, when so little else is going on, anyone attempting to weave such a complex and sinister web of deceit should not be too surprised if some strands of that web drift in the air as far as Baker Street.'

I confess I could think of no reply. The precise reasons for our visit to Pinfold were still unclear to me, although I was absolutely certain that it was not simply concern about the vicar's spectacles that had made Mrs Hudson so anxious to visit.

And if it *was* luck that had brought us here, then our good fortune held: Mrs Esterhazy was at home and happy to receive us. We were shown into a neat, unfussy parlour where the lady of the house was engaged in stitching together parts of a very tiny baby's smock.

'For one of our parishioners,' she explained, putting her work to one side. 'I sew very badly, and for some reason this failing, far more than any of my virtues, endears me to the congregation. Now, please, sit down, and tell me what it is that brings you here. Your first letter, Mrs Hudson, reassured me that my little problem was being considered, but I hardly expected you to visit me here in Hampshire.'

'Flotsam and I like to travel, ma'am,' Mrs Hudson told her solemnly, 'when our time allows it.' She had taken one of the armchairs indicated by our hostess, and I had placed myself genteelly in the other. 'As we were not far from here today, I thought we might put to you one or two further questions.'

'Well, please, ask me anything.' Mrs Esterhazy smiled warmly. 'But first, let me inform you of the most surprising development that has taken place since I saw you in London. I was just about to pen you a little note about it. You see...' And here she looked distinctly bemused. 'You see, all three pairs of missing spectacles have been mysteriously returned to us.'

It was, undoubtedly, a bizarre conclusion to a bizarre tale. After losing the curate's eyeglasses on the train to London, the vicar had replaced them with new ones, and had ordered yet another new pair for himself. But before his own replacements were ready, a small package with an Andover postmark had arrived in the post. It contained the spectacles Mr Esterhazy had lost in that town on the night when he gave his lecture. They were accompanied by a very short, anonymous message: *Taken in error. Apologies*.

'We were delighted to have the things returned,' Mrs Esterhazy told us, 'and were quite willing to believe that the whole incident had been a genuine error by someone too embarrassed to admit to it. But then, the following day, the second package arrived.'

This one had been sent from London and contained the curate's glasses, the pair that had disappeared from the London train. These, too, were accompanied by a note.

> *I return these with my most profound apologies. Although, my handsome reverend, you really must be told that you look so much more dashing without them.*
>> *With a smile and a dozen kisses from*
>> *The Lady in the Train*

'Well!' Mrs Esterhazy declared, 'You can imagine how outraged we were to receive such a message. Why, this De Witt woman practically confesses to stealing my husband's glasses! And yet we still have no idea why, nor why she should so suddenly return them.'

'And the third pair of spectacles?' Mrs Hudson asked. She seemed, I thought, less perplexed by these developments than I had expected.

'Well, that was the most worrying thing of all. The day after the second package arrived, Bertha, our parlour maid, came to see me in a state of great confusion. In her hand she held my husband's original glasses. She had found them pushed beneath the chair you are sitting on now, Mrs Hudson. Bertha was most upset, and assured me that she had cleaned under the furniture many times since they had been lost, and that they had never been there before. I assured her that her thoroughness was not in any doubt, but could offer no sensible explanation about how they might have come there.'

I saw Mrs Hudson's eyes turn towards the elegant French windows, which stood wide open to the gardens. Mrs Esterhazy must have noticed too, because she seemed to anticipate the housekeeper's next question.

'Yes, indeed, Mrs Hudson. The windows have been open every day for nearly the whole of the summer. And on Tuesdays – the day in question – Pinfold hosts a small market, so the village is much busier than usual. It would not have been very hard for someone to slip in unnoticed. But *why*, Mrs Hudson? Why?'

Before Mrs Hudson could attempt an answer, we were joined in the parlour by the Vicar of Pinfold himself, a man of perhaps thirty years, and every bit as good looking as the note from Mme De Witt had suggested – even *with* his glasses, which were in the round, Windsor style, with narrow horn rims. These, I noticed, were quickly removed while Mrs Esterhazy introduced us, and were placed firmly in the pocket of his rather smart linen jacket.

And again I had to agree with the mysterious Mme De Witt – without his spectacles the vicar looked even more handsome, there being nothing to distract from a pair of bright green eyes, and some very striking cheekbones. It occurred to me that church services in Pinfold were probably unusually well attended.

'It is so very good of you to call,' he told us as he shook our hands, 'although I worry that anyone should take our recent travails *too* seriously. There are far greater troubles in this world than a foolish vicar's missing glasses.'

He smiled as he said it, and even though it was the most warm and friendly smile imaginable, it was nevertheless strangely unsettling; I found myself suddenly beset by visions of highwaymen at dusk, and pirate captains, and loose-sleeved poets at dawn with duelling pistols. I hate to think myself a foolish young girl, but I confess that, on first acquaintance, I did find the Vicar of Pinfold quite distracting.

Then he told us in great detail about the meeting he had been attending with his church wardens about repairs to the clerestory, and his concerns for the ancient stonework in the north transept, and I was able to recover.

'So tell me, Mrs Hudson,' he went on, 'has my wife been able to answer all the questions that brought you here today?'

'Not yet, sir, although she has told us about the return of the missing glasses, and that in itself is very helpful. There was just one other little thing, really – about that day you travelled to London to give a talk to the Society of Antiquarians. I think your wife mentioned that you had hoped to travel up to town with Lord Digby?'

'That's correct.' The Reverend Esterhazy appeared to consider the question. 'I don't know his lordship personally, but he and I have corresponded over the years, and I was delighted to receive a telegram from him, suggesting that we should both travel up in the same carriage on the mid-morning train to town.'

'But that plan fell through, sir?'

'I fear so, Mrs Hudson. I found a seat in the appointed carriage, but Lord Digby never appeared. Indeed, he didn't even attend the lecture. I'm told that he was giving a talk of his own that day, somewhere on the south coast. His friends tell me that his lordship is growing increasingly absent-minded with the advancing years.'

'Thank you, sir.' To my surprise, Mrs Hudson rose from her seat and appeared to consider our visit at an end. 'You have told us exactly what we needed to know. It is a great relief. Now, we must get back to Baker Street. Mr Holmes will be wondering where we've got to. But I'm sure he'd want us to reassure you that there will be no further problems with your spectacles, sir. And I am sure, when his time is once again his own, he will be delighted to explain everything to you in person.'

If the Esterhazys thought our departure was at all abrupt, they showed no sign of it. The vicar even offered to drive us back to the railway station in his own trap, which was blissfully shaded and a great deal more comfortable than the station dog-cart. As we passed through the baking landscape, conversation was confined to the usual conventions. The vicar pointed out features of interest in the landscape and inquired politely about our own circumstances, about how hot London must be, about the advantages of country air. Only when he had handed us down from the trap and was saying his farewells did we return to the subject of our visit.

'There was one other question, sir,' Mrs Hudson told him, as he gathered up the reins. 'You mentioned that Lord Digby suggested that you both took seats in the same carriage, that day you went to London. Is it possible, sir, that you remember which carriage it was?'

'But, of course, Mrs Hudson.' He looked down at us, puzzled by the question, but still with a charming smile on his lips. 'His lordship suggested we should rendezvous in the first-class carriage nearest the front of the train. Which on that particular train happened to be the carriage nearest the locomotive. Does that help you at all?'

'Yes, sir.' Mrs Hudson was nodding, but I had the impression that his answer did not surprise her. 'Now, Flotsam and I had better be sure of catching the next train. We need to be in London as soon as we can. Among other things, we need to be finding Flotsam a ball gown.'

–

'Of course, Flotsam, it is generally only in the most desperate and inept works of fiction that one ever really encounters such a far-fetched device. Twins, indeed!'

The London train was a slow one, stopping at all the stations on the line, some of them so small and sleepy that even the arrival of a steaming locomotive barely seemed to wake them. Mrs Hudson and I had been lucky enough to find a carriage to ourselves near the rear of the train.

'The thought struck me as soon as Mrs Esterhazy mentioned a twin brother, but I tried to put it out of my mind, telling myself that there must surely be a more plausible and less outrageous explanation for her husband's travails. But, of course, Flotsam, just because something seems absurd doesn't mean that it can't be true, and the more I thought about those vanishing glasses, the less absurd it began to seem. Someone was clearly going to a great deal of trouble to make sure that Mr Esterhazy couldn't wear his spectacles, and I could only think of two sensible reasons for it. In fact, Mr Rumbelow summed it up very nicely for us: if someone did that to him, he said, it must either be to stop him from seeing something, or because they thought he looked better without his glasses.'

The train slowed for a moment, as though it were contemplating another stop, then thought better of it and built up speed again. In the shady carriage, Mrs Hudson was silhouetted against the passing countryside, her face dark against its brightness.

'Well, Flottie, it seemed highly unlikely that anyone would attempt the former. You can't hope to continue stealing someone's glasses indefinitely, and the vicar might quite easily have found other ways of reading whatever it was you were trying to keep from him. He might have equipped himself with a magnifying glass, for instance. But if, for some reason, you wanted to change someone's appearance on one particular occasion – if, for instance, you wanted to pass him off, for an hour or two, as an individual with excellent vision – then simply removing his spectacles might achieve your purpose very nicely.'

The pieces were beginning to fall into place for me now, but I was more than happy to let Mrs Hudson continue.

'So Mr Esterhazy had a twin brother, Flotsam. They were of radically different temperaments, but both had the same looks and the same athletic frame. The most obvious physical difference between the two, according to Mrs Esterhazy, was that her husband had poor eyesight and had worn glasses from a young age. So, if I wanted to convince someone that Mr Esterhazy's wayward twin was alive and well and living in England, I would arrange for that person to be shown – from a distance, mind – the mild-mannered Vicar of Pinfold. If the person I was tricking was unaware a twin brother existed, they would, very reasonably, be convinced that the dead man still lived. However, if the living man were wearing spectacles – when the dead man was famed for his perfect eyesight – that might well cause them to pause.'

'And that person being tricked was Mrs Barrington, wasn't it, ma'am?' I couldn't help but join in. 'On the platform at Clapham Junction. Someone deliberately arranged things so she was standing near the correct carriage – the first carriage of the train – knowing that she would mistake the vicar for her first husband.'

I paused, still working things out.

'But, ma'am, how could they have known that the vicar was her husband's twin? Mrs Barrington's first husband wasn't called Esterhazy. And even if he was, how could anyone have found out about his twin when even Mrs Barrington herself didn't know?'

I wanted it all to be true, but it still seemed impossibly far-fetched. Mrs Hudson patted my hand, then reached into her bag to produce two pears.

'To keep us going till we get to London,' she told me. 'Now, what was the question? Oh, yes. Mrs Barrington. Well, if you think about it, Flotsam, it's all very simple. Remember, we are dealing with people here who are very thorough, and who do not lack resources. So when Mrs

Barrington's cook discovered that her mistress had been married before, and that her scoundrel of a husband had died on the *Conquistador*, it was an easy thing for her co-conspirators to check. In fact, I did it myself, last night.'

I must have looked mystified because she smiled.

'On my way to see Sergeant Minders, Flotsam, I dropped in on Mr Rumbelow and asked him to look up the list of passengers who lost their lives on the *Conquistador*. It wasn't a difficult task. All the newspapers had carried the list, and a friend of his at the London Library provided him with a copy without any difficulty. By the time I returned, after seeing the sergeant, he had all the information I needed.'

'And you think Mlle Le Blanc's confederate did the same, ma'am?'

'I'm certain he did, Flottie. Because the list confirms that there really was only one Englishman on board the *Conquistador* when she went down, but that Englishman was not travelling as Dick Eastwood or Dick Heywood or Dick Vaizey. The official list states that the British citizen who drowned was one Benedict Esterhazy. It would seem our adventurer had reverted to his real name for that stage of his journey.'

'I see.' But I still wasn't convinced. 'Would that information be enough, though, ma'am? Even when they discovered the drowned man's real name, how could they know he had a twin?'

Mrs Hudson gave an approving nod.

'That is a perfectly reasonable question, young lady. But unfortunately for the Vicar of Pinfold and his spectacles, his scoundrel of a father placed a rather maudlin notice in the obituary section of *The Times* – a notice which appeared in the same edition as the final passenger list. It praised the dead man's physical accomplishments and his eagle-eyed marksmanship, gave the full name of his brother, mentioned that the two were twins, and even stated that Emeric Esterhazy was pursuing a career in the Church.'

She sighed and shook her head. She did not altogether approve of such notices.

'Now, Flottie, armed with that amount of information, and with a copy of *Crockford's Directory*, it would be the simplest thing in the world to locate our vicar and to begin to weave a plot around him. And once they knew he was to give a lecture in London, all they had to do was to make sure he was on a particular train and in a particular carriage, without his glasses on, and that Mrs Barrington was in the right place to see him.'

I considered this.

'So that telegram from Lord Digby, ma'am...'

'I've yet to hear back from his lordship, Flotsam, but the telegram was surely a hoax. They simply picked someone prominent in the Society of Antiquarians, someone who lived on the appropriate train line, and sent a telegram to Mr Esterhazy in his name.'

'And the Dutch lady, Mme De Witt, was one of the conspirators!' I declared triumphantly. 'It must have been her job to make sure Mr Esterhazy wasn't wearing his glasses when he arrived at Clapham Junction.'

'Ah, yes! Mme De Witt.' The trace of a smile played around the corners of the housekeeper's mouth. 'The mysterious Dutch lady who made sure she had left the train *before* it arrived in Clapham Junction. Have you wondered at all, Flotsam, why that might have been?'

'Well, no, ma'am. I suppose one stop was as good as another.'

'Perhaps, Flottie. But my basic knowledge of German tells me otherwise.'

I blinked. Of all things she might have replied, this was certainly one of the more surprising.

'German, ma'am?'

Neither of us had yet bitten into our pears, and now the housekeeper balanced hers carefully in the middle of her palm.

'Have you not wondered, Flottie, how I first came to connect Mrs Esterhazy's story with all that Bokara nonsense of Sir Torpenhow's? You see, I might never had thought of putting the two together, had you not told me the name of the mysterious foreign agent who Sir Torpenhow believes is at the heart of the Samarkand Conspiracy. The name he mentioned to you was Andreas Weiss – a man he considers a dangerous spy, and someone with a grudge against this country.'

The pear wobbled slightly as we jolted over some points.

'Now, when you repeated that name to me, I'd just been bringing up the Moselle. Perhaps it was reading the German on the labels that made me think of it, but it struck me that the name Andreas Weiss, in English, would be Andrew White. And it occurred to me, more as a passing thought than anything else, that I had once come across another Andrew White, another man of uncertain nationality, and that he too had born a grudge against Great Britain. Sergeant Minders, if you remember, confirmed that I had recalled the name correctly.'

But to me this seemed to be pushing coincidence too far.

'Those are both very common names, aren't they, ma'am? And there was no one called Andrew White in Mrs Esterhazy's story, was there?'

'Very true, Flotsam.' Mrs Hudson nodded approvingly. 'But there *was* a Madame De Witt. Now, I don't pretend to be a student of Dutch, but I've met a number of people from the Low Countries in my time, and I knew the name De Witt would be, in English, the name White. And that lady's story was a very thin one, Flottie. Mr Rumbelow has written to a number of institutions involved in the study of forestry, but none appears to have had a Dutch visitor by that or any other name in recent months. And then, of course, we come to the charming French cook at Frog Hall who went by the name of Le Blanc...'

'...And *blanc* is French for *white*!' I exclaimed.

'And the Latin for *white*, Flotsam?'

'Why, of course! *Alba!*'

Mrs Hudson's lips remained set, but her eyes gleamed. 'You might easily think our pair of conspirators lack imagination, Flotsam. But I think they enjoy the game. I think they use the same name in different forms because it's their own private joke. And, of course, when we understand that *De Witt* is also *Le Blanc*, then we understand how important it was for Mme De Witt to leave the train before it reached Clapham Junction. Otherwise Mrs Barrington would have been treated to the surprising sight of her own cook in a first-class carriage, chatting away to her deceased husband.'

'And *that's* why you thought Mlle Le Blanc was married to Mr Alba, ma'am. Because of their names.' Another piece clicked into place.

'Indeed.' The pear was still resting in her palm, but now she tossed it up, caught it, and returned it to her bag. 'Sergeant Minders and I had both heard a rumour that, at some point in Andrew White's long and dubious carrier, he had married a beautiful young French girl in the belief that she was a French countess. Last night Sergeant Minders remembered the French girl's name: Béatrice Flaubert. And what initials did you detect, last night, picked out of that very fine lace handkerchief?'

'B. F., ma'am! And the initial that replaced the "F" was a "W" – for Béatrice White!'

'Or Wiess, or Witte, or something along those lines.' Mrs Hudson gave a little shrug of her eyebrows.

'And yet, for all their cleverness, their plot was always likely to fail. For although they have succeeded in discovering a scandal with which to threaten the Barringtons, anyone who truly understands the nature of men like Harry Barrington would know that he would never put his own happiness – or even his wife's – above his duty to his country. So tonight, unless someone intervenes, this villain White will discover that no information has been brought to his rendezvous by the Serpentine, and he will then proceed to publish the information that will ruin the Barringtons.'

'But will it, ma'am?' I felt a sudden rush of hope. 'Because we know now that the whole story was a fraud. Mrs Barrington's first husband really *did* die on the *Conquistador*, so her marriage to Mr Barrington is all fine.'

'And that, I think, will be a great comfort to them both, Flottie. But the scandal will engulf them, nevertheless. Mrs Barrington's past will be picked over in every drawing room and every low tavern in the country, and there will always be some who believe the blackmailer. After all, they will say, how can we be sure that Mrs Barrington's first husband really was the man who drowned on the *Conquistador*? There will be many who say she could easily have made up the story about him writing to her from Havana.'

The rush of hope subsided.

'And the blackmailer will publish anyway, even though it isn't true?'

'Blackmailers do, Flotsam. It's one of the rules of their calling.'

I remembered Mrs Barrington's pale face as she'd told us her story, and I began to feel something very like anger stirring inside me. The thought that the same story would now be told by others, but twisted with lies against her, all because Sir Torpenhow's secret couldn't be told or wouldn't be told or shouldn't be told, seemed wrong and outrageous.

'It would be so unfair,' I complained.

And to my surprise, Mrs Hudson said nothing for some moments. She seemed to be considering my words, weighing them carefully, perhaps thinking the same things that I'd just been thinking.

'Yes, Flotsam,' she said at last. 'It would be most unfair. But don't worry, we can make sure it doesn't happen. I give you my word that Mrs Barrington's secrets will go no further than they have gone already.'

'But how, ma'am? What can we do?'

Both Mrs Hudson's eyebrows twitched at that question, but her expression remained as calm as ever.

'I really can't tell you, young lady. No, I'm not trying to be mysterious. It's just better that you don't know. But if you come with me tonight to Kensington Gardens, you can find out for yourself.'

I don't think she'd have told me anything more than that, even if I'd begged. But I never had the opportunity, for even as she spoke the train was drawing to a halt at the next station, and we were joined in our carriage by two farmers in tweed suits and a rather garrulous young lady carrying a cockerel in a picnic basket. In that company, listening to the lady chat about fowl pox and sour crop while the farmers grunted politely, any talk of spies or blackmail or mysterious foreign agents would have been impossible. And also strangely hard to believe.

Chapter Sixteen

We returned to Baker Street that evening a little after six o'clock, to find Mrs McFarland still gamely on duty downstairs, and, upstairs, a special gathering convened in Mr Holmes' study.

'You'd better go straight up, my girl,' Mrs McFarland told me with a puzzled smile. 'Mr Holmes keeps ringing and asking if you're back. You, too, Mrs Hudson. He seems very eager you should both look in on him.'

'You go, Flotsam,' Mrs Hudson told me firmly. 'You know as much as I do about everything, and one of us must stay down here to thank Mrs McFarland properly – with some iced sherry cup, I think, eh, Mrs F? And a large bowl of it, too, I would say, after such a long day, and such a hot one.'

So I went up alone, slightly nervous, and unsure who or what I would find there.

The first thing that struck me on entering the study was how unbearably hot it was, much hotter than I could ever remember. For some reason, the gentlemen had thrown open the shutters and pulled down the sashes, with the result that the heat from outside had filled the room. The room was very bright, too, even though the early evening sun was not falling directly upon it. Flushed and torpid in the heat, four gentlemen lounged in the armchairs: Dr Watson and Mr Holmes, and their guests, Harry Barrington and Sir Torpenhow Franklin. The study door was half open when I knocked on it, and I was able to hear Sir Torpenhow speaking.

'...So I'm forced to conclude, Mr Holmes, that the game is lost. Without the professor's part of the coded message, we cannot hope to receive the Emir's treaty. The month is almost over, and events today in Rumania make me fear the very worst...'

He broke off when he heard my footsteps, and Mr Holmes summoned me into the room with a jocularity that contrasted sharply with his companion's gloom.

'Come and join us, Flotsam. I've been telling Sir Torpenhow about recent events at Frog Hall, and about the unfortunate predicament Mr and Mrs Barrington find themselves in.'

'And I assure you, sir,' Harry Barrington interjected hastily, addressing Sir Torpenhow, 'that my wife and I are both agreed on the subject. Neither of us would dream for a moment of yielding to these despicable demands.'

Sir Torpenhow nodded his head gravely at this, acknowledging the younger man's sacrifice while somehow suggesting that he had never expected anything less.

'But we can still catch this fellow, can't we, Holmes?' Dr Watson asked eagerly. 'If we fill the park with special officers, all of them concealed in the dark, they can simply grab this blackmailer fellow when he arrives at the appointed spot. That should settle his hash, shouldn't it?'

Sir Torpenhow nodded again.

'Quite so, Doctor. Our officers are being briefed as we speak. I believe we have fifty men on the job. I guarantee that park bench will never be out of our sight.'

I heard Mr Holmes clear his throat, and something about the way he did it made me think that perhaps he didn't share his visitor's confidence in these arrangements. But it was me he turned to next.

'Flotsam, before we forget, a boy arrived earlier with a message for Mrs Hudson from Lord Digby, of all people. It was a verbal message, wasn't it, Watson?'

'That's right. Something about his lordship sending his compliments, and that he never planned to attended the lecture because it sounded deathly dull. And that he didn't send any telegram. I think that was it, wasn't it, Holmes?'

'Really!' Sir Torpenhow's patience was clearly wearing thin. 'We have more important things to occupy us, Mr Holmes!'

The great detective smiled.

'I have learned, sir, always to treat Mrs Hudson's correspondence with the greatest respect.' He turned back to me. 'So, tell us, Flotsam, how have you two been occupying yourselves today?'

I heard Sir Torpenhow tut under his breath, so I directed my answer most particularly at him.

'Well, sir, we went down to Hampshire to talk to that lady who was worried about her husband losing his spectacles. And before that, sir, we went to Revennings, to collect the last part of the Emir's coded message. Professor Broadmarsh sent it by pigeon, sir, to a young lady called Agnes. I have it here, if you would care to look at it.'

To say my answer caused uproar might be a slight exaggeration, but suddenly everyone seemed to be talking at once.

'What? You actually have the message? The actual message?' That was Mr Barrington.

'Care to look at it? Is this a joke? Surely, Mr Holmes, this must be nonsense?'

That was Sir Torpenhow, but I could barely hear him for Dr Watson chortling, 'I say, well done, Flotsam. Bravo!' then rising from his seat to pat me rather too heartily on the back.

Only Mr Holmes said nothing, but I could tell from the way he looked across at Sir Torpenhow that he had enjoyed my revelation without being entirely surprised by it. When the voices of the others had died down, he allowed himself a single comment.

'Only something unusually important would persuade Mrs Hudson to abandon her post at such short notice, wouldn't it, Watson? Now, come, Flotsam, that message. You can tell us all about *how* you obtained it later. For now we just want to see the professor's clue.'

So I produced the crumpled paper Agnes had given us, and passed it over to him. Mr Holmes studied it for a moment, nodding to himself as he read.

'Very interesting. And you say the girl's name was Agnes? Yes, of course. I see it now. *Silver-neon-sulphur*. Flotsam, would you be so good as to fetch that chalk-slate from the corner, and to prop it on the mantelpiece? I think we should see all three lines of the code together. Sir Torpenhow, you have the other two?'

Our visitor produced a crisp, cream-coloured card from his pocketbook, and passed it Mr Holmes; then the room fell silent, watching the great man write. When he had finished, he stepped back so that we all had a clear view of the slate.

M N H I A M T C T O E E Y V A U

D G L R Y N A U H S W T E N G T

I I T B R O R H E U T N S E U S

Dr Watson was the first to speak.

'Well, I'm sorry, Holmes, but if that's supposed to mean anything to me, I'm afraid I don't know what. Do we know if the Emir's message is even in English? That could be some dialect of Bokara for all I know.'

Our two visitors, though less willing to express their bewilderment, were also looking blank, so Mr Holmes turned back to the board.

'My apologies, gentlemen. I wrote the three parts in the order we received them. Let me now rearrange them into the order in which they should appear.'

And with a swift sweep of his cuff, he wiped away the bottom line, only to rewrite it in its entirety, this time squeezed between the other two lines of code.

M N H I A M T C T O E E Y V A U

I I T B R O R H E U T N S E U S

D G L R Y N A U H S W T E N G T

Mr Holmes stepped back to admire the end result, then returned the cream-coloured card to Sir Torpenhow, along with the slip of paper Agnes had given us. While Sir Torpenhow stowed both of them safely in his pocketbook, Mr Holmes allowed himself a small smile.

'And now, my friends, it is all very simple, is it not?'

And he drew a little arrow, pointing downwards, above the letter 'M' in the top left corner.

'All we have to do, gentlemen, is to read down instead of across, and the message is clear.'

It took me a moment to translate his advice into action, but as soon as I did, the words formed effortlessly before my eyes. And not only did I understand the words, I knew exactly what they meant.

MIDNIGHT LIBRARY
MONTRACHUTE HOUSE TWENTY
SEVEN AUGUST

'Why!' I declared. 'That's this Saturday! And it's the day of Lord Wymondham's ball! Everyone's been talking about it for months. So *that's* where the Emir's representative is going to hand over the document!'

I could barely contain my excitement, because it seemed to me that all Sir Torpenhow's difficulties were suddenly at an end.

'And that's all you needed to know, isn't it, sir?' I went on. 'Mr Barrington will be able to collect the signed treaty as planned, and you don't even need to worry about any foreign spies getting in the way, because they only have one line of the code, and we have all three!'

But the enthusiasm of the four gentlemen did not appear quite as great as my own. There were smiles, yes, and some nodding of heads, but clearly something was worrying them.

'You are almost correct, Flotsam,' Mr Holmes told me, 'but unfortunately we have not yet shared with you the recent news from Rumania. Professor Broadmarsh has been released unharmed, and is on his way home.'

I looked around, confused.

'But that's excellent news, isn't it, sir?'

Mr Holmes looked at Sir Torpenhow, who cleared his throat.

'It is, of course, excellent news that the professor is safe. His gardener, too, has been freed, and is travelling home with him. Our anxiety is caused by the ease with which we secured the professor's freedom.'

'It seems that you and I were extremely accurate in our map work, Flotsam,' Mr Holmes interjected, brightly, 'but no dramatic rescue from the hunting lodge was required. When our people at the Foreign Office hinted to the Rumanian authorities that we knew where the professor was being held, and pointed out that a major diplomatic incident could be avoided if he and his companion were released without delay, they complied at once.'

'Of course, they made up a story to smooth things over,' Sir Torpenhow explained, taking over the narrative. 'The official announcement was that two British travellers had been seized by bandits and held, possibly for ransom, in a remote location in the Rumanian mountains. Thanks to the diligence of the Rumanian police, these travellers have now been released unscathed, and are recovering at the British Embassy in Bucharest. Those responsible for this outrage were able to escape into the forests, but the authorities are confident that all will be brought to justice in the coming months.'

'But that's still good news, isn't it, sir? For the professor, I mean.'

'It's excellent news for Professor Broadmarsh,' Sir Torpenhow said again. 'The professor has conducted himself with great courage and with great presence of mind throughout. And it seems that he was indeed drugged on that special train, just as Mr Holmes surmised. He told our people at the embassy that he remembers passing through the station at Predeál, because he recalls looking at the crowds gathered there for the ceremony. But after that he remembers very little before waking up in the hunting lodge, with Rumanian officials reassuring him he was safe. He has a faint recollection of feeling very anxious, and of men asking him questions, but he readily accepts he might have dreamed those things.'

The great statesman pursed his lips for a moment before continuing.

'Now, none us believe for a moment, young lady, that Professor Broadmarsh deliberately gave up his secret message. But his recollections seem to confirm that he was questioned, and as he cannot recall anything about his interrogation, we can only conclude that he has told his interrogators everything they wished to learn.'

'But that's a terrible thing to say, sir!' I felt outraged on the professor's behalf. 'What would make you think such a thing?'

'Because they have let him go, child.' Sir Torpenhow's voice was stern. 'They want that line of code. They know the professor has it. If he had not given it to them, the Rumanian officials would simply have fobbed us off with more delays. They would be investigating his disappear-ance with the utmost urgency, they would be confident of securing his release within days. But they would not be letting him go.'

I considered that for a moment, and found myself agreeing with Sir Torpenhow's reasoning. And if Andreas Weiss and his conspirators had two out of the three lines of code, that definitely made their position stronger. But the advantage was still ours, surely? We simply had to make sure that the third line – Mr Barrington's line – was never allowed to fall into the wrong hands.

'That's absolutely correct,' Mr Holmes confirmed, when I said as much. 'Although I fear it is of little comfort to Mr Barrington here, whose wife's reputation rests entirely in the hands of Sir Torpenhow's special officers.'

I didn't like to mention that someone other than those special officers would be on duty by the Serpentine that night. Nor did it seem the right time to tell Mr Barrington that his wife was not a bigamist. There are times and places for these things. Mrs Hudson would know better than me when and where they were. Besides, I told myself, it would not be many hours before the Barringtons' blackmailer had been arrested in Kensington Gardens, and every cloud hanging over Harry Barrington and his wife had dissolved into the blue.

–

That August was the hottest month for many a year, and for those of us living our lives in the heart of London, the blazing sun and baking streets were enough to convince us that summer was at its height. But every evening we were reminded, as the days grew shorter and the nights longer, that autumn was gradually coming nearer. By eight o'clock that night, the sun had set. It was dark by nine.

Sir Torpenhow Franklin and Harry Barrington had left us long before that, sliding out into the lengthening shadows while the church clocks were striking seven, Sir Torpenhow bound for his townhouse in Belgravia, Mr Barrington for Waterloo Station and the mid-evening train to Frog Hall. As I watched him go, I wished that Mrs Hudson or I had been able to speak to him in private. So slumped were his shoulders, so defeated his demeanour, that I could imagine all too well the horrible evening he and his wife were to spend together, waiting for the scandal to break over them.

I consoled myself by imagining their relief the next day, when they discovered that the shadow had passed, that their blackmailer was apprehended, and that the man Mrs Barrington had glimpsed at Clapham Junction was not in reality her first husband, but a simple rural vicar with an interest in antiquities. Even so, I felt for them in their temporary suffering; but when I said as much to Mrs Hudson, she just brushed her hands together briskly and clicked her tongue.

'Don't you worry about them, young lady. They will be fine. You and I will see to that. And I've written Mrs Barrington a little note that will, I think, bring great joy to them both. I will post it tonight. So long as I catch the night mail, she will receive it in the first post tomorrow, and the first post is very early at Frog Hall, if you remember, so by breakfast time both she and her husband should be happy as larks.'

We had been putting away clean plates while we talked, and now Mrs Hudson stepped back to survey her neat and pristine kitchen.

'Now, Flottie, the two gentlemen have settled in for the evening, and I must say it's a relief. I was afraid they might form some scheme of their own, and would insist on accompanying Sir Torpenhow's men to Kensington Gardens. But I suspect Mr Holmes has no great opinion of Sir Torpenhow's measures, and no optimism that those special officers will succeed in making an arrest. And, of course, he knows that any plan he himself might make to apprehend our blackmailer would inevitably be sabotaged by the presence of all those burly men hiding in bushes.'

'So you don't think the special officers will catch him, ma'am?'

'If Andreas Weiss is the man I think he is, he is most certainly not going to blunder into such a crude trap, and nor will anyone he trusts to send in his place. Mr Holmes knows that, of course, and is assuming that the presence of so many police will simply scare the man off. And once scared off, his first action will be to send his incriminating allegations about Mrs Barrington to the newspapers, to her neighbours, and to everyone in society who can be trusted to spread the scandal.'

'But you can stop that, ma'am?'

Her confidence seemed remarkable, but I didn't doubt her for a moment.

'With your help I can, Flotsam. How fast can you run?'

The question was a little alarming, but I assured her I could run very quickly indeed, if required.

'Excellent, Flottie. It will most certainly be required. Now, it is far too early for us to set off, and it is foolish to try to work with this thing looming over us, so now would be a very good time to read a book. We'll leave at eleven o'clock, prompt.'

I thought that hour would never come. I tried to read, but my eyes simply passed over the words without really seeing them. I tried lying down and shutting my eyes, but in my imagination I was instantly in full flight, chasing villains around the Serpentine. I even tried going for a walk, but the streets were too dusty and the air too sticky for enjoyment. In the end, much to Mrs Hudson's amusement, I took it upon myself to polish all the gentlemen's shoes, though not one pair really needed it.

At four minutes to eleven, Mrs Hudson put down her own book and rose from her seat.

'Now, Flotsam, Mr Holmes let you have a good look at the blackmailer's directions. You can still remember the precise meeting place?'

'Yes, ma'am. The seventh park bench, walking south from the Italian Gardens, on the Kensington Gardens bank of the Serpentine. At midnight exactly.'

'Very good, my girl. Then let us be off!'

'But won't the parks be locked by now, ma'am?'

'They will, Flotsam, but that doesn't mean they are empty. Anyone locked in during daylight hours can wonder around for as long as they like, then let themselves out through the turnstiles. And for people who know the place well, there are ways of getting in and out at any hour. We know that somebody will be there at midnight, hoping to collect the all-important code from Mr Barrington – but I don't imagine for a moment that person has been hanging around in Kensington Gardens ever since the gates closed.'

'But what about us, ma'am? How will we get in?'

Mrs Hudson was an admirable woman in many ways, but I couldn't imagine her scaling high railings in the dark.

'We will use the gate by Porchester Terrace, Flottie. I know the man who keeps the key.'

And, sure enough, after a brisk walk across the centre of London which left me uncomfortably aware of the perspiration beneath my armpits, we arrived at the Porchester Terrace gate and found it closed but unlocked. The time, according to Mrs Hudson's pocket watch, was twenty-five minutes short of midnight.

'Plenty of time,' Mrs Hudson assured me, 'but we need to go quietly. Luckily, the eyes of Sir Torpenhow's men will all be focused on the bench in question, so if we hang back and make no noise, I think we can creep quite close without being noticed.'

The Royal Parks at night can be strangely eerie. I've been in there in winter, after the gates have shut, when the mist was rising from the lake, and I remember feeling there was no more lonely place in London. This night, however, as Mrs Hudson and I ventured forward, the gas lamps along the Bayswater Road threw a generous orange glow that reached quite a long way into the shadows of the park, and the grass itself, brown and parched by the summer, was light in the moonlight – so light that a late cat, stalking across the lawn beside the Italian Gardens, stood out clearly as a dark shadow against the turf.

And there was no sense of loneliness, either. Even before I saw anyone else in the park that night, I could sense them. More than once in my life, I've felt the emptiness that descends upon a busy place when the people leave it; but I felt none of it that night. If anything, the sense I had of people, present but unseen, concealed in the darkness, was more unsettling.

To my surprise, Mrs Hudson showed no inclination to skulk in bushes or creep behind trees. We stayed on the path, quite close to the lake, moving quietly and counting the benches as we passed them, until we could see the seventh bench ahead of us, about thirty yards away. There was enough light to show us that the bench was empty.

'One moment, Flotsam,' Mrs Hudson whispered, and the two of us listened.

Listening to the night is a funny business. At first you think that all you can hear is silence, then you become aware of your own breathing and your own pulse, and after that you begin to notice that the night is actually alive with sound – the flitting of birds, the sigh of the breeze or, in this case, the rustling of bushes and, once, the scuff of a boot against dry grass. We were certainly not alone.

'Do you remember, Flotsam, that trick we pulled off at the Blenheim Hotel, that time I wanted to have a look around the Satin Rooms?'

Her voice was very low, more a rumble than a whisper, and I nodded in reply. It was not an incident I would ever forget.

'Well, we're about to do something very similar. When I say the word, Flottie, I want you to walk up to that bench at an even pace. Sit down when you get there, and count to twenty. Then get up, stand still for a moment, and then start to run. Run back in this direction, back to the gate, absolutely as fast as you can. You're young and healthy, and I'm not convinced that Sir Torpenhow's men will have been selected for their speed. And you taking off like that, with no warning, will take them by surprise. But if anything goes wrong, Flottie, and they catch you before you reach the gate, say nothing, and just demand to be taken to Sir Torpenhow.'

'And if I do reach the gate, ma'am, what then?' I think my voice may have wobbled a bit as I asked it.

'Then all is well. I will see you at home.'

I don't think I replied, just nodded, although I remember feeling a sinking sensation inside me. The gate was a distance away, and I was only too aware that Sir Torpenhow had been talking of fifty officers concealed in the park.

'Very good.' Mrs Hudson held her watch very close to her face, angling it to catch the light. 'Four minutes to midnight. It's time, Flotsam. Off you go.'

I suppose it must have taken me less than a minute to reach the bench, but as I made my way towards it, it felt as though the whole park – not just me – was holding its breath. When I reached it, I sat down, and I swear I could actually *feel* the eyes fixed upon me. I waited, counting in my head, then stood up, still listening to my own breathing. Everything else was silence.

And then I started to run.

Almost immediately, a voice crashed out of the darkness, coarse and hoarse and appalling.

'Stop!' it yelled, 'Stop in the name of the law!'

For a fraction of a second, I felt myself filled with terror, but before the sentence was even completed I had recognised in the deep, booming cry the disguised tones of my companion, and I was away, running as fast as I have ever run, back down the pale path, the lights of Bayswater a beacon ahead of me.

It's hard to say exactly what happened then, and in what order. I was aware of noise all around me, of voices crying out, and of heavy bodies crashing through undergrowth, and then of a police whistle – terrifying and shrill – ringing out so that it seemed to fill the night. I think perhaps it was the undergrowth that saved me. The hidden officers had chosen their positions intent on concealment, not thinking that they might need to quit them at great pace; so by the time I was out in the open, sprinting for the gate with my knees pumping high beneath my skirts, I already had a slender but respectable lead. But I had not reckoned on the officers stationed on the park's perimeter, the ones who were not running after me but running *towards* me.

Perhaps I was fortunate again, for the majority had been stationed near Lancaster Gate, and were too far away to trouble me. But I was aware of two running forward from different sides of the Porchester Gate, intent on barring my way. One was coming from the left, the other from the right, and the one on the right seemed to me to be enormously large, and moving with surprising speed. As our paths converged, I watched him open his arms to engulf me.

But long ago, as a tiny slip of a child, before Scraggs found me, before Mrs Hudson took me in, I had run barefoot in London's alleyways. And perhaps I'd learned things then that I'd forgotten ever learning, things I would never forget and would never know I remembered. That is the only reason I can give for what happened next, for as the paths of the two police officers converged on mine, quite instinctively, and without hesitation, I swerved to my left, then, as the two men adjusted accordingly, I jinked sharply right, wrong-footing them both.

Even then, my fate was in doubt, for the colossus, caught off balance, flung himself backwards, his arm at full stretch, and I could see his huge hand reaching for my skirts, then feel his fingers closing on them, and I thought to myself that the game was up. But again my response was instinctive, and as his fingers grasped my hems, I spun myself around in a full turn, slashing down with the side of my hand at the same time, so that the fabric he held was suddenly tight and pulling from his fingertips just as the side of my fist caught his and forced it away from me.

And then I *was* free, still on my feet and moving as swiftly as before, with the Porchester Gate only thirty paces ahead of me. I didn't look back, even though I could hear footsteps gaining behind me, and could hear very close to me the shouts of my pursuers. I don't know how far ahead I was when I reached the gate – perhaps only ten paces, perhaps less – but I remember thinking, 'What now?' as I dipped out of the park, because out in the street with a pack of policeman behind me, I surely had no chance of escape.

But even before I'd finished the thought, I heard the iron gate clang shut behind me, and the twist of the key in its lock. Turning, I glimpsed an elderly man, his face hidden beneath a cloth cap, stepping away from the gate and leaping up into a waiting growler, while the officers pressed against the ironwork, baying for his blood. I think I must have stood for a full three seconds, gawping at the carriage, before I realised what was expected of me. But the door was still open, the man's arm holding it for me like an invitation. Running back, I threw myself in next him, and the carriage rumbled away, leaving the many arms of the law behind it. I didn't look back.

Chapter Seventeen

My rescuer's name was Mr Noakes, and that was all I ever really found out about him. He was chuckling as the carriage pulled away from the park gate, and he was still chuckling when it turned sharply right, into Queensborough Terrace, and out of sight of our pursuers.

'That was fun!' he told me then, chuckling again. 'There was a time there when I'd have gone fifty to one against you making it, young lady. But, my word, that was some excellent footwork. That big fellow, the one who nearly got you, he'll go to his grave still wondering how you got away. Feint left, step right, hand off, and away! Ha!'

It was too dark in the carriage for me to see his face properly, but I had the feeling that he might be very old indeed, yet he had leapt up into the growler with a genuine bounce in his stride.

I had just begun to ask him how he came to have a key for the gate when the carriage turned right into Porchester Gardens.

'Sorry, my dear, this is where I leave you,' he told me, still chuckling quietly to himself. 'Wilfred – that's the driver – will take you back to Baker Street. Don't worry about the fare. I've taken care of it.'

He stepped down into the street and waved to me as the carriage pulled away, then shouted, 'My compliments to Mrs Hudson. Tell her I wouldn't have missed it for the world!'

Strange though it may seem, it was only then that it occurred to me to wonder what had become of my companion. So intent had I been on carrying out her instructions, and so desperate to evade capture, that I'd never had time to ask myself what the rest of her plan involved. Clearly, my task had been to act as a decoy, to draw the hidden officers from the scene, but the second half of Mrs Hudson's plan – how she planned to trap the blackmailer and deliver him to justice – remained a mystery to me.

It was a mystery I was still pondering when the growler dropped me in Baker Street, right at the top of the area steps. Wilfred, a man of few words, grunted in reply when I thanked him, then rumbled off into the night, leaving me alone outside the darkened house. Mrs Hudson, whatever her plan, was still not home.

According to the clocks, I then spent nearly an hour fidgeting at the kitchen table, but it felt a great deal longer. It was certainly enough time for me to imagine a great many catastrophes that may have befallen my companion. Perhaps she had attempted to apprehend her adversary single-handed? Perhaps there had been a struggle? Perhaps he had been armed? Or had come with companions? Perhaps, his blackmail plan having failed, he had seized Mrs Hudson instead? When I finally heard footsteps descending into the area, I felt sure they must be the heavy boots of a policeman, come to tell me that a terrible fate had befallen my friend.

But, of course, the footsteps were hers, and she seemed rather surprised by the embrace with which I welcomed her.

'Why, Flotsam, whatever is the matter?' she asked solicitously. 'From where I was watching, you seemed to make your escape most effectively. Did anything untoward befall you after that? Did Mr Noakes not come to your aid?'

So I explained that everything had gone well, that the peculiar man with the key had swept me off in his cab, and that I was suffering from nothing worse than a little anxiety.

'Well, you have nothing to worry about, Flotsam. All has gone smoothly. I would have been home sooner, but I took that letter to the station sorting office, to make sure it caught the night mail. And my, it was a hot walk home! I don't believe the mercury has dropped by a fraction since the sun went down.'

'But what about the blackmailer, ma'am? Did you see him? Has your plan worked? Is Mrs Barrington's reputation saved?'

'Yes, I believe it is, Flotsam. My plan worked perfectly. After your sterling efforts, everything went precisely as I'd hoped. Of course, the blackmailer himself wasn't present, and I never expected him to be. He sent a proxy. But, once it was clear all the police officers had left the scene, there was no trouble at all in handing over the envelope.'

'The envelope, ma'am? What envelope?'

'Why, Flotsam, the one containing Mr Barrington's line of the code.'

'Mr Barrington's...?' But I couldn't even finish the question. Words really did fail me. 'But, ma'am, you haven't…? You haven't…? You haven't given away the code?'

'Of course, Flotsam.'

She was bustling round the kitchen now, undoing her bonnet, reaching down glasses and laying two small plates on the table.

'Think about it this way, Flottie. Some very unpleasant people have got hold of a nasty story about Mrs Barrington, who is a nice woman and deserves better. They have made it clear that they will make the story known to the wider public unless they are given the line of code that Mr Barrington brought back from Bokara. Mr Barrington's sense of honour won't permit this, and all the other gentlemen simply purse their lips and look pained. But unless somebody does something, Mrs Barrington's life will be ruined for the sake of a rather grubby piece of diplomacy.'

She paused in her movements and looked at me.

'So the solution was simple. I just gave them the code.'

There could be no one in the whole world who admired Mrs Hudson more than more than I did, but I confess I was aghast.

'But, ma'am! That was a national secret! The safety of the nation depends on it! You can't just give it away to our enemies!'

'Why ever not? Thanks to your deciphering of those telegrams, Sir Torpenhow now knows where that wretched treaty of his is to be handed over. At the moment he thinks his enemies are unaware of the time and place, but once he knows otherwise, he will simply have to take appropriate precautions. It shouldn't be beyond him to make sure that the library at Montrachute House is free of enemy spies for five minutes or so either side of midnight.'

'But, ma'am!' I said again. There seemed to be so many objections to Mrs Hudson's remarkable course of action that I was struggling to put any one of them into words. 'But, ma'am, what if they find out? What if they find out it was you? Isn't that treason, ma'am? Won't you be…?'

'Oh, come now, Flottie. Why should anyone find out? Thanks to you, there was no one in the park to see. Mr Weiss sent a very small boy to collect the envelope, by the way. A minute or so after you ran off, I was sitting on the bench with the envelope by my side, and this little urchin just popped up from out of the darkness, grabbed it, and disappeared. Even if anyone *had* been watching, they couldn't be certain what they'd seen.'

'But, ma'am…' I knew I was repeating myself, but I was certain I'd found a terrible flaw in the housekeeper's plan. 'Ma'am, if the blackmailer *doesn't* publish the story about Mrs Barrington tomorrow, and if it becomes clear later on that the conspirators know all about Mr Barrington's line of the code, won't the whole world think that it was the Barringtons who gave the secret away? And then they'll be ruined anyway!'

To my surprise, the question appeared to please Mrs Hudson greatly.

'Very good, Flotsam. That is undoubtedly the danger. But the letter I've just sent Mrs Barrington will help with that, I think. And with a little bit of help, we can kill two birds with one stone. Because we also need to make Sir Torpenhow aware that his enemies know about the rendezvous at Montrachute House, so that he can take sensible precautions. And I think I've worked out a way to do that *and* to place the Barringtons above suspicion, both at the same time. That's why you and I need to go out tomorrow to watch some cricket.'

'*Cricket*, ma'am?'

'Yes, cricket, Flotsam. You know – bat, balls, white flannel trousers. The difference between us and the French.'

I think I'd actually run out of ways to express my incomprehension, so I simply blinked and shook my head.

Mrs Hudson, however, didn't seem in the least put out by my reaction.

'Now, Flotsam, a quick slice of madeira cake and a cold drink are in order, and then to bed. We have a lot to do tomorrow.'

She nodded contentedly.

'I think you'll like Lord's, Flottie. It's all very soothing.

–

I awoke the next morning filled with a numbness that I thought at first might be lock-jaw but which I quickly realised was simply dread. Mrs Hudson had done something terrible, something that must soon be discovered, something that would succour the nation's enemies and bring our own country to its knees. I swung my feet out of bed with terrible reluctance, certain that I would emerge to find my whole world torn apart and in chaos.

But in fact the world beyond my little cupboard bed seemed a rather cheerful place that morning. I found, waiting for me on the kitchen table, three very perfect French marigolds in a glass of water accompanied by a scribbled note from Scraggs which read simply: *Don't forget to sort out about a dress*. Next to them, my breakfast was laid out for me, as well as a small bowl of peaches, with a note from Mrs Hudson which read: *Gone to Lord's to secure convenient seats. May be some time.*

And when the time came for me to take up a fashionably late breakfast to Mr Holmes and Dr Watson, I found them both in surprisingly good spirits.

'You won't be surprised to hear, Flotsam,' Mr Holmes told me with a considerable degree of satisfaction, 'that Sir Torpenhow's men messed things up royally last night. Seems a young girl was sent to collect the secret code from Barrington, but before they could arrest her, somebody got overexcited and shouted out, and somehow she was able to give them the slip.'

I felt the blood rush to my cheeks, but before I could offer any sort of reply, Dr Watson had intervened.

'And that's not all, Flotsam. We've had a telegram from Harry Barrington, haven't we, Holmes? Mrs Hudson took it in before she popped out. Seems everything's all right.'

'All right, sir?'

I felt sure that my voice must betray me, or if not my voice, my hands, for I was finding it very hard to hold the breakfast tray without it shaking.

'Yes, about the blackmail and stuff. What did he say, Holmes?'

'He said, Watson, that he was heading up here on the first train to explain it to us properly.'

And Mr Barrington was as good as his word. He arrived in Baker Street in the middle of the morning, before Mrs Hudson had returned, and it struck me immediately that he looked a good ten years younger than when I had seen him the previous day. Then, his shoulders had sloped and his face looked saggy and wretched. Now, he bounded up the stairs behind me with the freshness and enthusiasm of a puppy.

'Holmes! Watson! A very good morning to you both. Flotsam!' Seeing that I was still in the doorway, he beckoned me in. 'Come, come, I want you to see this. It is the most remarkable thing! Deliverance, and completely out of the blue. It is like a miracle!'

He was brandishing a sheet of writing paper which I took from him and passed to Mr Holmes, taking good care to read it as I did so. It was a clear and succinct communication, if a surprising one, written, like the other blackmail letters, in a crudely disguised hand.

> *Dear Mrs Barrington,*
>
> *I call you by that name as it is, in truth, your lawful title. Although your husband disappointed us tonight, we have no plan – and no longer any reason – to bring about your ruin. You may think this strange, but Sir Torpenhow Franklin will not.*
>
> *A Friend*

'Well, I must say,' Dr Watson declared, when he too had digested it, 'that's a rum business.'

'Indeed, Watson.' Mr Holmes was studying the postmark on the envelope in which the letter had arrived. 'This was sent last night, presumably after the failed ambush in the park. In those circumstances, you would expect a blackmailer to take a rather more vengeful course of action, would you not?'

Mr Barrington nodded, his smile lighting up his face. 'It is, as I say, a miracle!'

Dr Watson was still looking puzzled.

'But what's all this about Sir Torpenhow, Holmes? It seems to be saying that he'll know why the blackmailers have held their fire.'

The detective looked at the note for a second time, then shrugged.

'I can only suggest we ask the man himself. And we cannot do that today, as he was planning to catch the first train to Montrachute House, if you remember, and is unlikely to be back until very late tonight.' His eyes settled on me. 'What do you think of it, Flotsam?'

I was actually thinking that the disguised handwriting in the note looked very much like Mrs Hudson's disguised handwriting, so I said nothing and simply shook my head. Disappointed, Mr Holmes turned back to Mr Barrington.

'This letter would appear to relieve you of all your anxieties, sir. I congratulate you on a most felicitous outcome.'

But Mr Holmes' expression did not look particularly congratulatory. There was a frown on his forehead as he studied the note again.

'The implication of this letter is clear, however. It suggests that our adversaries are now in possession of your line of the code, which, if true, is a very significant development indeed.'

'But how can they have it, Mr Holmes?' Harry Barrington was looking perplexed. I tried not to look at him for fear of blushing.

'*How* they come to have it is not the pertinent question, sir. We need to ask ourselves what steps they will take now. But, in theory at least, we have very little to fear. Montrachute House is hardly the wild steppes of Asia, and the Lord Wymondham's summer ball is not the Carpathian Mountains. To collect an important document in an orderly way, in a comfortably furnished library, surrounded by people we know we can trust, should not be a particularly daunting challenge.'

'Quite right, Holmes,' Dr Watson concurred, 'and I for one feel we should be celebrating. Sir Torpenhow came to us because he had lost Professor Broadmarsh *and* the professor's vital coded message. Well, we've found both of them for him, and everything is back on a level footing. Sir Torpenhow and Mr Barrington here will handle things from now on, and they've got nothing much to worry about. The thing's in the bag.'

But however eloquently Dr Watson declared that Baker Street's involvement in the case was over, our shadowy adversaries appeared to think otherwise. And we didn't have to wait very long to discover for ourselves just how ruthless they could be.

–

I think it's fair to say that I was not greatly in the mood for cricket that day. Of course I knew Mrs Hudson far too well to think that her sudden desire to spend an afternoon at Lord's was purely a whim. But I think I was still a little shocked by the previous night's events, and had not entirely forgiven her for them.

Admittedly, she had, by meeting the blackmailer's demands, saved the reputation of the Barringtons. And even Mr Holmes agreed that no real harm was done to the nation's interests, so long as the handing over of the treaty at Montrachute House was managed competently. So perhaps, I reflected, my spirits lifting slightly, Mrs Hudson's solution might actually have been the sensible one after all. And as the two of us prepared a small picnic lunch to take with us, I took comfort from the thought that, whatever Mrs Hudson had planned next, it must surely be less scandalous than what had gone before.

Lord's cricket ground is hard to describe to anyone who has never been there. It is easy enough to describe what you can see – a circle of the most perfectly mown grass, a paler square where the wickets are marked, the high stands surrounding them, and the white-flannelled figures patrolling the turf. The sounds are easy, too – the satisfying *tock* of the ball against the bat, the crisp shouts that follow, the stirring of the crowd and the ripple of applause, then the gradual, settling silence as the bowler turns at his mark.

What is impossible to convey is the *feeling* of the place, the sense of somewhere where the world outside is forgotten; of a place where time has somehow been slowed, so that the past and the present jostle together, and the match you're watching becomes another tiny part of an ancient, densely woven fabric. I knew none of this that day, when Mrs Hudson dragged me there to watch Middlesex take on the Gentlemen of Kent, but as we settled in our seats near the pavilion steps and watched the players fanning out across the field after their break for lunch, I think I began to feel it. In front of me, an elderly gentleman tapped his stick in appreciation, and three small boys who had been squabbling over beetles were suddenly still, their eyes turned towards the wicket.

'Middlesex batting, and only three wickets down,' Mrs Hudson explained, though the words meant very little to me. Scraggs enjoyed cricket, I knew, and was able to bowl a potato at an apple barrel with unerring accuracy;

but my life contained so many other things to learn and understand that I'd seldom paid any interest.

'And Mr Lucas is well set,' one of the small boys added, without turning away from the game.

'Though if the Gentlemen can get rid of Mr Lucas, and then Mr Ford, they'll have a chance against the tail,' his rather grubby companion pointed out.

'Need to change the bowling,' the old gentleman with the stick opined, it being apparently well understood that in discussing the ebbs and flows of a cricket match, any differences in age or class or cleanliness were automatically set aside. 'They need to bring back Mr Raffles.'

All three boys nodded knowingly at that, and with those words I understood, with something of a sinking feeling, exactly why we had come.

AJ Raffles was, in those days, a celebrated and much-loved figure, the perfect embodiment of the amateur cricketer. He could bat and bowl with effortless grace, yet dig in on a sticky wicket with the grim determination of the most hardened professional. And then, when play was over, he could dance as gracefully as he could bat, and frequently did, enjoying all the invitations that society could shower upon him. People still talked about the time he danced all night at Ruthven House with Lady Haslemere's beautiful daughters, then calmly excused himself and took a cab to the Oval, arriving in perfect evening dress, breakfasting on a single peach and a glass of champagne, then scoring a defiant century on a disintegrating pitch.

It had therefore come as something of a shock to me to learn, not very long after entering Mrs Hudson's employ-ment, that Mr Raffles was also a jewel-thief, a cracksman and a highly resourceful burglar. The general public, of course, were unaware of this aspect of their hero's character, although it is quite possible, had they known of it, they might have idolised him to an even greater degree. More confusingly still, given her previous good character, Mrs Hudson appeared to be on very cordial terms with him.

That much was confirmed when, at the tea interval, I heard a pleasant voice behind me, and, much to the astonishment and admiration of the small boys with the beetles, the great cricketer himself was welcoming us to Lord's.

'I noticed you when we came out after lunch, Mrs H,' he told us cheerfully, 'and have spent the whole afternoon examining my conscience. That is probably why Slade Lucas has been able to do such terrible things to my bowling. 103 not out, and we've never looked like removing the fellow. On the positive side, you'll be happy to know, after the most minute examination, I am able to report that my conscience is completely clear. Whatever you suspect me of, I assure you I am innocent.'

He looked over at the small boys, who were very clearly trying to hear what the great Mr Raffles had to say, and then indicated the field of play.

'Come, lét us take a turn around the boundary rope. You can tell me whose pearls have gone missing, and I'll give you even money that I can work out who took them.'

But we had not come about any missing pearls, as Mrs Hudson explained. We had come on quite a different matter.

'You see, sir, I have a favour to ask. If you recall, that time I returned Lady Haslemere's emeralds to her bedroom, you were kind enough to say that if I ever needed anything, I had only to ask.'

Mr Raffles chuckled.

'Ah, Mrs H! The look on her ladyship's face that day, when she found her precious necklace untouched in its case! I swear that moment was worth more to me than the emeralds themselves! So, what is it that I can do for you?'

Mrs Hudson looked across at me.

'I'm a little worried that Flotsam here will be shocked by my request. You see, I need you to remove something from the pocketbook of Sir Torpenhow Franklin. While the gentlemen is sleeping. And it must be tonight.'

I think Mr Raffles was a great deal more taken aback by this request than I was, because I had seen it coming, and he had not.

'*Tonight*, Mrs H? That's asking quite a lot, you know. Did I mention to you that I'm pretty much retired nowadays? Oh, I admit that a particularly beautiful set of rubies or a perfect diamond might rouse me from my slumbers, but for now I'm terribly out of practice.'

'Sir Torpenhow lives in Belgravia,' Mrs Hudson continued relentlessly. 'I can provide you with his address, and I've made a point of gossiping with his manservant, so I can be pretty certain where his pocketbook will be.'

Mr Raffles was a good-looking young gentleman, and a debonair one, but I could see from the look in his face that he was harbouring genuine reservations.

'We may not be finished here until seven o'clock, Mrs Hudson. And then I'm supposed to be dining with Sir Henry Trubshaw at his club.' He turned to me with a sigh.

'I suppose I should be grateful that Mrs H isn't asking for it to be done yesterday.'

'I think, sir,' I told him, 'that it would have been better done yesterday, but we've both been a little busy.'

'Did I fail to mention, sir,' Mrs Hudson added, 'that the honour of a very beautiful young woman is at stake?'

'Is it, by Jove?' Mr Raffles stroked his chin and turned as if to study the wicket. 'I suppose I could try my hand at some leg spin after tea. It's about the only thing we haven't tried, and I seemed to remember Bosanquet taking wickets here after tea on a pitch like this one. If we could wrap up the Middlesex innings by a quarter to six, I could leave it to the others to bat out the rest of the day, while I take a stroll around Belgravia. Just to see the lie of the land, you know. And if all is going well at that point, Mrs H, perhaps we could discuss the matter further?'

I thought Mrs Hudson was going to smile, but she simply nodded.

'Anything you do to help would be greatly appreciated, sir,' she stated solemnly.

'Very well!' We had returned to the place where we started, and Mr Raffles began to say his farewells. 'I make no promises, you understand, Mrs H, no promises at all. Now, you are going to stay for the evening session, I trust? Or do you have to go and make old Sherlock his tea?'

'I fear, sir, that Flotsam and I have already been away from our duties for rather too long. And I think Flotsam has forgotten she is expected in Bloomsbury Square within the hour. But we will wish you the very best of luck, sir.'

'With my bowling, Mrs H?'

'With that too, sir.'

It says something about the peace of the place, about the strange calm Lord's can inspire, that I left the ground feeling genuinely optimistic. The previous day I had conspired with Mrs Hudson to betray state secrets to enemy powers. Today I had helped to commission a burglary. And yet I didn't feel bad at all. Everything was going to be all right. Mr Holmes would get his tea. Mr Raffles would surely find a way of dismissing Mr Lucas. And I was going to see Hetty Peters, to borrow a ball gown for the Survivors' Ball.

As we left the ground, before we had reached the street, a huge roar went up from behind us, followed by a round of applause much louder than any that had gone before.

'That will be Mr Lucas gone,' the old gateman told us. 'Mr Raffles must have got him at last.'

I nodded to him with all the solemn wisdom of one steeped in the game from the cradle.

'That's right,' I said. 'I knew he would.'

Chapter Eighteen

The following day was the last Thursday in August, which meant there were only two days until the Survivors' Ball; two days, also, until Lord Wymondham's ball at Montrachute House, where the whole fraught affair of the Bokara treaty would be brought to an end.

In other circumstances, I would have daydreamed shamelessly about attending Lord Wymondham's ball, for it was perhaps *the* most elegant event of the summer, and it was said that no experience on earth could match waltzing in the Montrachute ballroom at dusk, with the windows flung open along the whole length of the dance floor, so that if felt as though you were dancing outside, in a secret forest where every tree was hung with glowing lanterns.

But the ball of your dreams is one thing – a real, lavish, wonderful ball which you're actually invited to is quite another; and as consolation prizes go, the Survivors' Ball was better than the best.

A happy if chaotic hour had been passed the previous day in Hetty Peters' boudoir, trying on the most astonishingly beautiful – and often very lavish – gowns, and trying to decide which one I should choose. It was a decision made more difficult by the fact that everyone seemed to have a different opinion, and Hetty had a number of different opinions all at once. Even Reynolds, the butler, when he showed me up that afternoon had, after inquiring about the cricket score, lowered his voice to an urgent whisper.

'A word of warning about Miss Peters and her gowns, miss. A great many of them are rather elaborate affairs. But there is a very simple one in sea-green silk that I feel would be most becoming...'

A great deal of trying things on and taking things off followed, before we took a break for tea, which was laid out in the drawing room. There Mr Spencer, who hadn't been asked, expressed various opinions, and offered the advice that anything Hetty really liked should be treated with a great deal of caution.

'He only says that because he is a beast,' Hetty told me when we resumed our search, 'and a beast who knows more about beetles than ball gowns. Honestly, Flottie, the other day he told me he thought young Miss Grainger was looking very becoming, and when I went to find her, she was all wrapped up in apricot silk. And of course Miss Grainger is very lovely, and would look good in most things, but she makes some very unwise choices, and this one made her look like an off-colour milk pudding.'

For some reason, that phrase lodged in my mind, and quite a number of Hetty's gowns were quietly put to one side as a result. Then, just when I felt I couldn't face trying on even one more gown, we came to the very simple affair in sea-green silk, and miraculously even Miss Peters agreed that Reynolds had been right all along.

The ordeal wasn't entirely finished though, because one or two adjustments needed to be made for a perfect fit, and the following morning, after clearing and cleaning the breakfast things, and running various errands around town for Mrs Hudson, I set off for the house in Blooms-bury Square and an appointment with Miss Peters' favourite seamstress.

It was not till nearly eleven o'clock in the morning that I returned to Baker Street, just in time to bump into Dr Watson and Mr Holmes on the pavement outside our front door, attempting to hail a cab.

'Ah, Flotsam!' Mr Holmes welcomed me warmly. 'We hoped you would be back in time, because we'd like you to join us. We are going to see Sir Torpenhow Franklin about the security of this treaty of his.'

I think I must have hesitated, unsure of how to reply. Mr Holmes' recently acquired habit of including me in his deliberations with Sir Torpenhow was flattering, but a little overwhelming, and certainly extremely unconventional.

'But, sir, I'm not sure Sir Torpenhow…'

'You feel that Sir Torpenhow disregards your opinions because of your birth, age, occupation, gender, and your lack of an Oxford or Cambridge education? Yes, Dr Watson suggested as much. Which is precisely why you must come.'

He shot out his arm, and a passing hansom pulled to a halt a few feet past us. Mr Holmes, on lowering his arm, offered it to me.

'In this age of reason, Flotsam, such archaic prejudices are as destined for extinction as the dinosaurs and the dodo. I pay no attention to these things, Flotsam, and nor should Sir Torpenhow.'

'But, really, sir, I'm hardly dressed for such a visit…'

And in truth, after a morning running around London in the heat and the dust, I wasn't even very clean. But Mr Holmes dismissed this objection with a wave of his hand.

'Your current garments are perfectly serviceable, child,' he told me austerely. 'Now, come. I feel certain that, if we do not take a hand, Sir Torpenhow and his minions are extremely likely to... What was the phrase you used, Watson?'

Dr Watson gave me a smile that was very nearly a wink.

'Extremely likely to make a hash of it, Holmes.'

'My sentiments entirely.'

And, with that, the kingdom's most eminent detective handed me into the cab.

–

For all Mr Holmes' insistence that old social conventions should count for nothing in our modern times, it was certainly the case that the footman at Sir Torpenhow's house in Eaton Square appeared rather put out when asked to announce a dust-streaked young girl wearing the clothes of a domestic servant. And Sir Torpenhow, too, seemed a little taken back when Mr Holmes was ushered into his presence with me in tow.

'Mr Holmes, Dr Watson. Miss, er, Flotsam. To what do I owe this pleasure?'

Clearly my employer had decided to be blunt.

'We are here, Sir Torpenhow, because we feel certain that the agents working against you in this Bokara affair are now fully appraised of all three lines of code that make up the Emir's message. It is therefore vital that the most rigorous measures are put in place on Saturday night to make sure that the treaty can be handed over to Mr Barrington without any mishaps.'

'But, Mr Holmes!' Sir Torpenhow looked alarmed. 'How could the conspirators have possibly obtained the third line? Only a handful of people know it, and all of them are people who have my complete trust. Unless…'

And here, hugely embarrassed, the great statesman tried desperately not to look at me.

'Unless Harry Barrington chose to protect his wife instead of his country?' Mr Holmes eyed his host sternly. 'I imagine that is what you meant to say. But a note from the blackmailer, sent to Barrington's wife and seen by the three of us, appears to absolve him of all blame. In fact, Sir Torpenhow…' And here my employer raised an eyebrow to a neat point. 'In fact, the note would appear to suggest that you yourself might be able to explain this development.'

'Me?' Sir Torpenhow was the very picture of offended honour and aristocratic hauteur. 'Why, Mr Holmes, that suggestion is in extremely poor taste.'

'Oh, no one's suggesting you are in league with the enemy, sir. It would be absurd to think such a thing. But I remember, sir, that you put the note containing Professor Broadmarsh's line of code in your pocketbook. May I ask if you have removed it from there, or shown it to anyone, since then?'

'Not for a moment, sir. In fact I can tell you without a doubt that my pocketbook has not left my pocket since that evening.'

'So Professor Broadmarsh's message is still safely in your possession, sir?'

Sir Torpenhow rolled his eyes at such presumption, and, instead of answering Mr Holmes' question, simply reached into his jacket for his pocketbook.

'I have it here.' He pulled out a cream-coloured card and a folded piece of paper. 'The card is the one on which I'd written down the first two lines of code, and this sheet of paper is the one the professor sent by pigeon containing the third line.'

He handed both to Mr Holmes, who studied them with interest, then handed them back to him.

'Perhaps, Sir Torpenhow, you might like to examine these more closely?'

Of course, from where I was standing, a little behind Dr Watson, quietly trying to evade notice, I had no way of seeing what was written on either piece of paper; but I saw them later, and the first – the cream-coloured card – did indeed contain the first two lines of the Emir's code. But the second, which I remembered as a slightly tatty object, one that had spent quite some time folded tightly and secured to a pigeon's leg, had undergone a transformation. The sheet of paper Sir Torpenhow had handed to Mr Holmes was cleaner and less obviously tattered, and the writing on it was different too. Where there should have been a familiar sequence of letters and a PS about the professor's mulberry tree, there was instead a single line of handwriting.

> *Not even your pocketbook is safe from us.*
> *An Enemy of the State*

And so, I thought, Mr Raffles has lost none of his skill, despite his protestations to the contrary. I've been rather fond of cricket, and of cricketers, ever since that moment.

271

Of course, it was important not to let my relief show, although I don't think anyone would particularly have noticed it. Sir Torpenhow's utter astonishment gave way to something very like a howl of despair, and it was all Dr Watson and Mr Holmes could do to assure him that he was blameless, that the cleverness of our opponents knew no bounds, that the incident was a timely reminder that we needed to be on our mettle.

'For you can be sure, sir, that your adversaries will not be resting on their laurels. They know that one of the guests at Lord Wymondham's ball on Saturday will be acting as the Emir's envoy. They also know, if they can identify that person before the treaty is handed to Mr Barrington in the library, or if they can somehow intervene while the document is changing hands, then victory can still be theirs.'

Mr Holmes paused to allow his words to sink in.

'That will be their aim. But the odds are in our favour, and I believe there are steps we can take to improve our prospects further.'

'Please, Mr Holmes...' Sir Torpenhow was still very pale. 'Tell me what you feel needs to be done.'

Clearly my employer had given this some thought, for he barely hesitated.

'However comforting it may feel, sir, the temptation to fill Montrachute House with policemen in plain clothes must be resisted at all costs. When the Emir sent you the details of the rendezvous, sir, split between three messengers and written in code, it was a test of sorts. He wanted you to prove that your capabilities were as great as you claimed, that you could move men and information securely around the globe. So if, on Saturday night, his envoy sees we have flooded Lord Wymondham's ball with police officers, it will be taken as a sign of weakness – and rightly so. What hope have we of fulfilling our promises in Bokara, if we are so afraid of our enemies right here, in the Garden of England?'

Sir Torpenhow nodded.

'I see that, Mr Holmes, and it is an important point. But what would you propose instead?'

'Just this, sir. That we place a handful of people we trust in the very heart of Lord Wymondham's festivities, allowing them to observe events at close quarters while remaining invisible to our enemies.'

'Why, yes!' Sir Torpenhow nodded enthusiastically. 'It had already occurred to me that such an arrangement would be ideal, but I had hardly liked to ask... Tell me, Mr Holmes, are you happy to be there yourself, directing operations?'

'From the background, Sir Torpenhow, from the background. Our opponents are aware I have been engaged in this matter, so it is important I keep a very low profile. But we will need at least two pairs of eyes and ears out there on the ballroom floor and mingling in the entertainment rooms, so I suggest that Dr Watson is added to the guest list, accompanied by Flotsam here, in the guise of his niece.'

Dr Watson looked delighted.

'Why, yes, of course, Holmes. I'd be only too happy. Keep our eyes peeled and all that, eh, Flotsam!'

'But, Mr Holmes!' Again, Sir Torpenhow was looking in many places, but not at me. 'I have come to appreciate Miss Flotsam's considerable cerebral abilities, but to pass oneself off as the niece of a gentleman... Why, it is not

273

simply a matter of putting on a splendid dress. There are other things – manner of speech, culture, education – things that it would be impossible for this young lady, for all her talents, to master between now and Saturday evening. And we cannot afford for anyone we place at the Wymondham's Ball to attract even the slightest degree of suspicion.'

Mr Holmes looked at me, and then at Sir Torpenhow Franklin, and then back at me.

'Flotsam, I know you have a good ear, because I've heard you on many occasions impersonating me for the entertainment of that grocer's lad who goes by the name of Scraggs. Do you think you could also impersonate a young lady up from the country for her first ball?'

For some reason I thought of Miss Blondell from Revennings, who had a nice voice, and an easy one to replicate.

'It would be tremendously exciting to give it a go, sir!' I told him, slightly breathlessly but with very perfect vowels.

He tried not to smile as he turned back to Sir Torpenhow.

'A small wager, sir. I will put twenty guineas against your ten that Flotsam here will be successful in passing herself off as Dr Watson's niece for the entire duration of the Wymondham's Ball.'

He shot me a swift glance of approval, and I think he may also have winked.

'You accept those terms? Excellent! Flotsam's presence on Saturday will be worth far more than the ten guineas it will cost you, so you have done a shrewd piece of business. Now, in addition, my plan is also to have Mrs Hudson keeping an eye on things below stairs, while you yourself are free to mingle with the guests. Harry Barrington will be there too, of course, and other trustworthy individuals of my acquaintance are already on the guest list. Add to them a dozen officers waiting in the stables, in case of emergencies, and I think, sir, that we have taken ample precautions to safeguard the handover of the Bokara treaty.'

And so the plan was made. My role had been thrust upon me so unexpectedly, and with so little chance to decline it, that I didn't even pause to think of the implications. I was to attend the famous Wymondham's Ball, and as a guest. And I was being trusted by Mr Holmes to keep the nation's interests safe. It was far, far more than I could ever have imagined.

Sir Torpenhow Franklin, however, did still not seem entirely at ease, and accompanied us right out into Eaton Square, where his footman was attempting to hail us a cab.

'And can I just confirm, Mr Holmes, that you yourself will be present at Montrachute House on Saturday, to oversee operations?'

'I will, sir.' Mr Holmes nodded briskly. 'Wild horses wouldn't keep me from it.'

Just then we were accosted by a mild-mannered looking gentleman in a bowler hat, a hat he removed respectfully as he approached us.

'Excuse me, sir,' he inquired politely. 'Do I have the honour of addressing Mr Sherlock Holmes? I have a message for you, sir, from Her Majesty the Queen.'

'Indeed?' Mr Holmes swung round to face him, clearly believing him to be one of the many eccentrics who stalked the streets of London. It was his practice, I knew, to deal with them briskly but kindly, and send them on their way. 'How good of Her Majesty to send you. And what, pray, is the message?'

But the man appeared distracted by a hansom cab that was approaching us along Eaton Square, a cab I thought at first was out of control, so rapidly was it moving, until I saw that the driver was whipping his horse to a frenzy.

Although we were positioned safely on the pavement, I instinctively stepped back, away from the road, and Mr Holmes attempted to do the same, only to find his way blocked by the stranger.

'The message is this, sir.'

He spoke very calmly, as though nothing was unto-ward. But as he spoke he raised his hands and, with a ferocious shove, thrust Mr Holmes backwards, into the road, and beneath the hooves of the galloping horse.

—

It was not until the middle of the afternoon that I found myself back in the kitchen at Baker Street, telling Mrs Hudson everything that had happened.

'It is a miracle he wasn't killed, ma'am! It might have been luck, of course, but I think it was presence of mind. Either way, as he fell, Mr Holmes curled in his legs. He couldn't avoid the horse, of course, and the horse couldn't avoid him, but the cab passed right over without touching him.'

Mrs Hudson was polishing the glassware.

'Fortunate indeed,' she commented. 'And you say the leg is not broken?'

'Dr Watson thinks not, ma'am. But the knee is terribly swollen, and he can't walk on it at all, can't even stand up, without it causing him dreadful pain. And the doctor isn't sure if the ribs are broken or just bruised, but either way he says that Mr Holmes will need to stay in bed in Eaton Square for a week at least before he attempts to move around. Lots of rest, he says, and keep the knee up, and a cold-press on the swelling.'

Mrs Hudson straightened and gave a little tug at both her cuffs.

'He has had an extremely fortunate escape. And you say his assailant got away?'

'Yes, ma'am.' In the horror of the moment, and the confusion that followed it, none of us had thought to seize Mr Holmes' attacker, and by the time I looked up from where the detective lay, the man with the bowler hat had already disappeared. 'Sir Torpenhow says the man must have been a lunatic, and that the police must check the asylums for escaped inmates, but I'm not so sure.'

'You think an assault of that sort, in a busy street, in broad daylight, is the act of a sane man, Flotsam?'

'Well, yes, ma'am. And a very audacious one.'

'And I agree with you entirely. I fear we should have anticipated something of the sort, and have been on our guard.' Mrs Hudson took up another wine glass and resumed her polishing. 'Mr Holmes' involvement in the Bokara affair has clearly been causing our adversaries some concern. Mlle Le Blanc fled Frog Hall at the mention of his name. And Mr White, or Weiss, or whatever, came almost immediately to Baker Street to find out for himself if Mr Holmes had been instructed by Sir Torpenhow. Then, having identified a threat to his plans, he determined to remove it.'

'But at least he didn't succeed, ma'am!' I tried to sound as cheerful as I could.

'That is true, Flottie, but I fear Mr Holmes will play very little part in events at Montrachute House on Saturday.'

'Which reminds me, ma'am!'

The dramatic events in Eaton Square had been so shocking, they had temporarily pushed my other astonishing news to the back of my mind. But when I told Mrs Hudson all about the plans for the Wymondham's Ball she didn't seem as excited on my behalf as I'd expected.

'Mr Holmes' approach is surely the right one, and I know you will cope admirably, Flotsam. But if Mr Holmes is to be absent, that places an awful lot of responsibility on the shoulders of you and Dr Watson.'

'And yours, too, ma'am,' I reminded her. 'Mr Holmes was very quick to say that he wants you below stairs, keeping an eye on everything down there.'

'Then I'm afraid Mr Holmes will be disappointed, Flotsam.' She placed the polished wine glass on the table in front of her and selected another. I was aware of an air of sadness in the way she spoke. 'You see, Flottie, Sergeant Minders died last night. I've only just heard the news. And his funeral, followed by an evening memorial service of sorts, will be held on Saturday. So you will have to go to Montrachute House without me.'

'But, ma'am...' I began, horrified. To think that Mrs Hudson was going to absent herself from such a terrifically important event, with the reputation of the nation hanging in the balance, seemed too dreadful for words. But then I remembered Sergeant Minders, and the way the two had joked with one another, and although I was still horrified, I could raise no objection.

'But you can go, Flotsam. The Bokara treaty will be in excellent hands. And the Wymondham's Ball is considered the most magnificent social event of the summer. You will probably dance with a duke.'

I smiled at this, and Mrs Hudson smiled too, but there was still a little frown behind her smile.

'Just one thing, Flotsam. Have you forgotten that you are currently engaged elsewhere on Saturday evening?'

And at her words, I felt a stabbing pang inside me, and my mouth fell open. Incredibly, amazingly, unbelievably, amid all the excitement of Mr Holmes' arrangements, I had forgotten all about the Survivors' Ball.

'I rather think, Flottie,' Mrs Hudson concluded, 'that it should be you who tells Scraggs about your change of plan.'

Chapter Nineteen

The Friday before the Wymondham's Ball passed in such a confusion of activity that it is hard now to recall the order of events, and almost impossible to remember them all.

First of all, there was the planning.

Very early in the morning a messenger arrived from Sir Torpenhow Franklin, requesting the presence of Dr Watson and myself at Eaton Square. On arriving there, instead of being shown into a drawing room, we were ushered upstairs and into a very grand bedroom where Mr Holmes lay looking terribly pale, with his foot resting on a bolster so that his knee was raised above the bed. In the interests of propriety, the bedsheets had been arranged around Mr Holmes so that only the injured leg protruded. A bag of ice, dripping slightly, had been strapped around the joint, causing a damp patch that was slowly creeping along the leg of his pyjamas.

For all his pallor, however, the great detective's mind was as alert as ever.

'Dr Watson, Flotsam, I want you to meet Inspector Cavendish. He has been selected by the Home Secretary himself to join you at the Wymondham's Ball, and to command the small force of officers which will be held in reserve. His credentials for the job are impeccable.'

'By which he means I know which fork to use on formal occasions, and can handle myself on the dance floor without falling over,' the inspector added, with a rather charming smile.

He certainly seemed a very different sort of individual from the various police inspectors I'd previously encountered. Where they tended to be solidly built, rather serious men of a certain age, Inspector Cavendish was a loose-limbed young gentleman in his late twenties who did indeed look as though he would be more at home at Montrachute House than at Scotland Yard.

'The inspector is the grand-nephew of Lady Bulstrode,' Sir Torpenhow informed us, 'so his presence at the ball tomorrow night will rouse no suspicions. Now, before we start, I need to emphasise the importance of our task. Yesterday the French ambassador asked for formal clarification from the British government that we were planning no action that might destabilise the central Asian region. We denied it, of course. On Tuesday, the Ottomans did something similar. So if the Emir's treaty were to fall into enemy hands now – if our negotiations in Bokara were revealed to the world – it would have the gravest consequences imaginable. So we cannot, under any circumstances, allow that document to slip through our fingers.'

He cleared his throat nervously, and I realised how terrified our host was at the prospect of failure.

'Now, when I was at Montrachute House the day before yesterday, I managed to obtain a list of all those attending the ball, and I will have copies delivered to you later today, so that you may familiarise yourselves with it at your leisure. Many of the names on it will be those you expect, but there are a few less orthodox guests, and it is those you must look out for.'

Sir Torpenhow consulted a sheaf of papers that lay next to the bed.

'Lord Wymondham is a devotee of the opera,' he explained, 'and is a very frequent visitor to La Scala. During his visits to Italy he appears to have made a number of acquaintances we know very little about. Who, sadly, even his lordship appears to know very little about.' He read from his list. 'The Countess Colmar, the Baron Ville-franche, Don Federico of Portovenere… These may well be innocent opera-lovers, but they may also turn out to be frauds, adventurers or the agents of foreign powers.'

'And remember, sir,' Mr Holmes pointed out without raising his head from his pillow, 'that one of them might be the person you most want to meet. One of them may be in the employment of the Emir of Bokara, and charged with delivering the signed and sealed treaty.'

'You are right, Mr Holmes. That is why we must treat every guest with exemplary courtesy. To inadvertently offend the Emir's envoy would be a diplomatic disaster of the first order.'

Sir Torpenhow turned back to me and Dr Watson.

'Lady Wymondham doesn't share her husband's interest in the opera, but is a great patron of the dramatic arts. There are therefore a great many people on this list who you would not usually find at such a prestigious event – actors, writers, and that sort. I need hardly tell you to treat all of them with a great deal of suspicion.'

It seemed to me that Sir Torpenhow must have reasons of his own for his low opinion of the theatrical profession, but I was rather excited at the thought. Mr Rumbelow had once taken me to see *Much Ado About Nothing* at the Mermaid, and I could still remember every single scene. Even so, I nodded obediently, and noticed that Inspector Cavendish was doing the same. When Sir Torpenhow turned away to put down the list, he caught my eye and smiled.

'If any of them come dressed as spies, we'll arrest 'em on the spot, eh, Flotsam?' he whispered cheerfully. Then he straightened, and put on a much more serious face.

'Now, I've been asked to brief you all about the scene of operations,' he explained. 'Montrachute House stands a mile or so from the village of Bedworth in Kent. By a quirk of railway building, the station is some distance from the village but adjacent to the grounds of the house, which makes it very convenient for guests. A select few will be staying at Montrachute House itself, many will be staying in the surrounding villages, and some – impecunious actors, no doubt – will be travelling back by train that night. There are regular trains to and from Charing Cross, and the late-night and early-morning trains all stop at Bedworth.'

He turned to me and bowed most gallantly.

'Arrangements have been made for Dr Watson and his young niece to stay at Montrachute House as guests of Lady Wymondham. That allows you to arrive tomorrow afternoon, and to get the lie of the land a little before the ball begins.'

I nodded again, trying very hard to look as though this information was no surprise. But inside a little voice was saying to me, 'You are going to be staying at Montrachute House. You are going to be *staying* at Montrachute House.' The prospect both thrilled and terrified me.

'Now, tomorrow evening, the plan is simple. Harry Barrington will be attending the ball as a guest in the normal way, although his wife will not be joining him. He wants to be able to concentrate entirely on his diplomatic role, and feels that he would be forced to neglect Mrs Barrington were she to accompany him.'

Dr Watson and I exchanged glances, and I knew what he was thinking. While it was perfectly natural for Mr Barrington to consider the event a strictly business affair, it was unfortunate that Mrs Barrington wasn't attending. She was, after all, one of the very few people to have set eyes on the mysterious Mlle Le Blanc. If one of Lord Wymondham's foreign operatic acquaintances turned out to be Mr Weiss' glamorous accomplice, it would be helpful to know from the start.

'At five to midnight,' Inspector Cavendish continued, 'Barrington will head to the library, and the three of us will go with him, simply to ensure that no ambush has been laid. When we are certain all is well, we will withdraw to allow the handover to be made. Of course, the Emir's envoy may be there already, which would be all well and good. He may even be happy to hand over the treaty in our presence. Either way, as soon as Barrington has the document in his hands, we will escort him to the stables, where my team of officers will be waiting to go with Mr Barrington to the station, and then on to the Foreign Office. You, sir, Dr Watson, and you, Flotsam, will then be at liberty to enjoy the rest of the ball to your hearts' content.'

'That sounds an excellent outcome, doesn't it, Flotsam?' Dr Watson chuckled. 'Should still be plenty of champagne left at that point, eh? But tell me, Inspector, what if anything goes wrong? This Weiss chappie is clearly a very clever fellow.'

'I shall have my whistle with me, Doctor. One blast will bring my men to our rescue. We can't be sure that this Mr Weiss or any of his agents will make it into Montrachute House, but even if he does, there's a limit to what one man can do. And Mr Holmes suggests you carry your service revolver with you, just in case.'

This prospect appeared to cheer Dr Watson even more than the thought of the Wymondham's champagne.

'Good thinking, Holmes! Should be able to squeeze it under the evening dress somehow.'

Sir Torpenhow cleared his throat.

'Come, I know there is still much to do. But before we part, does anyone have any suggestions about any additional steps we should be taking?'

Very timidly, I put up my hand.

'Please, sir, I wondered if I could have two more people added to the guest list. They don't have to actually attend the ball, but if there was somewhere they could lurk where they could watch the dancing, I think it might be very helpful indeed.'

Sir Torpenhow looked at me sternly.

'And these two people are…?'

'I don't know their surnames, sir, but they are called Elsie and Leonora, and they are both kitchen maids at Frog Hall.'

For a moment I thought Sir Torpenhow was going to dismiss my request out of hand. He opened his mouth to speak, closed it, opened it again, then shut his eyes and swallowed hard.

'Inspector Cavendish,' he sighed at last, 'perhaps you would be good enough to make those arrangements?'

–

After the planning, there was the packing. It had taken Mrs Hudson and I less than a quarter of an hour to pack our bags for our visit to Revennings; it seemed to take us half the day to pack enough for my one night at Montrachute House. Not only did we have to think about nightwear and underwear, but also the day clothes I would wear to arrive in, the clothes I would change into after arriving, the clothes I would wear at breakfast the following day, and the quite different clothes I would wear immediately after breakfast, to travel back to London.

'For it's no good you playing the part of a young lady to perfection,' Mrs Hudson warned me, 'if you turn up with the under-garments of a scullery maid. The servants who unpack for you will know nearly everything about you by the time your things are put away. So they are the ones you need to convince. If you can make them believe you are Dr Watson's wealthy and vivacious young niece, then the rest will be easy.'

We quickly agreed that the only practical way of assembling all the things I needed in the time available, and all of them of a sufficient quality, was to allow Miss Peters to take charge, and I honestly think the squeal of delight she let out on hearing the news was audible most of the way across Bloomsbury Square.

'Why, of course, Mrs H!' she gushed. 'It will be a pleasure. We will need to go to Harkner's, of course, to pick up one or two things, and to Stourbridge's and to Peck's, and probably also to Campbell & Cutler's, but don't worry, we'll put it all on Rupert's account, and he can settle things with Sir Totpenhow when that treaty thing of his is safe and sound.'

A thought seemed to strike her.

'Oh, my! We'll have to choose a second ball gown too, won't we? And I really have no idea which one it should be. We should probably ask Reynolds, I suppose, since he got it right last time. Yes, of course, you'll need another, Flottie, dear, because this is a weekend away and anything can go wrong. A distant cousin of mine was staying with the Mintons the night before their daughter's coming-out ball, and the maid who was hanging her ball gown thought she saw a spider in the wardrobe, and was so terrified of spiders, poor thing, that she had a terrible fit of panic and while she was panicking managed to rip my cousin's gown completely in half. And my cousin hadn't thought to take a spare, and it was impossible to repair the first one, and no one could lend her one because she's quite an unusual shape, bless her, and in the end he had to borrow something from Lady Minton's great aunt, which was black and shapeless and made her look like one of those women knitting under the guillotine.'

She paused for breath and regarded me warmly.

'Oh, Flottie, I'm *so* excited you're going to be coming too!'

So items were purchased and borrowed and folded into cases, and a second ball gown was chosen that was surprisingly becoming, although not at all like the first. And when everything was packed and I looked at the number of cases stacked in the hallway of the house in Bloomsbury Square, I felt a moment of panic and told

Miss Peters that it was absurd, and that I couldn't possibly take so much.

But instead of looking worried, she just laughed.

'Nonsense, Flottie. There is no surer way of being looked down upon at a country house party than by taking too little luggage. I've half a mind to fill three more cases with extravagantly beautiful things you'll never need, just to make a good impression. And don't, whatever you do, forget yourself and try to be tidy. If the room doesn't look like a Turkish harem by the time you've finished undressing, then you're not properly in your part. If it will help, just imagine you're me.'

Which was actually rather good advice.

After the planning and the packing came the hardest part. It was time for me to find Scraggs, to tell him that I would no longer be able to accompany him to the Survivors' Ball; and I don't think the walk to St Pancras has ever been completed more slowly or more reluctantly by anyone since the station was built.

But in the end, he made it easy for me.

I found him packing up his things by the ticket barrier to platform three, and he welcomed me with a quiet but friendly smile.

'Hot again, eh, Flot?' he began, then carried on before I had time to reply. 'I've heard on the grapevine – from someone who is stepping out with one of Sir Torpenhow Franklin's footmen, actually – that you've been ordered to attend the big bash at Montrachute tomorrow night. It's all hugely important, and Sir Torpenhow is so anxious about it that he can't hold down his breakfast, or so I'm told. So I don't suppose you'll be needing that invitation to the Survivors' Ball after all.'

'Oh, Scraggs,' I told him, finding myself reduced to the brink of tears by his kindness, 'I'm so sorry about the way things have turned out. Mr Holmes just announced I was going, and I was so pleased to be asked, and so excited by everything, that I just forgot to even think about anything else. And then it was all too late to change anything. And, of course, a little part of me *does* want to go, because such things just don't happen to people like me, so I'd be lying if I tried to pretend it was all someone else's fault…'

I tailed off, feeling more wretched than I had ever felt before.

And, of course, it was in Scraggs' power to make me feel more wretched still, but instead he just reached into his bag and pulled out one of the paper fans he was selling, and held it out to me.

'For the journey down,' he told me. 'And come on, Flot, no tears. No one in the history of the Wymondham family, which is probably about a thousand years, has *ever* turned down an invitation to their summer ball.'

The journey back from St Pancras that day took me a lot less time. I walked with a spring in my step, because Scraggs had forgiven me, and I could travel down to Montrachute House with his blessing. And all our plans were laid, and a great adventure beckoned, and I was the luckiest girl alive. Which is why I was so surprised, somewhere near Wimpole Street, to find I had to stop, and step into a doorway, and burst into tears.

After that, though, I was fine. Scraggs was more than capable of enjoying the Survivors' Ball without me, and afterwards, no doubt, we would sit around Mrs Hudson's table and compare notes. So I stepped out briskly and carried on towards home. The sky was blue, and the future beckoned.

Chapter Twenty

When I look back, after all these years, on the Saturday of the Wymondham's Ball, I am amazed to find that I remember almost nothing at all about the start of that momentous day. I must have woken and breakfasted, and presumably carried out my usual chores, and must no doubt have talked a great deal about the challenges ahead. But if so, I remember none of it. Nothing until the moment Mrs Hudson tapped my shoulder and told me it was time to dress.

Even then, although I can recall putting on the unfamiliar travel clothes selected for me – starting with underwear and petticoats so gossamer-soft I could hardly feel them – and although I can recall Mrs Hudson fussing about with powder, and pinning up my hair, my main recollection of those hours is the constant stream of interruptions. It seemed as though there was a knock on the area door every four or five minutes, and in every instance, when Mrs Hudson opened it, there would be an elderly man outside, thick-set and grey, sometimes bald, never with very much neck, and always with the same message.

'Told to tell you, ma'am, six of us from Clapham, and a dozen youngsters still serving, managed to get the time off...'

'Thought you should know, ma'am, there'll be four of us from the old Putney station, and seven or eight of the young men have taken special leave...'

'Hope it will be all right, ma'am, if all five of us what's still alive from the Battersea beat can come along...'

And in each case, Mrs Hudson would reply with almost exactly the same words.

'Thank you for telling me, Sergeant. The Flying Goblin in Charing Cross, just off Trafalgar Square, starting at seven o'clock. It has three floors and a cellar, so room for everybody.'

Then she would return to my hair, and tell me – by way of explanation – that Sergeant Minders had spent a lifetime making friends. And finally, when all was done, she stepped back, smiled a warm, tender smile, and said, 'You'll do, Flotsam. You'll certainly do. Now go out and enjoy yourself, and don't worry too much about that wretched treaty.'

'I do wish you were going to be there, ma'am! And Mr Holmes too. So much depends on everything going to plan!'

'But *you* will be there, Flotsam,' she told me sternly. 'And Dr Watson. And you'll be keeping your eyes open and your wits about you.'

She reached out and adjusted a lock of my hair.

'Yes, Flottie, you'll do very nicely.'

–

I recall very little else until I was sitting with Dr Watson in a first-class train carriage, with the train slowing to a halt at Bedworth station. That was the moment the doctor looked up from his paper, grinned at me cheerfully, and said, 'In character from now on, Flotsam. Lady Wymondham knows that I am here at the request of Sherlock Holmes, but she believes you to be nothing more than my niece. I expect she'll have sent someone to meet us at the station.'

And she certainly had. We were greeted by a liveried footman so grand that my nerve almost failed me. But thankfully I was required to say very little; Dr Watson handed me up into the carriage, a splendid and dashing open-topped four-wheeler, and was most attentive, arranging the cushions and helping me to open my parasol. I don't suppose that footman heard me say more than a dozen words, which, by chance, was precisely as it should be, for I soon learned that by saying very little and looking suitably aloof, it was extremely easy to pass for a lady of breeding.

My next test was our hostess herself. I think I had some vague idea that Dr Watson and I would arrive, and would immediately scuttle off to our rooms, like commercial travellers in cheap hotels. I hadn't anticipated Lady Wymondham in person, advancing across the most exquisite marble floor with her arms extended towards us, intent on making us both feel as welcome as any duke.

'My dear Dr Watson! It has been more than two years since our paths crossed!' She was a lady in her early seventies and round as a tennis ball, but full of vigour, and exuding a warmth that seemed touchingly genuine. 'How pleased I am that you have come. And this must be your lovely niece. We are delighted to welcome you to Montrachute, Miss Flotsam. I understand your uncle is here on some sort of secretive business, but I do hope that will not detract from your own enjoyment of the ball. Your first, I understand?'

I told her, in my best Miss Blondell voice, that it was, and that I was more excited than I could say – and I didn't feel at all guilty for deceiving her, because both things were undoubtedly true.

'Then I shall make a point of introducing you to some lovely people, so that if this old rascal deserts you in the course of his duties, you will be in perfectly safe hands. Now, you will both wish to refresh yourselves after your journey, and then you must join us in the Orangery for a glass of madeira. The Boothroyd girls are here, and so is the Marquis of Donnington, but I'm afraid we also have the Bishop of St Asaph, so you may find it hard to get a word in.'

And that was all. I had imagined being quizzed through a lorgnette by a fierce and haughty aristocrat of dragon-like demeanour, of stumbling over my answers, of forgetting my vowels, and being frog-marched from Montrachute before I had really stepped inside. But instead Dr Watson and I were being led to our rooms by footmen so respectful they barely looked at us.

'Good work, Flotsam,' Dr Watson whispered quietly, as we ascended Montrachute's magnificent rosewood stair-case. 'I'm proud to have you for a niece.'

Then, the next test. Before I knew it I was alone in a bedroom so vast and so luxurious that it could quite easily have housed a family of six – alone but for the presence of Betty, a quiet and mouse-like maid, whose job it would be to look after me, dress me and generally fuss around me for the duration of my stay. At first, more embarrassed by the situation than I could possibly describe, I simply tried not to look at her. Then, when I realised that her eyes were permanently cast down, I allowed myself a quick glimpse, and saw that she was a small woman of perhaps twenty-five or thirty, slim, and with features that might be rather lovely if they had not been so tightly drawn into an expression of bland timidity.

'Your bags will be brought up from the station any time now, miss,' she informed me. 'Is there anything I can do for you now, miss?'

I very nearly gave myself away straightaway, for I was on the very brink of replying to her in my normal voice, telling her that everything was too lovely to be true. But I caught myself just in time, and felt my spine straightening and my chin tilting upwards, as Dr Watson's rather reserved niece remembered who she was.

'Thank you, Betty,' I told her graciously. 'I am a little tired and shall lie down for a few minutes. I shall ring for you when I wish to change.'

I think I half expected her to laugh in my face, and to ask me who I thought I was, talking to an honest girl like that? But to my surprise and relief, she bobbed and turned for the door in one movement, as though she herself were grateful to have survived our initial interview without any difficulties.

'Tell me, Betty,' I asked, stopping her just before she made her escape, 'have you worked here at Montrachute for very long?'

'No, miss.' Her eyes remained firmly pointed to the floor. 'This being such a big event, miss, they needs extra staff. So I was sent by the agency, miss. I've only come up from London yesterday. Will that be all, miss?'

I told her that it would, and watched her go with a strange mixture of relief and pity and guilt. I had thought it would be fun to act a part. But it wasn't all going to be fun.

However, I can't deny that I began to enjoy myself a great deal more as the day wore on. Dr Watson and I joined Lord and Lady Wymondham in the Orangery and were introduced to the son of a duke, three beautiful young women who were all destined to marry lords, and a bishop who wanted to talk about nothing except missionary work in China. When he asked me what I knew of that country, I had the presence of mind to pretend I knew nothing, which was exactly the right thing, and clearly endeared me to the Marquis of Donnington, who drew me to one side and told me it must be great fun to have such a dashing uncle.

'I don't really think of it,' I told him carelessly. 'I know he often embarrasses Mama, who says chasing criminals all day is a little vulgar. Do you think so too?'

Even in the loftiest of circles, people are loth to judge you harshly if you ask them to talk about themselves.

'I think it's a jolly exciting thing to do. *My* uncle does nothing at all but shoot pheasant during the season, and talk about shooting pheasant out of it! I say, shall we get some more madeira?'

So things passed off more comfortably than I had ever dreamed, and I quickly discovered that the less I said, the more smoothly I was able to glide through polite society. I had dreaded dressing for the ball, but Betty, perhaps impressed by the quality and quantity of my packing, was quietly attentive, and, growing in confidence, even made suggestions about the arrangement of my hair. It being a summer ball, and in the country, we started early, while the evening was still light, so I was spared an agonising wait till ten o'clock or later; but I can't deny I was still very nervous when Dr Watson called for me to lead me to the ball. But I was excited too, and perhaps a little less nervous than I had expected to be.

Those next few minutes – the first minutes of my first ball, and one of the grandest balls of the season – should surely be printed indelibly on my memory; but again, much of it seems lost in a whirling confusion of names and greetings and more names and more greetings. I do remember the Great Hall at Montrachute, bedecked for the occasion in countless candles, already busy with people moving and mingling, even though we were two of the first to arrive. And I remember being announced, and being introduced to a former prime minister who patted my hand, and I remember receiving a great many compliments from a number of gentlemen, all of which would probably have gone to my head had I not been too anxious about my own behaviour to listen properly. In this, too, I think fortune favoured me, because in Britain nothing is a surer sign of breeding, nor a surer sign of supreme social confidence, than to absent-mindedly ignore a good-looking young man whose family members, between them, command more wealth than a small nation.

And then, just when this parade of strange new acquaintances was beginning to overwhelm me, I was swept up by Miss Peters, who appeared from nowhere in a surprisingly restrained and incredibly beautiful dress of duck-egg blue.

'Flottie,' she gasped, 'you look adorable! Truly, I didn't recognise you. Your hair! Why, you are the loveliest thing here! Come with me. Quickly! Rupert is talking to a man about crop rotation, and I want to make sure he can't find me when he's finished!'

So I allowed myself to be carried off, and to be furnished with champagne, and to listen to Miss Peters' plan to flirt with a rather dashing second lieutenant until Mr Spencer noticed, or until supper was served, whichever came first.

It may perhaps have been a full half an hour after our arrival before Dr Watson and I found ourselves alone by a potted lemon tree – a welcome chance for me to catch my breath and to remember who I was and why I was there.

'My word, Flottie,' the doctor told me, 'you are a tremendous success! You will certainly not lack for partners tonight. Where on earth did you learn to be so effortlessly aloof?'

Perhaps it was my embarrassment at his praise that reminded me of what was really important that evening.

'Sir...' I began, then corrected myself hastily. 'Uncle, we are supposed to be keeping our eyes open for suspicious characters.'

'We are, niece.' Dr Watson surveyed the bustling scene around us. 'Although that sounded a lot easier when we discussed it in Eaton Square than it does now. How the devil are we supposed to keep an eye on all this lot?'

I knew exactly what he meant, for looking at the multitude around me, it began to feel as though Mr Holmes' plan was seriously flawed.

'Perhaps Sir Torpenhow should simply have flooded the place with policemen, after all?' I wondered.

We were rescued from these doldrums by the appearance of Inspector Cavendish, looking extremely at ease, and glowing with confidence.

'Good work,' he told us crisply. 'I was watching your entrance. Perfect. Poised. Nothing to arouse any sort of suspicion. Now,' he went on, 'I think it's important that you dance as much and as often as you can, Miss Flotsam, because one of us will need to keep an eye on the ballroom. But first, there are some characters over there I would like you to talk to, to find out if they really are who they claim to be. That one with the beard looks shifty, don't you think? I'd love to know if it's real. So I shall bring my great aunt over in a moment and ask her to introduce you. She knows who everyone is, because she has the knack of listening when the names are announced and actually remembering them. It's a formidable talent.'

He was as good as his word, appearing from the melee a few minutes later with his great-aunt, Lady Bulstrode, at his side.

'Miss Flotsam, isn't it?' she asked me politely, as though my name had been familiar to her for years. 'And Dr Watson. We have all of us, of course, heard of you. Now, Oliver says you require some introductions, so follow me, please.'

She moved through the crowd with the slow certainty of a battleship leaving harbour, oblivious to the much smaller craft scattering around her, and we followed until we arrived in the presence of the bearded man Inspector Cavendish had pointed out to us, who was standing with two companions near the door to the ballroom.

'Dr Watson, Miss Flotsam, let me introduce you to Mr Shaw, who is a theatre critic, and to Mr Martin Harvey, who acts. And to Mr... er... Grahame, who I believe is a man of letters.'

'Who works in a bank,' Mr Shaw corrected her a little gruffly. 'Don't you, Grahame?'

'For my sins,' the other man confirmed with a smile. He was a tall-ish, pale gentleman with a thin moustache, while the other had striking eyes and a pleasant smile, rather hidden behind a large beard. Neither looked like my idea of a dangerous foreign agent.

'These gentlemen are friends of our hostess, who predicts great things for them,' Lady Bulstrode told me in a stage whisper, and then, with a vague smile, left Dr Watson and I with our new acquaintances.

'Lady Wymondham predicts no such thing,' Mr Martin Harvey told me with a rueful smile.

He was smaller than his two companions, with a sharp, sensitive face. All three of the gentlemen were in their late thirties or early forties, but Mr Martin Harvey was the most obviously good-looking of the three.

'Lady Wymondham only invited me because she couldn't get Henry Irving,' he went on, 'and she only invited Grahame here because we've persuaded her he has a great novel in him.'

'And Mr Shaw?' I looked across at him very solemnly. 'Why did Lady Wymondham invite him?'

'To keep this pair in order,' he replied. 'But tell us, why did she invite you, Miss Flotsam?'

'Miss Flotsam is my niece,' Dr Watson stated rather stiffly, as though that explained everything.

'And does Miss Flotsam dance?' Mr Martin Harvey asked, rather eagerly, I thought.

I did, and I was longing to, but I had more pressing things to attend to, because two small figures in the minstrels' gallery had caught my eye. Parting from the theatrical gentlemen with a graceful nod of my head, I attempted to find my way to the gallery, and might have wandered the hallways of Montrachute House for an eternity had Inspector Cavendish not come to my rescue, with Harry Barrington at his shoulder.

'The minstrels' gallery? Yes, I know the way. We can talk as we go. Barrington here has news.'

'I certainly do, Miss Flotsam. You know how we're supposed to be on the lookout for anyone who could be the Emir's secret envoy? Well, a few minutes ago I was approached by a fellow who introduced himself to me as a Monsieur Karam. He's a large, jovial fellow who told me he was from the Lebanon, and had become acquainted with Lord Wymondham at the Beirut Opera.'

I listened intently, while Inspector Cavendish led us from the Great Hall, and down a lengthy corridor lined with alabaster pillars. Monsieur Karam already sounded a great deal more promising as a spy than Mr Shaw or any of his companions.

'Well, we exchanged one or two pleasantries in the usual way,' Mr Barrington went on, 'and then the fellow leaned towards me and opened his jacket slightly, allowing me a glimpse of a scrolled document. "I believe you and I have an appointment later on," he told me in a whisper. "*À plus tard*, Mr Barrington, *à plus tard*." And the fellow gave me a little wave and sauntered off!'

Inspector Cavendish was looking delighted.

'It's excellent news, isn't it, Miss Flotsam? Knowing the identity of the Emir's envoy makes things much simpler for us. We can simply keep an eye on Monsieur Karam all evening and make sure that nothing untoward happens to him, and at midnight he'll hand it over and everything will be fine!'

'But couldn't we just ask Monsieur Karam to hand it over right now?' I asked, and I noticed Mr Barrington flushing slightly.

'That would, of course, be the most sensible course. In fact, Cavendish here suggested it too, so I went back and found Karam. But when I pointed out that it would be easier all round, he just looked a little roguish, and tapped his chest where the treaty is, and said "Emir's orders, my dear fellow. Emir's orders."'

We had reached a small room decorated with *chinoiserie* wallpaper and small tables, and Inspector Cavendish came to a halt.

'The delay is certainly frustrating, Miss Flotsam, but it is not the end of the world. I've suggested Barrington and Dr Watson take turns to stay close to the fellow. Rupert Spencer will help too, now he's here. We might even get Sir Torpenhow to take a turn. I confess that once or twice today I've felt distinctly nervous about Mr Holmes' absence, but now we've identified M Karam... Well, if we can't keep him safe here in Montrachute House, there really is no hope for us! Now, that minstrels' gallery...' And to my surprise the inspector reached out and tapped a panel, which opened as obediently and smoothly as if it had been imported straight from one of Lady Wymondham's beloved theatres. 'Up there, young lady. I don't think you'll be disturbed.'

I don't know if the minstrels' gallery above the Great Hall had ever really been used for minstrels, but it certainly wasn't being used for that, or for anything else, on this particular occasion. Its sole occupants were two young girls dressed in black, sitting right at the back so that they merged into the shadows, and appearing to me much smaller in that lofty space than they had in the kitchen at Frog Hall. But Elsie and Leonora had lost none of their high spirits.

'Flottie!' Elsie squealed when I appeared at the top of the stairs. 'This is all your doing, isn't it?'

The pair ran to embrace me.

'That nice inspector told us as much when he showed us up here. And you can imagine the look on Miss Perch's face when the message came that we were wanted at the Wymondham's Ball. She was so surprised, her eyes bulged out!'

'She looked like a trout, not a perch,' Leonora added.

'Or like one of those salmon that Old Froggatt used to roast whole.'

'Or like the stuffed moose on the wall in the library.'

The pair of them laughed, then suddenly, at exactly the same moment, opened their mouths in horror and turned back to face the gathering below.

'We promised the inspector we wouldn't take our eyes off things for one moment,' Elsie told me. 'And we haven't, have we, Lee?'

'Except just now.'

'And when the inspector came up.'

'And for calls of nature. The inspector says calls of nature are all right, so long as they aren't at the same time, or for too long.'

'Leonora can take a very long time,' Elsie added.

'But Elsie makes worse smells.'

303

'And have you yet seen anyone who resembles Mlle Le Blanc?' I asked, bringing them back to the matter in hand.

'Not yet,' Elsie confessed sadly. 'But we will.'

'If she's here, we will,' Leonora confirmed.

'We look at every lady as she's announced, you see, and when no one's being announced we watch all the people milling around and talking.'

'Of course, we can't see the dancing from here. I'm sure the inspector would want us to take a look at the dancing later, wouldn't he?'

Their disappointment when I told them to stick to their orders was very great, but quickly forgotten as a number of new arrivals appeared and waited to be announced. As I left the gallery, they were still chattering away.

'That's not her.'

'*That's* not her.'

'That's not her.'

'That one looks like a pig in a big, pink sack.'

'That one looks like a pig that's just come out of the oven…'

Down in the Great Hall, I found Dr Watson waiting for me, and mopping his brow while he waited, because even in the Great Hall, the heat was mounting.

'Ah, Flottie! Just the person. I'm supposed to be keeping an eye on this Karam fellow, and he's taken it into his head to dance. Would you join me in a waltz?'

And so we danced, in the famous ballroom with one whole wall open to the gardens, so that it did indeed feel as though you were dancing in a forest. It was already dusk, and as we danced the lanterns were being lit in the trees, lit by invisible hands so that it appeared they were spontaneously sparking into life. My first dance at my first ball, safe in Dr Watson's steady hold, and nothing could have been more wonderful! Dr Watson had steered us into the vicinity of Monsieur Karam, who was waltzing with a plump lady in her fifties, but I was barely aware of the other dancers. The ballroom swirled around me, and for a full five minutes I thought of nothing else.

And after that there were more dances – waltzes, polkas, mazurkas – with any number of different partners. I danced with young men whose names I couldn't remember, and older men who couldn't remember mine. One young man, who claimed to be the nephew of a lord, danced with me twice and was seeking a third when Rupert Spencer, slightly disapprovingly, took me to the floor himself. I danced with Inspector Cavendish, who waltzed divinely, and Mr Martin Harvey, the actor, who told me he had recently had a bit of luck and that after tonight he was sure his life would keep on getting better and better. I think I danced with the Bishop of St Asaph, because I remember talking a lot about China, but sometimes I wonder if I just imagined that bit.

Through it all, I tried to keep an eye on Monsieur Karam, who appeared to be enjoying himself immensely. So immensely, in fact, that he was not an easy person to follow – dashing from the ballroom to the Great Hall, then into the gardens, and when supper was served, always teetering on the edge of the supper room, undecided about when to go in. That's why, when Sir Torpenhow Franklin made his first appearance of the evening, looking gaunt and weary, and something of a ghost at the feast, none of us was entirely sure of Monsieur Karam's whereabouts. It was not until Miss Peters spotted him in the rose garden – with a giggling lady of sixty-five – that we were all able to relax.

I made a point, throughout the evening, of visiting Elsie and Leonora in the minstrels' gallery, only to be told that none of the guests even vaguely resembled the French cook from Frog Hall. By ten o'clock it was clear that their enthusiasm for the task was greatly diminished, but they stuck with it, making up for their disappointment with observations that became ruder with every moment that passed.

'That lady looks like a tangerine balancing on a water melon.'

'And her friend looks like a grapefruit.'

'I bet you anything they chose their dresses over a bowl of fruit salad...'

For me, their disappointment was enormously cheering. If Mlle Le Blanc was present at the ball that evening, I would want to know about it; but I was much happier finding she was absent.

At a little after ten, when Inspector Cavendish, Mr Barrington and I were comparing notes under the lemon tree, I was startled to see a familiar face bustling towards us, beaming delightedly: Miss Blondell of Revennings, resplendent in a scarlet ballgown, her arms wide open as though intending to embrace us all. Such had been my excitement over the last few days, I had completely forgotten that Miss Blondell was planning to be present at the Wymondham's Ball; and watching her approach us, I braced myself for uncomfortable explanations.

But it was Mr Barrington she had noticed, not me, and she greeted him with a cheery cry.

'Harry! I have such wonderful news!'

She paused while Mr Barrington introduced us, but the name 'Miss Flotsam' appeared to jog no memories, and I don't think she really noticed me at all.

'It's Prof,' she told him eagerly when the formalities were complete. 'He's back! He's been away in some godforsaken part of Asia and hasn't been terribly well, but he's back at Revennings now, and I can't tell you how much jollier the place is since his return! I tried to persuade him to come tonight, because he loves a dance, but he says he isn't up to it. I left him sitting under the mulberry tree, and I can't tell you how wonderful it feels to see him there again!'

'My word, Miss Flotsam,' Inspector Cavendish declared as we watched her walk away, 'she sounds exactly like you do!'

'She seems very pleased to see the professor,' Mr Barrington commented. 'She's clearly very fond of him.'

'More than that,' I told him, understanding it for the first time. 'I rather think she intends to marry him.'

Before I'd even worked out what I thought of that, the three of us were then joined by Dr Watson, and shortly afterwards by Sir Torpenhow himself, who had been taking his turn at observing Monsieur Karam.

'The man has gone to relieve himself again,' he explained. 'I must say, I don't envy him his bladder! But I can't follow him there a second time, can I? He'll get the wrong idea. Anyway, I don't think he's in any danger. I'm beginning to think there isn't anyone here who's a real threat to us.'

'Please may I introduce myself, gentlemen?'

It was a pleasant voice, and a strangely familiar one, but at first the speaker was hidden from me. Then he stepped forward, his hand held out towards Sir Torpenhow, and I recognised him at once. He looked very different in evening dress, and the surroundings could not have been more dissimilar, but there was no mistaking the man who, only a few days earlier, had introduced himself to me as Egbert Alba.

'My name is Andrew White,' he went on, as calm and as debonair as though he were addressing a casual acquaintance in the park one Sunday, 'although some of you may know me as Andreas Weiss. I answer to either name, and to various others, so you may take your pick. And I thought I would introduce myself now, early in the evening, so there need be no unpleasantness later.'

I saw Dr Watson's eyes open wide, and Mr Barrington's blink rapidly, while Inspector Cavendish's jaw actually dropped open, in the way you read about in novels but never actually see. But it was Sir Torpenhow Franklin who reacted first.

'My God, sir!' he spluttered, outraged, pulling his hand away from the newcomer's. 'How dare you intrude here so brazenly! I shall have you thrown out. I shall have you horsewhipped for your impudence! In fact, I shall have you arrested! Inspector, we all know why this man is here. He is an enemy of our country, and a traitor to it. Inspector, do your duty!'

But before the inspector could do anything at all, Mr White smiled patiently and held has hands out, as though inviting handcuffs.

'Please, inspector, do what you must. To arrest me now will cause a scene, of course – I'll make sure of that – and I don't imagine that the Emir's envoy will be impressed by a scuffle here, in the Great Hall of Montrachute House, on the very night he is supposed to hand over the treaty. What would that tell him about the control you exercise over events? But, please, go ahead. Before you do though, I will be interested to hear the charge against me.'

'Why, trespass to start with!' Sir Torpenhow declared. 'How dare you set foot in this building?'

Mr White lowered his arms, then reached for a glass of champagne from a tray carried by a passing footman.

'I hate to disappoint you, Sir Torpenhow – it *is* Sir Torpenhow, isn't it? – well, I hate to disappoint you, sir, but I was invited by Lord Wymondham himself. Late in the day, I grant you, because I only met his lordship a week ago, at an event to raise funds for retired tenors. But if you check the list at the door, you will find my name is on it.'

'I don't give a hoot where your name is, sir!' Sir Torpenhow exploded. 'Inspector, this man is a traitor. The charge is treason, which is a capital offence. Make your arrest.'

I sensed Inspector Cavendish's hesitation. Clearly he, like me, had realised that Mr White would not have launched such an astonishing, head-on challenge to his enemies if it were so easy to have him locked up. And, perhaps sensing the inspector's doubts, the newcomer smiled at him.

'Not guilty, sir. I'm a citizen of more than one country, but not of this one, so no charge of treason can be levelled against me. I am no more a traitor to this country than you are to mine.'

His eye moved around the circle of his adversaries, and fell for the first time on me. And that, at least, surprised him, because I saw him struggling to place me.

'I don't believe I have been introduced to this young lady,' he told Sir Torpenhow. 'I know that Dr Watson here is accompanied by his niece, but this lady is surely far too good-looking to be any blood relation of his, and, besides, I'm sure I've seen her before somewhere.'

'Never mind who she is, damn you! Inspector, I'm asking you for one last time to do your duty.'

'I fear, sir,' Mr Barrington intervened, very calmly, 'that the inspector would be unwise to attempt an arrest unless there is a reason to suspect this gentleman of a crime. As he points out, it is not in our interests to create a scene. So unless anyone knows of any actual crime he has committed...'

'But the train, sir!' So angry was Sir Torpenhow, that he was struggling to find words to express his outrage. 'All that nonsense in the Carpathians! The kidnapping of Professor Broadmarsh! The whole Samarkand Conspiracy!'

But Inspector Cavendish was shaking his head.

'I cannot arrest this man for a crime committed in Rumania, sir, however devious or unsavoury. And in this country...'

'What about attempted murder?'

They were the first words I'd spoken, and Mr White looked across at me sharply.

'Murder?' he asked, unruffled. 'What an imagination the child has! Really, Dr Watson, you should not allow her to stay up so late.'

'The attempted murder of Mr Sherlock Holmes in Eaton Square on the twenty-fifth of this month,' I continued.

Inspector Cavendish looked from me to Sir Torpenhow, then back to Mr White. I could see this new suggestion interested him. But Mr White himself looked supremely untroubled.

'Yes, I heard about that. The appalling violence one encounters on the streets of London nowadays is a national disgrace. It was the work of a lunatic, or so I'm told. In fact, a little bird informs me that is what you yourself have been telling people, Sir Torpenhow.'

Sir Torpenhow hesitated, wrong-footed, and the moment was lost. Inspector Cavendish stepped back.

'As I say, until I have reasonable suspicion to make an arrest, then we must hold our fire. What I would like to know,' he went on, keeping his eyes fixed very firmly on Mr White, 'is why this gentleman has revealed himself to us in this way. If I may say so, it makes me anxious.'

'On the contrary, Inspector,' Mr White assured him. 'I have made myself known to you now because I like to be generous in defeat. I admit I had hopes of snatching that treaty from under your nose. I had even identified Monsieur Karam as its bearer. But on arriving here, it quickly became evident that I am outgunned and out-manoeuvred. I have no intention of attempting some undignified snatch at the thing, like an urchin stealing apples from a barrow. So I offer you my compliments, gentlemen, and promise you a better contest next time. And now, if you will allow me, I intend to enjoy the rest of the evening. I have nothing but contempt for the British aristocracy, but I have no objection to drinking their champagne.'

There was a brief silence as we watched him go, then I heard a growl from deep in Sir Torpenhow's throat.

'Inspector Cavendish, do not let that man out of your sight until the danger is over. And, the rest of you, do the same. I don't like the cut of his jib.'

Chapter Twenty-One

'So let me get this clear, Flottie…'

Miss Peters was wrinkling her nose in a rather endearing fashion, as she studied the scene below her from the darkness of the minstrels' gallery. I had sought refuge there after my encounter with Mr White, and Hetty had followed me, and had so overawed Elsie and Leonora that they had fallen totally silent in her presence.

'So let me get this clear,' she said again. 'That rather handsome man down there is a foreign spy, and admits he is a foreign spy, and has come to steal the treaty that everyone is so desperate to get hold of, but no one can do anything about it because he hasn't actually done anything wrong yet?' She gave an exasperated sigh. 'That's so very *British*, isn't it, Flottie? We must have fair play, mustn't we, even if it's a totally stupid thing to do?'

I agreed that was the case, and reminded her that any sort of unpleasantness in front of the Emir's envoy might ruin everything.

'But it's still totally stupid, isn't it, Flot? All those gentlemen down there, allowing him to walk around as though nothing is the matter, just because the rules say they should. I think it would be a great deal more sensible to *do* something.'

I began to explain again why Mr White hadn't been arrested, but Miss Peters interrupted me.

'I didn't say anyone should *arrest* him, Flottie, darling. I just don't think it's a very clever plan to have half a dozen people watching him eat canapés all evening. I'm sure I can come up with a far better idea.'

Slightly worried by this suggestion, I pointed to where Monsieur Karam was helping a dowager duchess to fan herself.

'Mr White can't do anything so long as that man's safe,' I told her, but Miss Peters was looking at a different part of the Great Hall.

'Down there, Flottie, do you see? That man is looking at you. The one with the beard. Now he's waving. I think you have an admirer.'

'His name is Mr Shaw,' I told her. 'He's a theatre critic.'

Hetty looked disappointed.

'And theatre critics don't really admire anything. But all the same, you'd better go down and see what he wants.'

It took me two or three minutes to make my way from the gallery to the far end of the Great Hall, where the three theatrical gentlemen had taken up position. From where they stood, they could watch the dancing in the ballroom without committing themselves to taking part.

As I approached, Mr Martin Harvey was speaking, and making dramatic gestures with his arms.

'Petrushka's, I say, and damn the expense! We'll go there tomorrow and I'll buy champagne. No, don't laugh, Grahame, I really will. I'm doing a bit of work for a man, and it's incredibly well paid. Money for nothing, really. You must come too, Miss Flotsam,' he concluded, seeing me approach.

'Not if you wish to preserve the tiniest morsel of reputation,' Mr Shaw warned me. 'We noticed you up in the gallery, Miss Flotsam, and Martin Harvey here says he wants to ask you something.'

The actor flushed a little, and so did I. He'd been extremely free with his compliments when we danced, and I was a little concerned by what might follow. Happily, it was not what I thought.

'Couldn't help but notice you were a friend of that fellow over there,' he said, pointing, 'and I wondered if that was Harry Barrington?'

With the barest nod of my head, I confirmed it was, and then waited for him to explain his question.

'It's just that his wife was once pointed out to me, and I was struck by what a remarkably graceful lady she was.' He blushed a little more.

'My friend is an admirer of beauty in all its forms,' Mr Shaw explained. 'That is why he lives in such an ugly flat. To be surrounded by beauty every day would be a terrible punishment for one so sensitive, wouldn't it, John?'

His friend ignored him.

'You are well acquainted with the Barringtons?' he asked me, still watching Mr Barrington very keenly.

'I was a guest at Frog Hall only the other day,' I replied truthfully.

'Frog Hall?' Mr Grahame interrupted with a smile. 'What an excellent name! Did you come across any amphibians during your stay?'

'Sadly not.' I smiled back. 'Although I'm told they once employed a cook called Froggatt.'

All three smiled at that, then Mr Shaw indicated the dance floor.

'Now, come, Miss Flotsam, would you do me the honour?'

I confess I found Mr Shaw a little more intimidating than his friends, but I agreed to dance anyway, because being asked was still a novelty, and because I felt sure he had not yet danced at all.

'John Martin Harvey is a charming and harmless fellow,' he advised me, as we set off around the floor, 'but you mustn't take his flirting too seriously. He flirts with everyone.'

'Is he a very good actor?' I asked.

'No idea. His roles are too tiny. But there's a rumour Henry Irving might be giving him a decent part in his next production, and if true, I shall give him rave reviews.'

'Because he's a friend of yours, Mr Shaw?'

From the proximity of a waltz, I could be certain beyond doubt that the beard which had worried Mr Cavendish was a real one.

'Perhaps. But I always try to be kind to actors who are making their way. It is the playwrights who should live in fear of me.'

I raised a stately eyebrow.

'Perhaps you have ambitions in that area yourself?'

He looked at me sharply.

'I have written plays, Miss Flotsam. I have written many plays. Once I even had a great success in London. Perhaps you saw it? It was about a soldier who prefers chocolate to fighting.'

'I fear not.'

'Well,' he shrugged, as the waltz drew to a close, 'perhaps one day I shall have another success here, and you can come to that one.'

316

He gave me his arm to escort me from the floor, but before we had rejoined his companions, we were intercepted by none other than Mr Andrew White himself, whose face was lit up by a rather smug smile.

'Ah! Miss Flotsam, is it not? The loving niece of Dr Watson of Baker Street. It has taken me all this time, but now I remember where we have met before!'

I felt a terrible hollow feeling begin to open up inside me, but before I could reply Mr Shaw spoke, his expression very grave.

'You are acquainted with this gentleman, Miss Flotsam?' he asked quietly.

'She is indeed, sir! She answered the door to me only the other day! What if I were to tell you, sir, that you have been gulled by a very tasteless practical joke? That this woman is not Dr Watson's niece, she is Sherlock Holmes' housemaid!'

'Then I would say, sir,' Mr Shaw told him firmly, 'that Mr Holmes is extremely fortunate in his housemaids.'

But Mr White ignored him, turning to me instead.

'I really must congratulate you, young lady. I know a little about imposture, and your performance tonight is magnificent. I was taken in completely. Presumably you are here on a whim of the great detective. But Mr Holmes' fortunes must have sunk very low if he depends upon his parlour maid to do his business for him!'

I watched him walk away, filled with horror and shame and despair, my whole, perfect evening turning to ashes. Everything had seemed to be going so well that I'd begun to forget what I was. And now I had been firmly, horribly reminded. I was not a young lady, not a guest of Lady Wymondham, not anyone's niece. I was what Mr White had just called me – an impostor. And, until that moment, a shameless one. I felt my eyes begin to fill with tears.

'Steady.' Mr Shaw's voice was very low. 'We'd better dance this one.'

And he pulled me back to the dance floor, the most private place in the whole of the ball, a place where I could close my eyes and dance, and say nothing to anyone, and have no one interrupt. A second dance followed that one, and it was only during the third that the playwright spoke to me.

'If that oily and unpleasant individual speaks the truth, Miss Flotsam, how on earth did you learn to dance so well?'

The tears were under control by then, but I replied in a very small voice.

'Servants dance too, you know. Would you be surprised if I told you that most of them can dance better than their betters?'

'Not in the least. Dancing, I've often said, is only a vertical expression of... Well, never you mind, young lady. Tell me, did you have to study very hard for the part? To learn to annunciate so beautifully, for instance?'

'Study? No, not at all. Only to listen, and to watch, too, I suppose. You see, I hear so many different voices, working where I do. It would be different if I were a flower girl or something like that. "Listen and observe," I suppose Mr Holmes would say. He had a wager with Sir Torpenhow Franklin that no one would guess the truth.'

'And no one has.' We danced in silence for a moment longer before he spoke again. 'Tell me, Miss Flotsam, that gentleman up there in the gallery, is it you he's waving at?'

And of course it was, so when the music ended I excused myself from my kind playwright friend in a far better state than I deserved, and hurried to join Inspector Cavendish.

I found him at the back of the minstrels' gallery, having apparently dismissed Elsie and Leonora from their posts so he could convene an emergency meeting. With him were Sir Torpenhow Franklin, Dr Watson, Rupert Spencer and a very flustered looking Harry Barrington, who was pacing nervously and running his hand through his hair. When I appeared at the top of the stairs, he turned to me eagerly.

'Miss Flotsam, I don't suppose you have noticed Mr White anywhere in the last ten minutes have you? The truth is, I've lost him!'

'Calm yourself, Mr Barrington.' Inspector Cavendish's voice was soothing, but I could see the tension in his face. Around him, Sir Torpenhow was clearly seething, Dr Watson was biting his upper lip and shaking his head, and Mr Spencer was looking out over the crowds below. His expression, I thought, was extremely troubled.

'Calm yourself,' the inspector repeated. 'We have made only a cursory search so far. We will spread out now in a more systematic way, and if needs be, I will get my officers to search the grounds.'

'Barrington here says the chap was talking to you in the ballroom, Flotsam,' Dr Watson explained. 'Don't suppose you saw where he went afterwards? Barrington lost him in the crowds after that.'

'No, sir. He came to tell me that he recognised me from our meeting in Baker Street, and he was a bit horrible about it. That was three dances ago, and I haven't seen him since. Perhaps…'

But I was interrupted by a familiar voice.

'Oh, *really*! You lot should be *so* ashamed of yourselves! There is a simply *lovely* ball going on down there, and instead of enjoying it, you are all sitting up here in the dark, pulling faces at one another. Is it that horrible Mr White you're looking for?'

None of us had heard Miss Peters come up the gallery steps, and now she was standing in the doorway, looking rather pleased with herself.

'Because if you are, you're never going to find him.'

'We're not?' Sir Torpenhow was clearly angered by the interruption. 'Why not? Where's he gone?'

But before Miss Peters could answer, I heard Mr Spencer give a low, agonised groan.

'Oh, no! Hetty, please, tell us exactly what you've done.'

With every eye on her, Miss Peters took her time, lowering herself onto one of the gallery benches with a look of beatific calm.

'Well, Flottie told me that you were all trying to keep watch on him, because you don't want him to steal your treaty thing. And that seemed to me like the most terrible waste of everyone's time when you could all be dancing, so I did the sensible thing. I can't imagine why none of you had done it already.'

Mr Spencer closed his eyes.

'What did you *do*, Hetty?'

'I locked Mr White in the Music Room,' she told us calmly. 'It's quite secure, with no other doors, and no windows or anything, just some terribly ancient musical instruments. And the key was in the door, and the lock is old-fashioned but terribly solid, so I thought it would be the perfect place. And so I went to find Mr White, who was walking away from Flottie with a contemptible little smile on his face, and I asked him if he knew Mr Barrington, and if so, had he seen him, because he was needed urgently. And Mr White looked quite interested by that, so I told him a gentleman had been taken ill in the music room, and was saying that he had something incredibly urgent he had to give to Mr Barrington, and the servants didn't know who Mr Barrington was, but I did, so I'd offered to go and find him. And Mr White smiled an even more horrible smile and said he'd come at once, to see if he could be of assistance.'

Hetty paused for breath and fanned herself for a moment.

'And, of course, the next bit was terribly easy, because he followed me into the Music Room, and it was obviously empty, and I said the man had been lying behind the piano, and when Mr White walked over to the piano to look, I slipped out behind him and locked him in. I have the key here, if you'd like it.'

There followed a remarkable silence, while the gentlemen exchanged glances but said nothing. Finally, Inspector Cavendish cleared his throat.

'Well, I have to say, gentlemen, this strikes me as a very sensible course of action.' He nodded his head. 'Yes, very sensible indeed. We'll have to let him out again, of course, when we have the treaty. And we'll apologise profusely for such an unfortunate accident. But until then, well… I think this young lady should be congratulated.'

'But, Hetty,' Mr Spencer asked, 'are you *sure* there's no other way out?'

Miss Peters looked at him and narrowed her eyes.

'Well, really, Rupert, I may not be a scientist like you, but I think I'm able to count the number of doors in a room. But perhaps you would like me to let Mr White out so you can check for yourself?'

'I should like to see this room,' Sir Torpenhow declared. 'From the outside, naturally. Inspector, I don't doubt this young lady's account for an instant, but there must be someone in Montrachute House who can confirm that this room is indeed secure?'

And so Inspector Cavendish scuttled off in one direction while the rest of us followed meekly behind Miss Peters while she led us to the Music Room, which turned out to be a long way from the part of the house where the guests were gathered. So far away, in fact, that we could hardly hear the orchestra. But as Hetty led us towards an enormously solid-looking door, we became aware of strains of music emanating from the other side of it. Mr White, it appeared, was occupying himself during his captivity by playing the oboe.

Of course, once we'd all looked at the door and seen how solid it was, there wasn't very much else we could do, so we stood around looking foolish and listening to the oboe music until Inspector Cavendish returned with two uniformed constables.

'It's all right,' he told us. 'The butler is certain that there is no way out of the Music Room except through this door. Not even any hidden panels or anything. And Miss Peters' key is the only one. There is a chimney, but rather worryingly the butler remembers the days they used to send small boys up there, and apparently the Music Room flue is unusually narrow.'

He turned to the two constables, who were quite young men with eager, intelligent faces.

'Now, you two, I want you to put your backs to this door and let absolutely no one in or out until I say. And when I do say, I will tell you in person, with at least one of these gentlemen present to confirm that I really mean it. And don't leave your posts for anything. Not for food, fire or flood. I don't care if the Prince of Wales comes down here and begs you on your knees, your backs stay against this door!'

And with that he led us away, all of us convinced that the room was sealed beyond any doubt, and that there was no way Mr White would leave it before midnight unless he could walk through walls.

Later, though, we were to change our minds.

-

Time passed surprisingly quickly at the Wymondham's Ball. With Mr White incarcerated and Monsieur Karam under close surveillance, even Sir Torpenhow appeared to relax a little. The orchestra continued to play, supper continued to be served, and the champagne never stopped flowing. Miss Peters danced with Mr Spencer, Dr Watson danced with Miss Blondell and I danced five times with the Marquis of Donnington, until Miss Peters intervened and told me that any more waltzes with him would begin to raise eyebrows.

On three occasions I accompanied Inspector Cavendish to the Music Room, to reassure myself that everything was still in order. And on each occasion, the response from the two constables was the same.

'Nothing to report, sir. The gentleman's made no attempt to get out. Hasn't stopped playing that infernal instrument in all the time you've been away.'

On the third occasion, the inspector and I continued on to the library, which was on the same side of the house as the Music Room, and was therefore reassuringly free of wayward ball-goers. Not only was it unoccupied when we arrived, but it had that sort of deep-settled hush which suggests that no one had been there for the whole of the evening.

'This handover business isn't going to be interrupted, at least,' the inspector concluded happily. He checked his watch, and announced that it was already twenty minutes past eleven. 'Time for us to get ready, Miss Flotsam. We should find Harry Barrington and get him down soon. There's no harm in him being early, is there?' He stopped and listened. 'My word, though, that's a bit eerie, isn't it?'

I realised he was referring to the sound of Mr White's oboe, still drifting through this side of the house, like a constant and mournful complaint.

But we didn't return directly to the ballroom. Instead Inspector Cavendish led me outside, into the balmy night air, and introduced me to the group of uniformed police officers gathered in the stable block, waiting to be called into action.

'This is Miss Flotsam, boys. Follow my orders at all times, but if Miss Flotsam tells you to do something, do it. And listen for the whistle. As soon as we need you, I'll give a long blast, then you lot get yourselves out of here at top speed and find where it's coming from.'

'They're a good bunch,' he assured me, as we returned to the house. 'Quick witted, fast and fit. Picked 'em myself. Don't want a repeat of that fiasco in the park, when the plodders let some young girl slip through their fingers.'

We made our way back to the open windows of the ballroom across a soft and velvety lawn, with the woodland lanterns dancing in the trees behind us, and I thought to myself as we stepped inside how beautiful it all was, how ordered and reassuring and safe.

It was then that we heard the cries.

If we had been on the dance floor or at the other end of the ballroom, we may not have heard them at all, because the efforts of the orchestra in a lively mazurka might well have drowned them out. But where we stood, near a door that led away from the Great Hall, towards the library and the Music Room, those cries crashed upon our ears like raw murder.

'Help me! Help me!' A man's voice cried. '*Au secours! Aidez moi!* Stop! Stop, thief! Stop!'

Inspector Cavendish and I moved almost as one, swerving past a cluster of startled guests, through the door, and out into one of Montrachute's long corridors, where we were able to pick up speed. At one point, though, the acoustics of the corridor confused us, and coming to its end we were uncertain which way to turn. By then, the cries were less loud and less frequent, but in unison we made the same decision, turning left and running on. By now we could hear other voices ahead of us, anguished and excited, and I was surprised when the inspector held out his hand to stop me.

'Listen, Flotsam!' he ordered, and at first I thought him completely mad, because all I could hear was my own breathing and those other voices, and still one or two weakening cries for help. But then I realised what he had noticed, and I noticed it too – more worrying and more sinister than all those other sounds combined. For the first time since it had begun over an hour before, the oboe had ceased to play.

The next thing I knew, we were running again, turning a corner into a place where the corridor ended in a long, wide open window. Underneath it lay the fallen figure of Monsieur Karam, one hand to his head, and I knew for certain it was his cries that we had heard. But we weren't the first to reach him; Rupert Spencer was kneeling over the prone figure with Dr Watson beside him, and Harry Barrington was gazing intently out of the open window.

'He assaulted me! He hit me!' Monsieur Karam gasped 'Robbed me of a precious document! A document belonging to the Emir of Bokara!'

'Calm yourself, sir!' Dr Watson exhorted, attempting to examine the fallen man's head, while at the same time Mr Spencer was demanding: 'Who, sir? Who hit you?'

'A gentleman. A gentleman in evening dress. He struck me with his oboe!'

'And where did he go, sir?' Mr Spencer almost begged. 'Which way?'

'I warned him! I told him, "you will not get away with this!" But he just laughed as he picked my pocket, and said that he had horses waiting for him near the village, and a boat waiting in the channel. He said he would be in France in time for breakfast!'

He was cut short by an urgent cry from Mr Barrington, who was still peering from the window.

'I think I see something! Out there on the ridge. Let's go!'

And with that, the night dissolved into a confusion of chasing. Mr Barrington was first out of the window, but Mr Spencer was quickly after him. Inspector Cavendish waited in the window long enough to blow one long blast on his whistle, then he too was gone, with me in his wake, leaving only Dr Watson to stay with the patient.

We ran, that night, with the fury of the possessed, and with the frantic energy of people who had spent many hours waiting for something to happen. Mr Barrington was our leader, but the rest of us followed close behind, and when the officers in the stable block responded to their inspector's whistle, we formed a chasing pack that was formidable in both speed and in numbers. To keep up, I had to kick off Miss Peters' lovely little ball shoes, and even then the complications of my ball gown made it hard to stay with them.

The path we followed, which wound up a low ridge towards a line of trees, lay white in the moonlight, and was easy to make out. Only when we reached the top did we hesitate, scanning the landscape below us for signs of a fugitive. But Inspector Cavendish seemed to know no doubts.

'We must split up!' he told us. 'From here, there are two ways out of the park, and either would take him to the village. Barrington, you go left, I'll take the right.'

A moment of confusion ensued as the pack divided into two parts and then they were off again, running, it seemed to me, very much faster than those officers I'd eluded in Kensington Gardens.

And it was then, as I watched all those athletic young men taking off in pursuit of their unseen quarry, that the thought struck me – an image of Mrs Hudson on the banks of the Serpentine, calmly explaining my part in her plan. 'How fast can you run?' she had asked.

'Flottie? Are you coming?' Mr Spencer turned to call out to me, and I tried my best to stop him.

'He's not there, sir! We've got to get back!' But it was too late. My voice was lost beneath the noise of the chasers. 'Stop! Come back, sir! Inspector! Come back!'

But no one stopped. No one even paused to listen. So I took a very deep breath, turned, and ran back to the house alone, as swiftly as my lungs would allow.

As I reached the lawn that led up to the glowing ballroom, it seemed astonishing to me that the festivities were continuing exactly as before, with all but a tiny handful of ball-goers completely oblivious of the drama taking place around them; and suddenly I was aware of my own, changed appearance – barefoot and panting, with my skirts dust-streaked from the chase.

Luckily, I could remember the location of the large window from which the chase had started, and I ran to it, expecting to find Dr Watson still tending the fallen Monsieur Karam. But both men had disappeared, so I rushed on past the spot, past a startled-looking footman, to the door of the Music Room, where the two young officers were still on guard.

'Mr White!' I cried. 'He's still in there, isn't he?'

'Why, yes, miss,' they reassured me.

'Please, open the door! I just need to see for myself.'

The two men exchanged glances.

'With respect, miss, the inspector said...'

'Open this door right now.'

I didn't shout it. I didn't even raise my voice. But I must have said it with such ominous, icy authority that, after another hasty exchange of glances, the taller man turned the key.

Inside the Music Room, Mr White was sitting at the piano, the oboe resting beside him. He remained immaculate in his evening dress, unflustered, poised and clearly very amused.

'Why, it's the housemaid! And what a state you're in! Breeding will out, I suppose. What have you been up to? Chasing the will o' the wisp?'

And he was right, of course. We had fallen for the simplest trick.

Mr White, meanwhile, was rising from his seat and stretching.

'I'm pleased to see you, though,' he went on. 'You and your uniformed friends form a very welcome rescue party. A rather pretty young lady inadvertently locked me in here some time ago, but now, with your permission, I would like to get back to the party.'

My mind raced. I think I hated the man then, in that moment – hated his cleverness and his condescension and his utter self-confidence; and I knew I would hate myself, too, forever, if I let him leave that room.

'Officer,' I ordered, 'arrest this man.'

Mr White rolled his eyes in an exaggerated way.

'Oh, really, child! I've been through all this with your betters. There is absolutely no charge you can bring against me. Not unless you believe playing the oboe in a locked room is now a criminal offence?'

But something had stirred in my memory, something Mr Rumbelow had said once when we were gathered in his office. It seemed so long ago now, and I'd thought it funny at the time. But now, suddenly, it stood crystal clear before me.

'It was you who arranged all those tricks to deprive the Vicar of Pinfold of his spectacles,' I told him firmly.

And he smiled at that, clearly amused at the recollection.

'Yes, I rather enjoyed all that. Very neatly done, you have to admit. And what fantastic serendipity to discover the dead man had a twin brother! But if you think you are going to lock me up on for stealing a pair of spectacles, you can think again.'

He turned to the policemen who stood behind me.

'Officers, this excitable child is referring to a little entertainment of mine which may, I admit, have caused a certain gentleman a little inconvenience, and made it a bit more difficult for him to conduct his Sunday service. But even my comely accuser will have to confirm that absolutely no theft was involved. I may have arranged for certain pairs of glasses to be temporarily relocated, but all have now been returned to their rightful owner. Is that not the case, Flotsam?'

'Officer,' I said as calmly and with as much authority as I could muster, 'arrest this man at once. By his own confession he is guilty of an offence under the Offences Against the Person Act of 1861, Section 36, obstructing a clergyman in the performance of his duties.'

Then, while a look of utter astonishment spread across Mr White's hateful features, I turned to the hesitating police officers and, for the first time that evening, abandoned my Miss Blondell voice.

'Come on,' I urged them, sounding like a scullery maid, 'put the handcuffs on him and let's wipe the smile off his face. Even without the blackmail or any of the rest of it, any decent judge will give him a couple of years.'

Mr White was too stunned even to struggle while the arrest was made, but I didn't have time to gloat. As I turned to leave the Music Room, the clocks of Montrachute House were striking midnight, and I was off, running again, as fast as I could, towards the library.

With the ball still in full swing at the front of the house, the corridors to the rear were empty, or should have been, but as I turned the first corner, I ran slap into Dr Watson, hard enough to bounce back off his shirt front.

'Ah, Flotsam!' he declared, looking extremely pleased to see me. 'Where is everyone? Did Cavendish catch that White fellow?'

'No, sir,' I explained, grabbing his arm so that he fell into step beside me. 'But I did. Has Monseiur Karam disappeared, sir?'

'Well, that's most extraordinary! He has, Flotsam. Stepped out for a breath of air and vanished into the night. How did you know?'

'Because Monseiur Karam is not the Emir's envoy, sir. He just made us think he was. He's working for Mr White, you see. They convinced us Monsieur Karam had the treaty, knowing that we wouldn't be looking for it anywhere else. And the attack on Monsieur Karam didn't happen, sir. They simply staged an attack a little before midnight, to draw us all away from library.'

'But Mr White hit the fellow with his oboe, Flotsam!'

'Monsieur Karam *said* he did. But Mr White hadn't actually escaped from the Music Room, sir. Monsieur Karam added the bit about the oboe to make it more convincing.'

I tried not to sound too approving, but in truth I couldn't help but applaud. Not only had the man posing as Monsieur Karam managed to work out the whereabouts of his employer, but when the oboe music stopped, he had taken his cue with exquisite timing. I couldn't help but admire the artistry in his villainy.

'So Barrington and the rest are off chasing shadows! Goodness, Flotsam, we'd better get to the library. It's just gone midnight.'

And we would have got there more quickly had we not come face to face with Mr Shaw and Mr Grahame as we rounded the next corner.

'Miss Flotsam? You haven't seen Martin Harvey have you?' the playwright asked as we approached him at speed. 'We've lost him, you see. My goodness! Look at the state of you!'

I think I had time to mutter something about the library as I stepped past him, with the result that the two gentlemen fell in behind us and the four of us reached the meeting place together.

It should have been so simple. As the clock struck midnight, Mr Barrington would have risen from the sofa, received the all-important scroll from the Emir's envoy, and our job would have been done. Instead, at two minutes past midnight, we discovered an overturned armchair, a tray of glasses and decanters scattered all over the floor, and John Martin Harvey, the struggling actor, kneeling amid the wreckage with blood flowing down his face from a gash on his forehead.

'Good God, man! What's happened?' Mr Shaw leapt to his friend's side, followed closely by Dr Watson, while Mr Grahame simply gaped.

'Got hit on the head,' the actor mumbled.

'But why? By whom?'

Mr Martin Harvey winced as Dr Watson began to examine his wound.

'Had a job to do. Man offered me a hundred guineas to give something to Harry Barrington. Library at midnight, he said, and if there were any funny business with police or anything, not to give it to him at all.'

He winced again, and I could see that the blood was still flowing freely.

'So I got here two minutes early. No sign of Barrington, just a little maid by the drinks tray. Asked her if she'd seen him and she said no, so I asked her for a whisky and soda water, and as I turned away she brained me with the whisky decanter. Took the document from my jacket, ran off.'

'Which way, sir?' I asked, before realising there was only one door leading from the library. 'And what did she look like?'

But the actor had no time to offer any description because just then the library door was flung open and the tiny figure of Leonora stumbled through it.

'Flotsam!' she cried. 'There you are! Come quickly! It's Mlle Le Blanc, and she's getting away!'

And so I followed, and Mr Shaw and Mr Grahame followed me, though I'm not even sure why, and there was yet more running. My first ball, and I'm sure I sprinted more than I danced.

Leonora led us out of a side door, into a part of the gardens that were not illuminated for the ball, talking as she ran.

'The inspector stood us down, you see, because we'd looked at every lady here. So we went to watch the dancing. But in the end we felt hungry, so we thought we'd find our way down to the kitchen, and we were just looking for the servant's door when we heard a man shout from one of the rooms, and when we turned round to look, there was Mlle Le Blanc, running out of the room dressed as a maid, with something in her hand. So I said, "Follow her!", and Elsie said, "Fetch Flotsam!", and look, there she is!'

And when we looked up to where she was pointing, we were greeted to the unforgettable sight of Elsie, some hundred yards away, on the crest of a low ridge and silhouetted against the moonlit sky, jumping up and down, and beating very loudly what turned out to be the Montrachute House dinner gong.

I don't know how long it took us to reach her, scrambling through the darkness as best we could. Every stray stone reminded me of my bare feet, and at one point, when Mr Grahame stumbled into me, I heard my dress tearing ominously.

'She went that way!' Elsie gasped when we finally come up to her. 'Down the lane. I think that's the way to the station. I was going to follow her, you see, but I thought there's no point in me catching up with her, so I stayed here to point the way.'

'You did well,' I told her, then started off again, down a little footpath that led to the lane. Behind me I heard Mr Shaw urging on his friend.

'Come on, man. There's bound to be a novel in this!'

'Not my sort of novel. You two go ahead, Shaw! I'm out of puff.'

And so in the end it was just the two of us on that last, dreadful charge down the hill towards the station. We were far too out of breath to speak, though at the stile that led to the lane, Mr Shaw helped me to free my dress from a nail that had snagged it.

'Don't know who she is,' he panted. 'Don't know what she's stolen. But the frenzy of the hunt is upon me!'

When we rounded the next bend, there was enough light in the sky for us to see the station, and to my despair there was a train already at the platform. And then, not too far ahead of us, hurrying into the bright circle cast by the station lamp, I saw our quarry, and even from that distance, I recognised her at once.

'Betty!' I cried out. But the little maid who'd dressed me for my first ball showed no sign of hearing, she just hurried across the platform towards a third-class carriage. With a sinking heart, I watched Béatrice Flaubert, or Béatrice White, or Béatrice Weiss, boarding the London train.

'We can still make it!' Mr Shaw declared, and with a burst of speed both unexpected and frankly quite unlikely in a playwright of middle years, he sprinted away from me, towards the waiting train.

I'll never know for sure what arguments he used or what threats he uttered to delay the departure of the 12:27 train from Bedworth, but Mr Shaw was always good with

335

words, and when I finally rounded the corner and scuttled onto the station platform, the train was still there.

I'd arrived at the end of the platform by the rear end of the train, by the guard's van, and it was by that carriage that the bearded playwright was engaged in a lively altercation with the station master, while the guard hung from the open door of his van looking utterly mystified.

'The point is moot,' I heard him conclude, 'because here she is, so we will never test your theory. Quickly, miss, into the guard's van. I've argued that you are royal freight, and of course any courier carrying royal freight has the right to delay any steam vehicle for up to three minutes if the freight in question is to be carried in the guard's van.'

I had no idea what he was talking about, and nor, evidently, did the station master, who seemed relieved to wave the train off and have done with.

It was already beginning to roll forward as the guard pulled me up, and I saw Mr Shaw making to clamber up behind me.

'No, sir,' I cried, 'not you. Someone needs to tell Sir Torpenhow. Tell him...' At this point I began to raise my voice, as the distance between us was already growing. 'Tell him to telegraph ahead. Tell him to have some officers at Charing Cross to meet the train!'

He replied with a wave as the train curved away from the station, and then he was lost from sight, leaving me to explain matters to an uncomprehending guard.

I had already realised that confronting Béatrice White on board the train was pointless. I had no power to arrest her, and even if the guard were to assist me, I was far from certain that we could carry it off. A timid maid being bullied by a train guard and a lady in a tattered ball dress would undoubtedly have the sympathy of other passengers in a third-class compartment, and it might well have been us, not her, who found ourselves being manhandled by the crowd. We could, of course, have halted the train at any point before Charing Cross – in a station or in the countryside – and waited for help to come, but I felt certain that Mme White would not hesitate to take to the fields if the train stopped unexpectedly. And my bare feet told me that she would have the advantage if it came to another chase, especially without a tangled ball dress to slow her.

So, I knew it was a much better plan to sit tight and hope that Sir Torpenhow would have reinforcements waiting in London. I was at the back of the train, and Mme White much nearer the front, and the ticket barrier at Charing Cross is at the front of the train, so I knew she would be off the platform and onto the station concourse before I could stop her. But if there were a dozen burly constables looking out for her…

At every stop between Bedworth and Charing Cross, I peeped from the guard's van to check that my quarry made no attempt to leave the train, but I didn't really expect her to. I was sure she had no idea she was being followed, and that was greatly to my advantage. Even so, as the train slowed approaching Charing Cross station, I felt incredibly nervous and a little sick.

And I felt a lot worse when I looked down from the guard's van and saw the reception Sir Torpenhow had arranged for us. Instead of a dozen hefty officers blocking the exit from the platform, there were three rather slim ones waiting at the end of the platform furthest from the ticket barrier, just at the point where the guard's van drew to a halt.

'Miss Flotsam?' one of them asked, as I began to scramble down. 'The sergeant had a message that he was to raise every available officer to meet this train, so here we are.'

But I was already despairing, and had no time for niceties.

'That way, quickly!' I cried, leaping down and setting off up the platform. 'We looking for a dark-haired maid in uniform. We've got to catch her. The safety of the nation depends on it!'

'Yes, miss. Very good. Usually there'd be a lot more than us, you see.' Even as we chased up the platform, the safety of the nation clearly seemed less important to him than the need to apologise for his paltry force. 'But an awful lot of the older men here, and at all the other stations, seem to have taken special leave today to go to funerals. It's odd, isn't it, Frank?'

'That's her!' I shouted out in triumph. 'There, at the ticket barrier. Quickly, before she gets away!'

'I see her, miss,' Frank assured me. 'Don't you worry, we'll catch her in no time. She's only a little thing. Where's the sarge, Bill?'

'Dunno. Took himself off somewhere. He should have been here, helping out. Stand aside there! We're coming through!'

The ticket inspector at the barrier looked up in alarm at this bellowed command, then made himself scarce, and we dashed past him, and out into the station concourse.

There, in front of us, only ten paces away, stood Mme White, still dressed as a lady's maid, and in her hand, visible to us all, was a scroll of parchment sealed up with dark purple wax. Unfortunately, she was not alone. In front of her, taking possession of the scroll, was a man in a bowler hat, and I recognised him at once as the person who had assaulted Sherlock Holmes in Eaton Square. He had struck me as a mild-mannered gentleman then, but now his face was set in a hostile and suspicious scowl, and in one hand he held what was clearly a swordstick.

And *he* was not alone, either. Arrayed behind him was a group of seven other men, all also wearing bowler hats, and all of them wearing similar scowls. They didn't appear to be carrying swords, but every one of them held a heavy, leaded stick. They looked like the sort of men well skilled in the art of affray.

I felt the officers alongside me shrink back slightly at the sight of them, but the one called Bill shouted out bravely.

'Stop there, you lot, in the name of the law!'

No reply came, but Mme White mumbled something in French, and the man holding the scroll nodded. Then, at his signal, his companions raised their sticks and began to advance upon us.

To give credit to my meagre force they held their ground stoutly, reaching for their truncheons, preparing to give as good as they got, but I could sense their apprehension.

'Step back, miss,' Bill ordered tersely. 'Behind us, if you please.'

'Could do with the sarge making an appearance,' muttered Frank. 'Good man in a brawl.'

I could still see the end of the scroll, protruding slightly from pocket of the ruffian-in-chief as he edged towards

339

us. Perhaps, I thought, if someone were swift enough and nimble enough…

'Don't hurt the girl too badly.' Mme White's voice was calm and cool, and completely devoid of any compassion. 'We might take her with us, to guarantee a safe passage.'

The man with the swordstick nodded, and drew the blade.

'Hit straight, lads,' Bill muttered. 'That one's mine.'

But before the two sides could close, I saw my moment. With a little shout, I made to dart to the left, as if to evade the line of brutes in front of me, and saw the two men on that side begin to move across, to intercept me. But before they had moved more than a few inches, I cut back – just as I had that night in the park – and flung myself straight at their leader. Speed and surprise stood me in good stead once again, as I was upon him, too close for sword work, before he knew what was happening. I even felt my fingers close over the end of the scroll.

Behind me I heard a cry of 'Quick, lads!', but before those words were even completed, I felt the man's arm go around me, as steely and unforgiving as a clamp, and with his leg suddenly behind mine, I was thrown backwards, hard and fast. As I fell, I felt the scroll slip from my fingers, and then the shuddering impact of landing made me close my eyes, certain that at least one blow from those heavy boots must surely follow.

And then, with timing so perfect Mr Shaw would have been ashamed to put it in one of his plays, a whistle blew, and no kick landed. Everything seemed to stop as though frozen, with me on the ground and the two sides still a yard or two apart, the young constables looking past all of us with expressions of utter bewilderment on their faces.

340

Then the brutes in front of us turned too, and behind them, where, a moment before, the concourse had been empty but for one or two loiterers, it was suddenly full of old men.

But not just any old men. As I peered in astonishment between the legs of my assailants at the rank they had formed across the station, a rank long enough and deep enough to block any possible exit, I was immediately struck by a certain uniformity in their size and shape, and by the fact that every single one of them was wearing a very dark suit and a black tie. The only exception was the blue of the station sergeant's uniform, standing out very clearly in the very middle of the front rank. The rest looked as though they had come in mourning.

And then I realised that they had.

The Flying Goblin public house was only thirty or forty paces from Charing Cross station, so it must have been easy for the station sergeant to recruit his additional forces. And they had answered the call to a man, whether in their forties or fifties or eighties, an impregnable barrier of ageing courage and fortitude and decency.

The louts in the bowler hats looked at them, then looked at their leader, then very slowly lowered their sticks to the ground.

On the day of his own wake, Sergeant Minders had been responsible for a final set of arrests.

–

It didn't take very long for Mme White and her accomplices to be marched from the station, nor for the cohort of retired police officers to return to their positions at the Flying Goblin. Soon Charing Cross station was quiet again. It was a little after half past one in the morning.

Apart from the station master and one or two of his men, only Mrs Hudson and I remained on the echoey concourse.

'It was clever of the duty sergeant to remember the Flying Goblin when he got Sir Torpenhow's telegram, wasn't it, ma'am?'

Mrs Hudson nodded gravely, and a thought struck me.

'Or had you reminded him you would all be there? Is *that* why you chose a place for the wake so close to Charing Cross station?'

Mrs Hudson, looking very serious in her black clothes, simply pursed her lips.

'The Flying Goblin is a very fine establishment, Flotsam,' she told me firmly. 'And if it did occur to me to remind Sergeant Bacchus of the location of tonight's event, well, there was no need. Someone had already thought to do it. A certain Mr Holmes, apparently, knowing where and how I was passing my evening, had sent him a note. It seems it had occurred to Mr Holmes that some additional forces at the train terminus might possibly be required.'

'And they saved the day, didn't they, ma'am, all those retired policemen? And the younger ones too, because they weren't all retired. If it hadn't been for them, Mme White would have got away with the Emir's treaty, and there might have been terrible consequences.'

And with that, a terrible thought struck me.

'The Emir's treaty! I completely forgot about the Emir's treaty! What happened to it, ma'am? That horrible man had it! Did anyone remember to take it off him?'

Mrs Hudson put an arm around my shoulder.

'The station master keeps a small stove burning at night, Flotsam, even in this heat. He drinks a lot of tea, apparently. I'm happy to say that the Emir's treaty ended up in the stove.'

'The stove, ma'am? You *burnt* it?' I looked up at her in disbelief. 'But, ma'am, after all that work, all the time we've spent getting it! All that *chasing*! And it was vital to the nation's interests, ma'am! Remember everything Sir Torpenhow told us about securing the frontiers of India for years to come? You surely can't have just *burnt* it?'

Mrs Hudson reached into her bag.

'You clearly haven't seen this evening's late editions, Flotsam.'

She produced a copy of *The Clarion* and showed me the front page. One headline in particular leapt out at me.

Outrage in Bokara
Emir Locks Up Missionaries
Sussex Curate Whipped on Emir's Orders

'In the circumstances, Flotsam, I can't think an alliance between our two nations is very likely now. The British public would not permit it. When Sir Torpenhow reads this, I think he will be extremely relieved to discover that the only evidence of his rather foolhardy negotiations has been destroyed.'

I read the headlines again. It was certainly true that the Emir didn't sound like a very nice man. And now we'd never again have to worry about the treaty falling into the wrong hands.

'So everything that the professor did, and Mr Barrington, travelling backwards and forwards across all sorts of countries, chased by spies...' I imagined again the minarets of Samarkand, the lofty towers of Tashkent, the camels and the covered bazaars, the long dusty trails leading westwards. 'All that was for nothing?'

'That,' Mrs Hudson told me firmly, 'is diplomacy.'

She gave my shoulder a little squeeze.

'And now, my girl, what about you? Your face is dirty, your dress is in rags and you've got no shoes. But all those things can be sorted out. Thanks to Miss Peters, you have spares of everything waiting for you in your room at Montrachute House. I'm told there is a mail train leaving in a few moments, and the station master will be happy to arrange for you to travel in the brake van. Why, you'd be back before supper finishes, and there'd still be lots of time for dancing.'

I thought of the beautiful ballroom at Montrachute House, open to the trees, made magical by the gleaming lanterns hidden among the leaves. Mrs Hudson was right – the orchestra would still be playing. Hetty would still be there, and Mr Spencer, and Dr Watson too. I would be able to dance till dawn in the arms of any number of handsome young men.

Dawn.

It was still some way off.

At the Survivors' Ball, it was a point of pride to still be dancing when the sun rose.

–

The orchestra at the Mecklenberg Hotel was playing a waltz when we arrived. At that hour, guests were no longer being announced, but a team of Lady Townsend's footmen, on duty near the door, closed ranks promptly when they spotted the grubby, ragged figure climbing the steps towards them.

But Mrs Hudson had come with me, and at a few words from her, the young men stepped aside with alacrity and let me through. I didn't even look at them as I went by. I think perhaps I had fallen into some sort of trance, so intent was I on my purpose; certainly I didn't look to right or left as I approached the ballroom, although I was aware, on all sides, of couples falling silent and stepping aside to let me pass. The Mecklenberg's marble floor felt cool and smooth beneath my toes.

The ballroom itself was filled with music and was packed to its edges with dancing couples, and at first no one noticed the tattered waif pushing her way through. But I didn't hesitate for a moment, because I had seen him at the far end of the room, looking out over the dance floor. In his borrowed dress suit, Scraggs looked much taller than usual, and older, and straighter.

Concealed by the whirling flurries of dancers, I came within a few paces of him before he noticed me, and then I saw his face light up with a grin. I'm not sure he even noticed my torn dress, or my bare feet, or my hair straggling down my back. He just walked forward and held out his hand.

And then we danced.

A Holmes & Hudson Mystery